Praise for

REPUTATION

"What an addictive, juicy novel, with a whip-cracking plot full of twists and turns. *Reputation* is packed to bursting with all of the best elements of commercial fiction. Read this one!"

—Sarah Pekkanen, #1 *New York Times* bestselling coauthor of
An Anonymous Girl

"Sara Shepard reaches delicious, vicious heights with *Reputation*. I felt like I was sucked into a video game, slipping into different skins in every chapter. It's the love child of *Dead to Me* and *Scream*, a creepy tale about modern technology and good old-fashioned human flaws. We're so lucky that Shepard is out there watching the way we live, seeing the best in us, and, oh yes, the cringe-inducing, often laugh-out-loud worst as well."

—Caroline Kepnes, author of *You, Hidden Bodies*, and *Providence*

"A modern murder-mystery that exposes our deepest fears about how vulnerable we are to the parts of ourselves we hide online. As the secrets pile up, Shepard writes her calculating antiheroines with sharp clarity, daring the reader to keep pace alongside her. I, for one, was breathless."

—Chandler Baker, *New York Times* bestselling author of
Whisper Network

"Deliciously diabolical. Shepard spares no one in this breakneck thriller as dark secrets and shocking scandals lead to murder."

—Liv Constantine, international bestselling author of
The Last Mrs. Parrish and *The Last Time I Saw You*

REPUTATION

a novel

SARA SHEPARD

DUTTON

DUTTON

An imprint of Penguin Random House LLC
penguinrandomhouse.com

Copyright © 2019 by Sara Shepard
Penguin supports copyright. Copyright fuels creativity, encourages diverse voices,
promotes free speech, and creates a vibrant culture. Thank you for buying an authorized
edition of this book and for complying with copyright laws by not reproducing, scanning,
or distributing any part of it in any form without permission. You are supporting writers
and allowing Penguin to continue to publish books for every reader.

DUTTON and the D colophon are registered trademarks of Penguin Random House LLC.

Produced by Alloy Entertainment LLC, 1700 Broadway, New York, NY 10019

LIBRARY OF CONGRESS CATALOGING-IN-PUBLICATION DATA

Names: Shepard, Sara, 1977– author.
Title: Reputation: a novel / Sara Shepard.
Description: New York, New York: Dutton, [2020]
Identifiers: LCCN 2019014647 (print) | LCCN 2019015499 (ebook) |
ISBN 9781524742911 (ebook) | ISBN 9781524742904 (tr pbk.)
Subjects: LCSH: Murder—Investigation—Fiction.
Classification: LCC PS3619.H4543 (ebook) | LCC PS3619.H4543 R47 2020
(print) | DDC 813/.6—dc23
LC record available at https://lccn.loc.gov/2019014647

Hudson Exclusive Edition ISBN: 9780593182567

Printed in the United States of America
1   3   5   7   9   10   8   6   4   2

Book design by Alison Cnockaert

This is a work of fiction. Names, characters, places, and incidents either are the product of
the author's imagination or are used fictitiously, and any resemblance to actual persons,
living or dead, businesses, companies, events, or locales is entirely coincidental.

To K + H

REPUTATION

LOOK WHAT YOU MADE ME DO

Maybe you got it at birth. Maybe you gained it through hard work. Perhaps you have yours because you're charitable, or ambitious, or an asshole. It's your reputation. Everyone's got one. And if you think reputations don't matter, you're wrong.

Good reputations lift velvet ropes. They get you approved for loans; they're your ticket to prestigious universities. Good reputations land jobs, find you a spouse, earn you the right friends.

But have a *bad* reputation—well. Here come the whispers. Here come the slammed doors. Just try to shake off your bad name: Ten years later, a girl will still be known as the sophomore who had the affair with her track coach. Twenty years later, the only thing neighbors know about the man down the street is that he beat his wife; or that the woman in the grocery store is a frigid spinster; or that the lady on the library steps had something *awful* happen and she went crazy.

So it makes sense to preserve a good name, sure. But how far would you go to preserve your reputation—especially when you fear you're about to be exposed? Would you work on a good cover story? Would you lie? Would you *kill*?

You're shaking your head: *I'd never do that—I'm a* good *person*. But until you're in the thick of it, you have no idea what you're capable of. If something needs to stay hidden, you just might do whatever it takes.

PART
1

1

KIT

I've already had two strong martinis before hitting the rooftop bar at the Hotel Monaco in Old City, Philadelphia, which isn't like me at all. But my foundation's clients, the very reason I'm on this business trip? They bailed on me at the last minute. Decided to go to a horse show instead. I tried to insinuate myself into their outing—not that I wanted to go to a horse show—but either they didn't get my hint or they didn't want my company.

I take my job very seriously. I raise money for Aldrich University, one of the best private colleges in the whole United States—it's up there with the Harvards and Stanfords of the world, and actually tougher to get into. Ever since my first husband passed away, I've been the university's leading ensnarer of Big Fish donors. I seek out alumnae far and wide, vetting their newly minted positions as heads of hospitals or as CEOs, tracking the science prizes they've recently won, making it my business to know if the books they've written have hit the *New York Times* Best Sellers list. And then I pounce, stroking their egos, showering them with praise, reminding them of the prestigious academic roots from which they hail and that the right thing to do, when enjoying their kind of wealth and success, is to *give back*. I get a rush when I receive a huge check from a new donor—it's my version of doing drugs. So when I find out that Dr. and Mrs. Robert Hawser of Devon, Pennsylvania, will be watching dressage instead of coming out with Kit Manning-Strasser of Aldrich University Charitable Giving for some wining and dining, I take it pretty damn hard.

Have I done something wrong? I'm not even the one who groomed these people—it was Lynn Godfrey, a pushy, grating, competitive woman from my department. I consider calling her and chewing her out, but I don't chew people out. I am graceful and humble and know when to back off. Next week, I will reach out to the Hawsers again. I will be kind and forgiving and gracious. We will start over.

But right now I have nothing to do in Philadelphia. I've checked in with my airline: All flights back to Pittsburgh tonight are booked. I don't feel like seeing the Liberty Bell. I don't feel like walking down South Street. I could finalize the plans for the Aldrich Giving Gala this Wednesday, but the party is such a well-oiled machine that there isn't much *to* do.

I've never been great with idle hands.

I uncap the first airplane-size vodka bottle in my room and call my daughters. First, I reach sweet, cheerful Sienna in her dorm room (she's an Aldrich freshman, and I've interrupted a study session). After a forty-two-second conversation in which Sienna profusely apologizes for not being able to speak longer, I then speak to quiet, sullen sixteen-year-old Aurora. She's at home but getting ready to go out. "Where?" I ask, suspicious. It's a school night. Aurora assures me she's just going to Sophie's house to study for a physics test, nothing to freak out over.

I mix the next drink as I dial Greg, my second husband of two years. Our conversation is short and about nothing but the basics. I don't tell him that my clients have bailed on me because, well, it isn't the picture of myself I want to paint. Greg doesn't ask me why I sound so down because that isn't the man he wants to be for me . . . though I believed he did, once. I confirm I am alive. He tells me the same. I remind him that the giving gala is in two days. It's kind of like an adult prom, the university's biggest fund-raiser of the year, and Greg is a no-brainer choice for my date, not that I'm exactly looking forward to it.

My phone pings shortly after I hang up with him. When I look down, it's a text from an unlisted number.

Get ready.

That's all it says. Frowning, I write back: *Who is this?*

No answer. A chill runs up my spine. Get ready for *what?*

A loud horn honk outside startles me. I turn and notice that my window curtains are flung open, affording me a view of the rooftops and the bridge beyond. A pigeon flaps from a nearby roost. I have a tingling sensation that I'm being watched.

I leap up and yank the blinds closed. I need out of this hotel room. I want company, noise, and maybe another drink. The closest place is the hotel's rooftop bar.

———

"You should try a naughty mule," says a voice beside me after I slide onto a barstool.

A man sits catty-corner to me on one of the gray couches, half-hidden behind a large marble post. I'm irked that he's been eavesdropping. I've been debating with the bartender—a discerning, fiftyish man with half-mast eyes who is pretentiously overdressed in a three-piece suit—between a Moscow mule and a gimlet. After that strange, anonymous, cryptic text I'd received in my room, the last thing I want are random eyes on me.

But my eavesdropper smiles jovially enough. I twist around to get a better look at him. By the way his legs stretch from the couch, I can tell that he's quite tall. His face is square and friendly, and his dark hair curls over his oxford collar. The corners of his eyes turn down in a way that seems trustworthy, and he has a big, wide, straight smile, with good, square teeth. He looks like a preppy, naughty schoolboy, as if he might be hiding a slingshot behind his back. I notice he's wearing Vans sneakers instead of loafers with his suit. Still dressed for my meeting, I am wearing Yves Saint Laurent pumps that paralyze my toes.

"It's vodka mixed with jalapeño and cayenne pepper," School-boy explains, holding up a copper mug. "If you like spicy, you won't find anything better."

My eyelashes lower, then lift. "What makes you think I like spicy?"

One eyebrow rises. His eyes drift down to my exposed legs, my high heels. "*Do* you?" he asks, in a voice that, unless I'm crazy, oozes with flirtation.

"Wouldn't *you* like to know," I shoot back. Then I chastise myself. Kit Manning-Strasser is not a woman who flirts with random men in hotel bars. I catch the bartender's eye. "Just a Tanqueray and tonic, please."

The bartender turns to mix it up, with a smirk on his face. He sets down my cocktail silently, and I swear I hear him snicker. My cheeks are on fire; even a sip of the drink can't extinguish the heat.

As the bartender turns away, there's a voice behind me: "Don't mind Bertram. He's a judgmental prick."

Schoolboy again. I can feel his gaze on my back as though it's a heat lamp. "You know him?" I ask nonchalantly.

"Nope. Just met him today. But I can tell. I'm good at reading people."

I pretend to be interested in the flickering votive candle on the bar. I'm still trying to process why this man thought I like spicy things. Or perhaps this is his line to every woman he meets.

Schoolboy interprets some tiny movement I've made as a cue to slip off the couch and take the stool next to mine. "I'm Patrick," he says, those crinkly, downturned eyes slow, careful magnets drawing me toward him.

"Kit," I answer.

He does not offer his hand to shake, so I don't offer mine, either. "So are you here on business?" I coolly ask.

He holds up a palm to say, *Halt.* "Come now. We're going to have *that* conversation?"

I blink. "Pardon?"

"We're at a hotel. We don't know each other. We can make boring chitchat, or we could actually have an interesting talk." He leans back and crosses his arms over his chest. He has nice forearms, I notice. Muscular. He's also not wearing a wedding band.

"And what, in your estimation, is an *interesting talk*?" I ask. "You want to talk about politics? Global warming? Health care?"

"I want to talk about who we *really* want to be." His eyes gleam. "It's a game I play when I travel. It's not often that we get the opportunity to be someone other than ourselves, you know? I'm not going to tell you where I'm *actually* from, but where I *want* to be from. You won't tell me what you *actually* do for a living, but what you *want* to do, in your wildest dreams."

A Tiffany lamp, perhaps authentic, sends glittering trapezoids across the marble bar. Out a long set of floor-to-ceiling windows, a rooftop deck beckons, though it is too cold to venture outside. I think of that line from "Eleanor Rigby," one of my mother's favorite songs. The title character puts on the face she keeps in a jar by the door whenever there are visitors. Who is Eleanor when she doesn't have to be Eleanor? Who am I when I don't have to be Kit Manning-Strasser?

"Interesting." I turn away slightly. "Except I'm not feeling very creative tonight, I'm afraid."

"It's not a matter of creativity. It's about looking into yourself. *Knowing* yourself. So you're saying you don't know yourself?"

In the background, the soft, unobtrusive electronica song ends, and another begins. Kit Manning-Strasser, I want to tell him, is not a woman who has these conversations. But it does beg a question: Do I know myself? Do I know what I want?

I think of all I have. But I also think of all the wrong paths I've taken. I think of how hard I pretend. Everything I haven't said. Everything I've wanted. Everything I've gained and lost.

"Fine," I say slowly, without quite realizing it. I settle back in my seat, and I ask him the very same question. "Where you are traveling from, Patrick?"

His eyes sparkle. "A little town in the South of France. It's known for its lemons. You?"

"Marrakesh," I answer, because I went there once with my parents when my father was on sabbatical—just a few years before I had to identify my mother's mangled body in the morgue after a drunk driver T-boned her car at ninety miles an hour. Marrakesh was the most magical place I've ever been. I've always meant to go back, and though my new husband has the cash to make such a trip happen, it's a little exotic for his taste. "And what do you do?"

"I'm a weather pilot. I fly into the center of hurricanes." He answers swiftly, like he's done this before. "And on the weekends, I race antique cars professionally. Preferably around old, crumbling cities with lots of tight turns."

"So you like danger." I crunch down on a piece of ice. "Thrills."

One eyebrow lifts again. "You could say that. And what do *you* do, Kit?"

I think of *Pulp Fiction,* which my sister, Willa, and I used to watch obsessively in high school, especially in those months after our mother died. "I'm the keeper of the meaning of life. It's in a box in my room right now, and I have to guard it with my life. I get paid very handsomely for doing so."

"Did they let you in on what the meaning of life *is*?" Patrick asks.

I nod mysteriously. "If I told you, I'd have to kill you."

"So you're a woman who likes to hold all the cards, then."

I shrug. "I like certainty."

Our eyes meet. Even in our lies, we have told one another some-thing real.

There is lime residue in my teeth. The bartender has his back to us now, perhaps having written us off as flirtatious philanderers. And then Patrick—is that even his real name?—glances at my left hand and says, "And what's your husband like?"

I turn my fat diamond ring to the inside of my palm. "Actually, I'm a widow." This isn't a lie. "Do *you* have a husband? A wife?"

There is something about the way he's looking at me that makes me feel scooped out and raw. "Neither."

Is he serious, or is this just what he *wants* to be true? I'm not sure which answer I want more.

We have two more drinks and spin tales about ourselves. He has jet-setters for parents. I have distant relations to royals. I say I com-mitted a few stealthy murders in my youth. Patrick says he was once shot off into space and spent days in orbit before NASA figured out he was missing. Midway into drink number three, we turn somber. Patrick tells me he has never fallen in love and isn't sure love is real. I tell him that I have, when I was young, but then I discovered it's a fallacy. This is actually my truth, which I know isn't the rules, but I'm tipsy, and Patrick is inching closer to me with every word he breathes, and something is happening, something I can't quite understand.

Naughty, the cautious part of my brain reminds me again and again. I'm married to a handsome, successful man. I have two smart, successful teenage daughters. From an outsider's perspective, I have it all. But here in the darkness of this strange bar, it all feels so far away. When I look back at that life, the one I'd been steeped in only twelve hours before, it's *that* Kit who seems false, not this one.

Patrick's chili-infused breath could ignite a forest fire. He looks at me as though he's known me forever. I'm so dazzled, and I won-der if he somehow *has.* "And what, royal murderess keeper-of-truth, do you want to do right now?" he asks.

The world is my oyster. I could tell him anything: that I want to cliff-dive off the moon, buy out a Chanel boutique, time-travel to Benjamin Franklin times, crawl into a cocoon and transform into a butterfly. But I know in those acorn-brown eyes what he's really asking, and it's what I want, too.

I let him take my hand and lead me out of the bar. Our lips touch as soon as the elevator doors close, and quickly, the kissing goes from tentative to full-on passionate. His fingers fumble for the tiny, delicate buttons at the neckline of my blouse. My hands are on his waist.

"Oh God," Patrick moans into my ear.

But then, coming to my senses, I push away. "Wait," I whisper. "No. I can't."

His eyes are two tragic pools. "Okay . . ."

I look down, panting. Adjust my blouse. Pull down my skirt. I fumble for my key card, deliberately not inviting him back to my room. I want to—believe me. I'm *dying* to.

"I'm sorry." I shake my head and give him a sad, regretful smile. "This just isn't me."

2

LYNN

TUESDAY, APRIL 25, 2017

After being Mystery Reader in my son's class, after a workout at Flywheel, after a blow-dry touch-up and makeup reapplication, after strutting out of the gym and getting double takes from nearly every man on the street—something I've become used to—and after popping into the gourmet grocery next door to my office, I get a lovely compliment. I pass a bottle of wine for tonight's dinner across the scanner at the checkout counter, and the shopgirl asks me for ID.

"Me?" I blink hard, grinning. "Goodness, I'm almost forty! I have two kids!"

"Oh." The girl—she can't be much older than twenty-two—squints at my face, then my ID, then back at me again. "Well, whatever you're doing, it's working."

This makes everyone else in the line inspect me just as thoroughly—including an almost-as-skinny, hawk-nosed mom who was a row behind me at Flywheel. *Good.* I swish to the office in a cloud of smugness, wondering if this moment is Facebook-worthy. It certainly reaffirms that all of my renewed efforts in my appearance and fitness, which I've redoubled since moving here, are paying off.

But as soon as I reach my office floor, my mood dampens. Kit Manning-Strasser's office, the first room I pass on the way to mine, is still dark. She isn't back from Philly yet? Late night with the Hawsers, maybe? That seems unlikely—in the pictures I've seen of the extremely wealthy couple, they look like the type who have already picked out their funeral plots. I wonder if my name ever came up over the course of their lovely evening out together—oh, you know, just the woman who groomed the Hawsers in the first place? The woman who nurtured a relationship, listening for hours as Lucy Hawser talked about her sick corgi and her girlhood years of riding dressage, practically falling asleep as Robert Hawser told her, time and time again, about the round of golf he'd had with Warren Buffett? *That* lady—remember her, people? Because guess what: She's not the same woman who took you out to dinner. We are very, *very* different.

Kit is more senior than you are, and that's why she gets to go on this trip, my boss, George, explained to me last week. And while it's true I've only been working in Aldrich's giving department for six months—my husband, kids, and I moved to Pennsylvania from Maryland about a year ago because my husband's company was offered great tax breaks here—I don't like coming in second.

I sit down at my desk, open my e-mail, and scour my messages for updates on the Hawsers. There's nothing—not from Kit, not from George. There are plenty of last-minute details about the Aldrich University Giving Gala, which is happening tomorrow at the Natural History Museum. *Is the guest list finalized? Are the speeches ready? Has the planner updated me on the final details?* Yes, yes, yes—I've always been excellent at throwing a party.

All that done, I open Facebook and sign into my account. The post of me, my daughter, Amelia, and my son, Connor, standing at the overlook of Mount Washington, the city of Pittsburgh glittering beneath us, has garnered quite a response: *Beautiful,* says my high school boyfriend, Brock, who married a woman who got a big ass after having three kids. *Your kids could be models!* writes an old friend from Maryland; poor thing went through a nasty divorce last year. I consider writing a response saying that I couldn't care less if my children grow up to be classically beautiful—it's their accomplishments, hopes, and dreams that fuel my fire. I also wish a few more of the moms from school had weighed in. Perhaps they think the post is too boastful? Or they find it inappropriate that I've let my nine-year-old daughter wear lip gloss and just a touch of mascara? Or I'm being paranoid. They're busy. That's all.

I click around to see if there's any dirt on anyone I know—a girl's night out that got messy; an inflammatory political argument between family members, all played out in comments. I see pictures of someone's new house (smaller than mine), someone's new baby (uglier than mine were), and a vacation photo of one of my sorority sisters and her husband (I've been on bigger yachts, and I have a better body). All is right with the world.

My phone buzzes, and I reach for it, figuring it's my husband texting to check in. He's on a flight back from somewhere—Denver? St. Louis?—trying to find another angel investor as kindly and generous as the first anonymous individual who'd poured tons of money into his business years ago. I suspect he'll be successful, eventually; his business is great and innovative, and rich people sometimes just need a little cajoling.

Except the text isn't from my husband. Instead, it's from an unlisted number. When I open it, it says, simply, *Get ready*.

I can just make out my ghostlike reflection in the phone's screen. I wait for a follow-up text of explanation. Nothing comes.

I look out the window. The sky is flat and gray. The air seems oddly still. The message gives me a chill. It feels like a warning. An explosion. A mass killing. A plague of locusts. I tap the phone icon on my phone, tempted to call my kids' school to check if everything's okay.

Then, as if in answer, my monitor goes dark. My head snaps up in surprise and then annoyance, because I can hear that winding-down sound of the hard drive shutting off. *What the hell?* Outside my office, I hear my assistant, Betsy, make a similarly startled sound. I stand just as she's rolling back her chair and peering under her desk to look at the power strip on the floor. Her monitor is dark, too.

I wander into the hallway. Everyone is staring in bewilderment at their monitors.

"A power outage?" Jeremy, one of our grant writers, says.

"But our lights are still on," Amanda, Kit's assistant, says, pointing upward.

Betsy's screen snaps to neon yellow, and she lets out a little yelp. I hurry back into my office. My screen is also yellow, and no matter how many keys I press, I cannot restore it to factory settings. Even turning the computer on and off does nothing—it's as though someone has taken over our power grid. I glance out the window, down onto the Aldrich quad. Terrorists? Aliens? All I see are students walking sleepily to class.

The flashing on the screen stops, and a message pops up. *You can't hide, hypocrites,* it reads in old-school eight-bit font, the type that used to blare across arcade screens. Below this is a freakish, pixelated drawing of a screaming face with hollowed-out eyes.

The hair on the back of my neck prickles.

Murmurs from the hall: "Who's doing this?" And then: "It's a hack. Holy shit, we're being hacked!" And then: "There's probably malware on our computers. Our systems are probably dead!"

Hacked? Why would someone hack the Aldrich Charitable Giving Department? To expose our donors? Most of that stuff is public record. Perhaps someone is looking for donors' bank information, or their SSNs? I reach for the phone to call security—but then, what is Glen, the sixty-five-year-old guard, going to do?

I put the receiver to my ear before I realize the office phone is dead, too. I grab my cell. That weird text message is still up. *Get ready.* Why would the hacker text *me*? I want to send a reply text, but I'm afraid. Replying could be as bad as clicking on those pop-up windows that unleash a virus on your hard drive. My phone contains more crucial information about work than my computer does.

On the monitor, the cryptic message dissolves, and a URL appears. I hover the mouse over it in anticipation. If my computer's already dead, what's the worst thing that can happen if I click on it? But when I try, the link isn't active. I'm not directed to a browser.

I click the mouse over it again—still nothing. Frowning, I grab a pen and copy down the web address. Moments later, my screen goes dark. No new messages pop up. I flip the switch of my computer, but when the computer reboots, a small question mark blinks in the middle of the screen. I'm no IT expert, but even I know that means the operating system has been wiped.

Outside my office, everyone is exchanging numb glances. "Is this bad?" Betsy sounds frightened.

"Do you think they got our social security numbers?" That's Bill, who deals with international donors.

"Did anyone write down that website that was on the screen?" asks Oscar, the youngest and techiest of the group.

"I did." I step forward to show him the slip of paper on which I'd copied the link. "What do you think it is?"

Oscar squints at what I've written. "It looks like a file that's hosted on Planett." He types the file-sharing juggernaut's address into his cell phone browser.

"Wait!" I cry. "What if your phone blows up?"

"Then I'll blame you," Oscar says. When he notices me scrambling to take the paper back, he quickly adds, "Jesus. I won't. I'm curious, too."

A crowd has formed. Oscar finishes typing the website into his phone and hits GO. I hold my breath, half expecting his phone to explode or the building to go up in flames. The screen shifts and, indeed, a Planett page appears. There is a list of folders, each of which seems clickable. *Aaron, Boyd. Aaron, Corrine. Aaron, Desmond.* Whose names are these?

Oscar scrolls down a little, and the Aarons disappear, and then I see a flash of *Antonishyn, Magda,* and *Apatrea, Laura D.* Wait, I *know* her—she's a nurse in the Aldrich Hospital Department of Cardiology. She and her husband RSVP'd for the giving gala.

Then I see another name I know—*Boyd, Sydney.* Dr. Sydney Boyd is a professor in the journalism department who recently won a Pulitzer—I've been talking him up to a tech CEO and Aldrich grad who is considering making a major donation.

"Me?" Betsy's finger stabs at the tiny screen. And there she is: *Breck, Betsy.* She looks terrified.

Oscar glances at Betsy hesitantly. "Do you want me to click on the folder?"

"No!" Betsy cries, but then she lets out a whimper. "Or, yes. Or, I don't know! What if it says something awful?"

I appraise Betsy—late thirties, dumpy, a self-proclaimed Jimmy Buffett parrothead. What is her *something awful*?

Oscar hands Betsy his phone. "How about *you* click on it? Tell us what's inside."

Betsy gratefully takes the device and steps a few paces away from us. I've never been so curious about her in my life. What can I say? I'm a sucker for dirt on people.

"It's . . . e-mail," Betsy says slowly. "My work e-mail. *All* my work e-mails. And it goes back . . . for*ever.*"

Jeremy hurries over. I do, too. The screen shows the inbox of her Aldrich.edu account. Most of the e-mail topics are about scheduling or the Aldrich Giving Gala; they're dated as recently as five minutes ago.

"Are *all* your e-mails here?" Jeremy cries. "Does this mean everyone's e-mails are?"

"If your name's on that Planett list, then I'm guessing . . . yes?" Oscar sounds dazed.

"B-But I have sensitive information in my e-mails!" Jeremy's voice rises an octave. "People's account numbers! Telephone records!"

People murmur. Since Oscar's phone doesn't seem to have caught a virus, everyone sprints to their own phones to check for their names on the drive site. I do the same, and my name is there, *Godfrey, Lynn L.* I click on the folder. Inside, I see the same party e-mails I've just read on my monitor. There is a sent tab, too, and even a deleted folder, which is full of ads for Saks, Tiffany and Co., and reminders that I need to get my BMW serviced.

I return to the main folder, my heart in my throat. It doesn't give me the best feeling to know that my whole department can read my e-mails if they want, especially because I tend to be a little biting about some of my colleagues in digital missives. But unlike Jeremy, I haven't e-mailed sensitive bank information or exposed any of our clients' personal details. Nor have I exposed any of my *own* personal details—at least not much beyond the odd exasperated rant to the boss.

It feels like I've dodged a bullet. Then it hits me—if my gynecologist and a journalism professor are in this database, too, did their computers also go down? Did they also receive the link to all those folders on the cloud?

I think about our donors finding out. I think of the money we could lose if any secrets come out—because, c'mon, there are going to be secrets. I hit my phone icon and move to call my boss. We need to do damage control. IT security will shut down this database before it can become too widespread—but still. We should have an action plan in place until that happens.

But wait.

I stare at the Planett page again. If I thought Facebook was a good place to troll for random gossip, then this database, with its millions of electronic messages never meant to be seen by the public, is a gold mine. IT security is probably working to shut it down this very moment. I only have a few minutes to look through it.

My finger hovers over the scroll bar. Is there someone I want to find out more about? The mother of the most popular girl in my daughter's class, who works in administration? There's something about her that screams *swinger,* and maybe I could somehow use that to my advantage to get my daughter invited to a few key sleepovers. Or what about the Aldrich hospital-affiliated marriage counselor my husband and I went to twice before I deemed her a biased crackpot? I can see if she kept notes on us. I can see what she *really* thinks about our marriage.

Then I get a brainstorm. *Of course.* Trolling for random gossip is one thing, but finding something that could finally give me leverage in this job—well, that's *useful.*

I'm going to look up Kit.

3

RAINA

TUESDAY, APRIL 25, 2017

I'm in line at the Aldrich University Bursar's Office when my school is hacked. It's like a beautiful piece of choreography seeing the computers flashing in unison and then that spooky picture of the eyeless man popping up where everyone's Facebook feeds and food blogs used to be. All the machines go dead at once. The woman behind the payments desk frowns, swears under her breath, and then stands to address the students standing in line.

"System's down, people. Unless you got cash, you gotta come back and pay your bill another day."

Groans. Mutters. I raise my hand. "Um, I've got cash."

Everyone in line turns to look at me. I hold my head high, trying to project an air of mystique. *Maybe I'm so wealthy, it's nothing for me to carry around fourteen grand in my pocket,* I think haughtily. *You people don't know.*

I glide toward the bursar's window. The lady, who's heavyset and has sumptuous lips and thick brown hair piled on her head, still has her fingers curled over the keyboard as though her computer's about to spring back to life. I hand her the thick envelope of bills. "Raina Hammond," I say in a perky voice. "This is a payment for the summer and fall sessions. Do you need my ID number?"

She does, so I rattle it off. She makes a note of it on my account and stuffs the cash in an envelope, old-school style. As we're finishing up, the man at the next window lets out a sharp gasp. "Lorraine! Our e-mails are on some kind of *server!*"

The person helping me swivels her chair. "Whose e-mails?"

"Mine! Yours! All of ours!" The guy taps at his phone, his eyes the size of golf balls. "Bethany just texted me! Everyone's business is up on some public website for everyone to see! And she said that she and a few other people got this creepy text beforehand that said, *Get ready.* Nothing else!"

"Get ready?" Lorraine murmurs. "Get ready for what?"

"Isn't it obvious?" The man shakes his head. "This is like what happened with that cheating site—what was it? Ashley something? All those married men were exposed?"

"Ashley Madison," I say dully.

"Bingo." He points at me. "That's the one. Or remember what happened with Sony, Lorraine? All those e-mails on that public site? Remember that executive's Amazon receipts for that dye for her pubes?"

The guys in the room titter at the word *pubes*—most of the girls look uncomfortable. I'm still dwelling on the phrase *sensitive information. Data breach.* A chill goes through me. And what does she mean, *everyone's* e-mails?

I can't get out of there fast enough, but on the sidewalks is the same kind of chatter I'd heard inside: *Hack. Public Google site. E-mails!* The panic is fizzy around me: *Is there any way to delete this website?* people cry. *My mom cannot read my e-mails, dude.* And just: *Oh shit, oh shit, I could get* expelled! A local news van has pulled up to the corner— wow, they caught on to the hack *fast*—and a cameraman points his lens at a petite, freckled girl in a cropped denim jacket. I recognize her—she and I spoke at a party at her sorority house about me rushing next fall. She is also talking about the hack. Jeez, it only happened five minutes ago, tops. Is this what it was like to watch the plague wreak havoc through London? I hear one of the reporters say the names Harvard and Princeton. I always appreciate when Aldrich is compared to those schools, but the mention of them at this moment jars me a little. I move closer to eavesdrop.

"Raina!"

I whirl around. Sienna Manning is jogging toward me, and a smile freezes on my face. I pray she hasn't seen that I've just come from the bursar's. I realize how paranoid this is—she'd have no reason to question me even if she *had* seen me go in there—but still. Too close for comfort.

"Hey," I say, gesturing to the news vans. "This is wild, isn't it?"

"What's wild?" Sienna blinks innocently.

"This hack thing. All the systems went down. And someone says there's some sort of e-mail breach—everyone's e-mails are on a public server." I search her face. "You didn't know?"

Sienna frowns. She and I met because I used to work for her grandfather. She's a total knockout with her porcelain skin, big green eyes, and—I'm thinking this happened only recently—gorgeous boobs. Upon meeting Sienna, I thought she'd be a wild, fun friend, but actually, her idea of a crazy night is going to poetry slams and drinking too much coffee. But she's grown on me all the same. Her innocence is refreshing. It kind of makes me feel bad for everything I'm not telling her.

"You mean even *our* e-mails?" Sienna asks. Her face has lost a little of its color. "Like, students'?"

I shrug. "Yeah, I guess. Students ... admin ... I don't know who else. I haven't looked at it yet."

I'm about to say more, but then my phone rings. When I glance down, my heart shoots to my throat. The caller ID shows Greg Strasser's name—Sienna's *stepfather.* I stab IGNORE in shock. Why is *he* calling? I just saw him.

A moment later, my phone rings once more. Greg again. I glance at Sienna, certain she's going to spy the guilt that's written all over my face, but she's busy with her own phone, her brow furrowed at something on the screen. "Excuse me for a sec," I murmur to her, walking a few paces away.

"Hello?" I answer cautiously. Just in case it's Kit, Greg's wife—Sienna's mom—on the other end instead.

"Raina. Thank God you answered."

Greg's husky voice is halting but concerned. I feel a pull in my chest. "Uh . . . hi?"

"Are you okay?" Greg asks cautiously.

A gust of early spring wind whips my chiffon scarf into my face. Down the block, another news van jerks to a stop. Reporters jump out and approach some more kids on the green.

"Why would I not be okay?" I ask evenly. I don't want to raise my voice and arouse Sienna's interest.

"This hack thing," Greg says. "You've heard, right?"

"Sure. All of the Aldrich systems are down."

"Yes. And all the e-mails are on some sort of . . . database. Are you . . . is everything okay with yours?"

I slide my tongue into the space at the back of my mouth where, years ago, I'd had a tooth pulled. My parents had no dental insurance, so I'd never gotten a bridge or implant, but now I've gotten used to the smooth, gummy absence. It's my secret worry stone. "I'm not worried," I say smoothly. It's not a lie.

"Are you *sure*?"

"There's nothing in my e-mails." I'm starting to feel annoyed. "You don't trust me?"

"No, but . . ." There's murmuring on his end. "Shit, I have to go," he whispers.

And then he's gone.

I stare at the phone for a long beat, trying to read between the lines. Is Greg trying to warn me that *he's* exposed something in his e-mails, something linked to me?

"Everything all right?"

Sienna has trotted over. She looks shaken, but not suspicious—at least I don't think so. I drop my phone into my pocket as if it's made of lava and hurriedly fix a smile on my face. "Yep, it's all good." And then I link my arm through hers. "Wanna get a cold brew?"

She leans into me, affectionate and trusting. She knows nothing. And she *won't* ever know. There's no way Greg slipped up in his e-mails—he's as careful as I am. It's why we understand each other. It's why we *work*. The Raina Hammond on the Aldrich e-mail server? She's the Raina I aspire to. Ambitious. Dedicated. Academic. Moral. The kind of girl who has nothing to hide.

It's everything else about me—everything those e-mails *don't* say—that I worry about leaking. But if I have anything to do with it, that's stuff people will never, ever find out.

4

LAURA

WEDNESDAY, APRIL 26, 2017

My six-month-old won't eat. I sit on my queen-size bed trying to force him to my nipple, but nothing. I try a bottle—same. I grab a squeezy pouch from the nightstand and see if he'd like a taste of pureed carrots. Nope. Now he won't have anything in his stomach when he goes to day care. He'll be cranky by midmorning. A bear for the day care providers.

"Come on, noodle." I undo the snaps on my nursing bra again. "Freddie, just have a little, please?"

Freddie arches away from my breast. There's an almost teasing look on his face, like he knows he's pressing my buttons. "Freddie, come *on*!" I moan.

"Geez, babe."

My husband, Ollie, stands in the doorway, a look of disdain on his broad, ridiculously good-looking face. "You're being kind of pushy, don't you think?"

I let the flap of the nursing bra fall over my nipple. "It's just . . ."

Ollie lifts Freddie from me and cradles him in his arms. "Is mommy being mean?" he says in a goo-goo voice. "Is mommy forcing you on her boob?"

"He needs to eat," I say petulantly, buttoning up my shirt again.

"You should *like* mommy's boobs," Ollie goes on in Freddie's face. "*I* sure do."

Our baby giggles. I unclench my fingers from the handful of comforter I've unconsciously grabbed. Ollie's just being nice. He's not chiding me. I don't know why I instantly assume he's about to attack every little thing I do these days. When I peer at him again, his eyes are kind, and he's handing Freddie gently back, murmuring kindly, "If he's not hungry, don't worry about it. He'll eat when he eats."

I nod and stand. There's no more time to waste, anyway. I have four minutes to get into the car or else I'm going to be late. I stuff everything into the baby bag and shrug on my coat over my scrub pants, feeling frumpy and sweaty and really, *really* not in the mood for work. Dr. Greg Strasser's latest e-mail flashes in my mind, and I stop short and wince.

"Babe?"

I jump and whirl around. Ollie lingers in the hall. He's dressed in his police uniform, though his gun holster is empty. There is something inscrutable in his eyes as he stares at me. Dread flutters through my chest once more. "Y-Yes?" I squeak.

"Just be careful," he says. "With that hack stuff from yesterday, I mean."

I smooth down my scrubs. Try to breathe. "There's nothing in *my* e-mails that could have caused any trouble." At least I have that solace.

"I just hate that you're part of the server they targeted," Ollie says as he starts down the stairs. I follow him. "And I hate that we haven't been able to shut it down yet. But it's like, the more we dig into this thing, the more we realize that whoever did this had a beef with higher education as a whole. And whoever did this might not be finished."

I feel a chill down my spine. "What do you mean by that? Like . . . another wave of identity theft? Some kind of . . . *attack*?"

Ollie shrugs. "Just watch your back, okay? Until I crack this, that is."

I smile nervously. "Well, if there's anyone who can figure it out, it's you." My husband has been an officer in Blue Hill—where we live, though we own one of the cheapest homes in the township, a run-down fixer-upper that we can't exactly afford to fix—for ten years. It's a sleepy precinct to work for, and most of his business is breaking up teenage parties and issuing speeding tickets. Though recently Ollie shut down a rambling, vacant old house that was being rented out for sexual deviants. This was *huge* news in the neighborhood—but Ollie mentioned he has a feeling the operation is back in business, simply moving into a new house a few streets away.

His good police work got him noticed, and his boss asked him what sorts of cases he *really* wanted to work on. Ollie said he was particularly interested in cybercrimes . . . and now a huge case has fallen into his lap. So the hack is a boon for us, in a crazy way. Still, I hate what has happened that's giving him the opportunity to advance his career. The fallout from the hack has brought Aldrich University to a grinding halt. *All* of Aldrich University—including the enormous, esteemed university hospital, where I'm a nurse. Because all the systems are down, we have to rely on our paper records for scheduling, which we haven't kept very diligently because, well, why would we, when it's all in digital form? And try recalling patient surgery histories and prescription records and past appointment notes off the top of your head. Try calling the insurance companies for every single patient because all those records are lost.

Not to mention the mess with everyone's e-mails on that server. That's wreaked havoc on other parts of the school, and scandals have broken right and left: like how the admissions department kept digital documentation of Aldrich applicants' every personal detail, from their medical history to their arrest records to their transcripts to their parents' tax returns. Or a report I saw about the dangerous cover-ups that are surfacing—like how everyone in the theater department knew that a certain professor/director is a known sex offender, but no one did anything about it. The longer those e-mails stay on that server, the more dirt people are going to find about everyone.

And that's not even the half of it. The news broke yesterday that not only was Aldrich hacked, but several Ivies up the Eastern Seaboard were as well. Harvard. Princeton. Brown. In each of those university enclaves, students, teachers, and administrators are dealing with their own versions of hell. The fact that so many schools were hacked calms me a little—not that I would wish this upon anyone else, but it seems less likely that this was for Aldrich *specifically* and that the hacker is lurking around a nearby corner, ready to strike with physical weapons instead of digital ones.

"Oh my God, I almost forgot. Watch Freddie for a sec, will you?" I place the car seat in the foyer and dash back up the stairs. In my closet hangs the black dress I've chosen to wear to the gala tonight. I grab it, my nicest pair of pumps, my makeup bag, and my curling iron and hair spray, shove everything but the dress in a gym bag, and clomp down the stairs again. Ollie eyes my new loot quizzically, especially the short dress, its flirty hem swinging.

"The Aldrich benefit," I remind him. "Did you forget?"

Ollie looks blindsided. "You mean it's still *happening?*"

I reach for the doorknob. "As far as I know, yeah. Why?"

Ollie scoffs. "I'm just surprised, with the hack."

I drape the dress over my forearm and pick up the baby car seat again. "Well, I'm not the one who makes those decisions. But we have tickets. We should go. It'll still be fun."

Ollie tips his head toward the ceiling. The joints in his shoulders crack, a sound that always reminds me of breaking bones. Ollie sometimes works out at a boxing gym and fights against guys mixed-martial-arts style; on one of our first dates, he admitted that he'd broken a few of his opponents' bones. It's an image I struggle to reconcile with my soft-spoken, teddy bear Ollie. He claims it only happened a few times. Apparently, sparring is a great stress relief for the pressures of a job in which, literally, you have to prepare every minute to be aiming a gun at someone, or screaming your guts out, or fearing for your life. Still, I can't quite picture him behaving that way.

"I'm just so slammed," Ollie says. "We're no closer to shutting down that database than we were when the hack broke. And I don't know how it will look—the guy on the task force going to the Aldrich gala instead of burning the midnight oil to take down the hacker? Doesn't seem right, babe."

I run my tongue over my teeth. "I didn't think of it like that."

"I'll try and come, okay? But don't hold your breath. I won't know until later tonight."

My smile wavers. I want him to come with me. I don't know if I can do this particular event alone. Almost nine months ago, when the doctors in the cardiology department bought the more senior surgical nurses tickets to the gala, I'd felt honored. Dr. Greg Strasser and I were—well, our schedules didn't intersect as much, but the shit hadn't hit the fan yet.

But now, all that has changed. Going alone will leave me exposed. I need Ollie as my shield.

But how can I explain that without giving something away? I've been excited about the event—it will look strange if I suddenly have a change of heart. "No problem," I say, tucking a piece of hair behind my ear. "Your black suit's clean. Grab it just in case."

He nods, and we kiss goodbye. I carry the cumbersome car seat out the door. The morning is sunny but below freezing—spring is taking forever to arrive. I snap the car seat into its base, and my baby lets out a giggle. I look into Freddie's huge blue eyes and feel the rush that will never cease to amaze me—this little man, this *miracle,* is mine. Such an amazing little treasure. It hadn't been easy for us, making him. A year ago, we never thought we'd get a baby at all. And now . . . look. Our world is so shiny and bright.

Except it could crack open and smash on the sidewalk.

I swallow hard. *No, it won't.* I can't think like that. Nothing's going to change.

I slide into the front seat, feeling a whoosh of conviction. I can't fear Greg Strasser. This is my life, my future, and I need to set the tone. I pull out my phone and look at the e-mail I sent Greg earlier this week. *I've received your research. Definitely taking into consideration. But I have all I need for now—thanks.* It's popped up in the hack, but if anyone asks about it, I have a ready excuse. The problem is, Greg didn't write me back.

There's no way I'm going to e-mail him again and risk it turning up on a hack site. So I compose a new text: *Please. We need to talk. Are you going to the giving gala?*

The phone whooshes to indicate the text has been sent. My heart pounds, waiting for Greg's answer—in the old days, he used to get back to me almost immediately. I need to get a grip. I need to fix this. And I have a fleeting, powerful thought that passes through me like lightning: *It would be so, so much easier if Greg Strasser were just gone.*

There's an excited bubble of conversation at the nurses' station as I clock in. Tina, a surgical nurse who has as much tenure as I do, notices me and grins mischievously.

"What?" I ask—she's said something I haven't caught. I'm distracted. I've checked my phone relentlessly, waiting for Greg's reply, but he still hasn't answered.

Tina's eyes dance. "Have you heard about Dr. Strasser?"

Her voice is teasing, *knowing.* My stomach flips. Terrible things come to mind: Greg broadcasting the truth on the marker board the nurses used to keep track of who was attending to which patient.

Blaring it over the hospital loudspeaker. Telegraphing it in a hospital-wide e-mail.

"N-No . . ." My throat has gone dry. "What happened?"

Marjorie steps forward. Her mouth is twisted into a smirk. "Some crazy shit came out about him in the hack," she whispers. "Apparently, he's having an online affair with someone—and, man, does he talk dirty to her. It's gone viral. Like *really* viral."

Tina pretends to fan herself. "The things he wants to do to her on the MRI machine! I'll never look at that thing the same way again."

"I wonder how Kit's taking it." Marjorie crosses her arms. "Gorgeous woman like that? And remember when they started dating? It was only what, two, three years ago? He was like Tom Cruise when he jumped up on Oprah's couch, ecstatic about Katie Holmes."

"Men," Tina spits. "They always want 'em younger. Up for anything."

"Well, if these e-mails are true, this girl certainly was *that*," Marjorie chuckles. She looks at Laura. "Chauncey is furious. Says it makes the whole department look unprofessional." Chauncey is the head of the hospital, a man we all quietly fear.

"This hack makes *everyone* look unprofessional," Tina says with a shrug.

"Wonder who exposed him?" Marjorie turns to the coffeemaker to refill her to-go cup. "Someone put Greg's shit all over Facebook. There are tons of e-mails on the hack server, though—why'd they target him?"

"Guess he has some enemies." Tina's gaze returns to me, and there's something about it that seems smug. *Could she know?* "I'd be surprised if Strasser came in today. If that happened to me, I'd hide under a rock forever. Move out of the country."

As if on cue, Marjorie's phone pings. Her eyebrows shoot up. "Speak of the devil. Dr. Strasser has come down with the flu. Awfully convenient! He's asking Alice to reschedule his surgeries."

"Coward," Tina spits. She glances at me once more. I pretend to fiddle with my Fitbit.

In a fragrant cloud of bubble gum and hand sanitizer, Tina hurries away to speak to Alice in scheduling. Marjorie is off to attend to recovering patients. I busy myself at the desk, staring at the stack of memos that temporarily replaces some of the data we'd stored on the network, but my mind is thudding. I need to know.

I head for the ladies' room and shut myself in a stall. It's not hard to find the link to the database where all our Aldrich e-mails have been dumped. I find Greg Strasser's folder right away. After scrolling through his inbox and finding nothing incriminating, not even a weird Amazon purchase, I open his trash folder—and voilà. There they are, a whole list of them, practically the only messages Greg threw out. His e-mails are titled things like *Sucking your sweet tits* and *I came over and over just thinking about you* and *I love looking at your juicy ass.* I feel dirty just reading the words.

But maybe this scandal is a good thing. Greg will focus on it for a while instead of me. It might make him pliable. Agreeable. I might be able to effectively get my point across and get out of him what I need.

My breathing begins to slow. Yes, I'm going to speak to Greg. And I'll make him see my side. I *have* to.

5

KIT

WEDNESDAY, APRIL 26, 2017

On Wednesday morning, pre-work, I wander the cheese department of Whole Foods with Aurora in tow. My daughter searches out a brand of low-fat mozzarella string cheese she insists she must have in her school lunch. I'm still in a fog from the night in Philly. All I think about are Patrick's dancing eyes. The strong grip of his hand. The feel of his lips on mine.

Did it really happen?

That night in the hotel, I'd lain awake, praying he'd knock on my door. I both wanted it and dreaded it. After he didn't show, I felt disappointed. Our bond had been so instantaneous, so powerful—the opposite of what I have with Greg. I can't even recall the last time Greg looked at me with such intensity . . . and I don't know if he ever will again. Maybe I shouldn't have squandered the opportunity.

But then I told myself, thank *God* nothing happened. I have everything I want right here. Okay, so my husband and I had a truncated honeymoon phase. Greg and I got together during such a fraught—though terribly romantic—time, but it's hard to keep those intense feelings up. I fell into Greg's arms after my first husband died very young and very unexpectedly. Greg was a white knight on a steed. But I don't need rescuing anymore.

Or perhaps our disillusionment with the marriage is because we didn't vet one another properly before making a commitment. I was busy being the shocked and fragile widow, Greg was so good as the character of the admired hero . . . but those aren't our real selves. Once we stripped off those costumes, maybe we weren't as interesting to one another?

Still. I'm not giving up. Perhaps Greg and I just need a vacation alone, a better one than the trip we took to Barbados over the holidays. Maybe we need to take up a new hobby together. Or maybe I should push couples counseling again. I'd brought it up as recently as our Barbados trip, insisting that a friend from college had used a great therapist who was only a few blocks from our house. Greg's reply had been "Oh great, we'd tell her all our problems and then see her out later at the local grocery store, buying toilet paper. No, thanks."

I pick up a wedge of Gouda. Drop a box of crackers into my cart. Then my phone buzzes. I hope, irrationally, that it's a text from Patrick—that he's somehow found me. But it's Amanda, my assistant. *You need to see this.*

Attached is a screen grab of the hack database I already know about—I was briefed about the Aldrich hack as soon as I got off the plane from Philly and have already met with the PR team to strategize talking points if I happen to be interviewed, as the university president's daughter. On a server, for public consumption, are the inner lives of more than twenty thousand students like my daughter Sienna; administrators such as myself; athletes; my father, the president; and even students from years ago, like my first husband, Martin.

And speak of the devil . . . it's Greg's folder of e-mails that's open. As a hospital employee, he is on the server, too. Several e-mails to someone named Lolita Bovary are circled.

I frown. I've already looked through Greg's e-mails. I looked at my own, too, and Sienna's, just to be sure there isn't something I'm missing. But these e-mails are from Greg's trash folder, which I hadn't thought to open.

A second text pings in, and then a third. I squint at the new images Amanda has sent, not understanding what I'm reading. More e-mails are circled, dated as recently as a few months ago. They say things like *I want to bend you over on the MRI machine. I thought of you today and went into the bathroom to masturbate. You look so sexy in that short skirt. Do a dance for me, next time I see you.*

These e-mails aren't to me.

I sink against one of the cheese cases. The woman Greg is writing to signs her name *Lolita.* And she submits to him like a child. *Thank you,* she writes. *I'm flattered. You're so cute.* She never has any requests of her own, but it's clear she's enjoying the attention.

Bile rises in my throat. I can't believe this is happening.

Then I realize something else: Amanda wouldn't have trolled for dirt on my husband. Someone sent this to her. Someone *made her aware.*

"Mom? You okay?"

Aurora's face is full of alarm. She so closely resembles Martin with her dark hair and her green eyes and pouty mouth—it's like looking at a ghost. Before I can hide what I've read, her gaze falls to my phone screen. Her brow furrows. A vein in her neck pops.

I press my phone to my chest. "I'm fine."

But Aurora's skin has gone pale. It's clear she saw Greg's name in the address line. "Mom?" she asks, her voice hoarse. "Was that in the hack?"

I turn to a display of blue cheese, grab the biggest hunk, and drop it into my cart. I hate blue cheese. It will rot in our fridge for weeks. But I need a distraction from Aurora. I can't look at her. "It's nothing. Don't worry about it."

My heart pounds as we go through the checkout line. I hold it together as I drive Aurora to school. She gives me a long, inquiring look before she gets out of the car, but I pretend to be very committed to a story about the economy on NPR. After she trudges into the school building, I speed out of the school parking lot and merge onto the highway, typing while driving.

Who knows about this? I write to Amanda with shaking hands.

Amanda's reply bubble is meek and regretful, like it wants to blurt out what it knows and then run quickly away, don't-shoot-the-messenger style: *Everyone.*

—————

That night, I stand at the foot of the Aldrich University Natural History Museum stairs, gazing at the royal purple banner that announces the evening's event. The night is everything I imagined when I put together the plans: It's a beautiful, early spring sunset. Limos wait at the curb. The city twinkles magically. I pictured myself standing right here, hand in hand with Greg. I figured people would see an attractive woman in a slate-gray, low-cut silk gown that showed that, at thirty-nine, I'm still as fresh and beautiful as any undergrad, definitely too young to have a nineteen-year-old daughter. I imagined my glossy lips curving into a dazzling smile, and my husband giving me a lingering kiss at the corner of my mouth. It would be enough of a gesture to show everyone that our marriage is rock-solid, nothing to see here.

Now the only accurate prediction is the dress.

I glance once more at my reflection in my compact. Inside, I am trembling—*raging*, really—but I don't have a hair out of place. I drop the compact back into my clutch, hold the hem of my gown, and start up the stairs alone . . . as though I meant to come solo all along.

"Mrs. Manning?" A guy stops me, and for a moment I think it's *him;* I've been seeing Patrick ghosts everywhere. But this is a young kid in jeans, a black T-shirt. "Do you have a comment about the hack?" he asks. A reporter, then. He must recognize me as the president's daughter.

"Nope," I murmur, hurrying past.

"Have you been in touch with any of the universities that were targeted?" another voice dogs me. "Any idea who's behind it?"

I duck my head. *If I knew that, don't you think I'd have already done something about it?*

But Kit Manning-Strasser does not bark at journalists. I duck my head and push through the door, where, thankfully, the reporters aren't welcome. My chest buzzes. At least the reporter didn't ask about Greg's e-mails. He's practically the only person who hasn't.

Inside, among a backdrop of dinosaur bones, paintings of woolly mammoths, and plaques heralding Arthur Aldrich, the nineteenth-century railroad baron, for funding paleontological digs all over the world, the party has begun. The student waitstaff looks presentable enough in their tuxedos, despite their Technicolor hair and stretched-out earlobes. I look around at the guests. People are drinking and laughing, but many look . . . *off*. They keep worriedly glancing at their phones—it's obvious why. I want to tell them for the love of God to just *stop*.

"Kit, darling!" Judge Packard and his wife, Johanna, approach, breaking me from my spiraling memory. I straighten up—these are some of my biggest donors, and I need to focus. I give the Packards a convincing smile and, as they move forward to kiss my cheeks, I can smell that the judge has had a couple of vodkas already.

"Lovely party," the judge says, the ice cubes in his drink clinking noisily.

"Such a fun locale!" Johanna agrees. "I haven't been here since my kids were little. Where's your gorgeous husband?"

I curl my toes. *Way to be subtle.* "Greg couldn't make it," I say brightly. "He's not feeling well."

"Really? What a shame . . ."

There's a feisty, don't-bullshit-a-bullshitter expression on

Johanna's face. So Johanna knows. She must have read the e-mails—for some reason, Greg's e-mails to Lolita, along with a few other sordid gems, made it onto a "Worst of Aldrich University" post on Facebook. It's likely no one else outside our universe cares—though I can bet money that Harvard, Princeton, and Brown have put together their own "worst of" lists—but everyone around here definitely knows everything.

I went straight home after dropping Aurora off at school because I knew Greg didn't have surgery scheduled until later. I found him in the kitchen, reading a recent issue of *Golf*. He barely looked up as I approached. It's a sharp contrast to how he used to greet me: springing effusively from his chair, peppering me with kisses, sometimes even sweeping me into the bedroom.

"I read those messages of yours in the hack," I said in a dark voice to him. "Care to explain who Lolita is?"

Greg's face clouded. His eyes lowered. "If you must know, I've never seen those e-mails before today."

If I must know? It's suddenly a *privilege* to be let in on a husband's dalliances? "They were *in your deleted mail*. Of course you saw them."

"Someone must have hacked me. Planted them there. Honestly, Kit, I have no idea." He ran his hand through his hair. "But I could lose my job because of this."

His voice sounded plaintive—even afraid. But his eyes blinked rapidly, something that always happened when he was in a bind. *He's lying.* I thought of the last e-mail I read from Lolita: *Don't shut me out. The only thing getting me through this quotidian existence is you.* Greg didn't even write her back. Had he broken it off with her? Had he *ghosted* her? Should I feel sorry for this woman? Is she even age appropriate?

Quivering with rage, I told Greg not to come to the gala. I wanted it to be *my* decision, not his. Then I went upstairs. Greg didn't follow. He didn't try to defend himself, prove to me he hadn't written the e-mails. When I went downstairs again, he was locked in his office, on the phone. My first thought was: *He's calling her.* But he was probably on the phone with his boss, the chief of surgery at the hospital. He was probably trying to save his position.

Now I wonder if I've made the wrong choice in letting Greg stay home tonight—it's as if I've given him a gift. It would be satisfying to see him squirm. For Johanna Packard to ask *him* her questions. For *him* to suffer some of the whispers and looks instead of me.

A hand touches my shoulder. My father, the Aldrich University president, looks dapper in his tuxedo—he's whittled off his belly in the past few months, probably due to one of the exercise fads he's always trying. If I were in a better mental state, I'd ask him which one it was. "Oh." I feel my throat catch. I was hoping Dad wouldn't be here, considering the hack. Then again, maybe he's showed up because he doesn't want to spook our donors. "Dad. Hey."

My father gives Johanna Packard his million-watt smile, which seems to have some kind of voodoo effect on women of a certain age. "I realize Kit's probably in the middle of a grand speech, but may I borrow her for a moment?"

Already a few paces away, Dad turns back, raising one eyebrow at me as if to say, *You're coming.* All around me the volume is beginning to rise, and I catch snippets of conversation. One man waves a supersize iPhone at his wife. "How long has this been going on?" A robust man has his own iPhone pressed to his ear. "Do you realize those pictures are now on a *public website?*"

I feel worse with every step. Why hadn't I asked Patrick's last name? Why hadn't I woken up when he did and followed him down to the lobby? If only I could call him right now, hear his voice, escape this nightmare . . .

My father stops at a reproduction of a prehistoric crocodile and gives me a stern, almost reproachful look. "So where's your husband?"

Your husband. He can't even say Greg's name. I work hard to keep my shoulders back. "I told him not to come."

"I see."

I wave to the Lowrys, another Big Fish couple, across the room as a way of distraction. "So has the IT team shut down that Planett page yet?" I then ask my father. "What's the status on getting the systems up and running? The donors are freaking out."

Dad's eyes narrow. "I'm handling it. Don't worry." Then he sighs. Shakes his head in shame. "I just can't believe he'd *do* this to you, Kitty."

I nod. I play the role of the humiliated, gutted, heartbroken woman. But there's more to how I feel than just that. As the hours go on, a new feeling has supplanted my heartbreak. Knowing what I know, I should have fucked Patrick all night. I should have had a grand time, the best sex of my life. And I would have been way more discreet about it, too. I wouldn't have put it on my goddamn *e-mail*. It's bad enough that Greg cheated, but he'd cheated so foolishly, so sloppily, almost like he wanted to get caught and humiliate his family.

Now everyone will think our marriage is a sham. People will feel sorry for me. They'll whisper speculations about why Greg strayed. My daughters might even get drawn into the gossip. People might dig up how Greg and I met, how that connected to my first husband. They'll think, *Well, well, well, isn't* that *ironic?*

"Kit? Hey! Kit!"

It's Lynn Godfrey, my coworker. Tonight, she wears a sleeveless, floor-sweeping red dress and five-inch pumps, and her white-blond hair is piled on top of her head in a French twist. She waves at me from across the room as though we're old friends, though I'm certain Lynn is brimming with schadenfreude—she definitely knows about Greg's e-mails. It wasn't lost on me how bitter Lynn felt when I got to go to Philadelphia to attend to *her* clients.

I murmur an excuse to my father that I have to go. Then I cross the room to Lynn. She's watching me, holding two filled martini glasses.

"Got this for you." She proffers one of the cocktails as I approach. "It looks like you need it."

I wave it away. "I never drink at the gala."

Lynn snorts. "I went through quite an ordeal to get this. It's a madhouse at that bar."

She points a manicured fingernail toward one of the bars, and I see my daughter's friend Raina Hammond mixing a cocktail. Raina gives me a cheerful wave, almost like she's been waiting to catch my eye. I don't smile back—something unnerves me about that girl. Before I left for the gala, I'd called Sienna; she'd told me she might go to a party with Raina later. Sienna also mentioned the e-mail hack, pausing awkwardly as if she wanted to bring something up but was afraid of what my reaction might be. Greg's e-mails, naturally—so she read them, too. I'd nearly hung up on her, I was so desperate to get off the call.

I want that cocktail after all. I take a long sip, about to ask Lynn how the night is going—we should compare notes about donors. Suddenly, someone slams into me from behind. The martini splatters my arms and bodice. "Oof!" I cry out.

"Oh my God, Mrs. Strasser!" A dishwater blonde steps back, her eyes round. "I am so, *so* sorry!"

It's Laura Apatrea, a surgical nurse in Greg's department. She wears an ill-fitting black shift and blocky, churchgoing heels; her dark blond hair seems tragically undone for such a formal event, almost like she quickly styled it in a public bathroom.

"Did I splash you?" Laura grabs some napkins from a nearby table. "I can't believe I—"

"It's *all right*," I say through clenched teeth. "It's not a big deal."

She looks mortified, but I swish her away unsympathetically. I don't have time for doe-eyed Laura right now. But Lynn assesses Laura over the lip of her cocktail as the nurse scuttles away. "A little bird told me the doctors paid for some of the nurses to come." A mischievous look crosses her features. "Maybe your *husband* sponsored her?"

There is something about the way she says *husband* that needles me, but I'm not about to delight her with a reaction. "So," I say briskly, "I already spoke to the judge and his wife, and I'm about to pitch the Lowrys, which means you should cover . . ."

But then I trail off. Lynn, only half listening, has turned to put her hand on the shoulder of someone walking past. The man's back is still to us, but there's something familiar about him that resonates with me on unspoken, subconscious levels. "Kit." Lynn's voice is honey. "I'd like you to meet my husband." She strokes the man's arm. "Darling? This is Kit Manning-Strasser. We work together."

The man turns, and it feels like I'm falling down an elevator shaft. Here is that schoolboy grin. Here is that same adorable dimple in his left cheek. I blink hard, certain my mind is tricking me, but no . . . it's *him*.

Patrick the hurricane pilot/auto racer. Patrick of the no last name. A man whose scent I can still smell in my nostrils, who is driving me so wild I drifted aimlessly around a grocery store. I almost drop my drink. My legs feel boneless.

A startled look flickers across Patrick's face, too, but then he reaches out his hand. "Kit, is it?"

My tongue feels fat in my mouth, but I say, somehow, "Yes."

Lynn beams obliviously. I remember everything she told me about this man: He's a successful businessman, her college sweetheart. They have an eleven-year marriage and two young children. I should be mad that Patrick lied to me, but how can I be? He *told* me he was lying. That was the game.

"Nice to meet you," I add, because I have to say something. Then I grab my drink and down the rest of it fast. The world wobbles. The alcohol hits me instantly. I am certain, suddenly, that I'm going to throw up.

"Excuse me," I say. And then I turn . . . and run.

6

LYNN

WEDNESDAY, APRIL 26, 2017

*W*hen asked to name the deadliest sea creature, most would probably guess a shark, but it's not true. The best hunter in the sea—and I am reminded of this as I pass a glass case featuring a fossilized version of one at the giving gala—is the sea horse. Their heads are shaped in such a way that they slice silently through the water, causing almost no disruption to the current. They can sneak up on their prey completely unannounced. If a creature can't sense danger coming from behind, how will it know to flee?

Just another reminder that sneaky always, *always* wins.

I've been talking with Rupert Van Grieg, one of our biggest donors, for almost thirty minutes. Would rotund, pink-cheeked, already-soused Rupert enjoy my sea horse evolutionary tidbit, or does he just want me to tell him another slightly off-color joke about Catholic priests? I'm babysitting Rupert because Kit's not at her best right now. She's stumbling vertiginously. She's slurring her words. Our boss, George, has cast a couple of alarmed glances her way. This isn't the Kit Manning-Strasser we all know and adore.

Slow and stealthy, that's how you win. Slow and stealthy.

Besides the martini I drank earlier in the night, I haven't had another drop of alcohol. And because of that, I'm nailing it tonight, hack scandal be damned. I've locked down four major donations for the next quarter. Even the Hawsers, the couple Kit had purportedly gone to see in Philly but with whom she hadn't closed the deal? They came tonight from all the way across the state, and I won them over, too.

I watch as Kit almost face-plants into a table full of tiramisu. When you can't handle the heat, you should get out of the kitchen.

Rupert purses his lips at me, and I can tell he's about to beg for another joke (and, let's face it, brush his hand over my ass). Then I sense someone to my left. My husband is not sea horse–stealthy, so I turn as he approaches, reaching out to draw him in. My stomach flips at the way his tuxedo hugs his body. Patrick hasn't aged a day since we met—which, considering all I've had to do to stop the hideous march of time, is a great indignity.

But something's off. He doesn't take my hand. He doesn't smile. His eyes flicker around the room. He seems checked out. Almost as fossilized as the dinosaurs.

"You all right, honey?" I murmur, a slight note of warning in my tone.

The corners of Patrick's mouth turn down. "I don't think our appetizers agreed with me." He lightly touches his cummerbund for effect.

I frown. "*I* feel fine." I turn back to Rupert. "Patrick and I went to Or, The Whale before we came here. Split the seafood tower."

"Ah." Rupert nods. "Great food at that place, but terrible service."

Patrick was distracted at dinner, too. He kept looking at his phone, but when I peeked at the screen, all I could see was his screensaver—a picture of our two kids, Connor and Amelia, on the beach at Hilton Head. I'd wondered if he was communicating with the babysitter about something—Patrick often worries when we go out, regularly checking in with the sitter with reminders and tips— but he shook his head and said the kids were fine.

"I think I'm going to head out," Patrick says apologetically. "You mind if I take the car, babe? You can take an Uber—I don't want you driving."

"Why? I'm not drinking." I put my hands on my hips. I'm suddenly aware of how my Spanx are digging into my waistline. "C'mon, darling. It's a great party. Stay a little longer."

Patrick glances toward the door, his face pale. "I think you'd be better off without me."

Above us, a T. rex looms, its fossilized jaws open in mid-munch. I estimate the hours it took me to get ready for tonight: the hair and makeup appointments, the waxing, the skin brushing, the CBD oil I numbed my feet with so I could stand up in these shoes. The body shaper I contorted to get into, the jewelry I'd polished, the vintage Chanel clutch I'd searched for before remembering I'd put it in the safe-deposit box in the closet. I heard my mother's voice in my head the whole time I prepared, telling me I wasn't pretty enough, that I had to do *more* to hide all my imperfections, though when I looked at the end result in the mirror, I wanted to snap a selfie and send it to her—in her grave. *Here, Mom, you'd finally approve.*

And all that was on top of the hours I spent memorizing important details about donors—a wife's favorite opera, that a husband's family is from Hungary, that a couple has six poodles, that their favorite type of vacation is to go to Old West camps and pretend to be ranchers. I made fucking *flash cards* to remember all of it. And here I am tonight, looking gorgeous, killing it professionally—this is an important night for me. Patrick needs to stay. He needs to hold my arm and laugh at the donors' stupid jokes and choke down another glass of wine. He should know this by now. And usually he's good at following the gentle requests I make of him.

I'm not as controlling as I might sound—it's just that Patrick *needs* it. A mutual friend introduced us. I was in college at UVA; Patrick had graduated from Duke a few years prior. Patrick was handsome, athletic, and ambitious, launching his first business at just twenty-three, but he was lost without his mother and in over his head as a businessman, so he was looking for a personal assistant who would not only help him transform himself into a proper CEO but also run his life domestically. Patrick needed someone to organize his calendar, schedule his meetings, take his calls, but also shop for him, tell him what to eat at dinners, and even tell him how to socialize at events and not sound like a fratty buffoon.

I've always been good at running things and behaving properly—nonstop etiquette classes and hypercritical parents will do that to you. In high school, one of my closest friends wanted to become a movie star, and before she moved to Hollywood and established a very respectable career as a character actress, I was her manager. It didn't even feel hard. I bullied my way into getting her auditions and interviews—even setting her up with some producers in LA. All I had to do was act like I'd been in the business for years, and people believed it. I had a good little business going for a while, though I stopped it after I started college because it was taking up too much of my time.

Anyway, after months of a strictly professional relationship, things deepened between Patrick and me, we got married, blah, blah, blah, happily ever after. And now I see myself as Patrick's PA, life coach, and sexpot all rolled into one. Because of this, I am the envy of other mothers and wives—they are stunned by how *agreeable* my husband is. They're like, "He's compliant *and* handsome *and* wealthy *and* he's a stellar father?" (That part I never had to school him on: Patrick is over the moon for those kids, sometimes to a fault.) His buddies might call him *whipped*, but I like to think that we whip one another. Not literally—horrors—but there are certain things I do to hold up my end of the bargain, too. I haven't eaten bread in years, for example. I close the exercise ring on my Apple Watch every day. I go to bed with a full face of makeup and wipe it all off only after he's fallen asleep—again, another tip from my late mother, who always said my naked face was too flat and plain.

"Just take a Tums," I murmur to him now.

Desperation flashes across Patrick's face. "Nice to see you again," he says to Rupert, as he backs away.

Rupert loops a fleshy arm around me. "If you leave, I might just take this one home!" He squeezes me tighter. His skin smells like Scotch and, underneath it, Bengay. I laugh along, but inside, I'm rolling my eyes. If I suggested that Rupert and I get naked, he'd probably piss his pants.

"But seriously," Rupert adds to Patrick, "you've got a real gem with this one. She can tell a joke, speaks four languages, and she was telling me earlier that she's skilled in French cuisine! Watch out, Julia Child!"

Patrick laughs halfheartedly. "Yep, Lynn can pretty much do it all."

He squeezes my arm, gives me one more kiss, and heads to the door. I glance around to see if anyone's seen. It doesn't seem so, but I wish Patrick weren't walking out of the museum so damn quickly. I mean, he's practically jogging away from me.

I wish Patrick's e-mails were on that hack server. I want to believe that he's faithful—he'd *better* be—but after trolling so many accounts on that hack database, I don't have much trust in humanity. Kit's husband's dalliance was far from the only transgression I found—totally unassuming people are having affairs, people I would have never guessed. Like my sweet, slightly naïve neighbor Charlie in Aldrich University medical research? He's banging his research assistant. And Tomiko Clarke, who has an executive role in Aldrich Alumni Relations, is cheating on her wife with a *man*. I even found a dozen long, deep, emotional letters to a person named Sadie in my boss George's drafts folder. I don't know who Sadie is—and considering that George's wife is with him tonight, either they've worked it out or she hasn't trolled his e-mails yet.

But Patrick would be a fool to play with fire. It's not even worth dwelling on—I have a job to do. I have donations to bring in and money to make. I also still have the Kit Show to watch. And so I turn to her, watching as she staggers about, arms flailing, body listing. I have a good feeling that after tonight, everything is really going to change.

7

KIT

THURSDAY, APRIL 27, 2017

The first thing I smell when I come to is bleach. Which is unfortunate, because I *hate* bleach: It always reminds me of being in the morgue all those years ago. A dry heave wells up inside me, and I press onto my arms. My eyes feel reptile-dry as I open them. There is the taste of death in my mouth. Where the hell *am* I?

The world spins. I see the overhead light blaring, the tile work, a dust ball, a strand of my highlighted hair. And then I see the photograph. It's an Ansel Adams print of Siesta Lake in Yosemite Park. The real deal Ansel Adams, not some lame print you buy in a mall art shop—Greg bought it for me as a wedding present. I even remember the card: *A cool, tranquil respite for* my *cool, tranquil respite.* Greg was such a Lord Byron back when things were fresh and new.

Okay, then. I'm in my downstairs powder room. In my craftsman-style home tucked on Hazel Lane in Blue Hill, one-point-six miles from the museum, where the gala was held. How did *that* happen? Did I *walk* here?

I struggle to my feet. The world lurches, and I catch the side of the sink. I'm definitely still drunk from the gala. *What* did I drink? All I can remember is one martini. I notice my reflection in the mirror: My gray gown is as wrinkled as elephant skin. My makeup is ghoulishly smudged around my eyes. My lipstick has long been eaten away.

It feels like the tundra in the front hallway, and I'm quick to discover why: My huge, arch-shaped craftsman-style door stands wide open. A crisp breeze gusts in the smell of earth and mulch. *Jesus.* Did I really leave that open? And then I spot my car crookedly parked in the driveway. I close my eyes, desperately wanting to blot out what my brain now knows. I *drove home.* I can't quite believe it: I *never* drive drunk.

I twist around, peering back into the bathroom. My clutch lies facedown on the tile, a lipstick and my keys fallen out. I scoop everything up, pull out my phone, and look at the time. It's past 1:00 A.M. Cold, clammy panic overtakes me. The last I remember checking, it had been only a little after ten. I've lost *three hours.*

I retrace my steps: I'd gone inside the gala. Talked to Dad. Drifted over to Lynn Godfrey. And then . . . *Patrick.* I shut my eyes. I've temporarily forgotten.

I recall dinner, sort of—talking to the Farrows, the Reeds, the Lechters—but I also remember hiccupping loudly. All eyes on me again. Someone laughing unkindly. Someone mentioning an MRI machine. Lynn Godfrey watching me, amused, from a few tables over . . . with her husband. But I couldn't look Patrick's way. I didn't want to know if he was watching me—or if he *wasn't* watching me.

At some point, the Lewises tapped my arm and said they were leaving—and, oh yes, they were reconsidering their donation this year, considering all these hack scandals that were coming out. "You mean about my husband?" I'd blurted. God, had I actually *said* that? They'd looked at me partly pityingly. Maureen, the wife, said I should go home and get some rest.

But everything else . . . all those other hours and minutes . . . I can't remember. At *all.*

"Aurora?" I call out into the hallway. No answer.

"Greg?" I sound like a witch, my voice craggy and sick. As I look down, I realize I'm only wearing one shoe.

The kitchen light is on, which is a huge red flag. Among his other lovely qualities, Greg is a stickler about energy efficiency; he has a conniption if we leave lights on when we aren't in rooms. Did *I* leave this on? Did I come in the kitchen first? There's nothing.

And then I see it.

Feet splay out on the travertine tile. I stop short, wondering if this is some sort of drunken delusion. These are Greg's feet. And they are connected to Greg's Adidas around-the-house pants. Which are connected to a T-shirt from Bar Harbor, Maine, and then . . . oh Jesus. Greg is lying facedown in a pool of . . . *something*.

"Greg!" I scream, dropping to my knees.

His back rises and falls erratically, and he makes a gurgling sound. Now that I'm on the tiles, I have a clear view of what the liquid is: blood.

"Oh Jesus. Oh fuck. *Fuck*." I'm suddenly sober. I touch my husband's cheek. It's cold and clammy. "Greg!" I scream. "Can you hear me? Who did this?"

I roll his face to the side so he can look at me, and I nearly puke. I have never seen someone so pale. I have never seen lips so blue. His eyes have a milky glaze. Blood seems to be pouring out of somewhere on his abdomen, but I'm afraid to roll him over to find a wound. My gaze crazily scans the kitchen floor, the island, the huge farmhouse table. I don't see a sharp object. I don't see *anything* incriminating.

"Greg." I hold his clammy cheeks. "Greg, *please*! What happened? Who did this to you?"

There are goose bumps on my arms. My whole body is wet and sticky with blood. I wonder if I'm going into shock. "Honey, oh my God, I . . ." And then it hits me: Aurora is home, too. I clap my hand over my mouth. "Aurora," I say to him. "Is she okay? *Where is she?*"

Greg's eyes search mine. They blink once. Is this some sort of code? I need to check on my daughter, but her bedroom is three flights up, and I'm afraid that if I leave Greg, he'll die. Or will he die regardless? I feel like an asshole for wholeheartedly hating him tonight. I feel like an idiot because I have no first-aid or CPR skills.

I'm in such shock that it seems to take me forever to find my phone. Blood from my fingers smears the screen, making it difficult to punch in the digits for 911.

"Stay with me," I tell my husband as I speak to the operator. *This cannot be happening.*

The ambulance comes blessedly fast. I open the door for the EMTs and say some words, but the panic and fear and my breath muddle everything in my mind. They march in with their equipment jangling, smelling like Axe body spray and McDonald's drive-through, which turns my stomach again, reminding me, *Oh no, Kit, you aren't sober by a long shot.* And then, suddenly, they're kneeling down next to him. One shouts stats—that Greg's blood pressure is low, that his pulse is "thready," that his oxygen level is "dangerous." And in another blink, one of them is looking at me. I realize he's asked me a question. I make him ask it again: "What sort of weapon made this wound, ma'am?"

I blink. "I-I don't know," I finally say. "I *found* him like this."

And then, I remember: *Aurora.* I need to find her. I dash upstairs.

The second-floor landing is dark. The hectic sounds from downstairs fall away. The wood floor makes a spooky *creak* under my feet as I travel down the hall. I stop halfway down, my eye on a shadow in the guest room. *Shit.* What if whoever did that to Greg is hiding up here now? My heart pounds. I snap on some lights. The hallway is empty, lined with perfectly even photographs.

I head up the second flight of stairs to the top level, where Aurora and, until recently, Sienna sleep. After moving in here, Greg paid to have the top floor remodeled, breaking down the walls of the chopped-up little bedrooms and creating one big loft space that the girls share. The room is full of Lovesac beanbags, a ballet barre, a giant-screen TV; and we carved out two big walk-in closets. But there's no Aurora in the pink Jenny Lind bed by the window. My heart nose-dives. "Aurora?" I call weakly. Nothing.

I fumble for my phone and manage to successfully dial her number after the third try. The phone rings once, twice . . .

"Mom?" Aurora sounds sleepy. "What time is it?"

"Where are you?" I screech.

"I'm at Lilly's." Aurora sounds confused. "Why? What's wrong?"

"Ma'am?"

The voice floats up the stairs. I glance down the staircase. It's not one of the EMTs but a short, muscular police officer. He has close-cropped red hair and squinty eyes, and he's blinking hard like a man who's drunk too much Red Bull.

"Aurora, I'll call you back," I murmur. I blink at the officer. I'm sweaty suddenly. I wonder if I stink of booze.

"Are you his wife?" the officer asks.

I nod. I think I nod.

"Mind coming down here for a sec?"

I nod, but I don't move. It feels like I've just been dropped into a bucket of ice. I don't know how I suddenly know, but I'm positive my husband is going to die. Maybe he's already dead.

And then I think of how I'd ordered him not to come with me to the benefit. "Why are you punishing *me*?" Greg had protested. "You're really going to believe some stupid website?"

"You really think a hacker went to the trouble of making up e-mails in *your* account?" I snapped. "Just admit it, Greg! Just admit you did a terrible, terrible thing!"

But he wouldn't. He kept shaking his head. *Deny deny deny.* I was so humiliated that I threw a shoe at him. A high, spiky-heeled shoe: I flung it right at his head. "What the fuck?" Greg screamed, ducking before the thing clocked his skull.

Those will be the last words he ever says to me: *What the fuck?*

I rake my hands down my face. I remember, too, the thought that kept drifting into my mind for the past day. In the cheese section, after I read those e-mails. At the benefit, when everyone was staring. And if I'm honest with myself, maybe even before that, too. In Barbados, when Greg refused to go to therapy and acted like an asshole. In Philly, when Patrick and I pressed together in the elevator. *It would be so much easier if Greg were just . . . gone.*

I thought it over and over again. It became a fantasy. A best-case scenario. And now, here it is, happening for real. I got my wish.

PART
2

PART

2

8

WILLA

FRIDAY, APRIL 28, 2017

It's 6:00 A.M. in Pittsburgh when I step out of the airport, but because I'm still on California time, I'm feeling like a skin-snapping, pupils-going-in-two-different-directions swamp creature. A rickety Ford minivan with the logo IRON CITY CHECKER CABS rolls out of the gloom like something in a haunted house ride. The driver, a gap-toothed, yellow-skinned fellow with a Marlboro 100 balanced between two fingers, leers at me out the window. I step back a little, a dangerous whoosh going through me. "Need a ride?" he asks in a kind-enough voice.

I, Willa Manning, can't get in a car with a smoker. I drink cold-pressed beet juice. I check for parabens on my shampoo label. Climbing into this car is my equivalent of sitting in a bathtub of plutonium. I really should never leave Los Angeles.

Except this guy is the only cab this time of the morning—and for some reason, my Uber app isn't working. Sighing, I climb in and perch on one of the minivan's captain's chairs, trying not to look too closely at the mysterious stains on the upholstery. My eyes water as the cigarette smell wafts out the vents. I can practically feel the cancer cells growing in my lungs. "Colton Street," I tell the driver as he pulls away from the curb. "One block from Aldrich University." And then, even though it's only 21 degrees outside, I roll down the window and stick my head out like a Labrador.

The driver raises a bushy eyebrow. "Aldrich, huh?" He whistles. "You hear about the murder?"

I almost laugh out loud. *Um, yes, Marlboro Man. You might say I heard.*

"They got any leads on that yet?" the cabbie asks. As if I'm a cop.

I mumble something ambiguous, shut my eyes, and pretend to go to sleep. I still can't wrap my mind around what's happening. Yesterday morning, I'd been minding my own business, driving to my job at the West Coast office of "The Source," a highly respected news site that specializes in deep, intense investigative reporting. I was pissed because there was a mysterious leak in my apartment, but the landlord wasn't taking my calls about it. And then I'd heard an annoying, nosy-aunt voice in my head saying, *If you had a man in your life, Willa,* he *could fix the leak instead of you having to bother Mr. Jenkins.*

Who *was* this woman in my head? I'd been hearing her voice for months, and she pissed me off.

Then my father called. I don't often answer calls while I'm driving, but something told me it was important. And he told me, in a panicked, jumbled rush, that my older sister's husband had been murdered. I should probably come home.

And here we are.

Apparently, Greg was stabbed in his kitchen. Kit came upon him after getting home from a work gala. (Side note: I had a couple of missed calls from Kit at about 5:00 P.M. Pacific time. I'd been in an interview with my latest subject, a female arsonist about to get out of prison.) At about 2:00 A.M., Greg died in the ambulance on the way to the hospital. The funeral is set for tomorrow.

My first thought, when my father told me all this: *Kit's now a widow twice over.* My second thought: *Blue.* But then, I've been wondering about Blue lately anyway. I pushed him out of my brain fast.

Before getting on the red-eye, I searched to see if the story popped up on any of the news feeds yet. Yep: "Prominent Surgeon Murdered in Pittsburgh Home—Possible Hack Link." As I read the story, I felt a little jealous. Not because of its content, but because this is actually the sort of investigative story I like to report on for my job: a tragic murder of a prominent person in society, with an unclear culprit and motive. I like the puzzle of figuring them out. They're always more complicated than you think, and they often have surprising endings.

The story went on to talk about the Aldrich hack, the database full of e-mails, and how someone had leaked some of Greg's onto a bunch of social media portals. Seems that Dr. Greg wrote some filthy fantasies about sex on the MRI machine to a woman who wasn't my sister. *Classy.* Full disclosure: I never really got why Kit fell for Greg Strasser. He's good-looking, he's successful, he has money . . . *had* money. Jesus. But he always struck me as . . . fake. Deceitful. Maybe even predatory. Not that I wished him dead or anything, but . . .

Changing planes in Chicago, I tried calling Kit. Her mailbox was full. After getting through some work voice mails of my own, I trolled the news again. There's a new story featuring an interview with a man named Maurice Reardon; he would be the lead detective on Greg's case. Detective Reardon hinted that Kit might be a person of interest—but that was ridiculous. The chance of my sister murdering someone is about as great as the chance of me ingesting anything colored with blue dye #1 or #2. (Don't even get me started on what just a few Froot Loops can do to your immune system.) Though here's an unnerving little blip: I finally got around to listening to my voice mails from yesterday, and one was from Kit. When I played it, I heard fuzzy, blurry sounds, the phone shifting around this way and that. Almost twenty seconds in, I heard Kit's voice. I *think* it was Kit's voice—it sounded slurred, despairing, not like this shiny thing my sister has become. "Should I get revenge?" Her voice echoed. "*Should* I?"

Probably best not to turn over that voice mail to the detectives.

My cabbie sets his radio to a local news station. I listen as a reporter quietly updates us on Donald Trump, a failed uterus transplant, and then new details about the multi-university hack. My heart jumps. I lean forward to hear.

"Analysts haven't yet been able to trace the hacker who stole hundreds of thousands of e-mails linked to those working at and attending Aldrich University in Pittsburgh, Pennsylvania; Harvard University in Cambridge, Massachusetts; Brown University in Providence, Rhode Island; and Princeton University in New Jersey," the reporter says. "Alfred Manning, who has been Aldrich University's president for more than fifteen years, has reported that an IT task force has been working around the clock to fix the breach. Other presidents have weighed in as well, saying their security teams are taking similar measures."

My shoulders tense. Scandals are starting to leak right and left— at all the colleges, but I only tune into the ones about Aldrich. A professor at Aldrich's medical school actually doesn't have a medical degree. The head of the history department is selling cocaine out of his office. A few players on the school's prestigious basketball team are paying kids to take their tests.

Lives are crumbling. I listen as the reporter floats a few theories of who might have done it: A kid who'd been rejected from every Ivy he applied to. ISIS. North Korea.

The driver continues down 376, and soon enough we cross through the Fort Pitt Tunnel and drive toward the steep embankment to Blue Hill, the neighborhood where I grew up. *Home sweet home*—or not. Dread and shame rise inside me. I come back to Pittsburgh only when it would be ridiculously inappropriate not to— Christmases, the birth of my sister's daughters, Kit's first husband's funeral, her weddings—otherwise, I stay far, far away.

We drive past the neighborhood's main drag, which is peppered with trendy boutiques and yoga studios. I can list the stately order of homes before my parents' by heart: first the Queen Anne Victorian with turrets and third-floor decks, then the Arts and Crafts splendor with stained glass, then the marble monolith that looks like the Metropolitan Museum of Art. At the end of Logan Street is the house I know best: a huge, stately colonial of brick and slate standing on a freshly mown lot. My parents bought the place in the 1970s using every scrap of savings—this was long before my dad made bank at Aldrich. "It's the kind of house one sacrifices for," my mom said. "As soon as I saw it, I knew we'd make wonderful memories here."

I can still hear her voice all these years later. She's one of the reasons I find it so hard to come back. Every landmark I pass, every bend in the road—it still makes me think of how she was taken too soon. My mother never visited LA—she never even knew I'd chosen to move there. This means I can pass through the city untouched by her memory, not suddenly and unexpectedly plunged into sadness.

Two news vans are parked in front of the house. As my cab slows, two reporters step toward us. "Holy shit," my driver says.

I toss him some crumpled-up twenties and wrench the sliding door open. Popping flashbulbs assault me. I hitch my carry-on over my shoulder and jog toward the house. The reporters jog alongside me.

"Excuse me?" a male reporter with a microphone asks. "Do you have a comment about the murder?"

"Do you know Kit Manning-Strasser?" cries another voice. "Is it true she found Greg's body?"

"Do you think she did it?" someone shouts. "Because of the e-mails?"

The front door is unlocked, so I wrench it open and hurry inside, slamming it behind me. Someone rings the bell. "Dude," I shout to the closed door. "It's not even seven A.M.!"

I bolt the lock. Then I turn and look at the house. The foyer still smells like it did when Kit and I were kids: leather, dust, furniture polish. There's the notch on the railing where Kit chipped her tooth when we'd been flying kites down the hallway. There's the spot against the radiator where I sat for what seemed like days after I found out that a drunk driver killed my mother. I shut my eyes. This is too much.

I hear a creak. I can smell my father's Old Spice before I see him. "Willa," he says as he walks forward from the kitchen, his arms outstretched, his eyes sad. "Thank you for coming."

He looks even thinner than he was at Christmas, when he'd started a juice cleanse to "lose the whiskey belly." His sandy hair, normally so groomed—Dad is one of those men who used to take longer to get ready for an event than my mother—is Einstein-crazy around his face. I step closer to him, and he pulls me in for a hug. I feel the same as I always do—like we are distant islands, not really familiar to one another anymore.

"Where's Kit?" I ask, pulling back.

"Still asleep."

I nod. I can't fathom what Kit's day was like yesterday—hospitals, morgues, police stations, funeral homes. She can't go to her own house on Hazel because it's crawling with forensics people. I bet she took something to knock herself out last night. I would have.

"So I'm supposed to be at the college—this hack thing." My dad pinches the bridge of his nose. "You heard?"

"Of course. Hacks are our bread and butter at work."

"Kitty didn't do this, you know."

I fix my gaze on a knot in the stair finial. At first, I think my dad means my sister didn't do the hack, but then I realize—he means she didn't kill Greg. "*I* know that," I say.

"We need to keep her safe right now. Away from the gossip. And whoever *did* do this? He's still out there."

That tagline would definitely bump Aldrich University up a spot on the *US News & World Report* Best Colleges ranking: *Come for the e-mail hack, stay for the serial killing!* I sigh. "Go to campus, Dad. They probably need you."

"Are you sure?" His eyes are concerned. Unsteady.

I nod. "I've got Kit. It's fine." Then I scrutinize his thin face. "You look terrible. Are you sleeping enough?"

"Of course."

"Eating enough?"

But then we're interrupted. "Aunt Willa?" says a shocked voice.

On the landing stands Kit's nineteen-year-old, Sienna. Behind her, like a smaller Matryoshka doll that could nest perfectly inside her older sister, stands sixteen-year-old Aurora. It's only now that I remember my father said on the phone that the girls are staying here, too—even Sienna, who could technically escape to her dorm room. They are negative images of one another, Sienna fair and blond, Aurora with more olive skin, like her father, Martin, but they both have the same bright, upwardly sloped eyes, Cupid's bow lips, and rounded faces. Aurora looks as ballerina-scrawny as ever, but Sienna wears a tight black dress that reveals curves. Shit. When did *that* happen?

"Oh my God," I say, rushing for them. "You guys."

I'm assaulted by a mixture of smells: fruity bubble bath, sour bedding, sticky-sweet hair products. Their bodies feel frozen stiff, like they've turned to wood. Their skin is cold. Beneath my arms, Sienna is trembling.

There's a cough a few risers up, and here is Kit. There are circles under her eyes, and she looks dazed. Despite the fact that she is wearing a thick oatmeal cardigan and wool pajama bottoms, she has her arms wrapped around her body like she's spent the night in a snowdrift. She sees me and stops short, her eyes going wide. "Why are *you* here?"

Somewhere in the room, a gasp. Maybe it's me. This isn't exactly the welcome home from her I expected.

But then again, I also kind of deserve it.

9

KIT

FRIDAY, APRIL 28, 2017

I'm sorry," I say to Willa. "I didn't mean to say that. I'm just . . . surprised."

"It's okay," Willa answers in a clipped voice, then turns. "Come on. Let's get out of this drafty foyer, okay? Do you need coffee?"

She heads toward the kitchen, and I wilt against the banister. *Willa.* Just looking at her makes me well up. I so rarely see her. She only turns up at sad events—funerals, accidents, divorces—so of course I'm plunged into memories of the sad moments I saw her last. But more than that—*Willa.* The tie to my past. The tie to my *mom.* She has Mom's eyes, and they're looking back at me, but I don't know what they're thinking. Who's at fault for the emotional chasm between us? Or maybe it's no one's fault. Maybe we are just normal sisters who don't speak as much as we should. Yet that makes her being here now even more momentous. I know she didn't want to come. I know it was a huge sacrifice to get on that plane. My chest feels tight with a mix of embarrassment for the charity I didn't ask for as well as gratitude that she's done the difficult, uncomfortable thing just for my sake.

Also, with Willa being here . . . it makes it all *real.* Greg is dead.

Someone murdered him. I don't know why the murder happened, or what motivated it, or if the person plans to strike again. I don't know how narrowly I escaped being murdered myself. I've become aware that until the cops find who actually did it, they're going to suspect me—at least a little bit, anyway. With Willa here, the past few days suddenly aren't a dream. It's as real as it gets.

I'm not ready to deal with that.

Willa bustles around the kitchen, knowing where everything is kept by heart because my father hasn't changed a thing. As usual, my sister's small, angular face is makeup-free. Her reddish-brown hair, cut to the shoulders, has streaks of blond through it—from the sun, most likely, as Willa isn't into the whole salon scene. Her body radiates with health and athleticism, and not just because she's wearing leggings and a hoodie that shows off her taut waist. It astonishes me that she's still single. I get that a lot of women in LA are size zeros and look like supermodels, but Willa is truly a catch.

After the coffee is made, she carries two mugs and walks down the hall. Without discussing it first, she heads to the back room of the house, our favorite place. It's where my mother let her interior decorating freak flag fly: All of the furniture upholstery is busily patterned, and nothing matches. The shelves are crowded with bird's nests, pine cones, wood carvings, old egg-crate artwork Willa and I did in preschool, an old Bakelite rotary telephone in sixties orange, and a framed diorama featuring two tiny train-model people trapped in two separate test tubes reaching out to touch one another but never quite connecting. Mom's old sketchbooks are piled in a corner. A few unfinished paintings, both of them still lifes of junk on our kitchen table at the time, rest on easels along the wall. Time hasn't touched this room. It is one hundred percent 1997, the year of her fatal car crash.

I sit down on the leopard-print couch. Willa perches on the slipper chair stamped with hallucinogenic poppies. Our usual spots. My gaze moves down the hall, where I notice Willa's suitcase resting on the front mat. "Wanna take that upstairs?" I ask, gesturing to it.

"Oh." Willa shifts awkwardly. "Actually, I got a room at the Marriott. I'll take my stuff there later."

I run my tongue over my cracked lips. What is it with her and that freaking Marriott? Every time Willa visits—at least since she's had enough money to do so—she's stayed there. She says it's because she doesn't want to get in our way . . . but it feels so impersonal, especially now.

I sit dumbly on the couch. My mind crawls. Finally, I pick up the Coffee mate creamer I grabbed from the kitchen and pour a hefty amount into my mug. Willa gives me a horrified look. "What?" I ask.

"Do you know how many chemicals are in that?"

I shrug, then dump the rest into my coffee. The liquid is vanilla-colored by now. I take a long sip, but now, of course, the creamer tastes like piss. *Buzzkill.*

"So are you still surfing?" I finally say, remembering that the last time I visited Willa in LA, I'd seen two surfboards leaning against her back deck. One of them, she said, belonged to a guy friend. I never did get to meet the guy.

My sister blinks. "Not in a while. I've been busy with work."

"Oh." I wrap my sweater tighter around me.

"I can't wait to get back into it. It's why I moved to Venice. Surfing . . . grounds me."

I never know what people mean when they say something *grounds* them, but then, Willa and I have always been on different planets. We were closer when we were young, but that was only because we lived in the same house with the same rules and routines. Our personalities were nothing alike. Despite our shared last name, some teachers were surprised to learn that we were sisters. I was the friendly one who had so many friends there was hardly autograph space left in my yearbook by the end. A girly girl, I hated to get dirty in chemistry lab; I walked the track in gym instead of participating in sports. I had a head for math and history, but English bored me—much to my father's chagrin, as he'd been in the English department before becoming an administrator.

Willa, on the other hand, was an English teacher's dream. She also played every sport there was, including on boys' teams when girls' weren't offered. She was one of those strong-looking, slightly scary girls who walked into a room and just dominated . . . but you didn't exactly want to be friends with her.

After our mom's death—I'd been a freshman at Aldrich University, and Willa a junior in high school—Willa got . . . *weird*. She dropped out of sports. She bought a pet tarantula, Stewie, and let him walk up and down her arm, hoping to freak people out. She started hanging out at the punk club downtown. She wrote angry poetry on her bedroom walls, and she regularly told people to fuck off. Though she didn't toe the line, my dad never punished her—I guess he figured this was her version of grief. Besides, her grades were always great, which was what mattered most to our dad. He so wasn't equipped for the emotional parts of having teenagers. It's probably why I got married so quickly—I needed someone to rely on. And maybe it's why Willa left.

The year after my mom's death, I threw myself into my friends, activities, and my boyfriend, Martin. Martin was my everything: handsome, sweet, loyal, funny, empathetic. He was my nursemaid as I grieved, helping me get through the days. I was practically living in his dorm room when Willa made the announcement that she was reneging on her acceptance to Aldrich and going to California instead. Maybe I should have tried to connect with her about this sudden change of heart—Willa had always said that she was going to apply to Aldrich and nowhere else. Maybe I *did* try, but I don't recall us having any meaningful conversations about it. Willa was resolute. She was leaving.

After Willa moved, we talked even less. The tragedy with our mom became sealed off, rock hard. We went on our separate trajectories, doing our own things. I became the Kit Manning who married Martin and got pregnant at twenty, who scrambled to find child care so I could finish my last year of college. Willa became the Willa Manning who, well, I don't really know. Works as a reporter? Avoids nondairy creamer? Is celibate? Even though she comes home for holidays and weddings and such, she never shares much.

Out the window, three news vans shimmer through the lifting fog. The reporters sit on the curb with cups of coffee and a box of Dunkin' Donuts, having a little party. "Have you seen Facebook?" I ask. "It's the weirdest mishmash of posts about Greg ever. There are all these judgmental comments about his e-mails . . . and then once the murder story went up, some of those same people also posted stuff like *OMG, RIP, he was always such a good man.*" I shake my head. "Such hypocrites."

"Wasn't that what the hacker said, too? Called everyone hypocrites?"

My head snaps up. "Where'd you hear that?"

"I read it in the news."

God, all the stories: the hack, Greg's affair, his murder. It's almost too much to keep track of.

"Have they let you see him yet?" Willa asks.

"Who?"

Willa cocks her head and gets an uncomfortable look, as if to say, *Who else?* I feel a tug of dread. "Not since the hospital. They're performing an autopsy. I don't understand *why.* I mean, he obviously died of blood loss from the stab wound. What else do they think they're going to find?"

"Maybe they can find out what he was stabbed with. They didn't find the murder weapon, right? Or maybe to see if he'd taken any medications. If he was drunk."

"And what, stabbed *himself*?" I sigh. "The thing that's the hardest? I'm still so angry with him. Those *e-mails.*"

Willa averts her eyes. I feel embarrassed, though I know I

shouldn't. Everyone's read them, probably even my ninety-two-year-old grandmother in the nursing home. "What did Greg say about it?" she asks.

"That he'd never seen them before. His theory is that someone hacked into his account—a spammer or something—and planted them in his deleted messages."

Willa looks skeptical. "May Greg rest in peace, but I bet every guy who's been caught in an affair says that exact same thing."

"I know. But I'm not sure I blame him for cheating. Our marriage had hit a rough patch."

Willa blinks. "Really?"

"Lately, all we did was roll our eyes at one another. All the things I found adorable about him at first became annoying. He was just so cynical. Nothing was ever right. It was with everyone, everything. The attitude began to wear on me."

"Huh," Willa says.

"But I sat with my irritation for months. It's not like I said to him, 'Hey, Greg, you're really negative, and that needs to change.' I just . . . quietly seethed. It wasn't until Philly that I had a moment of clarity. I knew I had to snap out of it." I sigh. "But I guess it was too late."

"Philly? What happened in Philly?"

I feel drunk. Jesus, I can't tell Willa about Philly. "Just a wake-up call in the form of too much to drink," I hedge. "I came home even more committed to fixing things. Or at least broaching the subject with him again—I brought up therapy a few months ago, but . . ." My eyes lower. "And then I saw those e-mails. So . . ." I shrug.

"God, I can't imagine what this is like for you." Willa's spine is bent. "I mean, to be mad when everyone expects you to be sad . . . it's a roller coaster."

"Exactly."

A motor starts on the street. Mr. Leeds, one of our dad's neighbors, is off to work. The reporters jog alongside his car. I wonder what Mr. Leeds is saying about me.

Willa takes a breath. "So what happened that night? I mean, you went to the benefit. I had some missed calls from you. Greg didn't go, I guess? And then I got a message where you sounded kind of . . . drunk."

I forgot about calling Willa until this very moment, but now it rushes at me like a freight train. It had been after I'd seen Patrick at the gala. I had thought, fleetingly, that maybe I'd book a plane ticket to LA and head straight to the airport. Disappear for a little while. So I'd called Willa in the ladies' room, but when her voice mail came on, so did the pressing need to vomit. So I dropped my phone, and . . . I can't remember the rest.

"I actually *didn't* have that much to drink," I say. "But it was like I was suddenly bombed. Nerves, I guess." I sigh. "The next thing I remember is waking up on my powder room floor, and it was hours later. I was back home."

"How'd you get home?" Willa looks horrified. "Did you *drive*?"

I stiffen. "I'm not proud of it. But yes, they have me on a surveillance camera driving my own car out of the museum parking lot." I don't like to think about that. The idea of operating my car while wasted is terrifying.

"But you don't remember anything else from the benefit?"

"Not really." I stare at my fingernails. "Talking to donors, stumbling, feeling paranoid. Everyone knew about Greg's affair, and I was so *embarrassed*. I hated that my daughters were going to read those e-mails, too—everything just felt hopeless. I remember wanting to leave, and looking around for Dad to see if he'd give me a ride. But I couldn't find him. And I *think* I remember sitting in my car before I left . . ."

I definitely remember sitting in my car, actually. I was *sobbing*. About what, I wasn't even sure. The messed-up state of my relationship. The building fury in my chest for what Greg had done. The humiliation of seeing Patrick with Lynn Godfrey.

"What happened after you woke up on the floor of your powder room?" Willa asks.

I lick my lips, explaining how the house seemed eerily silent. "I walked into the kitchen . . . and found Greg."

"I'm sorry to ask, but . . . did Greg . . . say anything to you?"

I shake my head. I walk her through calling 911 and the EMTs coming, and running upstairs to see that Aurora was still okay—I hadn't yet known she'd gone to a friend's. I don't tell her the weird relief I'd felt after the ambulance took Greg away. Or the nagging feeling that I'd brought on Greg's death.

"Did the police find forced entry into your house?" Willa asks.

"I don't think so. But I'm not sure. They're checking."

"Was anything stolen?"

"The cops had me look around when I went back to get some clothes. My jewelry was still there. Everything was in the safe. They didn't take any TVs or computers."

Willa jiggles her leg nervously. "Maybe the Lolita person killed him?"

I shrug. "She was embarrassed by being outed in the hack?"

"In the e-mails, Greg comes on strong at first—there's a lot of dirty talk on his end, but she's more . . . demure. But she never tells him to stop, either. Later, it shifts. She's begging him by the last e-mails. Maybe he broke up with her and wouldn't see her."

I shut my eyes. I hate that Willa has read the e-mails so carefully that she has a detailed analysis of them. Then, a strange feeling comes over me. I give her a steely look. "Are you doing a story on this?"

Willa's eyes widen. "*No!* How could you say that?"

When struck by sunlight, the gold thread in the couch cushions gleams. *Our 24-karat settee,* our mother used to joke. "A lot of people have been calling me. They're dying to know what happened, and I'm not sure it's always with good intentions."

Willa crosses her arms over her chest. "So you lump me in with everyone else?"

"I'm sorry." I don't know why I'm picking on Willa. I want to talk to her about this. I need to talk to *someone.* "Forget it." I look down. "I'm sorry. And okay, sure. Maybe Lolita did it, I don't know. But I have no idea who she is. I've thought about women Greg is around at the hospital, at the gym, at this charity he volunteers for . . . but nobody fits. No one is his type."

"Who *is* his type?" Willa asks, a little begrudgingly. I can tell she's still hurt.

Me, I almost say, but I am no longer sure.

I flash on the moment Greg and I met, three years before. Martin was dealing with the congenital heart issue he'd battled since birth—something he was cavalier about when we'd gotten together but which quickly revealed itself as a very big deal. He was hospitalized three times in a row that winter. Most people who had his condition dropped dead with no warning; doctors only figured out what they had in autopsy. Martin was already living on borrowed time, and he'd become so weak and frail. He'd cut back on teaching hours, which slashed our income. Many doctors suggested a transplant, but we didn't want to take those risks. According to online reports and Best Doctors awards, Dr. Greg Strasser was the best. We felt lucky to get an appointment with him.

When the nurse called out Martin's name to be seen, I had to help him up from the waiting room chair. He hobbled toward the exam room, his back stooped, his breathing labored. In the office, we slumped in the chairs and stared at one another wearily. I figured we were in for a long wait—the more important the doctor was, it seemed, the more behind schedule.

Martin frowned. "Did you see what this costs? *One hundred seventy,* just for a consultation."

"Actually, that's a bargain," I argued. "My dad talked them down to half their usual fee." Dr. Greg Strasser didn't take our insurance, but because he was affiliated with Aldrich University, my father was able to pull some strings.

Martin ran his hand through his thinning hair. In college, it had been so thick, almost unruly, but the surgeries and medications had ravaged it. "So everything's going to cost that much? Even at half, we can't afford this."

"It's your *health*," I hissed. "We can find the money."

Martin set his jaw like he knew what I might suggest next: We could always borrow from my father. It had always been a bone of contention, whether in arguing to buy a bigger, better house, or get a newer car whose brakes didn't squeal, or take the kids to Disney World. I knew my father would bail us out, but Martin wouldn't hear of it: He wanted to support us on his own. Though both of us had grown up comfortably, we gave little thought to money or choosing careers that would put us in a high tax bracket. I admired that Martin wanted to teach elementary school; I didn't care—then—that it paid barely enough to support a family of four in our expensive suburb. I also loved the idea of being a young parent, having the energy to actually have fun with little kids.

But once I had Sienna, and then Aurora so quickly after, I started to notice that everyone else around me had more for themselves and their children. The mothers who could afford a cleaning lady so they could spend weekends taking their kids to museums and playgrounds. The parents who didn't sneeze at sending their kids to arts camps and fancy dance classes, or taking the whole family to Europe for two weeks of cultural enrichment. The moms who didn't freak out when they saw the costs of sports uniforms or overnight field trips or even a babysitter for a night out. I was around easy excess constantly. It wasn't hard to want those things, too.

Yet Martin remained content with where we were. He questioned why I'd changed; I questioned why he hadn't. It was a rift between us—the wanting and not wanting. It was like Martin didn't seem to understand what I was craving. Sure, it was just *stuff* . . . but that stuff sometimes made the difference between a miserable day-to-day experience and a pleasant one. Or at least I thought so, then.

Suddenly, the door to the exam room swung open. Dr. Strasser walked in, startling us both—especially me. He was taller than his picture in *Pittsburgh* magazine made him out to be. He was imposing in his white coat and disarming with his big, straight smile. He shook Martin's hand first—"Call me Greg"—and then mine. And I hate to admit this, but when our hands met, when he looked me straight in the eye, I felt a stirring in my chest.

"So you have quite an extensive medical history for someone so young." Dr. Strasser settled into a stool in front of the computer.

I touched the heavy purse at my feet. "I've brought all of his paperwork. It goes back almost seven years."

Strasser looked surprised. "You two are old enough to be married seven years?"

"We've been married for fourteen years, actually," I admitted. "Straight out of college."

Martin sent me an annoyed look, as if he didn't see the point to disclosing personal details.

Strasser glanced at the papers in my hands. "I received some of your history, but certainly not seven years' worth." He held out his hands and gestured for the files. "May I?"

"Oh." I pushed the purse forward. "So these are doctors' notes, scans, dates of surgeries, and then I kept this separate log of medications Martin was taking and when they stopped working, or the side effects he got from them, that sort of thing. It includes blood pressure information as well."

"My. *Very* thorough. Good job with this."

God, how he'd looked at me, even then. *Where have you been hiding, you divine thing,* his eyes seemed to say. Where had that love gone? And when did it go?

"Did Greg have any other enemies?" Willa asks, jolting me from my thoughts.

My mind feels sluggish. "He was really well liked. Truly, the only enemy of his that I can think of is . . ." I trail off. Wave my hand.

Willa frowns. "Who?"

"Forget it. Never mind." But I was about to say, again, *Me.*

Has my sister read my mind? Given the guarded way she's looking at me, I think yes. I laugh offhandedly. "I am on the cops' suspect list. I certainly had motive. And I was the one who found him."

"But you didn't do it." Willa sounds resolute. Thankfully.

"They're just covering all the bases. They have surveillance of me leaving the parking lot at a certain time of the evening, and if I drove really quickly—like ninety miles an hour—burst into the house, and stabbed Greg *immediately,* the timeline could fit."

"But you said you passed out on the bathroom floor."

"I know. I did. Except no one *saw* me do that. Then again, there are no witnesses saying I came home at a different time than when I did, either. And like I said, that surveillance image in the parking lot doesn't give me much time to get back here and stab Greg."

Willa sits back, her hands curled around her knees. "What about your girls?"

I pause. "What *about* my girls?"

"Where were they the night it happened?"

"I thought Aurora was home, but it turns out she was at a friend's house two doors down." I turn my head from side to side, feeling my neck crack. "Lilly. They usually sleep in the guesthouse in the back-yard. The police already talked to both of them. Neither heard a thing."

"And what about Sienna?"

I look at my coffee. The creamer is a congealed layer on top. "She was on campus. At a party."

"They seem really out of it today."

"Do you blame them? It's a shock."

"They seem more than shocked, actually."

I frown. "What do you mean?"

Creak.

A figure has stepped into the hall: a beautiful twentysomething girl with bouncy red hair, wearing a dark blue leather jacket. It's

Raina Hammond, Sienna's friend from school. I jump to my feet. What the hell is *she* doing here?

"Mrs. Strasser." Raina's eyes are full of sorrow. "Oh my goodness, Mrs. Strasser. I was standing right there with Sienna when she heard the news. I am so, *so* sorry."

"Raina . . ." How did this girl get in? I'd just checked the door—it was locked. Did she say anything to the reporters? Is *she* a reporter? "This isn't a good time."

Raina's eyebrows arch. "Sienna invited me. She's upstairs, right? Staying here for a little while instead of the dorms?" She makes a strange choking sound. "I really, *really* need to see if she's holding up okay."

I notice Raina's red eyes and blotchy skin. Has she been crying . . . about Greg? I'm confused. Raina barely *knew* Greg.

Raina wipes her eyes. Her gaze shifts to Willa. "Are you Sienna's aunt Willa?"

"Yes . . ." Willa says cautiously, seemingly picking up on my vibe.

"Nice to meet you. Sienna thinks you're the bomb." Raina sniffs, then points upstairs. "Can I go up just for a sec? Please?"

"Um . . ." God, I'm too tired for this. "Fine. Sure. Whatever."

To my horror, Raina wraps her arms around my shoulders. She smells like flowery perfume and expensive leather and vodka. A tendril of silky hair slithers across the back of my neck like a spider, and I jump back. "Okay, okay," I say. "Go on."

Raina's booties thump on the risers. Willa's gaze is on me, and I sigh. "That's one of Sienna's college friends—she was out with Sienna the night Greg died, actually. They go to Aldrich together. Raina used to work for Dad—that's how Sienna met her, I believe—but she doesn't anymore, I don't know why. But I don't get a great vibe from her."

"Why?"

I shrug. "I came home one time to find her in my bedroom, standing near my dresser. The drawers weren't open, there was no sign she'd touched anything . . . but I don't know why she was in there in the first place."

Willa's eyes linger on the stairs again. We can't hear any noises coming from all the way up there. "Was she close with Greg?"

"Not that *I* know of. Though . . ." I glance upstairs again. Those tears in Raina's eyes. That heartbroken voice.

And suddenly I realize something. The night Greg was killed, I'd called Sienna when we reached the hospital. Before blurting out what happened, I'd asked where she was. "At this party," she said. "But it's winding down. And I'm not drunk. As soon as I find Raina, I'm leaving."

As soon as I find Raina. But Raina just told me she'd *been* with Sienna when my daughter heard the news. She'd implied that she'd been standing right next to her. Witnessing it all.

She just lied.

10

RAINA

FRIDAY, APRIL 28, 2017

I know I should stay away from Alfred Manning's house—for a lot of reasons. It's not like I'm his favorite person these days. But I saw him pulling out of the street before I turned in, so at least I knew I'd avoid *that* minefield. I came for Sienna. I need to be around people who are as shaken as I am. I wish I could tell her the truth . . . but I'm not an idiot. Sienna wouldn't understand. She'd take offense. I would, too, if I were in her shoes.

But still, for all intents and purposes, she's my friend. And as a friend, I have the right to console her. So here I am.

When I climb the stairs to the bedroom where Sienna is staying, I find her sitting on the floor, a yellow fleece blanket bunched in her lap. She's not crying. Practically not breathing. Instead, she's staring at something on her cell phone. Her finger keeps scrolling, down, down, down—it's a long text. Or a homework assignment. I really hope Sienna isn't worrying about homework at a time like this, but then again, she's obsessed with grades. The day I met her, when I was working in her grandfather's office, she'd run into the lobby near tears because she didn't understand an organic chemistry assignment and was sure she was going to fail the required class. Alfred was out, but I'd stepped in to help her. Organic chemistry isn't that hard if you understand the equations. Sienna was so grateful for my pop-up tutoring session that she instantly made me her friend . . . which worked to my advantage.

Now, Sienna looks up and sees my tears, and a confused expression flutters over her features. Maybe she's thinking, *drama queen.* Maybe she's speculating about Greg's hacked e-mails—I'm sure she's read them. Who hasn't?

Or maybe she's wondering who killed him.

I drop to my knees next to her. "How are you holding up, baby?"

Sienna blinks slowly, like a turtle. She looks at my tears and, once again, her face registers confusion. "Sorry." I wipe my eyes, growing self-conscious. "I've got PMS. And I'm scared shitless. There's a killer on the loose, you know?"

Sienna's mouth twists. Still, she says nothing.

"Have the police figured anything out?" I ask. "Do they have a suspect?"

"I don't know." Sienna's voice is emotionless. "Our whole house is being dusted for fingerprints. Even my bedroom. They're probably going through my drawers. Looking at my underwear and tampons."

Her eyes lower almost catatonically. She reminds me of a barnyard animal that sleeps standing up. It makes my heart twist. My friendship with Sienna might have started out less than sincere—I saw her as yet another stepping-stone to truly get close to Alfred Manning—but she's grown on me. If I'm rocked by Greg's death, I can't imagine how I'd feel if Greg were my stepfather.

"Are you okay?" There's a hitch in my voice.

Another slow blink. "I took some NyQuil," Sienna admits. "It's making me feel . . . I don't know. Like my bones have turned to vapor."

I breathe out. It's just pills, then. She doesn't know anything. And I'm actually glad she's taken something. It's probably better just to blur these next few days . . . or even weeks.

"Do you want me to call anyone?" I ask. "Friends from the

dorm? Maybe Anton?" That's the boy she admitted she had a crush on but was too nervous to act on it. They were just friends, for now, but Sienna could totally snare him if she tried.

Sienna closes her eyes. "No." Her voice is soft and faraway. Her features slacken.

"Okay. Sleep it off." I pat her shoulder. "Let me help you into bed. Where's Aurora?"

"Don't know." Sienna lets me pick her up and walk her over to the little bed by the corner. She is a rag doll as I move her legs onto the mattress. "She's pissed at me. She didn't even sleep in this room last night."

"Why would she be mad at *you*?" I ask, but Sienna is snoring as I finish the sentence.

Ten minutes later, I'm walking around Aldrich campus. The place is a shitshow. Classes are still being held, but a lot of kids are using the hack and the downed systems as an excuse to go home for a long weekend. Many who are still here are protesting about things that have come out in the hack—there's a group by the library up in arms about some uber-racist remarks one of the people in housing made to his staff. Over by the Campus Life building, a stately brick house with columns, girls are holding signs bearing Greek letters with slashes through them—something must have come out about a frat. There's a news van on every street corner. It all makes me a little sad. I adore Aldrich. I don't want its reputation to be tarnished. I don't want people to stop applying here. I went through enough to get accepted; I want this all to be worth something.

But will I get to *stay* here? What am I going to *do*?

As I turn a corner, I get that prickly feeling again. *Someone is watching me.* I stop short and glance over my shoulder, but the sidewalk is empty.

I pull my hood down. *No one sees you. No one knows what you know. You have to believe that.*

Around the corner from the hospital is a coffee shop called Becky's. I push through the door, relishing the darkness and dankness. Greg and I used to meet here a lot, actually. We sat at one of the back tables, looking around to make sure no one we knew came in. I had as much to lose as he did, after all—it's one thing for an Aldrich girl to be seen with an upperclassman, even a grad student. But a man old enough to be her father? I had an image to uphold as a good, dutiful coed. I'd told Greg I wanted the whole Aldrich shebang: dorm life, an editorial position on the literary magazine, maybe even student government. I wanted to go to football games, fencing matches, rallies. I had three purple Aldrich sweatshirts hanging in my closet, and I wore them with pride. I loved the appreciative nods I sometimes got from people on the street when they saw the school's name. *That's right, people, I go here. I'm smarter than you.*

I think of the first time I met Greg. Ironically, it had been in passing. I'd been at my interview at President Manning's office; he was looking for a new executive assistant because his last girl, Tara, unexpectedly quit. I might have had something to do with that. Some careful spying on Tara's weekend activities and drug use, a strategically worded e-mail telling Tara that she resign as Manning's assistant or else I spill the beans—it was that easy.

I'd called his office the day she quit, before he'd even had time to post the job online. Naturally, I was the very first interviewee. I knew Manning would choose me. Not because he needed someone immediately—he was the type of man who seemed to flounder without an assistant—but because I'm just that enticing, that good.

I was sitting in the waiting room outside his office, staring at the paintings on the walls. They were of presidents of Aldrich Past. All men, of course, sitting on their tufted chairs with their pipes and their smug smiles. I'd read online that the president of a top-notch college made more than three million dollars a year. With that kind of cash, I'd be pretty damn smug, too.

The door to the back office opened. "Raina Hammond?"

It wasn't Manning but a haggard, fake-smiley blond woman. She introduced herself as Marilyn O'Leary, Manning's deputy. "He and I work very closely together," she said. She looked me up and down, and I thought I caught a little disapproval in her gaze. "Whatever gets to Manning goes through me first."

I didn't like the sound of that, and I also didn't like that she followed me into Manning's office. There, at his desk, was Alfred Manning in the flesh: that golden skin, those sparkling, dancing eyes, those expressive eyebrows I'd seen rise so comically in the many interviews he'd given on CNN or *60 Minutes* as the leader of a progressive, esteemed university. He wore a button-down shirt and well-fitting wool trousers, and he seemed to ooze superiority. Instead of feeling insignificant—or off my game—I was proud. I'd infiltrated a top school's inner sanctum. I knew I was going to get this job. *That's right, all you assholes who thought I was going nowhere,* a voice taunted in my head. *Look at me now.*

A look of delight crossed Manning's features when he saw me. He was coy about it, but I knew he was taking in my face, the size of my breasts, and my long, shapely legs. "Why don't you come in?" he said, gesturing to the door. Then he turned to Craggy Blonde: "Marilyn, we're all set here. Thank you." Craggy O'Leary made a pinched face and left the room.

Alfred Manning's office was kitted out in warm cherry bookshelves, a low-slung leather couch, and a grand desk that spanned the width of the room. Upon the desk was, among other things: a bust of William Shakespeare, a photo of a younger Alfred Manning and Robert De Niro, who'd received an honorary Aldrich doctorate, and a gold Rolex that was flung so haphazardly you'd think it was a Swatch.

My fingers crept toward it. Maybe I could just steal it, sell it, and not have to go through the rest of this bullshit. But then Manning sat down, and my hand snapped back.

"So." Manning said, looking at his notes. "Miss . . . Raina."

I reached into my oversize purse and handed him a résumé. "I heard you weren't a fan of e-mail, so I figured I'd better print this for you to read again."

"You heard I didn't like e-mail?"

There was something challenging about the man's smile, like he found this all a game. That was okay. I liked games. "I mean, I know you *use* it. I just knew it wasn't your preferred mode of communication. And in fact, I'm *very* tech-savvy—I can do all of your computer responsibilities, if you want. Social media and all that." I lowered my lashes in the way I'd practiced in the mirror. "If I get the job, I mean."

"I like people who show some initiative," Manning said in praise. Was he flirting? I decided yes.

Manning glanced at the paper in front of him. "You studied at Columbia's Summer Creative Writing Program. Who'd you work with?"

My mind scrambled. "Professor Cordon. Among others."

"Ah. Yes, I know Gerald."

His name was Archer, actually, but I'd let it slide. It wasn't like I knew the guy, either. "I want to be a writer," I added. "Like you."

Manning looked surprised. "You've read my books?"

"Are you kidding?" I leaned in a little closer. "I'm a huge fan."

Manning pressed his hand to his chest. "You *are*?"

"I especially liked that mystery about the state fair you wrote in the eighties." I cocked my head just so. I felt a carefully positioned tendril of hair kiss my bare shoulder.

"My word." Manning seemed flustered. "Most students don't even know I've been published. It's just my hobby, really. It's not like my books are with large presses."

"You're being modest. You're very good."

Manning shrugged, but it was obvious he was delighted. He looked up again, and we locked eyes. He looked away first. "So, um, can you tell me a little about the position?" I asked.

"Ah, yes." Manning walked me through the details of the job. "It's pretty standard, really. Answering calls. Scheduling. Making sure I'm where I'm supposed to be." He gave me a serious look. "There are a few circled dates every month where I'm out of range and not to be disturbed. I expect you to be my guard dog in those instances."

I didn't like being called a dog—I would leave that role to Craggy O'Leary. So I said, "I'll be your gatekeeper."

"Very good."

The older man's blue eyes had flecks of orange through them that reminded me of a wolf. I bet when he was in his prime, he was gorgeous. Even better-looking than Dr. Rosen.

"I'm eager to prove myself," I purred to Manning. "It would be such an honor."

"Excellent." Manning's eyes crinkled. "You know what? The job is yours. Do you mind if I see your student ID? You earn course credit for your assistance. It helps offset the shockingly low pay. Don't blame me—that's up to the school's budgetary committee."

"Oh." I patted my pockets. "My ID is lost—I keep meaning to get a new one. But don't worry about the course credit. I'd rather take classes. And I don't care about the low pay."

Manning looked puzzled. "How did you get into the building without your student ID?"

I gave a sheepish shrug. "The guard and I are kinda like this." I held up two fingers tightly pasted together. And Manning believed me. Sweet guys like him always do.

"You okay?"

I jolt up, and I'm back in the coffee shop. A girl stands over me, her face bathed in shadows. She's holding a coffee cup and has a substantial leather tote slung over her shoulder.

"I said, are you okay?" she repeats. "You're crying."

I touch my cheeks and find them wet. *Shit.* I thought I was all cried out.

I sniff and turn away. "I'm fine. It's nothing."

"Is it because of the hack?" Her voice is low. "Did something bad come out about you?"

Nosy much? "I'm not stupid enough to put anything personal on my Aldrich e-mail."

She nods. "I know, right? What were people thinking? *And* did you hear that doctor was murdered? It was, like, blocks away." She shivers and looks around. "The killer could be *in here* right now."

"Let's hope not," I say, and sip my coffee.

She sits down in the chair opposite me. "Here." She passes a plate across the battered coffee table. "It's the lemon blueberry, right out of the oven."

The scent of lemon and sugar wafts in my nostrils. When I look at the girl, I see sparkling blue eyes, pale skin, dark hair held back with a headband, and rosebud lips. She's a dead ringer for Audrey Hepburn, whom I've always had a crush on. But I don't need a distraction. I need a plan.

Still, I tell her thanks. "Lemon blueberry really is the best." I break off a piece and offer her some. "I'm Raina."

"Alexis Barnes." She takes a bite of the scone, chews. She's one of those people who look pretty even when eating.

"How'd you know I go to Aldrich?" I ask between bites, recalling how she asked about my e-mails in the hack.

"I go there, too. I've seen you around campus." Her lips curl into an embarrassed smile. "You're sort of hard to miss."

A grain of sugar melts on my tongue. There is something about the way she's looking at me that reminds me of how Alfred Manning looked at me in his office months ago. Or, for that matter, the way Greg Strasser looked at me that very same day. My eye darts to the blueberry-size diamond studs in Alexis's ears. Her camel trench, slung over the back of the chair, looks like Tory Burch. Her black leather purse lacks a label, but I think I saw it on the Celine website. I have a trained eye for these things; I can size up someone's net worth with only a few clues.

Alexis tells me that she's an art major. She lives in Hudson dorm—a different hall than where I'm living—and is considering rushing a sorority—"though they all seem kind of lame."

"Really?" I ask. "I think they seem fun."

Alexis shrugs. "If you're into the whole school spirit thing. I find it kind of meh."

I tell her my usual lies: that I'm from outside Philly, dad's a professor at Penn, mom's an artist, we grew up in an old farmhouse, and I went to a private alternative school. I tell the old chestnut about studying at the Columbia Writing Program last summer. Wanting to be a novelist isn't a lie—I see myself writing someday. I'm already such a fabulist, it shouldn't be that hard.

After a while, I *do* feel better. Not because of the scone, but because of Alexis's adorable pink cheeks and her enormous eyes. She has hitched forward on the couch so that our knees almost touch. Another thing I'm highly attuned to: when someone is into me. But I've never been with a girl before. The possibility is intriguing. Maybe a distraction is *exactly* what I need. And as she recrosses her legs, I get a look at the bloodred underside of her high-heeled bootie: Louboutins.

Perhaps the answer to my problems has dropped right into my lap, blueberry lemon scone and all.

Alexis checks her watch and declares she needs to get to a class. As she's sliding on her coat, she glances at me like she wants to say something. "Listen, if you're crying about a guy, he doesn't deserve you."

I almost laugh out loud. Like I'd *ever* cry over a breakup. But her concern is touching. "Thanks. But it wasn't a guy." I almost want to tell her I'm not into guys. I want to know what she'd say to that.

"There's a party tomorrow off-campus," Alexis adds. "It's like a burn-the-candle-at-both-ends, let's-go-down-with-the-ship because-we've-all-been-hacked sort of thing. Wanna come?"

"Sure," I say.

We exchange information. Alexis touches my hand in goodbye, her fingers lingering on my skin. I watch her saunter out of the coffee shop. As soon as she's gone, I look her up on Facebook. Her account isn't private—it's almost like she *wants* me to find it. There are pictures of a summer spent in southern France. Glamour shots of her standing on a yacht. And—Jesus Christ—one from Christmas where she's hugging a freaking Mercedes with a giant bow around it. Caption: *Santa was good to me!*

I'm back in the game. I wonder what Greg would think if he saw me now.

That day at Manning's office, Alfred Manning and I parted on a lingering handshake and a plan for my first day to be next Monday morning. As he walked me out—Marilyn What's-Her-Face, blessedly, was nowhere to be seen—a devastatingly handsome man with dark wavy hair and wearing a blue blazer that matched his eyes burst into the lobby. And there he was. Greg Strasser, Alfred's son-in-law. I'd done my research. I knew everything about him. I knew everything about the whole Manning clan.

"Alfred." Dr. Strasser waved a cell phone. The irritation was plain in his voice. "Kit and I have been waiting for you downstairs for a half hour."

Manning blinked in surprise. "You have? Why?"

An annoyed sigh. "Lunch at the Duquesne Club? Remember? We're late."

"Oh." Manning held up his hands in frustration. "Well, no need to be impatient. I've been a member there for forty years. I'm sure they'll hold our table."

"It's not about them holding the table," Strasser growled under his breath. "It's that *some of us* have other things to do today."

Either Manning didn't hear or he was feigning obliviousness. He gave me a bright, enthusiastic smile. "Anyway! See you Monday!"

"Right," I said, scurrying out of there.

I reached for the door to the hall, glancing back one more time. Manning's back was turned in his office, but that doctor? He was still looking at me. As our eyes met, he gave me a half-exasperated, half-conspiratorial smile.

It was like he knew what I was up to without me having to say a word. Like he knew my kind. Greg knew my endgame with that old guy. And in that look, I could tell he thought it was delightfully naughty indeed.

11

LAURA

SATURDAY, APRIL 29, 2017

The morning of Greg Strasser's funeral, I stand in my bedroom in my underwear. I feel like someone has glue-trapped me to the floor. My baby is screaming on the bed, but I can't go to him. I am fastened here, staring into the black depths of my closet, my body on pause.

There's a knock. "Everything okay in there, babe?"

Ollie pushes the door open and sees the flailing baby and me. His brow knits. He storms over to Freddie and scoops him up. "What the hell, Laura?"

His flash of moodiness snaps me out of my state. "I'm fine." I'm suddenly contrite. "Sorry. Freddie's just fussy. But it's not a big deal."

"He's been carrying on for five minutes at least." Ollie gives me a strange look while rubbing figure eights on our baby's back. "You're not even dressed?"

I turn back to my closet. My whole body feels like it's stuffed with tiny pins. *Just pick something,* I tell myself, but my mind is moving so slow. Is this really happening? Am I really going to *Greg Strasser's funeral*? It's inconceivable to think that Greg didn't wake this morning to go on his predawn bike ride. That he hadn't gotten his regular hard-boiled eggs at the hospital cafeteria, thanking Gladys, who ran the cash registers, on his way out. That he was no longer breathing. No longer *thinking*. No longer hating me.

Ollie stands at the full-length mirror, Freddie still in his arms. "I'll take him," I offer, reaching out. It's paranoid, probably, but I don't like him standing with Freddie in front of a mirror.

Ollie angles the baby away. "It's fine."

Cowed, I turn to the closet again. But then I feel eyes on my back. "Babe." Ollie sounds worried. "What's that on your leg?"

"What's what?" I ask, feigning ignorance.

"There's a big scratch."

I don't have to look down to know where he's pointing. The jagged scratch on my calf is redder today, scabbed over. I touch it gently. "Tree branch, I guess. Freddie and I went walking in the woods yesterday afternoon." I make a quick mental calculation: Yesterday afternoon, the weather had been gray but warm. A walk could have occurred.

Ollie nods. The tension has loosened from his face when he sees that I'm choosing a dress and shoes. "So everything went okay with Reardon yesterday?"

I'm glad I'm facing the closet, for I wouldn't want Ollie to see my stricken expression. He means Detective Reardon, the lead detective working Greg's case. Reardon called me in for questioning because Greg and I worked together.

"It was fine." I hate the hitch in my voice. "It's not like I had anything to tell him." I yank a cardigan from a hanger. "Do they have any leads on the killer?"

I can sense Ollie stiffening. "You know I can't discuss that with you, babe."

My stomach contracts. I try to nod, to understand, but I wish he'd tell me something, anything. Whom do the cops suspect? How much do they *know*? And how much, by association, does Ollie know?

"I will say that it's been more complicated because they can't find the weapon," Ollie suddenly pipes up. "Once they do, they'll have their guy. Or girl."

I feel the muscles in my cheeks twitch. "What if the weapon *isn't* found?"

"Oh, they'll find it." Ollie swings around for the door, Freddie in tow. "Reardon's search team is the best. They're really digging into Strasser's life. I have a feeling those e-mails that broke in the hack are just the tip of the iceberg of what he was hiding." He shakes his head ruefully. "Goes to show you really don't know anyone."

I open my jewelry box. I'm not really an accessories girl, but I need to do something with my hands. Ollie is right, though. Greg was hiding things. Things far bigger than those silly e-mails. A heat comes over me, prickling behind my eyes. I feel I might faint. *Keep it together, Laura,* I tell myself. *Get through this.*

I need a moment alone to collect myself, so I give Ollie a warm smile. "Can you take Freddie downstairs and make him a bottle? I've already thawed some breast milk. It's on the counter."

When I went to the police station, I'd had all my answers worked out. Reardon had a kind, gentle demeanor, but I could tell he wouldn't go easy on anyone. "You hear about those e-mails of Strasser's that were leaked?" he asked me.

"We all did. A lot of nurses thought they would ruin his reputation as a surgeon."

"Any idea who the woman is?"

I shook my head. Did he believe me? It was hard to gauge by his unwavering expression.

Then he asked about the benefit. I told him about Kit Manning-Strasser hurriedly downing a martini, and how Greg was absent, and how the reporters were questioning everyone about the hack. I said how dreadfully stuffy and pretentious the whole night was, especially because I was alone. Then Reardon wanted to know where I went *after* the benefit.

I halted. "Why does that matter?"

"We're trying to put together an accurate picture of where everyone was." He sipped his coffee. "Dotting our *i*'s, crossing our *t*'s."

I could feel my palms going clammy. "Am I a suspect?"

"No, no, of course not." He raised one of his bushy eyebrows. "Unless you have something to tell me . . ."

On the tip of my tongue was the simplest alibi—that I left the party at around ten and had driven straight home to my son. Except it isn't true. All Reardon would have to do was call up sweet Lucy, the babysitter, with her college textbooks and her nanny bag of special games and toys to entertain Freddie, and she'd tell him that I didn't come home until almost 2:00 A.M. Lucy was asleep on the couch, Freddie snuggled in next to her.

And how would *that* look?

Now, I swallow hard, thinking about what I'd told Reardon instead. Ollie couldn't have read my alibi statement, could he? He's too much of a Boy Scout to break police protocol. He knows nothing. Not about the benefit—and not about what happened a year ago, either. About Greg, that night. The night that started it all. These are things I didn't tell Reardon, either. Things I haven't told anyone. And now, Greg has taken them to his grave.

It was a bitter cold, early January evening a year and three months before. A snowstorm was imminent—the air tasted of it—but we'd had a hard day, and we were both eager for a drink. I pushed inside to the lush darkness of the Modern, the sexy hotel bar in the new boutique hotel across from the hospital. Icy crystals were stuck to my hat. Greg's, too.

Greg and I settled into a private banquette next to an aquarium full of exotic fish. I ordered a glass of wine. When we received our drinks, Greg held his up for a toast. "After a day like today, I needed this." He rolled his head on his neck. "I don't know how we stand some of those people in that hospital day after day, you know?"

It was always flattering when Greg said he saw me as "one of the good ones." I wondered *why* he saw me this way. I liked the idea that he detected something deep and special in me, something that set me apart from others, something I couldn't even see myself.

In the next hour, we covered our usual topics—benign patient gossip, the latest show on Netflix we enjoyed, funny trends from the nineties. I'd desperately needed this night. Things had been so tense and sad at home; it always felt like I was on the knife-edge of either throwing something at a wall or bursting into tears. It was as though every time Ollie and I looked at each other, all we saw was failure to become a family. I didn't know what was going wrong. Things seemed so healthy on my end. I ovulated normally. My periods were regular. I scheduled preliminary infertility blood work, without Ollie knowing, and the results were fine. A terrible thought had begun to creep over me—that maybe the problem was with my husband. But I had no idea how to broach the topic with Ollie and didn't want him to feel like I was accusing him. And so I just languished in wanting. I needed to be somewhere else, talking about something else. Not how badly we wanted and how cruelly we'd been denied.

By the time I finished my wine, I felt unleashed. I deserved to have fun, damn it.

Somehow, Greg and I got on the subject of porn. This was probably because one of his patients that day was a woman with porn-size breasts and a face for adult television—she had congenital heart disease and possibly needed surgery. "Do all men watch that kind of stuff?" I asked, dangerously close to crossing a line.

Greg reached for the bowl of almonds we'd ordered to share. "I suppose all men do. Unless their wives get pissy and forbid it."

I couldn't imagine telling Ollie what he could or couldn't watch, though the thought of him indulging in porn gave me pause. Our lovemaking had become prescriptive and uninspired—the moment I brandished a positive result on the ovulation predictor stick, he seemed to acquire sudden onset performance anxiety. I struggled just to get him to come, which led to him barking at me to back off, and that led to me bursting into tears, inevitably with my legs in the air because it was supposed to help sperm motility. If his sperm was even motile. Perhaps, though, porn would help take our minds off our troubles.

As a puffer fish darted past in the aquarium, Greg lifted his arms over his head. Stretched. Then gave me a saucy smile. "And what about *you*?"

"Me?"

Greg looked at me expectantly. "Women need to get off, too."

Get off. It was funny to hear Greg use that term; I wouldn't have imagined it. Here was yet another tidbit for my collection on what made Greg Strasser tick. I'd been a witness to so many intimate moments of Greg's life, but it was in a fly-on-the-wall sort of way— he probably didn't even realize. Did Greg remember I'd been there the day he and his wife met? *I* sure did. The way Greg looked at Kit in that patient exam room when she and her first husband came in. The way his magnetism pulled her in, paralyzed her. Afterward, I'd locked myself in a supply room, feeling like I'd just climbed out of a cold, choppy sea. It was the first time I'd ever seen Greg set his sights on a woman, and he was so determined—so *confident*. In contrast, Ollie was always so tentative, always asking if this was okay, that was okay. But didn't every woman want to be swept off her feet? Didn't every woman want to be just a little overwhelmed?

That was my porn: Replaying the memory of Kit and Greg meeting. There was no way I could tell Greg that, though. And so I thought of the opposite of that, a story that would bury my desire for him deep: I told him about my quest to have a baby with my husband.

It just spilled out of me. All those negative tests Ollie and I endured. All that heartbreak. The next step was to see a reproductive endocrinologist; one round of IVF was covered by my health insurance. But Ollie was digging in his heels. He said IVF felt like playing God.

Greg took a long pull of his beer. "I regret not having a biological kid," he said softly. "My wife and I talked about it . . . but she wasn't sure she wanted to go through the baby stages again. Sienna and Aurora are awesome—really, it's such a gift to have them in my life. But it's very different when it's your own." And then he slid his hand toward mine. "I'm so sorry, Laura. So fucking sorry. Of all people, you deserve to be a mother. You deserve everything good in the world."

His hand lingered on mine, and I didn't pull away. There were three empty bottles of beer in front of Greg, lined up like a fortress wall. A mirror reflected Greg's face in sharp profile as he looked at me hungrily, a new light in his eyes. I was reminded of the way he'd looked at Kit in the patient room years ago. His eyes had hooks in them. They drew me in.

If I had been smarter, I would have left. But the alcohol—and the flattery—blurred my judgment. It also awakened a sense of entitlement. I'd longed for this man forever. Why not indulge in the way he was looking at me?

So I let Greg buy me a shot. The vodka sliced its way through my veins, reviving me, dooming me, and when I found myself pressed up against the bar's sleek, sexy back hallway wall with him, deep in the shadows, my mouth clashing against Greg's, our hands mapping each other's bodies, I didn't think, only acted. In that silvery-lit corner, I was no longer Laura the nurse or the beleaguered woman who couldn't have a baby. A conquest like Kit had been in that exam room. I was whoever I wanted to be.

But then Greg pulled back. "Wait. Wait." His gaze slid sideways. A shadow loomed against the wall. We waited, but no one appeared. I stared at Greg hungrily. The inch of space between us felt like too much. Greg panted, waiting. After it was over, I wished I could go back to that anticipatory moment of Before, the heady tension of it, when it was just intoxicating possibility. When I hadn't chosen yet. When I was still pure.

There's a crash downstairs, and the baby laughs. I stare at my pale face in the mirror. My eyes have purple circles beneath them. The corners of my lips pull down. I look like a ghoul. I pull the dress over my head, slip on some heels, and fluff my hair. My phone sits facedown on the bureau, and I regard it suspiciously. Has it moved to the left since I set it there last? Has Ollie looked at it?

Fingers shaking, I unlock the screen. Something has occurred to me. Phones can track one's movements, recording the various locations where the phone has traveled. I need to make sure that hasn't happened. I need to erase all traces of where I've been and what I've done.

I'm able to find the location services in the settings. *Common locations,* reads the banner at the top. I see my home address, and then the hospital. But underneath, there are a few locations that stand out. If someone thought to look, they might grow suspicious. Nausea coils in my gut. I tap on two addresses in particular, horrified at their date stamps: *Wednesday, April 26.* The night of the benefit. The night of Greg's death.

A button in the upper corner reads *Clear History.* I press it, holding my breath. After a moment, all of the locations logged in my device are gone. I blink at the blissfully empty screen, praying this isn't a mirage. But they don't return.

The ringing in my ears begins to recede. I'd never, ever admit that I'm glad Greg is dead, but if I'm honest, it's a great weight off my chest. Without him, my life can continue as planned. Without him, I have a chance at happiness . . . even if I'm not sure it's happiness I deserve.

12

KIT

SATURDAY, APRIL 29, 2017

*M*y second husband's funeral falls on the day when the weather finally breaks for the first time. People don shorts to jog down Blue Hill's main drag. They troll plant nurseries and sit outside for brunch. It's a day to have a picnic, not to wear an itchy black dress and drive to a dark, stuffy church to stare at an empty casket that's supposed to symbolize a death vessel for my dead husband. We can't put his *real* body in there yet because the coroner hasn't finished his autopsy investigation.

"Are we ready?" Willa asks us as we pull into the parking lot of the church.

In the back seat, my daughters grumble. Neither has spoken since we got in the car. Are they on something? Did Raina sneak them pills? Maybe I shouldn't have let Raina see Sienna that morning Willa arrived. I still don't understand why Raina lied to me about being with Sienna when I broke the news about Greg.

I open the door and step out. As I swing my legs toward the pavement, I realize I've got a black stiletto on one foot and a brown one on the other. Willa seems to notice at the same time, and she quickly whips off her shoes and hands them to me. "Here. Take mine. We're the same size."

I shake my head. "Stop. It doesn't matter."

"I could give a shit about whether my shoes match. Honestly."

I flinch, taking the statement way too personally—like Willa doesn't give a shit if her shoes match because she doesn't give a shit about *Greg.* I could tell Greg found her toughness off-putting, and Willa thought he cared too much about what people thought. When I first introduced Greg to Willa, on a warm day when we'd visited her in California, Willa challenged Greg to a race on the beach, and he declined.

"Come on," Willa chided him. "Are you afraid I'm going to beat you?" She was just playing, but Greg gave her kind of a sharp look, and the mood just . . . deflated. Conversely, there was a moment at our rehearsal dinner when Willa rolled her eyes when Greg name-dropped that he was buddies with one of the wealthiest CEOs in Pittsburgh . . . and Greg *noticed* the eye roll, and things got tense pretty fast. It was obvious they only stomached one another out of their affection for me.

I stuff my feet into her shoes. It seems so bizarre, the need for me to look good going to a *funeral.* But people are going to be watching me. They're going to see how I behave. They're going to watch for a breakdown. More than a few people think *I* am Greg's murderer. It's easy to read between the lines on Facebook. A few times, I've wanted to comment on the posts, sometimes saying things like *It wasn't me, I swear!* Or maybe *Yes, it WAS me—you bitches figured it out!*

The feelings that have come over me in the past few days are surprising. I'm not sure who I am anymore. All I want to do is throw a big middle finger in everyone's faces.

The church lawn is eerily quiet; we've gotten here a little late. Behind us, another car rumbles up. I turn, thinking it's our father— he said he'd meet us in the parking lot—but a young couple climbs out of a white Subaru SUV instead. The woman wears a slightly too-long black dress and clunky heels and holds a baby with bright blue eyes that inexplicably strike a chord deep inside me. Her husband, a huge, shaved-headed dead ringer for Dwayne Johnson, takes her arm. As the woman raises her head and meets my gaze, I feel a ripple of memory, recalling the last time I saw Laura Apatrea: at the benefit, when she'd spilled my drink.

The man notices me and untangles his arm from Laura's. "Kit, right?" he asks, walking toward Willa and me. His face is open and kind, and his voice is higher than I expected.

I nod, shakily. He offers a hand. "Ollie Apatrea. I'm part of the Blue Hill precinct. I just wanted to let you know that I'm so, so sorry for your loss."

"Oh." I limply pump Ollie's firm, warm hand. I hadn't known Laura's husband was a cop. "I met with someone else when I was in there—Reardon?"

"Yep. Detective Reardon's the best in the business—he's going to figure this out for you." Then he glances at my sister. "Ollie," he says, offering his hand.

Willa fumbles awkwardly. "Kit's sister, Willa. Hi."

Ollie squints. "Do we know each other?"

"I don't think so," Willa says tightly, doing a half-turn away from him.

Ollie lingers on her for a beat and then turns back to me. "If he's ever busy, let me give you my card." He hands a card to me, holding my gaze. "This is a real shock for all of us. Everyone at the station is trying to pitch in."

"Oh." I smile shakily. "Well, thanks." Then I nod to Laura. "Nice to see you again."

She gives me a mousy smile in return. Ollie's gaze remains on me for a beat longer, and then they both turn for the church. I pinch the business card between my thumb and forefinger until it bends. That's one thing I'll say about the Blue Hill PD—everyone has been over-the-top friendly.

Willa watches them as they walk up the steps. "How do they know Greg?"

"Laura was one of Greg's nurses."

"Cute kid, but couldn't she have found a babysitter?"

I shrug. What do I care if a baby cries through the service?

We step into the lobby, which is empty because the service is about to start—it's possible everyone was waiting for us. The double doors of the church's main hall are flung open, and every pew is stuffed with people. Dr. Cho from cardiology. Dr. Rosenstein, the hospital chief—and a huge donor to Aldrich University. A horde of doctors' wives sit together, their eyes sharp and searching. Miles, Greg's best man at our wedding, stares at me like he's seen a ghost. Kristin, the sweet, sensible girlfriend my dad unexpectedly broke up with that previous August, sits in a back pew. Dozens of pretty women I don't recognize are here, too. I wonder if one of them is Lolita. I wonder if one of them is Greg's killer.

Faces turn when they see us and, just as I predicted, the farce begins. There are fake smiles all around. Murmurs of condolences. Pitying looks. I smile back, but in my head, I'm slapping cheeks, throwing drinks in faces. It's so obvious some of these people are here just for the spectacle of it all. I search the crowd, finding Greg's only living family, a dotty, out-of-touch great-aunt named Florence. Aunt Florence looks at me with pity, so I shoot her my only genuine smile so far today.

Willa touches my forearm. "Are you okay?"

"What do *you* think?" I whisper back.

"Do you want to leave?"

Yes, I want to say, but imagine how *that* would look?

Then another hand steadies me. "Come on, Kitty. Let's go."

It's my dad, dressed in a gray suit and a dark tie. His strong fingers curl around my forearm. Relief fills me—he's *here.* I fall into him in the same way I fell into him at my mom's funeral, when I could barely stand. At the front row, Dad heads for the middle of the pew, and we all slide in, me in the middle, Dad next to me, and then Willa and the girls.

There's a pause in the organ music. And then, like music all its own, come the whispers.

She looks like she's drunk.

She'd have to be to get through all this.

Do you really think she did it?

Of course. I can't believe she even showed up. It's monstrous.

Kit Manning-Strasser doesn't react to petty bullshit, I tell myself, but can't they wait until they're somewhere private? And worse, these are girls I socialize with, sit on sports sidelines with. Women who invited Greg and me to Christmas parties, festivals downtown, charity events. Will I ever be invited to those again? Or am I suddenly, irrevocably tainted, persona non grata?

A minister I've met only once—yesterday—appears at the podium. The crowd quiets down, and this man begins to talk about someone named Greg Strasser, who bears absolutely no resemblance to the man I married. He opens with a few words about Greg's big heart, then waxes about Greg's dedication to his work and family, then brings it home with some words about Greg's integrity and honor. I nearly burst out laughing. Where has this guy gotten this information from? Yesterday, when we spoke, he asked me to write a few words about Greg's life. I *tried* to think of positive things to say . . .

Like the memory of Greg the day of Martin's surgery. Martin and I appeared in the cold pre-op room at 5:00 A.M., bleary-eyed and nervous. The moment I saw Greg in the hall, scrubs on, surgical mask around his chin, I'd felt that same perverse buzz again. Greg held my gaze, and I felt like he actually saw *into* me—saw all my fears, my conflicted emotions, even my faults. And it's as if he said, *It's okay. I'll make this better.*

But then, hours later, after so much waiting for the results, Greg himself appeared over me in the waiting room, still in medical scrubs and a hairnet. There was a speck of something that looked like blood on his sleeve. I'd stood quickly, my heart dropping to my knees. I knew what he was going to say before he even opened his mouth. His expression said it all. And then I just sort of . . . *fell* into him.

"I'm so sorry," Greg whispered in my ear, holding me close. "Kit, I am so, *so* sorry I couldn't save him."

I held Greg much longer than probably appropriate. He didn't try to pry himself away. He didn't say he had patients to see or paperwork to fill out. He just . . . *held* me, for what seemed like hours. It was a tiny moment of grace during such a terrible time.

But after that day, I didn't speak to Greg for months. I was surprised when he reached out to me at work on a bright day in July, asking me out to dinner. "If you're not ready, I totally understand," he said.

But I was ready. It's terrible, but in some ways, I'd felt ready the moment he told me Martin was dead. I hadn't been alone since before my mom died. I had no skills for navigating life by myself. Perhaps I could have relied on my dad more, but he was so busy with his duties as president . . . and anyway, I'd never relied on him before. And so I accepted Greg's offer.

And oh, those first dates we went on! Greg took me to restaurants, and we ordered everything on the menu. We flew in a private plane to New York City and stayed in a penthouse along Central Park West. Greg took me on lavish shopping trips, where we bought presents for the girls, sparkly baubles from Tiffany's and cute quilted bags from Tory Burch. He invited the girls and me over for dinner at his town house in Shadyside, buttering up Sienna and Aurora, stocking the fridge with stuff they liked to eat. I remember how tickled I felt when Greg and Sienna sat at the table for hours after dinner to talk about which movie was better: *The Godfather* or *The Godfather, Part II*. He would always have art kits for Aurora, whose whole life was drawing—expensive Winsor & Newton paints, beautiful watercolor boxes, even a wooden easel, set up at his town house window. There were moments when I thought he was only doing this because my husband had been his patient and he had an exaggerated sense of guilt and duty. There was also the awkwardness of how it looked to be dating the surgeon who'd failed to save my husband. My father warned me to be careful, though after he got to know Greg, those warnings waned.

And I hedged the story for Willa entirely, just saying Greg was a cardiologist within the hospital and left it at that. Actually, I started hedging the story with everyone. And after a while, I began to believe Greg genuinely adored all of us. And it felt so . . . *good*. Greg tried so hard to make me forget that I'd just lost someone. He helped us *all* forget. And for a while, it was wonderful.

But I couldn't tell the minister those things, I guess because it didn't end up being the truth, when all was said and done. Instead, I'd hurriedly sent him some pictures of a trip we'd taken to Barbados a few months before, over Christmas break. I'd thought the pastor would use them as inspiration for a eulogy, but instead, to my horror, the photos are now playing on a slideshow on a screen behind his head. I see a selfie of me at the airport looking tired but optimistic. Then there's a blurry shot of Sienna giving a thumbs-up by the gate. Another flip: Aurora's waiting for our flight with her hat pulled down and her headphones over her ears. Down the pew, Aurora gasps. I shoot her an apologetic look. I didn't realize they were going to show our entire photo album.

Next on the screen are shots of the girls jumping off cliffs, standing on surfboards, and eating corn on the cob at a fish fry—Greg is in none of them. Why hadn't I weeded through these photos before sending? Why had anyone left the responsibility to me, *period*?

As the pastor glosses over Greg's later years, the Barbados photos devolve into shots of landscapes, flowers, and birds. Empty white beaches. Crisp blue-green water. Colorful tropical butterflies. From an outsider's perspective, the trip still looks heavenly, but by that time, we were all tired of one another. In the airport, Greg's disposition was sour, testy, and critical, which put me on edge—because we were on *vacation,* damn it, and couldn't he just enjoy it? He tried to rally at the resort, surprisingly pleased at the accommodations and the quality of the rum punch the bartender whipped up. But the girls were getting on his nerves with their selfies and constant Instagram hashtagging and squealing over the cute boys on the other side of the pool. He snapped at them for the dumbest things. Because of that—or so I figured—they gravitated toward other young people on the property and hung out with us very little. Greg and I ate a lot of dinners alone—silent dinners. I couldn't think of a thing to say to him, and in that beautiful, tropical oasis where romance should come easy, our silence seemed even more indicative of how much our relationship had fallen apart. By the end, Greg was a grump. Sunburned, tired, snapping at everyone, and spending several hours taking care of work e-mails in the afternoons instead of hanging out with us.

There's a commotion in the aisle, and Raina Hammond squeezes into our pew. Her hair is perfectly blown out; she wears a black dress far too short for church. She grips Sienna's hand, and Sienna squeezes back, but Aurora seems to shift closer to Willa, looking disgusted. I run my tongue over my teeth. Maybe she knows Raina is a liar, too.

More songs. A eulogy from a fellow doctor about the time he and Greg spent at medical school, that's as bland as can be. Then, finally, it's over. Everyone stands and exhales, and people turn to me. But there's no way I can talk to anyone right now. I've got to get the hell out of here. As soon as the people to my right file out, I hurry toward a side exit, not caring that I've left my family behind.

The warm air kisses my skin. I take deep, even breaths, running my fingernails up and down my arms; I'm tempted to break the skin just to feel *something.* Church bells gong. Two kids in Aldrich sweatshirts smoke e-cigarettes in front of off-campus housing. A local news van circles the block and turns into the church parking lot. *Jesus.* I hurry to the back of the building.

"*Kit.*"

I wheel around. Patrick stands with his hands in the pockets of a dark suit. He is alone, and he's looking at me with a mix of urgency and uncertainty. I stare at him, then at the church, then at him again.

"What are *you* doing here?" I finally splutter.

"I wanted to express my condolences."

"You came to my husband's *funeral?*"

"You and Lynn work together." He shrugs. "It would have looked weird if we *didn't* come."

We. I want to kick him.

"You said you weren't married," I whisper.

"*You* said you were a widow," he shoots back, his eyes aflame.

"That's true!" I place my hands on my hips. "And now it's even *more* true!"

Patrick's expression falters. "Jesus," he says in a low voice. "I'm sorry. Are you okay?"

I stare at a billboard across the street for a new hardware store a few blocks away. The tenderness in Patrick's voice is heartbreaking. Just like that, I want to touch him, bring him close. "Of course I'm not okay," I mumble. "I walked in on my husband bleeding out. Most of the people in that funeral think I did it."

"You didn't do it."

"*I* know that." Another tiny piece of me crumbles, but I have to resist. I raise my chin, my gaze purposefully nowhere near his face. "It's better we lied to one another in Philly. And it's good nothing really happened. It would be humiliating, considering Lynn and I work together."

"I regret that nothing happened," Patrick says quietly.

I clamp down hard on the inside of my cheek. *Do not react.*

But Patrick moves closer. "I kicked myself when I didn't get your phone number. And when you showed up at that benefit . . ." He lets out an embarrassed laugh. "I don't mean to be cheesy, but it felt like the universe was trying to tell us something."

"Don't bring the universe into this. Don't pretend this is fate."

But he senses me faltering. His suit jacket rustles, and before I know it, his fingers are twining through mine. Involuntarily, I grip hard. Then I let go. But then I squeeze again. There is a push-and-pull in my heart and brain. I know I should walk away, but I can't.

"Can I call you?"

"I . . ." I close my eyes. *Say no. You have to say no.*

"Patrick?"

People have begun to stream out of the church, and some have trickled around to the side lot. I have a clear view of Lynn Godfrey *click-clack*ing in her high heels toward a row of vehicles, her children in tow. *Patrick's* children. She's whispering to them, patting the head of the little boy, who's dressed in an expensive-looking child-size suit. Lynn's head swivels about as she looks around for her husband. I also notice Willa in the crowd . . . and she *does* see me. Her eyes narrow on Patrick. I step away from him, mustering a look of innocence.

Patrick backs up, too, but not before he gives me a deep, meaningful look. "Think about it, Kit. Please?"

"Um," I murmur, uncomfortable because Willa hasn't taken her eyes off us. Patrick jogs back to the parking lot. Lynn greets him with a surprised smile—she definitely hasn't seen that he and I were talking. She takes his hand, and they climb into a white Porsche SUV.

Willa marches to me, her brow furrowed. "Who was that?"

"Just . . . someone." I can feel the heat in my cheeks. "Expressing his condolences."

Willa frowns. Maybe she can tell I'm not being completely truthful. She turns to the car Patrick and Lynn have just climbed inside. Behind the windshield, I can see Patrick's lips moving. Is he giving Lynn an excuse for what he was doing behind the church? Is he telling her he loves her, and that he's a good man, and that *he* would never be like dishonest, philandering Greg Strasser?

He's a liar, I want to scream. I want to hate Patrick. But I don't. All I can think of is his fingers entwined in mine, his mouth saying, *I can't be away from you.* I am a terrible, terrible person, because the truth of it is, I don't think I can be away from him, either.

13

WILLA

SATURDAY, APRIL 29, 2017

*L*ook at this turnout!" I swing Kit's Mercedes E-class down
yet another filled parking lot row, narrowly avoiding two
young, muscled dudes in a Blue Hill Country Club golf cart. Every
parking space I pass is filled with a car. "I don't remember *this* many
people at the church. I guess most would rather drink to Greg's
memory than pray."

Kit's got her eyes closed. "For the millionth time, Willa, just
valet."

"All right, all right." I steer toward the front of the club. The
dashboard dings, though I'm not sure why. Kit insisted that I drive
after the funeral because she was feeling too woozy. I wonder if it
has anything to do with that George Clooney clone she was having
a tête-à-tête with after the funeral.

The club's main building is a sprawling, ivy-covered monstrosity
with long glass windows that look out onto the driving range. I wish
I didn't remember this place as precisely as I do, but it seems branded
on my brain. When I was fifteen and my father got promoted to
president of Aldrich University, he decided that our family should
join the club. Most of my memories from here are of sitting slumped

at a giant oak table in the dining room, watching preppy girls from my class snicker at me from behind straight, sleek columns of hair. After fulfilling her socialization requirement, my mom always sank down next to me and whispered, "God, these people are such *shits*."

Now, as we head toward the doors, Kit gazes around nervously. I wonder if she's looking for reporters. I'd bet any amount of money that some are staked out here—when reporting on cases like this at "The Source," I've slipped into all kinds of events like these, eager to listen in and absorb the mood. I'm about to tell her I'd be fine with skipping this entire event, but then my phone buzzes in my pocket. It's a text from my boss at "The Source," Richard. *Have you heard the latest about the frat stuff coming out in the hack?*

I frown, my fingers poised over the tiny keyboard. *What?*

It takes him several texts to get his point across. *Two local reporters dug up e-mails from two students about some rape cover-ups at the Chi Omega house. There's this trail of administrative e-mails essentially saying that everyone needs to get their story straight. There are definitely some violations taking place, and some people definitely knew.*

The words swim before my eyes. *Like who?* I want to write, but another text comes in.

Wanna tackle it since you're there anyway?

I roll my jaw. This is my sort of story, but no. *No.* C'mon, man— I'm at a freaking *funeral* for my sister's husband. Give me time to breathe.

I turn to Aurora and Sienna. The girls are sitting together on a bench, speaking in low, heated voices. Sienna massages her forehead with her hands. Aurora lets out a huff and turns away. Abruptly, Aurora jumps to her feet and storms off. Sienna takes her hands away from her eyes and watches her go, a scowl on her face.

I watch her go for a moment, then collapse next to Sienna. "What was that about?"

Sienna glances at me, and the scowl morphs into a wearier expression. "It's stupid."

"She looked pissed."

"She's just . . ." Her shoulders rise and fall. "We had a fight about this guy . . . it's dumb."

A muscle twitches in her cheek. I think about what Richard just told me about the frats. Sienna is an Aldrich student now. Has she ever gone to one of those parties? Has anything dangerous ever happened to her there? Were her dorms safe? All at once I hate that they're coed.

I wish I could bring myself to ask her. There's something so innocent about Sienna, despite her curvy body. She seems like a baby bird I need to shelter. But instead, I say, "Are you still writing?" A few years ago, Kit told me Sienna had taken an interest in fiction, so I'd asked her to send me some of her stories. They were quite good for someone her age. Sienna nods. "Can I read some?" I go on.

"I guess. I post them on Wattpad." She whips out her phone, opens a new text, and types in a web address. There's a swooshing noise. "I just sent it to you. But don't judge, okay? They're a work in progress."

"Me, judge?" I nudge her. "How about this: I'll read your stories, and I'll let you read some of my stuff from college. It's pretty embarrassing."

"Okay," Sienna says, though not as enthusiastically as I'd hoped. Her gaze drifts across the lobby. "You mind if I talk to my friend, Aunt Willa?"

"Sure. Go right ahead."

Sienna shoots me a grateful smile and stands. As I look across the lobby, I see she's heading for that Raina girl. They huddle together, talking. Raina glances at me, then looks away. I guess things never change at this club. All these years later, I'm *still* being whispered about.

Kit has left the lobby, so I drift into the club to find her. The building smells exactly how I remember—a nauseating mix of flowers, some chemical-laden wood polish that's probably giving all of us pancreatic cancer, and top notes of booze. It seems like all of Blue Hill have made their way to the big, horseshoe-shaped bar in the main room. Attractive, tanned men clamor around the bar. Thin, angular, lineless women who all have the same perky breasts guzzle white wine at bistro tables.

I elbow through the crowd. No one seems to recognize me, which is a blessing. Voices float into my ears, and I catch the mention of Greg's name. It's the usual let's-rehash-Greg's-greatest-hits jabber—business types muse about the time he got a hole in one on the fourteenth hole, another man remarks about a time Greg did a brilliant Sinatra impression during karaoke night at a local bar. In death, Greg Strasser seems cooler, friendlier, and larger than life. Though maybe that's unkind of me. Despite his philandering, Greg didn't deserve to be killed.

I also catch snatches of words like *murderer* and *on the loose*. Someone says, "I heard this strange noise outside my house last night, and I even brought my *dog* in—you can't be too careful!"

I've wondered about this, too: *Is* there a murderer on the loose? *Should* we be worried?

I order a pinot grigio and drift around the tables. Then I catch Greg's name again—but the tone is quite different. Hushed. Conspiratorial. *Gossipy.*

"I mean, this is the thing," says a voice. "Besides the whole . . . *e-mail* stuff . . . it's not like he was trying very hard with her."

I freeze by a window that overlooks a sand trap. The voice comes from a table of women of varying ages. One is tall and masculine, with a prominent brow and thick brown hair ending just past her ears. The second woman is petite and perky with chestnut-colored hair arranged in a French braid. The third woman—the one who's spoken—is about forty pounds overweight, wearing pink glasses, and glancing furtively back and forth.

"So true," French Braid pipes up. "He was *always* at the hospital, even when he wasn't on call."

Wine wells in my mouth. Are they talking about Greg and Kit?

"And at first, he seemed to *love* those stepdaughters, but at the end? It's like they didn't exist." That's Tall One. Is she one of Greg's coworkers? A nurse?

"And aren't *those two* a piece of work." Pink Glasses rolls her eyes. "Those pictures of them in the bikinis at his *funeral*?"

I press my nails into my palm. Should I intervene? Who gives these bitches the right to talk about innocent teenagers?

"Anyway," French Braid says. "Those e-mails, *whew!* Who do we think *she* is?"

"No clue," Pink Glasses says.

"My money's on her being the killer," opines French Braid. "Not Kit."

Tall One looks surprised. "You think?"

"Yep. Lolita gets obsessed in the e-mails. She was obviously unhinged. I bet she found him at home the night of the benefit. She wanted to get back together, but he didn't. They argued, and she stabbed him. I saw an *SVU* about this very same thing last week."

A man stands and blocks my view of them, though maybe that's a good thing, as I'm bubbling with outrage. So now we're using *Law and Order* episodes in lieu of real evidence?

"But what about how Kit and Greg got together?" I think it's French Braid talking. "I was more wondering if *that* plays into this, somehow."

"What do you mean?" That's Tall One's voice.

"You don't know?" I can barely hear her over the bar chatter. "That first husband of Kit's? Strasser was his surgeon, and the guy died on his operating table. Some say those two *planned it*—they'd been dating long before he died. They wanted the first husband out of the way."

I duck my head and try to blend into the surroundings. I feel jarred by what I've just heard. I knew Greg worked in the cardiology department when Kit's first husband, Martin, underwent the heart surgery that he didn't survive. But I wasn't aware Greg was Martin's *surgeon*. Was I supposed to just *know*? Why didn't Kit tell me?

I want to know more, yet when I turn back to the women, they're packing up their things. Should I follow them? Ask more questions?

"Excuse me?"

Behind me, a tall man about my age holds a tumbler of brown liquid. He has a mess of chestnut curls, piercing blue eyes, a prominent Adam's apple. He's also blinking at me with a big, expectant smile on his face.

"It's Paul," he says. "Paul Woodson? From high school?"

For a beat, I can't remember Paul Woodson—I've locked high school memories away so tightly, it's a wonder I even remember my school's mascot. But then I recall a cramped room where we held the lit magazine meetings. And Paul Woodson's beat-up Vans sneakers tapping as he flipped through poem submissions. And Paul wrinkling his cute nose at most of the abysmal entries. He used to quote Velvet Underground lyrics, which had inspired me to buy the band's whole catalog at Tower Records and listen to it on repeat.

"Oh," I blurt. "Jesus. *Paul.* Oh my God." I sound like a nervous eighth grader. "I just mean . . . shit, my brain is scrambled today. It's good to see you!"

He smiles sadly. His two front teeth still overlap, something I'd found unbearably hot at sixteen. "It's weird. I was just thinking about you the other day."

Paul Woodson was thinking about *me*? This seems highly improbable. Then I remember: Of course he was thinking about me. My sister's husband was *murdered*.

"When's the last time we saw each other?" Paul asks.

"Um, I think it was that dinner," I say, because I know for certain. "For lit mag."

"Yes, that dinner!" Paul cries. "At the Indian place!"

I nod as though I hadn't obsessed over that dinner for weeks, *months,* after it happened. "It's been a long time."

"And what are you up to now?"

"I live in California." I want to sip from my drink, but I'm disappointed to find it empty. "I have for years. I'm an investigative journalist."

"Oh yeah? Freelance, or for a paper, or . . . ?"

"This online news site called 'The Source.' You probably haven't—"

"*You* work at 'The Source'?" Paul looks thrilled. "It's the first e-mail update I click every day! I'm a journalist, too, actually. Well, a rock reporter—I cover the local band scene. But I'd *love* to get into more investigative stuff. You're my idol."

Is this happening? Paul was the king of the alternative kids, all army surplus gear and half-shaved head and Henry Rollins intellectual sarcasm. I spent lit-mag meetings slumped in the back, feeling sporty and preppy and nothing like the spidery, edgy girls who flocked around Paul like groupies. I haven't thought of Paul in years, but now that he's standing here in front of me, I can't *believe* I haven't thought of him in years.

Paul's expression shifts. "Shit. Sorry. I'm sure you don't want to talk about your job. I am so, *so* sorry about your brother-in-law. It's shocking."

"Oh. Yeah. Thanks."

He leans closer. "Do the police have any leads?"

"No." I tuck a strand of hair behind my ear. "Despite tearing Kit's house apart for clues. Crazy, right?"

"They aren't equipped to handle this sort of thing—they're more into white-collar crime and petty break-ins." An inspired smile settles over his features. "*You* should look into it. You'd probably do a better job."

"Oh, I don't know," I mumble, though he's right. I'm good at getting answers and facts. Good at noticing when people are lying.

Good at making the police tell me more than they should. But all at once I feel exhausted and confused. Seeing rumpled, fuck-it-all Paul Woodson in a country club is about as unlikely as seeing a shark in a kid's backyard swimming pool.

"So wait, how do *you* know Greg?" I ask.

Paul sips his beer. "I was his ghostwriter." Noticing my blank stare, he clarifies. "Greg wrote a medical column for the *Pittsburgh Post-Gazette*; he hired me when it got picked up for syndication, since I live close. The guy is great at deciphering blood-work numbers and repairing an aortic valve, but he needed someone to translate that into laymen's terms."

"Oh." I sneak another peek at Paul. He has grown handsomer since high school; he's still lanky, his jaw is still sharp, but his chest has filled out, and I like the flecks of gray at his temples. Then something hits me. "You *live* here? Near . . . Aldrich? You moved *home*?"

Paul jiggles the ice in his glass. "I was living in New York City, but then I got divorced, and . . . it's a long story. So yep. I'm back home."

A waiter passes with a steaming buffet tray of pasta; the smell of the vodka sauce makes my nostrils prickle. *Et tu, Paul?* I think. Of course my teenage crush would wind up only a few miles from where he went to high school. *Everyone* ends up back here, even hot punk-rock guys destined for greatness. It makes me sad. But more than that, it makes me really uneasy. No one has left. Around every corner, someone might know me and *remember.* All at once, I need to get away. Like *really* get away.

I shoot Paul a watery smile. "I should probably find my sister. But it's been really nice to see you."

Paul looks chagrined. "How long are you going to be here? Can I give you a call?"

How long have I waited to hear those words? But it feels like too little, too late. "I'm heading back to the West Coast soon. But drop me a message on 'The Source' website, okay?"

I snake through more people, elbowing a woman in a black maxi dress so sharply that she breathes in a gasp and shoots me daggers. It takes me an agonizing three minutes to find Kit, though when I do, she is blessedly alone. I scuttle up and slide in next to her. "Hey," she says, brightening at the sight of me.

"I need to get out of here," I say bluntly.

Kit places her empty glass on the bar. "I'll find the girls."

She reaches for her handbag so happily that I almost don't clarify. "Actually, I mean get out of Pittsburgh. There's a flight leaving for LA tomorrow morning, and I need to be on it."

Hoots of laughter explode across the room. A sudden, sharp smell of a cigar wafts into my nostrils. Kit has frozen. "You're *leaving*?"

"Work needs me."

"B-But you just got here!"

"I didn't, actually. I've been here for three days."

The muscles around Kit's mouth tighten. "Oh geez. Three days. Of course. I'm sorry I've taken up so much of your time."

"Kit, I'm sorry, but—"

"I mean, whatever; my husband's murdered, my kids are traumatized, I still could go to jail for it, but hey, three days of casual conversation and hiding out in your hotel room most of the time seems about the right level of support."

"I haven't been hiding in my hotel room!"

Kit swishes her hand. "Whatever, Willa. You do you. Like always."

"Kit . . ."

Kit pretends to be interested in the baseball game on television. "Why do you hate me so much, anyway?"

I step back, feeling slapped. "I-I don't hate you!"

"It sure feels that way. You always can't wait to get away from here. From *me*."

"That's not true." I start to dismantle a bar mat into little chunks. "How about you come to LA instead?"

Kit narrows her eyes. "*I* have a job, too. And two daughters."

"They can come." I shift my weight. "We both know I wasn't going to stay for very long."

I notice the lines around Kit's eyes. The beginnings of aging at her mouth. It's startling—for years I've held a high school version of her in my head, the fresh, perky, desirable girl everyone wanted to be friends with. I think she's about to say something, but then she tosses a napkin on the bar and storms away.

"Kit!" I cry, leaping up. I follow her into a bathroom, though she slams the swinging door in my face. Once I push my way inside, Kit has shut herself in a stall. I pound on the stall door. "Kit! Come on! Don't be *mad*!"

There's sniffling from inside. "Leave me alone."

"I'm sorry, okay? I just . . . I need to go. It has nothing to do with you."

She opens the door a crack. Her eyes are red, and her cheeks are blotchy, and she looks pissed. "Do you even realize I don't have anyone else right now? Did you not *hear* what people were saying? Then again, maybe you didn't. Maybe you were just thinking about how soon you could get out of here."

"No, I did hear, I just . . ." I trail off. I'd just hoped Kit *hadn't* heard all those whispers.

"And Dad's not helping. He's wrapped up with this hack thing. And the girls—I'm supposed to be the strong one for *them*."

"Kit, I didn't—"

But she cuts me off, points at me. "Look, I know we're not close anymore. I know you have a life in LA. I know that maybe you think my life is . . . oh, I don't know. Petty, maybe. Superficial. I have a lame job. A husband you've never really liked."

"That's not fair! I don't think those things!" Not really, anyway.

"And I get it—Pittsburgh is nothing compared to LA. There's no good takeout. Everyone's obsessed with sports. If I lived somewhere warm and amazing, I'd want to go back, too. But we're still *sisters*. And I have no one else right now, Willa."

The bar coaster I've torn up is in shreds in my hands, falling onto the tiled bathroom floor. There's an ache in my stomach that's possibly been there since I landed in Pittsburgh on the red-eye. It never occurred to me that it bothered Kit that we weren't close. I figured she was subsumed by her own issues—family, career, marriage, her brand-new, sparkly, rich-girl life—to give a shit about our relationship. I figured she had lots of support. I'd actually envied her, if I was being honest with myself. Gregarious Kit in the dependable same city she's lived in since birth, while I forged it alone thousands of miles away.

But now all I see is that I haven't been a sister.

I think about the text my boss sent. I'm not working on any stories right now, and I have almost three weeks of unused vacation time for the year, plus a bunch of carried-over days from years past. Would it kill me to stay here for a little longer and be the sister Kit needs?

Well, yes, it possibly might. But it might not. And whatever doesn't kill me will make me stronger.

I take another minute to dwell on it, then take a deep breath. "I'm sorry. I'll stay. I *want* to stay." There's a lump in my throat. "I didn't realize. I should have, but I didn't." I lick my lips. Swallow hard. How do I say I want to be close to her again? How do I bridge all the years, all the secrets? I have a feeling I have way more things to hide than Kit does. And I certainly don't want to divulge anything. Long ago, I'd made a promise to myself always to move forward, not look back. It's why being here is so difficult. There are too many reminders.

"Forget everything I just said," I tell her. "I won't book that flight. I won't book *any* flight."

She glances at me begrudgingly. "Really?"

I open the stall door wider. "Yes. Actually, maybe I can help with figuring out what happened to Greg."

Kit looks at me suspiciously. "For a story?"

"No. Absolutely not. For *you*."

As if on cue, I catch sight of those same women from before—the ones who were whispering about the rumors of how Greg and Kit met. I glance at Kit, wondering if I should ask her about it. Is Greg being Martin's surgeon a secret? What *other* secrets is she keeping? And what did those women mean about Greg acting like Sienna and Aurora didn't exist toward the end? What was with Sienna and Aurora arguing on the bench an hour ago?

There's a lot I'm missing here. A lot that lurks beneath the surface, ready to be excavated. And maybe, just like Paul suggested, I'm the person to do it.

Kit's brow furrows. "Are you going to speak to *everyone*?"

"I don't know. Maybe."

"Well, don't question the girls. They've already been through it. I don't want to retraumatize them."

I shrug. "Okay. Whatever." There's a lump in my throat. I've always been a person who relies more on action than words. Maybe if I can figure this out for Kit, then things will be okay between us. All of our neglect from years past will be wiped clean. "Now, can we get out of here? I think I'm starting to regress into my seventh-grade self."

Kit laughs weakly. When she takes my arm, I feel that we might be all right. For a second, I almost feel *good* about my decision. But then I remember: I've lied to Kit, just now. Yes, I want to investigate what really happened to Greg. But that's not all that made me decide to stay.

Years ago, in this same neighborhood, something happened that went unresolved. For years I've dwelled on that iniquity. I've thought about the rot that hides behind this pretty community's walls, the ugly secrets people keep. It's why I went into my particular career: To draw the truth from people. To tell things others are afraid to. To expose people for who they are, no matter how prominent they might be. Greg's murder occurred in the very same town where, all those years ago, something else happened that changed—damaged—someone forever.

That someone is me.

14

LYNN

SATURDAY, APRIL 29, 2017

My husband and I don't attend the reception for Greg Strasser. I'm curious about it—it seems like something interesting *always* happens at funeral receptions—but Patrick reminds me that our kids have a soccer game today, and it's the first time since the season started that both of us can attend. I can't argue with him: Our family comes first.

The games take place on a large swath of ground in a sports complex that also houses an ice rink and a climbing wall. "Take her down, Amelia!" I scream to my nine-year-old daughter, who's running toward a girl on the opposite team like a charging bull. I scan the field to my left: Connor, my six-year-old son, is a flash in yellow mesh. My kids are the best players out there. I used to be an excellent soccer player when I was young, and I taught them everything I know.

Marion Cummings unpacks the juice boxes I've brought for team snack. We might be new in town, but I've made sure to volunteer for parent duties in sports and school. It's a little trick I picked up when I was a new mom in Maryland: It's always the same group of four or five mothers showing up and signing up for everything, but because of that, they're perceived as better, more selfless parents.

When you're perceived as better, you start to *feel* like you're better. It's quite an empowering cycle, and I've found it's worked for me like a charm in this new city. See, when my kids were really young, I felt I had no handle on anything. I envied the calm, graceful women who just breezed through motherhood. In high school, college, my twenties, *I* was always the one people looked up to. Patrick announcing the move was a boon, actually, because here, I get to start over. And here, I'm nailing motherhood . . . nailing life, really.

"What was the service like?" Marion asks.

I look up. Patrick and I stopped home to change into more comfortable clothes, but all the other parents seem to sense that we've just come from the funeral regardless.

"Well, I don't want to criticize, but . . ." I chew on my lip. "They showed these inappropriate photos from the guy's family vacation during the pastor's eulogy. His daughters were practically naked. I had to cover my kids' eyes." I hated bringing my kids at all, but our nanny wasn't available on such short notice.

"Aren't you freaked-out?"

Marion is looking at me with such intensity that my skin starts to crawl. "Freaked?" I finally say, my voice a note or two higher than normal.

Marion rips open a Costco box of mini pretzel pouches with her stubby nails. "I'm considering moving us all into Gil's parents' house in the city until the murderer is caught."

Ah yes. The murderer. I raise my eyebrows, feeling a tug in my chest—because, after all, it *is* terrifying. "Well, we have a security system. And I'm not letting my kids out of the house for a *second* without Patrick or me watching."

"Or maybe the wife did it?" Marion moves closer, an excited expression on her face. She, like the rest of us, is taking advantage of the warm weather and has her mom-hoodie tied around her waist. She really should do something about those "bingo wings," as my mother used to call flabby arms. "Someone told me she was acting *very* drunk at that party. Then again, if my husband did that to me, I'd get wasted, too."

Your husband should *do that to you, considering you're only having sex with him once a year,* I think. That was a little gem I read about Marion in the hack e-mails. Lucky for me, her husband is an Aldrich employee, and it's all there.

I plop the last juice box into the cooler. "I haven't really kept up with the news."

This is a lie. I've read every story about Greg's murder that's been reported in the local news. Even a few bigger affiliates have picked it up because of the hack ties. I've stared at the surveillance image showing Kit's car leaving the benefit. I've speculated the math. Based on the severity of Greg's wound and the time of his death, the coroner placed the time of his stabbing at between 11:00 and 11:15. Kit left the lot at 11:06. If she drove fast, she *could* have gotten home quickly enough to kill him . . .

Marion drops the empty pretzel box beside the trash bin because it's too large to place it in the bin itself. "Anyway, I've been thinking about putting together a community watch program until they catch the killer. Do you think Patrick would be willing to take a shift?"

"Absolutely." My husband is just coming back from the bathroom. I loop my arm around his waist.

"Huh?" Patrick jolts up. "What's that?"

"I said you'd take a shift during community watch," I repeat.

Patrick squints. "Community *watch*?"

"Of course he'll do it," I tell Marion cheerfully. And then I turn back to Patrick. "There's a murderer on the loose. We need to keep our children safe."

Patrick looks like he wants to protest, but then says, resignedly, "Okay. Sign me up."

We turn back to the game. I glance to my left to make sure Marion isn't paying attention, then whisper, "You were in the bathroom for twenty-five minutes."

He looks startled. "It was more like five."

I make a harrumph noise that says I know otherwise, but it's as if Patrick has no idea what I mean. Does he really not see how bizarrely he's behaving? At the funeral, he kept swiveling around, looking at people, though when I asked whom he was searching for, he didn't give me an answer. And then there's the night of the benefit. It was strange enough that he left abruptly only an hour into the thing. I stayed for a few more hours, fulfilling all my work responsibilities; when I got home, the house was dark, so I'd figured Patrick had gone to bed. But then I noticed his car wasn't in the driveway. Or in the garage.

I let myself in. Patrick's suit jacket was slung over one of the counter stools in the kitchen, which means he'd at least stopped at home. I tried his cell phone, but it rang inside his jacket pocket. I found it and unlocked the screen—I'd figured out Patrick's password long ago. There were no illicit texts. No indication of what he was up to.

I wanted to confront him, but I was so exhausted that I fell into bed and drifted into a rage-fueled sleep. I woke up hours later, dim morning light peeking through the blinds. When I saw Patrick wasn't next to me, I panicked. I went downstairs and found him dressed in a T-shirt and pajama pants, scooping coffee grounds into a filter. "Hey," he said. "I'm going to pick up the kids from their sleepovers if you want to ride with me."

"Where were you last night?" I bleated. "You weren't here when I got back."

He hit the button to start the coffee brewing. "Walgreens. We were out of Pepto."

Out of Pepto? It was so clearly a lie. But then I glanced at my phone sitting in its charging dock on the island . . . and everything came to a halt. I'd received eleven texts since the night before; quite a few of them were from people from my office and others in the community. Most included a link from a local news website: *Prominent*

Surgeon Murdered in Home Late Friday Evening. I saw the face of the man I'd seen on Kit's arm at dinners and benefits. And the e-mails I'd trolled for in the hack.

Greg Strasser was . . . *dead.*

I read the details, the timeline. Then I looked up at Patrick in horror. He'd been out last night, too. He could have been killed just as easily. Everything felt so fragile and unpredictable, and I wasn't angry anymore—just grateful I wasn't the one who'd lost a husband.

"Mom!" Amelia sprints up to me now, a sheen of sweat on her forehead. "Did you see my goal!"

"Of course I did!" I cry, pushing a few strands of her blond hair from her face.

Connor runs up next, slapping Patrick a high five. "Do you have my granola bars?" he asks me, hopping madly from foot to foot as though he's still on the field.

"Right here," I say, pulling one from my bag.

I notice, as Patrick bends down to readjust Connor's shin guards, that we are the only mom-and-dad unit who's shown up today. Every other kid has one parent on the sidelines, not both. It's got to count for something.

"Go get 'em," I tell the kids, patting their butts as they run back onto the field. Honestly, I wish I were running around, too, because although it was balmy ten minutes ago, it's now downright freezing. Damn mercurial weather.

I lean into Patrick. "Babe, I'm cold."

He looks up, surprised. "You didn't bring a sweatshirt?"

I set my mouth in a stern line, and he sighs. "I think I have a jacket in the car. Want me to grab it for you?"

"Forget it." I wrench away from him. "I'll get it myself."

I can feel Patrick gazing at me the whole walk up the hill to the parking lot, but I don't turn back. Let him feel like he needs to make it up to me.

The complex is nestled in the middle of an office park, and bland, soulless buildings rise around me. It's a gloomy scene, which only compounds my malaise. I've looked everywhere for evidence that Patrick's up to something: his phone, his browser history, even what he's watched on Netflix, Amazon Prime, Hulu, and YouTube. Nothing. So why is my intuition pinging? Why do I feel a strange, sneaky uneasiness? Am I only suspicious because *I* have done something I'm not proud of? Am I turning my guilt outward, projecting it onto someone else?

I hit the key fob to unlock the SUV doors. The back seat is littered with juice boxes and empty snack containers, but when I open the trunk, I find Patrick's leather jacket lying under a few empty plastic grocery bags. I whip it out and put it on, running my hands up and down my arms to get warm. I'm about to head back to the fields, hoping I haven't missed another goal, but then I notice a small silver shopping bag tucked into the very corner of the trunk. I frown and pull it out. Inside is a small, lacquered box with a familiar, expensive jewelry store's name printed across the top.

I open it up and there is an exquisite, whisper-thin gold tennis bracelet with a line of channel-set diamonds. It looks like a glamorous handcuff. I draw in a breath. Our anniversary is in a week. Is this my gift?

I feel the corners of my mouth tugging into a grin. And just like that, I feel much, much better.

15

LAURA

SATURDAY, APRIL 29, 2017

After Greg's funeral, Ollie, Freddie, and I flop onto the couch. Freddie has finally, *finally* fallen asleep after fussing through the service. I carefully set him down in the pack-and-play. Then I back away, my chest clenching when I see his curled little form, his butterfly-wing eyelids. He looks so peaceful.

What would he think if he knew his father is dead?

The thought stabs me, but then I feel Ollie's arms circling my waist, his lower half pressing against my butt. "Mmm."

"Ollie," I say, stepping away. Ollie pulls me closer, cupping the sides of my face, kissing my mouth aggressively.

"*Ollie,*" I say again. "What are you doing?"

He bunches up my dress and fumbles at the waistband of my underwear. "Let's make another baby."

"Now?"

"Come on." He grips my wrist, pulling me back to him. "Right now. Let's do it."

"No," I almost growl. And this time I shove him. Hard.

Ollie's eyes widen. At first he looks rejected, even annoyed, but then he's contrite. "I'm sorry, babe. You just look so hot, and . . ."

Now it's my turn to feel guilty. "No, *I'm* sorry." I can feel the tears gathering in my throat. "I just . . . I'm a mess today, you know? My head is all over the place."

"I know." He runs his hands over the back of his neck. "But at that funeral, knowing that someone our age is dead—it made me think about how fleeting life is. How we have to seize it by the horns, and I love you so much. You know that, right? I love you *so* much."

I can only eke a nod. I am the worst person on earth.

We sink into the love seat. I let Ollie stroke my forearm. I keep my head down, feeling as though a heavy bag is pressed against my shoulders. Maybe I've made a mistake, pushing him away. Things feel so precarious, on the verge of being exposed. Ollie can't *know* anything, can he?

But the way he said, *Let's make another baby.* If only it were that simple.

After the mistake of a night with Greg, I vowed to change. I was careful around him. Polite, but distant. Two weeks after it happened, he asked me into his office. He closed the door. We went over the details of a patient, and he put his hand on my knee. I drew back. "No?" Greg cocked his head playfully.

"No," I said firmly. My attraction for Greg had evaporated; he'd fucked it out of me, maybe. Since then, I couldn't stand to look at myself in the mirror. My whole life, I'd held myself to certain standards, but now I felt my reputation was soiled, even if I was the only person who'd ever know.

Greg's eyes were pleading. "But you get me, Laura. And I get you, too."

Not long ago, I would have been flattered. Thrilled. But I shook my head. "We're better than this," I said quietly. "We're both *good people.*"

Greg drew back as though I'd slapped him. "Well," he said, crossing his arms. "I guess I have my marching orders." And then he dismissed me.

My period was due right around then. It was the only thing I could rely on being regular in my life, and yet the days kept passing, and it didn't come. I stared at the calendar, first puzzled, and then apprehensive. Two weeks went by. At that point, I was starting to feel nauseous, and my breasts were tender, and I felt strange, pulling sensations in my lower abdomen. I wasn't surprised when two lines came up on the test I took in the pharmacy bathroom three minutes after purchasing it. I stared at the little plastic stick, feeling nothing—not hope, not doom. It was fucking ironic.

Here was the thing, though: Yes, I'd cheated with Greg, and yes, the sex hadn't been protected, but Ollie and I had also tried plenty that month. It wasn't out of the question that this *was* Ollie's baby. Maybe we'd finally conceived. Maybe the Greg dalliance had nothing to do with anything.

I pocketed the pregnancy test. Steered my attitude toward something light and bright and joyful. It wasn't hard to get excited—*really* excited. I was *pregnant,* something I'd wished for forever. Ollie and I would finally get what we deserved. I told him that very night, casually dropping the test next to his plate at dinner. He stared at it long and hard, and then looked at me questioningly, almost worriedly, like he was afraid he was dreaming and would soon wake up. But I grinned. "It's happening! Really happening!"

A strange sort of whoop emerged from the back of his throat as he rose and hugged me hard. His shoulders shook with sobs. I cried, too, though my tears weren't any one pure emotion. It wouldn't be easy to erase the possibility of Greg from my mind. Years before, I'd heard a heart transplant patient use the term *brutiful*—a mash-up of *brutal* and *beautiful,* indicating an experience that was difficult but memorable and came with a certain amount of grace. That's how I felt: both brutal and beautiful. Thrilled and devastated at the same time.

The pregnancy stuck. I got through my first trimester with no complications. Eventually, I had to tell Greg the news. Nerves rippled through me like water through a sieve. Since I'd turned Greg down in his office, we'd avoided one another. If we were working the same surgeries, we were cordial, but there was no casual banter like before. I'd also noticed him in the hallway sometimes, typing on his phone, a wisp of a smile on his face. A new woman? Perhaps his wife? In hindsight, I wonder if it was that Lolita person.

In his office, I stared at the crystal paperweights on his bookshelf so I wouldn't have to look at him directly. "So I'm pregnant," I blurted. "Due October third."

"October third," Greg repeated, but there was a kink in his voice, like he was counting backward. A memory of Greg at the bar popped in my mind, all sharp edges: *I wish I'd had a biological child.* Sadness had wafted off him. Yearning.

"Ollie and I are really excited," I said. Because I had to. I needed to draw lines around this baby. Ascribe whom it belonged to.

"I'm sure you are," Greg said. And just like that, his eyes crinkled mirthfully. He opened his arms. I walked into a strange, tentative hug. A happy ending, then.

Until it wasn't.

By the time I went into labor, I barely remembered my worries about Greg. But when Freddie was born and the nurses placed him on my belly, his little eyes screwed tight, his big mouth stretched wide, I took one look at him and knew. Thank God Ollie's back was turned—he was washing his hands at the sink—there was no way I could hide my dismay. I'd heard that babies look like their fathers when they're born for biologically imperative reasons: It's so dads will see themselves in those new, tiny faces and feel compelled to protect them. The only face I saw in Freddie's squished little features was the face of the doctor I worked alongside in the operating room, not the husband who slept next to me every night. Not the man who yearned for this child as deeply as I did.

When Ollie turned and saw me crying, he assumed it was out of joy—our baby was finally here, healthy and strong. I did feel that. But I was also bitterly angry—and afraid of what Ollie might suspect. But Ollie held Freddie outstretched, marveling at his existence. When his mother arrived and declared that the baby was the spitting image of Ollie's deceased father, Joe, I began to breathe easier.

Still. *I* knew. I kept Greg from seeing Freddie for as long as I could. But just a few weeks ago, on one of my days off, I needed to pick up my paycheck, so I popped into the hospital with Freddie. Greg wouldn't be there—I was so paranoid about running into him that I knew his schedule better than my own. The nurses flocked around us, commenting on the baby's chubby cheeks, his bright blue eyes, his sweet disposition, the milestones he'd already achieved.

And then I sensed a presence in the doorway. My blood ran cold. When Greg clapped eyes on Freddie, it was as though he was hit with an electric current. "So," he said, "I finally get to meet the big man."

I tried to act like things were normal. But I felt a horrible twist in my gut at how recognizable my son's features were. Freddie had the same little bump on his nose that Greg did. The same long eyelashes. That same cleft in his chin. Greg could see himself in Freddie, and it was like a switch had flipped inside him. A rope had snapped.

I got out of the hospital quickly, unable to stand Greg's charged stare. But during my next shift, I found a folded piece of paper in my locker. It was a printout reminding new mothers to give their baby vitamin D drops. I stared at it for a few long beats, confused. Maybe Tina had slipped it in there? She was crazy about vitamins. But when I asked her, she looked at me like I was crazy. "I'm not going to tell you how to raise your kid."

Later that same day, I found another printout: studies on circumcision. I'd already circumcised Freddie, and how was it anyone's business? Two days later came a list of appropriate Montessori schools in the greater Pittsburgh area. A day after that, a sheaf of horror stories about SIDS cases at day care facilities.

A crack formed in my brain. During one of our nights out, Greg had talked about how *he'd* had a Montessori education. And last year, when a local day care had an infant suspiciously stop breathing while napping, he'd muttered to me, "Personally, I think day cares are evil."

The messages kept coming, sometimes two or three stuffed into my locker over the course of a single shift. They were about the Ferber method, how long a mother should breastfeed, the benefits of organic food. Each unwelcome piece of paper I unfolded felt like a ransom note, a letter of execution. Greg Strasser was not a man to reject. I learned the hard way.

"My poor, poor baby," Ollie says, dragging me back to the present. I look around. Dust sparkles through our living room. Our baby turns on the monitor screen, suspended in dreams. "But you don't have to be scared. I'm not going to let anything happen to you."

I frown into my lap, momentarily confused. *This* is why Ollie thinks I'm upset? But then, of course he does. He thinks I'm in a state because someone murdered my boss in cold blood. But it's not the murderer I'm afraid of. It's how relieved I am that Greg is gone.

And that I hold myself a little bit responsible.

16

RAINA

SATURDAY, APRIL 29, 2017

*T*hanks to the free cocktails at Greg Strasser's post-funeral reception, I'm still buzzed when I show up to Alexis's party. This makes me chatty with my Uber driver. I babble about movies I've just seen, my favorite neighborhoods in Pittsburgh, and wanting to be a writer when I grow up.

"What do you think about that crazy murder that happened near Aldrich?" the driver asks me as we turn onto a Lawrenceville side street. "Pretty scary the killer still hasn't been found."

"I *knew* that guy," I say, almost proudly. The driver looks at me like I'm a celebrity. Asks who I think did it. But that's a question I don't want to answer.

When I get out of the car, I realize I'm a hot mess. I need to sober up. I need to be *on* tonight for Alexis so I can see what she's all about.

I stare at my outfit. I've got on my highest heels. I'm still wearing my sexiest, shortest black dress—which, okay, probably wasn't funeral appropriate, but I thought Greg, wherever he is now, might appreciate it. Tonight bears so much promise. Every text I've received from Alexis in the past twenty-four hours has been increasingly suggestive and flirty. She's one of those girls who punctuates her texts with hearts and gives people flirty nicknames—*hottie, sexy girl, gorgeous*. I knew a few high school girls who did that, always screaming out, "I love you!" to their friends and creating over-the-top tributes in one another's yearbooks, but with Alexis, the nicknames take on a new charge. I feel she's calling me sexy because she *wants to have sex with me*.

And I'd like to make that happen . . . and more. I just need to figure out her stakes. How to ensure it doesn't go up in flames. Basically, I need to make sure it doesn't go the way of what happened with Alfred Manning months before.

I thought I'd read Manning right when I'd planned out the scam. I'd paid my dues by being his faithful assistant for months, enduring meetings with Marilyn O'Leary, endless coffee runs, boring discussions about policies and staff changes and budgetary blah blah blah and admissions requirements and a meeting with Barack Obama, which unfortunately I hadn't gotten to attend. I'd pretended, postured, become the perfect Aldrich girl he needed. Hell, I even audited classes in case Manning, for some reason, memorized my Aldrich schedule and quizzed me on the subjects. I knew what his stakes were—his milieu wouldn't look kindly on the news that the president of the university got busy with his student assistant. And that night in December, I was ready to pounce. This was going to be an even better version of Dr. Rosen. I was so ready to take his cash.

He'd invited me over to his house in Blue Hill to screen the latest Aldrich promotional video and make notes. We'd meant to do it in the office, but he was mired in meetings—and the notes were due that Monday.

It was almost too good to be true. His house, where we'd be alone? No cameras, no nosy Marilyn? He was almost *asking* for what I had in store. I was ready, too: the hemline of my blush-colored silk dress stopped at the top of my thighs. My shoes were high, pointy-toed, and expensive. My hair was blown out and soft around my shoulders, and my makeup was subtle and sexy. Ringing his bell, I shivered—I'd left my heavy winter coat at home. But big coats weren't sexy, and tonight, it was go sexy or go home.

The door swung open, and there was Manning, dressed in a fitted, long-sleeved tee and slim-cut jeans that seemed to belie his sixty-nine years. But he looked confused at my appearance. "Did you come here without a coat? Aren't you freezing?"

"I'm not," I said, trying to bite back my annoyance. I lowered my lashes and gave him a playful punch on the arm. "But I'd love to come in."

"Well." Manning tugged his collar. I couldn't tell if he was feeling bashful or awkward. "Yes, do. Come in and get warm."

I sashayed past him. I could tell he was looking at my ass. *Good, good, good.*

We walked through the house and into the basement, which was carpeted and smelled like lemon Pledge. Manning flicked on a light in a room to reveal a small theater with tiered rows of plush seats and a large screen at the front, framed by velvet curtains. "Wow," I said. "Swanky."

He found a seat. I slid right next to him, a notebook in one hand. The seats shared armrests, and I made sure to drape my arm over his armrest in hopes our hands would bump. My gaze drifted to the side of the room. A door was ajar, and inside I saw a long bathroom counter where several pill bottles were lined up. I wondered if anything fun was in those bottles. Something we could do together.

As Manning dimmed the lights, I pulled my cell phone from my pocket. Earlier that day, I'd downloaded a video app that could film in near darkness. Manning was busy fumbling with the remote and didn't see me prop the phone on the far arm of the adjacent chair at such an angle that it would capture both of us in the frame. I felt a pang of regret. It was starting. There was no turning back now.

The opening credits to the promotional film filled the screen. Ever so slightly, I angled my legs toward Manning's. He didn't move. My heart was a jackhammer. I could sense the video counter ticking upward, logging every moment. I slid my left hand down our shared armrest toward his lap. On the screen, Alfred appeared, speaking about Aldrich's long tradition of excellence.

"Oh!" I cried, grabbing his hand. "It's you!"

He chuckled. "In the flesh."

Then he turned to me, a curious sparkle in his eye. *You can do it,* I urged him telepathically. *I won't bite.* I pushed out my breasts. *Touch me. Nobody will see. Nobody will know.* I glanced toward the open door to the little bathroom again. *Let's pop some of those pills. Get crazy.*

Then Manning's eyes darted to the seat past me. "What's that?" He pointed.

"What's what?" My voice was a strange, high-pitched warble. Now that my eyes had adjusted to the darkness, I realized that my phone was more visible than I'd anticipated. The screen glowed faintly, reflecting the resplendent campus meadow in the film.

I palmed the phone and tucked it into my bag, then turned to the screen. "Oh my God, the quad looks gorgeous with all those cherry blossoms!"

Manning was still staring. A strange glaze came over his eyes, and his features seemed to distort. "Raina," he said in a low voice. "Perhaps it was a mistake for you to come."

"W-What?" I could feel the smile melting on my face.

"I want you to leave."

I was thrown that he'd figured me out so fast. "I-I don't know what you're talking about!" But then I stared down at my bare legs, my tits hanging out. I looked ridiculous.

And then it was just . . . over. I couldn't go to his office that next Monday. I wondered, actually, if I'd ever set foot on Aldrich campus again. The prospect gave me chest pains. Aldrich University had seeped into me. I didn't want to leave its walls. I sat down on the frigid curb outside his house, too numb to cry. It felt like I'd run into a brick wall. Like I'd fallen down a deep, endless hole.

But I'm not going to make the same mistake twice.

The Uber has dropped me at a detached three-story house painted a Wedgwood blue. The doorway is narrow, dark, and kind of grim. When I ring the bell and the door swings open, though, the house widens into a big space with exposed-brick walls and ceiling beams. The space is packed, and the kitchen is new and swanky and way nicer than anything a college student should be living in. Cool, funky music swirls through the speakers.

"You made it!" I feel a hand on my arm and there is Alexis, her eyes looking extra huge and sultry, her dark hair piled on her head, and a slinky black jumpsuit clinging to her curves. The tag pokes out the back: Tory Burch again. She looks me up and down, then pouts. "No fair. You look prettier than me."

I swish my hand. "I've been at a funeral all day. I probably smell like church."

Alexa's eyes widen. "Was it that doctor who was murdered?"

I blink. "How'd you know?"

Her gaze drifts to the corner. Of all people, *Sienna* sits in profile, speaking to a guy in a Thom Yorke T-shirt. I watch as she tips the bottle of wine she's holding to her mouth and takes a long drink. *Whoa.*

"I know you guys are friends," Alexis says in a low voice. "And a bunch of people asked her about her stepfather's funeral today, so . . ." She looks puzzled. "You didn't know she was coming?"

I shake my head. Sienna didn't mention anything about going to a party tonight . . . not that I'd asked. But this party seems way out of her league. Just as I'm about to head over there, Alexis catches my arm. "Can I show you around?"

Alexis's eyes are hopeful. "Okay," I say. "Just a sec."

I quickly open the Uber app and type in all the details, charging a ride for Sienna to my account. Then I send Sienna a text: *A friend says you're at a party but maybe need rescuing. There will be a car waiting for you outside in five minutes. Please get home safe, and call me in the morning.*

There. Now it's up to Sienna to actually heed my advice.

I peer around the house. A spiral staircase leads to a second level. The floors are a dark, expensive-looking wood. "Whose place is this, anyway?"

Alexis leans so close I can smell her citrus perfume. "My boyfriend's."

I keep my smile pasted on, but inside, my spirits sink. "He must be some baller."

"His name's Trip," Alexis says, as though this tells me everything I need to know. She looks around the room. "There he is."

She points to a tall guy with floppy hair. His skin has a healthy glow, his teeth are straight and white, and there's something about his bone structure that screams WASP. On one hand, I can totally see them together. On the other, I can't at all.

Alexis takes my hand and leads me through the crowd. I figure she's going to introduce me to Trip, but instead, we walk through the kitchen and to a set of dark back stairs. I glance over my shoulder. Sienna's still in the corner, talking to that guy—I've never seen him before. She's also moved on to a new bottle of wine.

I bite my lip hard. Did she even see my text? I open the phone and send another one. *Sienna, seriously. You should go home.*

I watch as she pulls her phone out and squints at the screen. Then she peers around the room. Looking for me? Looking for the "friend" who told on her? To my relief, she gets up, sets the wine bottle on the table, and wobbles out the door. *Good.*

Finally, I can follow Alexis. Our shoes clonk against the bare wood on the stairs. It's hotter on the second floor and has that stuffy smell of a grandmother's house. The staircase winds around past the second floor, and Alexis follows it until we reach a door in the ceiling. She pushes it open, and a blast of cool air rushes in. I can see a sky full of stars. The only way to get to the roof is to climb a rickety metal ladder, which I can't manage in heels.

Alexis senses my hesitation and points to my shoes. "Take those off. You have to come up. It's the best view in the neighborhood."

I kick off my heels. The ladder wobbles vertiginously as I put my weight on it, and once I'm on the roof, I have a sudden, sharp fear that something terrible might happen. It's not like I know Alexis very well. She could close the hatch, lock me up here, and leave me for dead. I glance down at her nervously; she's still on solid ground at the ladder's base. But then she follows me. I breathe out.

Once we're both up the ladder and on the sooty, tacky roof, we look around. Low buildings rise around us, but farther beyond, I can see the string of buildings downtown and the glittering lights on the bridges. The cars on the highway across the river look like tiny jewels.

"Nice," I whisper. Even nicer: When I look down, I spy a car chugging at the curb. Sienna stumbles down the steps and lurches for the door. "You Sienna?" I hear the driver say. The door slams, and the car pulls away. I let out a breath I didn't quite realize I was holding.

Alexis leads me across the roof to two plastic chairs and a folded flannel blanket. "Come under this with me, babe. Sun's gone down, so it's chilly."

Babe. Her signals are all over the map. She drapes the blanket over our legs and pulls something out of a shoulder bag. A shiny wine label glints in the moonlight. "Screw top, luckily," she murmurs, twisting off the cap. An acidic scent fills my nostrils. My mouth waters.

Traffic swishes peacefully. Alexis's body presses into mine, and I feel the swell of her rib cage as she breathes. I want to snuggle with her, but I still can't quite read the situation—how much touching is too much? What is friendly, and what's romantic? I need to play this just right. As impatient as I am for things to move quickly, I have to bide my time.

"So are you feeling sad?" Alexis asks after we've both drunk from the wine bottle.

"Sad? No. Why do you ask?"

"You were at a funeral. Usually, after *I'm* at a funeral, I'm a little sad."

"Oh." I scrunch the scratchy blanket in my hands. My leg is falling asleep from the weight of Alexis's body, but I don't dare move. "I feel bad for Sienna, sure. She's a good friend. I was with her the night that guy was killed, actually." Although, actually, I wasn't with Sienna the *whole* night. I'd found her about twenty minutes after she found out about Greg. She was balled up in a corner, practically catatonic.

"Did you know him?" Alexis asks.

I turn my head away, staring at a smokestack on a nearby roof. "Sort of," I lie.

"He wrote some sexy e-mails to someone. Have you read them?"

"I'm not really into hack gossip." I don't want to talk about this anymore, so I tilt my head back. "Look at that red light up there. Think it's a spaceship?"

Alexis squints. "No, silly. That's Mars."

"Really?" I squint hard. "Nah. It's so bright."

Alexis swallows more wine. "The planets are always bright. And that's definitely Mars because of its reddish tinge." She gives me a cocky smile. "You're looking at the president of her astronomy club in high school, so I know for sure."

"You were an astronomy nerd?" I nudge her. "You're making that up."

"I was a nerd through and through." Alexis laughs. "I took all AP classes, on the Quiz Bowl team, in Model UN . . ."

I'm about to ask what Model UN is—my school didn't have fancy clubs. But that would make me look stupid. "Well, good for you."

"Were you a nerd, too?" Alexis asks.

I'm about to tell her yes, but maybe it's not the right play tonight. "Actually, I was a troublemaker," I admit. "I can't even believe I got into Aldrich."

"Your grades weren't good?"

"No, they were good. Great, actually. But, I mean, it's *Aldrich*."

Alexis frowns. "Aldrich isn't *that* great."

"Of course it is," I say proudly, my smile crooked. "I mean, it's gotta mean something that it was hacked along with Harvard and Yale, right?"

"Yeah, but." Alexis stretches out her legs. "All that stuff that's come out in the hack—everyone seems so skeevy, you know? Totally amoral. Half the professors are criminals."

"Well, *I* still love it," I say, feeling something clench in my chest. It's true. I love Aldrich desperately. I love the things I've learned, the taste of the world I've received. Maybe that's because it's about to be taken away from me.

Alexis chuckles. "Personally, I love *people,* not old, crumbling institutions run by old, crumbling white dudes."

I laugh, too. "So, like, you love your boyfriend, then?"

She snorts. "Oh God, no. Not him." And then she lowers her chin. Her eyelashes flutter. "But I might be into someone else. I'm not sure yet. It's all really . . . new."

I watch her carefully. Is she sending a message? If not, then what are we doing up on this roof together, alone?

"Hey," Alexis suddenly says with momentum. "Come with me to my parents' place next Tuesday. They live just a few miles to the north."

I stiffen. "Oh, I don't know. I'm not great with families."

"Please?" She grabs my hands. "It's my grandmother's ninetieth birthday—I have to go. We'd have so much fun! We could ride the horses, we have a great heated indoor pool, their bar is insane . . ."

The scent of a cigarette drifts up from the street. I try to wrap my mind around what Alexis is asking. Meet her *family*? What if Alexis's parents see right through me? What if I do something that shows my roots? It is so far out of my comfort zone I don't even know how to answer.

"But what about Trip?" I finally say. "Maybe you should take him instead."

Alexis's face darkens. "He's already invited. But I want you to come, too."

I frown. "Are you sure that makes sense?"

"My parents are crazy about Trip," Alexis explains in an almost woeful voice. "He's practically a son-in-law to them already. But I'm *tired* of him. He's just . . . I don't know. Not right."

I sit back. "Then why are you going out with him?"

She shrugs. "You know what it's like. When my parents like a guy, they'll move heaven and earth to make sure I stick with him. My parents have wanted to cut me loose for years, though—they're real assholes. Breaking up with Trip would be just the straw that breaks their backs."

I cross my arms. "So you're basically pretending to be with Trip just to make sure they don't disown you?" I say *disown* on purpose. I need to know if money's at stake.

Alexis taps her nails against the wine bottle. "You could say that. It would have to take someone really special to make me break away from them."

She looks at me, hope in her voice. I feel another flutter in my chest. And she's got to be indebted to her family because there's money involved. A trust fund, probably. Something her family would cut her out of if she didn't obey. And just like that, I've found her weakness.

Alexis grabs my hands. "So will you come next weekend? *Please?*"

Far above us, an airplane zooms. It's a plane and not a planet—I can tell by the blinking light on the wing. "All right. It sounds fun."

"Great!" Alexis cries, throwing her arms around me. "We're going to have a blast!"

I squeeze her tight, inhaling her scent, feeling her hair tickling my shoulders. It's hard not to be excited. It's hard not to leap up and scream to the universe, *Thank you, thank you, thank you.* Maybe, after twisting Alexis around my finger, I'll get to stay at Aldrich after all.

I think about that cold, bitter night after I'd left Manning's house.

I called Sienna because her family lived close by and I needed to get out of the subzero air. I had no intention of telling her what had happened with her grandfather or anything. At that point, I'd actually liked Sienna as a person, and I didn't want her to think less of me.

Sienna said she was on her way back from a ski weekend with friends; she said she was pretty sure no one else was home but that I could let myself in with the garage code to warm up.

I rushed into the warm, big house. Hot water would help my numb fingers, so I set off to the bathroom. When I passed the kitchen and saw the figure by the fridge, I screamed. He looked over and screamed, too. Then came the shattering sound of breaking glass.

"Jesus!" Sienna's stepfather backed up against the fridge door. He was wearing med scrubs and white sneakers, and his eyes were round with surprise. "Who are you?"

"I'm so sorry!" I cried. And then: "I'm Raina. Sienna said I could come in. She gave me the garage code. She said no one would be home."

Sienna's father's brow furrowed, taking in my skimpy outfit. "Were you outside in just *that*?" I nodded miserably. There were goose bumps on my arms.

He found a sweatshirt, some heavy wool socks. I changed in the powder room, staring at my naked body, then a black-and-white photograph of some lake in Yosemite. When I walked back into the kitchen, Sienna's stepfather was mopping up the glass that had broken on the floor.

"I'm really sorry," I said again. "I can reimburse you."

"Don't be silly. It's kind of my fault. I was skulking around in the dark, trying to figure out what to do." He paused. "I'm supposed to go out with my wife's friends tonight—stupid holiday tradition. I really, *really* don't want to."

The floor smelled yeasty from the beer. Sienna's stepfather had an impressive mop of hair, thick and wavy. I remembered my encounter with him in Manning's office the day of my interview. That smile he'd shot me when I was leaving. My skin began to tingle.

"Why don't you want to go out?" I asked softly, leaning against the counter.

He brushed the pieces of glass into a dustpan and carefully slid it into a chrome trash can. "Have you ever gone out with people not because you want to but because you have to? Except if you had to choose, they wouldn't be the people you'd ever want to hang out with?"

"All the time."

"Well, it's like that."

"Then don't go if you don't want to. Life's too short."

His lips twisted into a smile. "You know, you're right. I think I'll say my surgery is running late." He touched his phone. The screen glowed to life, showing a family photo of himself, Sienna, Aurora, and his pretty, polished wife. After he tapped a few words, the phone made the telltale *bloop* noise that the text had been sent. "There," he said.

I took in his height, his handsome bone structure, his name across his chest. *Dr. Greg Strasser, Cardiology.* His eyes roamed from my hair to my bare legs to the way the sweatshirt clung to my boobs. I could feel the heat of his gaze and practically see the thoughts forming in his mind. Dr. Strasser was gorgeous. Dr. Strasser seemed willing. And most of all, Dr. Strasser, a cardiologist, was probably *loaded.*

And just like that, I shifted gears. It was so easy.

Greg's phone beeped; he glanced at it, and his face clouded. "Is that your wife?" I asked, coiling a piece of hair around my finger. "Did I get you in trouble?"

Greg sighed. "No one said marriage was easy." Then he looked at me as if realizing something. "You're at Aldrich like Sienna, right? How are you liking it?"

"I love it. I'm on the Dean's List."

"Good for you." Dr. Strasser held my gaze. "And you work for Kit's dad, right?"

"*Worked*." I felt a corkscrew of regret. "We've . . . parted ways."

He snorted. "Well, Alfred Manning is a cantankerous old coot." He leaned in closer, smelling like clean clothes. "I don't think he likes me much, either."

I gave him a skeptical look, wanting to ask why not. Instead, I pointed at the bottle of wine on the counter. "Mind if I have some of that?"

Strasser glanced at the wine, then crossed his arms. "How old are you?"

"How old do I look?" And then, after a beat, "I'm almost twenty-one, honest. Birthday's March nineteenth." A lie. My birthday was in March, but I would be only twenty.

The teakettle whistled. Strasser switched off the burner. He poured me a half glass of wine. "Cheers."

"Cheers." I sipped. "And thank you."

"Nah, thank *you*." His eyes twinkled. "I am way, *way* too tired for a night out." He rubbed his forehead and temples, grimacing.

I lowered my lashes. "I can help you relax, if you want."

Dr. Strasser froze, the wine halfway to his lips. The ions in the room seemed to rearrange. If there was a moment to just act, it was now. I took a step toward him. I would start with a little massage. I'd comment on his musculature. Ask if he worked out. Men loved that. As I stepped closer, I momentarily left my body and saw this scene as a stranger peering through the window: a pretty girl in a sweat-shirt and socks and an older man in surgical scrubs stood in the kitchen.

"Aldrich doesn't have a Dean's List, you know," Greg suddenly said.

I stopped halfway across the floor. "I'm sorry?"

"Aldrich doesn't have a Dean's List. It's one of the school's quirks."

"Oh." An oily sensation spread through me. "My bad. I was thinking of my high school's honors list, I guess." I raised one shoulder in an *Aw shucks,* but my heart was starting to beat hard. "And I just wanted to impress you. Is that so wrong?"

Dr. Strasser was looking at me like I was one of those Word Find games; the longer he stared, the more likely it was that the answer would reveal itself. Finally, he said in a voice that wasn't quite angry but wasn't quite friendly, either: "Do you even go to Aldrich at all, Raina?"

I felt a cold draft on my thighs. How had he figured *that* out? But maybe it didn't matter. I could still feel his yearning. All I had to do was push a little harder, and I'd have him.

"You got me," I said, pouring myself another half glass of wine. "It's . . . complicated. Still, I'll be your Aldrich coed, if that's what you like. I'll be whatever you want."

Alexis snuggles close. I conceal a grin. A new plan is forming, just like it had that night with Strasser. That plan had worked. Worked really, *really* well.

But now Strasser is gone. And I have to move on to survive.

17

KIT

MONDAY, MAY 1, 2017

The moment I step through our office doors on Monday morning, I feel the same way Alice must have when she walked in on the Mad Hatter and the March Hare having the tea party. All activity on the floor stops. Jeremy stares at me as though he's seen a three-headed frog.

"Kit!" George rushes over to me. "What are *you* doing back?"

"You guys need me." I nervously stuff my key card back in my purse. "Is that all right?"

"Of course, of course." George follows me as I unlock my office door and walk inside. "I just didn't want to push you to come back until you were ready." His gaze slides to the big window that overlooks the street. A few reporters have followed me here. I don't know what they expect. If I haven't talked to them yet, what makes them think I'm going to change my mind and suddenly give a statement?

My office has a dusty smell as though it's been shut for weeks. I can feel my boss watching me. I've ignored his calls and e-mails, even the ones about work matters, which mostly had to do with such-and-such donor pulling out because of the hack news. That's not like me. Kit Manning-Strasser is on point in her job, even in a crisis.

It was Willa who urged me to come back. Create some normalcy again, she said. Even if you stare at your computer for six hours, doing nothing, it'll get easier with each passing day. Willa said she'd take care of the girls, grocery shopping, and even moving us back into my house, if forensics ever finishes up. Not that I'm sure I want to move back. I'm not sure I can ever go into my kitchen again.

George updates me on some of the pressing hack scandals that most threaten donor support. I offer to make some calls, assuaging the benefactors' fears and persuading them not to back out of their financial commitments. "You realize they may want to know how you're holding up," he says carefully. "Quite a few of them are . . . curious."

A muscle in his cheek jumps. Is he trying to tell me that a lot of the donors suspect I'm the killer? But the donors are smarter than that. And besides, if I were bad for business, George would have had a conversation with me about it last week. Suggest I take some time off, maybe. He isn't the type who beats around the bush.

Then George says he has a meeting to get to, adding with a crinkly smile that it's "really good to have you back, Kit."

I settle into my desk. My computer is functional again—the Aldrich servers have finally been restored. The IT specialists still haven't figured out how to take down the hack database, but at this point it's moot, because the link has been replicated and reposted by a bunch of other sites like Snopes and Open Secrets. I launch my e-mail app, feeling a rush of holy-shit fear. Can I really do this? I've just buried my second husband, a murder happened in my house, the whole world knows that my dead husband had an affair, and a man I made out with is married to my coworker. Am I really going to keep it together?

My phone rings. The caller ID reads, *Unknown*. A reporter? Various news outlets are dying to get an interview with me because of Greg.

I let it go to voice mail. After a moment, I press the little triangle to play it, and some static noises crackle through the speaker. After about ten seconds, someone sighs. The hair on the back of my neck rises. Do I know that sigh? Is that Patrick?

Forget him, I tell myself. *He's married to your coworker. Stop thinking about him.*

My phone rings again. This time, I see my dad's landline number. One of my daughters, probably.

I pick up the receiver. "Sienna? Everything okay?"

"Actually, it's Willa."

My sister's gravelly voice makes me sit taller in my chair. "Oh. Hey."

"How's work going?"

"I just got here," I remind her. "I haven't really done anything yet." I idly navigate to Facebook, though that's a mistake. My feed is full of both Greg *In Memory* messages and a few hundred reposts of Greg's e-mails to Lolita. "How are the girls?"

"Well, they haven't come downstairs, even when I knocked." Then she clears her throat. "Maybe they should go back to school."

"They're still so shell-shocked."

"I wonder if it would be better for them if they went back. They'll be around friends. Classes will take their minds off things."

Out the window, a siren wails. I twist away from the noise. "Just because you convinced me to go back to work doesn't mean it's the right choice for them."

"I was serious when I said they've been off since this happened."

I ball up my fist. "What do you mean, *off*?"

"Don't you think they've been acting sort of weird? Distant? Kind of . . . cold?"

"Their stepfather was murdered in their home—a home we can't even go back to yet. I think that's a valid excuse for not acting like themselves."

"I wonder if they should talk to someone."

"A counselor?" I start to open the paper bag that contains a muffin I've brought for breakfast, then decide against it. I'm not hungry.

"Or even me. As a start. Maybe they're afraid to talk to you."

I scoff. "Why would they be afraid?"

"A lot has happened. Maybe they'd feel more comfortable talking to someone who isn't so close to the situation."

I've tried to reach my girls over the past few days. The morning after I found Greg murdered, I sat on the couch with them, cradling their bodies. I *tried* to say things to make them feel better, safe. But I'd been in shock, too. All of my swirling emotions of horror and loss and anger stewed close to the surface. Perhaps I was more concerned about my own self-preservation right then, but can you blame me? I basically bathed in a pool of my husband's blood. I was also the one who'd had those violent, angry thoughts about him just hours before he was stabbed.

I figured I'd just let them grieve on their own and then, in a few days, we'd talk. I also need to get that awkwardness out of my head first, so that I don't tarnish their opinions of Greg now that he's gone.

Unbidden, the image of Sienna and Greg sitting at his old kitchen table in Shadyside flashes back to me. How happy they were. How tickled I'd felt when I watched Sienna laughing for what seemed like the first time since Martin died. I flash on another memory, too: Aurora, at fourteen, rushing home from school so she could log into a website at precisely 3:00 P.M., when Beyoncé tickets went on sale. But the bus had been late; by the time she logged in, the tickets were gone. Greg and I watched as she bit back tears. Fast-forward to the next night: Greg slyly sitting down to dinner and, with a twist of his mouth, pushing an envelope across the table to Aurora. She opened it, and her eyes popped wide. "How did you *find* them?" she screeched, and got up and threw her arms around Greg . . . just as one would a father.

Willa clears her throat. "There are a few other things I want to ask you. Stuff I meant to ask yesterday . . . but things were so crazy . . ."

I swivel away from my computer to the window. Down on the street, the student bus, which takes kids to dorms all over campus, huffs past, kicking up a plume of black exhaust.

There's a long pause. "Who was that guy you were talking to after the funeral?"

I curl my toes. I had a feeling Willa might ask. "Just a friend."

"You looked . . . uncomfortable."

I peer nervously into the hall, fearful that Lynn Godfrey is lurking around a corner somewhere, listening in. "I'm not particularly good at accepting people's sympathy, that's all. I haven't exactly processed that Greg's dead."

"Okay," Willa says. And then, after a pause: "Also, this other thing. Maybe I have my information wrong, but was Greg Martin's surgeon?"

I roll a few inches back, my chair hitting the radiator behind my desk. The heat is on, and my spine is instantly too warm. "Yes. Yes, he was."

"Is there a reason you never told me this?"

"I . . . don't know. I didn't think it was relevant."

"You said Greg was part of the team that diagnosed him. Not that he'd been the guy who actually *operated on Martin's heart.*"

"You mean the guy who let him die," I say stonily. "You mean the guy who deliberately killed him so we could be together."

Now it's Willa who's silent. "Wait." Her voice is small. "You mean . . . it's true?"

"Of course not! But I know people talked. Of course they speculated about it after we got together. I guess *that's* why I didn't tell you what his role was. I didn't want you to judge him."

"Oh." Willa sounds both relieved and sheepish. "Okay. I mean, it sounded a little far-fetched to me, too." There's an awkward pause.

I stare at the family photo in a silver frame on my desk. It's of me,

Greg, and Sienna and Aurora on that disappointing Barbados trip, though we're smiling cheerfully for the camera. In my desk drawer is another family photo—of me, Sienna, and Aurora . . . and Martin. Not in Barbados—we never could have afforded Barbados—but at Ocean City, New Jersey. There's significance to why I saved that photo and why, sometimes, I pull the drawer open and look at it. Maybe I *do* feel guilty. I *was* unfaithful, in a way.

"I will say this," I tell Willa. "Greg did sweep me off my feet the moment I met him. He was just so vibrant. Larger-than-life, the doctor who could save anyone. And he was . . . complimentary."

"How so?"

"He kept saying how caring I was as a wife. He recognized that I had a lot on my plate and was impressed with how together I seemed." I sigh. "Martin hadn't recognized any of that in a long time. Which, I mean—it makes sense. He was so sick. *Scared.* But I'm still human. Greg's attention felt good. And also . . ." I trail off, not wanting to tell her the rest.

"Also what?" Willa asks.

I lace my fingers around my coffee mug. There are certain limits to what I'll admit. What will Willa think if I tell her that, when my eyes drifted to Greg's expensive shoes and slick watch, I felt a deep, envious desire? And when the appointment was over and Martin's surgery was set, when we were walking through the parking garage to find our car, I saw a beautiful Porsche parked in the RESERVED FOR DOCTOR spot and almost blushed with lust? I'd fetishized Greg's wealth and possessions. I'd become ravenously material.

"Greg called quite a bit, but we always talked about Martin," I say instead. "Or, well, *mostly* all about Martin."

"What's that mean?"

There's a lump in my throat. Sometimes, during those phone conversations, after a barrage of questions about Martin's chances of recovery, or if whether perhaps a heart transplant *did* make more sense at this stage, I'd talk about my daughters. I felt so alone in navigating Martin's illness; Sienna and Aurora were more concerned with their friends and social media minutiae. I remember sitting on my kitchen floor one night, talking to Greg about how I'd asked Sienna if she wanted to be there in the hospital during Dad's surgery. Sienna shrugged and said callously, "But homecoming is that night, Mom."

"She's just scared," Greg assured me. "She's distancing herself from the situation so she doesn't have to face the tough emotions."

It was weird to be telling this to my husband's cardiologist instead of my husband, but how could I share it with Martin? It would break his heart to know that his beloved Sienna was pushing him away. Those two always had a special bond, with inside jokes and special hobbies and interests they pursued together. I wouldn't be surprised if Martin wanted Sienna and Aurora by his side even more than he wanted me. We loved each other, sure, but marital love is complicated, whereas love between parent and child is pure.

"It just felt so good to be listened to," I say softly, knowing how poorly I'm explaining this. "I was so, *so* scared."

"Of course you were," Willa says softly, sympathetically.

I remember looking up at Greg in the hospital, after he'd told me Martin hadn't made it. I'd drunk up the strangeness of him—his full head of wavy hair, the smattering of freckles on his cheeks, the bone structure of his clean-shaven, youthful face. Our gazes locked, and something stirred low inside me, something both lustful and shameful. It almost felt as if we were going to kiss. We didn't, of course. I turned in the hall and saw that my daughters were standing there, watching.

"Did you ever ask your girls what they thought about all of this?" Willa asks, as if reading my mind.

I crinkle my muffin bag between my fingers. "What do you mean?"

"What did they think about you dating the surgeon who couldn't save their dad?"

I don't like the way she's phrased that. "He didn't . . . look, I don't think they would have liked anyone I dated." I blow out a breath. "What was I supposed to do, Willa? Be alone forever? I didn't have any support system."

"You had the girls. And Martin was their father. They adored him."

"It wasn't like Greg *replaced* Martin." This just isn't something Willa can understand. "And, Jesus, they adored Greg. They were . . . I don't know, impressed by him. Their grades went up when he came into the picture, almost like they felt they needed to prove themselves. Also, Greg was able to give them things they never had. Cool clothes. Fancy handbags all the popular girls were carrying. Lavish vacations. Stuff we never got to enjoy before. And over the years, they really bonded. Half the time I'd walk in and Greg and Sienna would be talking about something I had no clue about. Aurora had him correct her science homework. She went to *him* when she got the best grade in her biology class."

"But what about in the past few months? I heard that Greg kind of acted like the girls didn't exist."

A shock goes through me. "Who said that?"

"Just . . . more reception gossip. People are assholes, but sometimes in gossip there's a kernel of the truth."

I rise from my chair. "Because you know the situation so well." I'm hurt. I'm shocked. But below this, I'm horrified. Was that how people saw us? *Did* Greg shut the girls out, just like he'd done to me?

No. The past three months, besides Barbados, were normal. We all went out to dinner as a family. Greg and the girls binged Netflix shows. He dropped Aurora off at school almost as much as I did. Sienna told us at dinner one night that she had a crush on Anton, a boy in the dorm, and Greg asked her a million questions about him—what's his major, is he athletic, what are his friends like, does he smoke pot.

"Are you sure I can't talk to your girls?" Willa asks quietly, break-ing me from my thoughts.

"About Greg? *No.*"

"But they're a part of this puzzle. They've had a lot of stuff hap-pen in a few short years—their dad's death, their mom's remarriage, stepdad's affair, his murder. It's a lot to unpack. And also," she goes on, perhaps sensing that I'm about to interrupt, "*I* just want to know, too. Personally, as their aunt. I regret not getting to know them better through the years. I've interviewed a lot of kids for some of my investigative pieces. I know how to do it without pushing."

"But they aren't your interview subjects. They might not open up to you. You might make it worse."

"But maybe I'll get *something* out of them. Like at the funeral, Sienna said Aurora's angry with her about something. Any idea what that might be?"

I glance back and forth. My thoughts are scattered.

"What are their thoughts on all that Lolita stuff? They're teenag-ers, they must be humiliated."

"I didn't get to talk to them about it." But this is a lie. I avoided talking to Sienna about it on the phone. And at the grocery store, I told Aurora nothing was wrong. *Deflect, deflect, deflect.* But my girls aren't idiots. They must have read those e-mails. Everyone did.

God, they were probably crushed. Maybe they saw an inevitable future hurtling toward them: Another broken family. A lonely mom. A mess. Maybe they even worried we wouldn't have nice things any-more. Some mom I was, instilling in them that only nice things lead to happiness.

Suddenly, I'm seized with uneasiness. "Leave the girls out of this."

"But *why*?"

"I appreciate what you're doing, trying to figure out what went on, but just . . . *don't.*"

There's a long silence. Down the hall, a shadow looms in the break room. A moment later, Lynn Godfrey's tall, slender form appears in the doorway. She holds a cup of coffee, the steam rising over her face. Her gaze holds mine for a moment, and one eyebrow raises. She tips her chin upward and marches away. My cheeks blaze.

"Get to know them, ask them questions about themselves, but please don't get into this with them," I repeat. "What happened is too fresh. *Please*."

"Okay." Willa sighs. "Fine."

After we hang up, I place my forehead on the desk. I wish I could tell Willa I don't want her to talk to the girls because I want to talk to them first . . . but I'm not sure if this is true. Lately, I've been thinking there are two Kit Mannings in one body: the Kit Manning from three years ago, the frazzled mother, the loving wife, the worrier. And then the Kit Manning of today: a polished, well-heeled doctor's wife, the head of the donations department who can throw a party and charm a room.

We're so different, these Kits. Do we treat our daughters differently, too? Which Kit Manning is it who doesn't want Willa to talk to Sienna and Aurora—the one who wants to preserve the shred of reputation she has left, or the fiercely protective mother? Maybe I haven't dwelled on Sienna and Aurora much because I know that if I dig too deeply into what they're feeling, I might not like what I find.

What if, deep down, they *were* furious with Greg for the e-mails? But what does that mean . . . and what did my daughters do with that anger?

18

WILLA

MONDAY, MAY 1, 2017

After I hang up the phone, I pace the downstairs rooms of my family's house. I want to respect Kit's wishes not to interrogate the girls, but leaving them out of this story is like only drawing half a picture. They lived with Greg.

And it's Kit's reluctance to let me talk to the girls that bothers me most. Is there something she isn't telling me? *Does* she think Sienna and Aurora are hiding something? Let's face it: The police can't figure out anyone who'd want Greg dead, but this is a man who came into the girls' lives only recently, after they lost a father they loved to death.

I need to figure it out. I hate the idea of making them uncomfortable. And I don't believe for a second either of them hurt their stepfather. But I do wonder if they know something they don't want to tell. Perhaps I need to draw it out of them before someone else does—like an unsympathetic detective, or an impassive, hard-nosed lawyer.

I climb the creaky stairs to the third floor. The top level holds three more bedrooms, a tiny bathroom, and an oversize closet in which my mother used to store her knitting supplies. The doors to the rooms Sienna and Aurora are staying in are shut tight, which seems symbolic—they've closed everyone out. I press my ear to Sienna's door, but I hear nothing. Same with Aurora's. My heart is thudding hard, and I don't know if what I'm doing is right—after all, I'm going against Kit's strict wishes.

Still, after a moment I call out, "Girls? It's Willa. Can we talk for a sec?"

After a beat, I hear footsteps padding across Sienna's wood floor, and her door opens a crack. There are circles under Sienna's eyes. The shirt she is wearing is rumpled and stained. "Hey, Aunt Willa," she croaks. "Um, I'm kind of not feeling well."

"This'll only take a minute." I rap on Aurora's door next. "Honey? Can you come out, too?"

Aurora's door creaks open, revealing the tiny bedroom with the slanted roof. I can't help but smile, poking my head in. "I lived in this room for a few years in high school, once Grandma and Grandpa trusted me in the attic." I point to the far wall. "That was painted black. And there was a big Nirvana poster on the ceiling. I used to love Kurt Cobain."

The corners of Aurora's mouth curve into a frown. "I was sleeping," she says moodily.

"This won't take long. I just have a couple of questions."

When I say *questions,* Sienna seems to flinch, and Aurora's arms tighten around her torso. "Sit down, sit down," I tell them. I gesture to the little love seat my mother placed in the hallway years before.

"You guys still mad at each other?" I ask.

Aurora chews on her lip. Sienna spins a silver ring around her finger.

"You girls need each other. You're going through a hard time. Don't forget, your mom and I lost a parent when we were your age, too—and just as abruptly. After all these years, it still hurts." I feel my throat close. Sienna's head lifts an inch. It's not often that I show emotion, and this has gotten her attention.

The house makes a series of small settling clicks and groans. "You guys have been through so much. It isn't fair. And I feel like a jerk—I barely got to *know* Greg. Is it awful to say that I was still kind of stuck on your dad as, like, Kit's soul mate? I mean, he and Kit were together for *so* long. I remember them snuggling up on the couch in high school, hogging the TV. But I should have gotten to know Greg better. Your mom talked a little bit about him back when your dad was really sick. Said he was this amazing surgeon. A really good, genuine person. He really dazzled you guys, huh?"

The girls nod but don't say anything.

"You know, I wonder what it feels like, as a surgeon, to have a patient not make it." I try to keep my voice light, contemplative, but my heart is pounding harder than I'd like. "How can they teach you to deal with that in medical school?"

Aurora frowns. Picks at an imaginary piece of lint on her knee. "There's no point in being angry at the surgeon. Sometimes things just happen."

I'm surprised at how well-adjusted she sounds. I glance at Aurora, and she's nodding, too. So maybe I was wrong, then. Maybe these girls don't harbor some sort of deep hatred for Greg for inadvertently killing Martin on the operating table. It makes me feel better.

But it still doesn't clear up all my intuition that they're hiding something. "So are you getting annoying backlash from friends about what you guys are going through now?"

"A little," Sienna admits. "People have a lot of questions."

I lean forward a little. "I hate to ask this, but did you guys *read* those e-mails?"

Sienna's jaw tightens. Aurora clears her throat. "They were pretty gross," she says in a loud voice. "Like, way, *way* more disgusting than I imagined e-mails like that would be. I can't believe she . . ."

But she trails off as Sienna gives her a hard, inscrutable look. I don't understand what's gone down, but suddenly I'm filled with new questions. *She?*

I cock my head. "Do you girls know who Lolita is?"

Sienna raises her chin. "No, she doesn't."

"Aurora? You can speak for yourself."

Aurora stares at her fingers. "No." But a hot, crawling sensation eases across my chest.

"Is it a friend of yours?" I deliver the next line very, very carefully, glancing at Sienna. "Like Raina, for instance. She's gorgeous. And she certainly seemed broken up about Greg's death."

Sienna sniffs. "Raina isn't Lolita."

But she covers her nose when she says this, an obvious tell that she's lying. I hold her gaze, and she looks away first. "You don't need to protect her," I urge. "We need to figure out the truth."

"I'm *telling* the truth."

"Okay, then, who is it?"

"Why would I know?" Sienna slaps her thighs, then stands. "Why are we having this conversation?"

I glance at Aurora, but she's staring blankly into her lap. "Okay. Well, whoever Lolita was, the cops will figure it out eventually, if they choose to look," I say evenly. "There are ways to track the origin of those e-mails. By certain markers in the language. Or by the IP address."

"The cops probably looked already," Sienna says, her eyes shining. "And the IP isn't going to tell them anything."

This is the most effusive Sienna has been my whole visit. There's even a sudden bloom of pink on her cheeks. "You seem to know a lot about computers," I say carefully.

She shrugs. "It's common knowledge. And I have a friend—he says IPs always just give you generalities about an area an e-mail came from, not the particular user."

"That's true. But sometimes getting a general location is a good clue. Did your friend tell you that?"

"Not necessarily."

Her combativeness surprises me. Sienna is typically the one who doesn't want to make waves. I glance at Aurora, but she's glaring as though the conversation irritates her.

I stand, sensing that I'm not going to get anything else from them. "Thanks for talking, girls. If you ever want to open up about Greg—about *anything*—I'm a sounding board. Seriously."

The girls turn in relief, and their separate doors slam mere seconds after I've released them. I stand in the silent hall once more, the tips of my fingers tingling. I go over what they've just told me. Did Sienna just show her hand? Is she trying to push me away from searching the IP because it'll lead me to Raina? Does this explain why Raina seemed so upset by Greg's death? What could this say about the murderer?

I clomp downstairs and find my laptop on the kitchen table. It doesn't take me long to pull up the hack database and find Greg's e-mails to Lolita. I grab a pad of paper and write down the e-mail's IP, a garbled mess of numbers and dots. I tap the next e-mail. It has the same IP—which seems like a good sign. It probably means Lolita—Raina?—wrote to Greg from a home computer instead of a cell phone, which would make it harder to track a location.

I navigate to an IP lookup database, my heart hammering. If I remember correctly, Raina lives in the dorms—where a lot of other kids live, too, so even if I do get an IP, it won't be a direct lead to her. Still, it could prove Greg's mistress was a student.

The results appear. I hinge forward, squinting at the screen. In broad font are about ten lines of text, starting with the continental location of the IP and narrowing all the way down to its specific longitude and latitude. My gaze fixes on the line that reads *Zip Code*. I have to blink a few times before it sinks in. This isn't Aldrich University's zip code, though. It's Blue Hill's. *Ours.*

But that makes no sense. I get that Greg's e-mails would come from here, probably his own computer in his study—and when I check, the IP is a different blend of numbers, though it still comes up as being a computer in Blue Hill.

Except Lolita doesn't *seem* like someone who lives around here—
at least not an adult. Her writing is ebullient but hesitant, submissive
and almost filial. It's the writing of a young person who idolizes an
older man. Not in the words Lolita uses—her vocabulary can be
impressive, like how, in one of her last e-mails to Greg, she says, *The
only thing that keeps me going through my quotidian day are my thoughts of you.
I'm so, SO sorry. Please don't shut me out.* But she's needy. Self-conscious.
Ashamed. Whoever wrote this knows what she's doing is wrong.

Something catches in my mind. I click to the link Sienna sent me
on the day of Greg's funeral. It leads to a Wattpad page listing all the
stories Sienna has posted. Last night, I read the first one, a gloomy
tale about an aimless girl who works in a diner. I spot it right away—
that word again. *Quotidian.*

Is it a coincidence?

A crack opens in my brain. On a hunch, I click back to Wattpad
again. Sienna has also misspelled the word *lose* as *loose* . . . in the same
way Lolita has in an e-mail. Again, this could all be happenstance.
Except . . .

My heart stills. I think over everything the girls said upstairs. On
shaking legs, I rise back up and walk to the landing. "Girls?" I call
out. "Come down here!"

I hear the creaks above me. Their steps seem tentative, maybe
even afraid. And eventually, when Sienna calls out, "What's wrong?"
I hear the edge in her voice. She doesn't need to ask—she already
knows what I've figured out.

19

KIT

MONDAY, MAY 1, 2017

There are a few reporters hanging out on the circle, waiting for me to return to my father's house after work. I duck my head and run past all of them, slipping inside the door before they can snap a photo. It's quiet inside when I step into the foyer, but I can tell the place isn't empty. There's kinetic energy within the walls, a vibe that puts me on edge. I drop my keys on the table by the door and slip off my shoes. "Hello?" I call out. No answer. "Hello?" I call again.

The hair on the back of my neck prickles. A terrifying notion crosses my mind: The killer is back. Maybe he's lurking around a corner, ready to take me, too.

When I turn into the kitchen, I stop short, my heart leaping into my throat. Willa sits at the island, her head in her hands. My girls are at the table, staring at me numbly. Sienna's face is blotchy. Aurora's skin has gone sickly pale. My gaze swings from Willa to them again, and then it hits me. She talked to them. *Unbelievable.*

I drop my purse angrily on the floor. "I asked you for *one thing.* You can't even do that for me?"

Willa holds up her hands. "Wait. I'm sorry. I know you didn't want to. But . . ." She looks goadingly at Sienna and Aurora. "Tell her what you told me."

I glance at my daughters, but it's as though a curtain has been thrown over my eyes. I don't want to see them like this—sobbing, secretive, *guilty?* Maybe I'm not ready for whatever this is. Maybe it's far worse than petty complaints about me being a shitty mother lately.

I look angrily at Willa. "I told you not to question them. I *told you.*"

"Kit," Willa pleads. "Just listen. Sienna wrote the e-mails."

Time slows down. Sienna's head is down, so I can see the grease in her scalp. Aurora is chewing on her lips like a feral animal. "Huh?" I splutter.

"The e-mails to Greg. Sienna is Lolita."

It feels like they've whipped the big wooden lazy Susan that sits in the center of the table straight at my gut. "*You?* And . . . *Greg?*" Horrible images flood my mind.

"No!" Sienna looks horrified. "I . . ." She glances desperately at Willa, and Willa makes an encouraging gesture with her hands for her to continue. "I wrote both sides of the conversation," she mumbles. "Greg's . . . and mine. From different computers, so the IP addresses are different . . . but it's all me."

I sink onto a stool. Sienna's face contorts with shame. I want to go to her, but all I can think of are the words in those e-mails. Greg said such gross things to that woman. I'm supposed to believe *Sienna* wrote that?

"*Why?*" I whisper.

Sienna's breathing is choppy. "I-I wanted you to see what he turned into. It's why I put them in the deleted folder. A-And I was hoping that you'd open up his computer one day and find them in there and it would end things for good. It's not like I knew the hack was going to break. And even then, I didn't think someone was going to find the e-mails. But then . . . they did."

There's a sour taste in my mouth. So Sienna *had* wanted to talk about the e-mails with me before the benefit. Not to process her anger but to confess what she'd done. But I hadn't let her talk. I'd shut her out, I'd drawn my own, incorrect, conclusions. I condemned Greg, left him alone to be murdered in our kitchen. Did I bring this on myself?

Something vile occurs to me, and I rush toward her. "What do you mean, you wanted to show me what he'd turned into? Was he hurting you? Or Aurora?" I glance at my other daughter; she has curled into a ball in her chair. *Please don't let it be that.*

Sienna shakes her head. "No. *No.* I just . . . I knew he was having an affair with someone, and I wanted you to know, too. I broke into his e-mail and looked around for incriminating messages that would prove it to you, but I didn't find anything. And then I decided to make something up. It's not a lie, really. I just needed to plant the seed, because you deserve someone better."

"Jesus," I whisper. I'm in such shock I can't even swallow. "Sienna, *you*? Really?"

"I'm sorry!" Sienna covers her face with her hands. "I didn't know what else to do! I wanted the best for you!"

"But how do you even know he was having an affair? Do you have proof?"

"K-Kind of." She sniffs. "There was this one incident, last winter. After a snowstorm. Greg was at a late surgery. I was up, watching Netflix. Past midnight, I heard the key in the door. Something crashed. I was freaked out that we had a burglar, so I ran to the landing. I saw Greg stumbling around."

"Stumbling," I repeat.

"He could barely walk." She twists her mouth. "Definitely drunk."

I chew on the inside of my cheek. Greg went out after surgeries, sometimes. He needed to blow off steam. He sometimes went to business dinners, too—with the head of the hospital, or pharma reps, or sometimes even for media interviews.

"It's not a crime to be drunk," I say.

"I know, but . . ." Sienna sighs. "He didn't see me on the stairs. He was *really* out of it. He went to the kitchen. And that's when I noticed." She pauses. "He *smelled* weird."

"Like . . . alcohol?"

"No. Like . . . like perfume, but not something *you* wear. Anyway, it made me feel . . . icky. And mad for you, Mom. I wanted to know who he'd been with. So I hid until he went to bed, and then I ran downstairs. Looked at his phone. But I couldn't figure out his password. I was about to go to bed, but then I saw something on his jacket. There was this really long hair." She pantomimes peeling it off fabric, holding it by the tip.

This all seems so unfounded. "The hair could have been from a waitress who'd brushed up against him while delivering his drinks. It could be from a patient. You don't know." Sienna shrugs, considering this, but doesn't look convinced. "Did you ever notice something like that again?" I ask.

"Just that one time."

I glance at Aurora, who hasn't moved. "Did you know about this?"

Aurora looks haunted. "About what?"

"Any of it!"

Aurora licks her lips. *Oh God,* I think. *She did.*

I slap my arms to my sides. "Were you girls in on it *together*?"

"No," Sienna insists. "Leave Aurora out of it. I told her the day of the funeral. I was dying inside. I had to tell someone. Those e-mails came out in that hack . . . and then Greg was killed. Because of *me*?"

I run my tongue over my teeth. My head is aching. My thoughts have ground to a halt.

Willa looks at Sienna. "This . . . drunken stumbling you heard. When was it?"

Sienna thinks for a moment. "Last winter. I don't remember the exact date."

I can feel Willa turn to me. She wants to ask me something, but I hold up a hand. I feel too exhausted to mine this any further. I hate her for exposing my daughter's duplicity. I also hate that these are things that have gone over my head. I'm supposed to know my girls better than anyone else.

"The night of the benefit," I say to Sienna, my voice croaking with fear. "I need to know. You really weren't here? You really didn't see Greg? You really didn't . . . ?" I'm not able to complete the sentence. It's like tossing a bomb into a field and then running away before the blast.

Sienna's eyes are wide, dark pools. Her lips part. "No way."

"Okay," I say, nodding and nodding. "Okay."

I tilt my face toward the ceiling, staring at the pendant lights over my family's old island, glowing like the sun. I have so many questions. How Sienna crafted the e-mails and hacked into his e-mail. Why she didn't just *come* to me with her suspicions. Did she think I wouldn't believe her?

Again, my fault. All my fault.

I think about the wording of those e-mails. Greg's aggression. Lolita's retreat. She begged him to take her back in the end. Could it really be *fiction*? How does this tie into who killed Greg? *Does* it even? Or maybe Sienna's right, and Greg *was* having an affair with someone—but not Lolita. And it's *this* person who felt cheated on.

Gravity presses down on me. This is too much to take in. I can't focus on my husband's killer. I still haven't wrapped my head around the fact that my husband's gone. And underneath that layer is how angry I am with him. And underneath *that* layer is the frustration that Martin had a bad heart and that now I've lost *two* people I loved, and how it doesn't seem like the universe has dealt me a particularly fair hand.

"I need a second," I say, rushing out of the room. But as I'm at the door, I hear a sharp, metallic buzz. My eyes dart to Sienna's phone, which lies faceup on the table. A name flashes on the caller ID: *Raina*.

Aurora frowns. Sienna grabs her phone and turns it over. The thing keeps buzzing, sending shock waves through the wood, the air, my teeth. *Buzz,* stop, *buzz,* stop. Finally, Sienna holds down the button on the side and turns it off.

I feel Willa watching me again, and finally, I meet her gaze. It's clear she saw the name on the screen, too, and she's making the same connections I am. *Raina.* The night Greg was murdered, I remember Sienna's voice on the phone, her quick assurance that she wasn't drunk. I remember how she worded the next part, too: *I just need to find Raina, and then we're leaving.*

Maybe Raina had tried to impress upon me that she and Sienna had been together when Sienna heard the news—together the whole night, essentially—because she needed to cover her ass, create an alibi. Aldrich is a half mile from my home on Hazel Lane. Someone could easily travel from campus to there and back again in the span of an hour or so.

I walk out of the kitchen, through the back door, and to the middle of the yard. My feet sink in the wet earth. Wind whips around me, stinging my skin. But I can barely feel it. I'm too caught up with the picture taking shape before me. The truth about Greg's mistress has been in front of me this whole time. Maybe the truth about his murderer has been, too.

20

LAURA

MONDAY, MAY 1, 2017

At 6:00 P.M., Ollie opens the refrigerator and proclaims we have nothing for dinner. "I can cobble something together," I tell him. "There's some chicken breasts in the freezer."

"Nah, that's okay. We need other things, too. I'll go out. You look tired."

I certainly can't argue that. Before he leaves, Ollie pulls me into a half hug and kisses the top of my head. I try to relish the affection, but all I feel is numb panic. Then I watch him shrug on his coat and head out the front door. After his car is gone, I collapse against the doorframe as though all my bones have broken. Ollie worked from home today, and because I've had the day off, too, we've been under one another's noses in this little house for hours. With him gone, it feels like I can finally breathe again. Finally *think*.

Except ten minutes later, I hear the keys in the lock again. The front door squeaks open.

"That was quick!" I chirp as I clomp down the stairs. "Did you just get takeout?"

But Ollie has no shopping bags in his hands. He's even left the front door open, a cold wind blowing in stray bits of leaves. When he sees me, he just stares. Except there is something empty about his gaze. It seems like he's looking through me.

Horror carves through me. "I-Is everything okay?"

"Give me the baby," Ollie says in a low voice.

I start. Then I press Freddie to my chest, my hand against his back. "W-What? Why?"

"*Give me the baby.*" He holds out his arms.

Something in his voice makes my stomach drop. I hand over the baby, staring down at my trembling hands. Ollie stands over me, his nostrils silently flaring. My heart hammers.

"I just got a group e-mail from Reardon about the Greg Strasser murder case—I guess they're looking for any tips they can get," Ollie says in a low voice. "Some images from a neighbor's security camera show the cars in the cul-de-sac the evening he was killed."

He sets his mouth in a wobbly line. My brain goes dark.

"Why, Laura?" Ollie's gaze is pointed toward the front wall. His hands look huge against our child's tiny body. "Why is it *our license plate* in one of the images?"

I open my mouth, but no sound comes out. My body feels hot with shame and terror. I don't want this to be the way I break the news. I wanted to do it on *my* terms, not with it forced upon me. But here it is, and here we are, and I have to.

"Because I was there," I admit.

Ollie's brown eyes blink rapidly, as if I've spit in his face. "You?"

"It's not what you think!" I cry.

"Then what *was* it?"

Years from now, I will see this moment as a great divide separating our relationship from what it once was to the muckish mess it becomes. Years from now, I'll also wonder why I didn't just say I was suffering from postpartum depression, or that I'd been seized with a bout of mania, or, hell, that I had a split personality and it was the *other* Laura who did what she did that night. But the truth was also polluting me, stabbing at me, scooping me hollow.

"J-Just a second," I say. And then I turn up the stairs. Ollie lurches toward me as though afraid I'm going to use this as an opportunity to escape. Is this how he sees me now? As a criminal? "I'm going into the office," I protest. "I just need to get something."

The office desk drawer groans as I pull it open. Through tear-streaked vision, I fumble to the very back and find the scrunched-up piece of paper I've hidden there. I'd hoped to never read this again.

The afternoon before the Aldrich benefit, I'd received three directives from Greg in my work locker. The first was about the pitfalls of co-sleeping. The second the benefits of a stay-at-home parent. And the third was an unsigned, typewritten missive that read, *I want to have more of a role.*

Like a goddamn ransom note. It felt like a death sentence.

I'd stood there, paralytic. If I denied Greg contact with Freddie, he would tell Ollie. He would demand a paternity test. When the test came back positive, he would go to the court and ask for fifty-fifty custody. Hell, maybe he could make a case for getting *full* custody. I didn't know how family court worked. Maybe judges favored the wealthier parent. Maybe judges favored the parent who didn't lie. I needed to talk some sense into Greg. We couldn't keep communicating through these messages; I needed to confront him and make him *stop this.*

And so I'd written him that text the morning of the benefit about talking face-to-face. I'd explain to him that he was scaring the shit out of me. He'd understand he was being irrational.

I remember walking into the benefit alone. It might have been the party of the year, but I was too anxious to notice. I barely took my gaze off the door, wanting to know the exact moment Greg entered so that I could immediately corner him. After about thirty minutes of anticipation, my stomach in knots, there was a flurry of activity at the entrance. Kit Manning-Strasser entered wearing a gray dress and perfect makeup. People surrounded her as though she was a celebrity, and Kit smiled and trilled and chirped, but her eyes seemed distracted. I thought of Greg's e-mails, that thing with Lolita. *Little do you know,* I'd thought with disdain. *That's only the tip of the iceberg of the secrets he's been keeping.*

Kit made a zigzag across the floor, dazzling donors, speaking privately to an older man in a tux, gulping down a martini. I kept my gaze pinned to the front doors, but Greg never appeared. And then it hit me: *He stayed home.* I was so stupid. Greg wouldn't want to come to this after the Lolita bullshit. He wouldn't want to face the whispers.

I felt like I was drowning in guilt and doom. And so I decided: If Greg wouldn't come to me, then I would go to him. I knew where he lived. I would leave the benefit and go.

I felt sudden, revived courage. Yes. *Yes.* It was good to have a plan.

I gave the valet my ticket and was inside my car. My head felt fuzzy, but there was no way I was going to wait an hour or two to sober up. Luckily, the drive wasn't long: Hazel Lane, the street where Greg lived, was just five minutes from the museum. I rolled slowly around the cul-de-sac, my heart like a gong in my chest. The moon glowed directly over the top point of Greg's roof. A light shone into an empty front room. Greg's car was parked in the driveway. A dim light shone in a top window.

Come on, a voice in me goaded. *Just do it. Just go and ring the doorbell.*

My dress felt heavy around my body. My shoes were suddenly too tight. I thought, too, about the ultimatum I would give Greg . . . and how he might not accept it. *Then* what? What if, after all this effort, Ollie still found out I'd been here?

I rolled away from the curb, the sobs rocking my chest. I drove blindly, talking to myself, feeling like I was going mad. I found myself taking the ramp for the Liberty Bridge to the suburbs. Traffic was sparse, and with the fog in the air, the bridge took on a ghostly feel. At the traffic light before the tunnel, I suddenly felt a rush of despair so forceful I let out a muffled scream into my fist. This night, this hell, it was never going to end. I couldn't bear it any longer.

The turn signal indicator made a ticking sound through the cabin. When the light turned green, I veered to the left and pulled onto the shoulder across from the bridge. In the glove compartment, I found the small notebook I always kept there, and a ballpoint pen. What did I write on that scrap of paper? I remembered writing Ollie's name at the top. The words *I'm sorry.* The confession spilled from me, but I didn't bother checking my punctuation or spelling or even if the letter made sense. Yet when I was finished, I felt even worse than I had before. The tears dripped onto my nose and into my mouth. My chest hurt from crying.

I thought long and hard, but I couldn't think of a way out. Every possibility led to disaster. Every choice was heartbreaking. And I wasn't sure I was strong enough to weather any of it.

I crossed the street to the bridge's edge. My thin dress did little to protect me from the whipping wind off the water. At the edge of the bridge, I stared down, down, down. It was so dark, I couldn't really tell where the water was. Jumping would be so easy. A mess left behind, but a mess everyone would get over.

I raised my chin to the sky then. Felt the wind on my face. It was cold. Slap-like. Cruel. Maybe the water would be warm. Forgiving.

A horn blared over my shoulder. "Excuse me?"

I turned, startled. A battered Volkswagen was on the side of the road, its headlights shimmering through the mist. A guy no older than twenty stuck his head out the window and gawked at me. I stared down at myself. There was no barrier between my body and the Allegheny River.

"Don't do this," the kid said in a trembling voice. "Please."

His car was so old that the muffler grumbled cantankerously. A faint jazz riff tinkled from the radio. The kid got out of the car and left the door hanging open. "Come on," he said. "It's going to be okay. Please get off the ledge."

He was a boy—with blue eyes, blond hair, sharp cheekbones, and wearing an Aldrich University sweatshirt. A student. He had the same coloring as Freddie; my son might even look like this kid when he got older.

Freddie. My child surged back to me. Good Lord, what was I thinking? Shakily, I climbed back over the guardrail, though I misjudged its height, and the metal slashed my calf. "Shit," I whispered, the pain bright and true.

The boy was now by my side, steadying me. He smelled like clove cigarettes and sour laundry, but his arms were strong. He held me up.

"Are you okay?" he asked. "Can I drive you somewhere?"

My eyes felt fat with tears. Normally, I would have felt embarrassed to cry in front of a stranger, but this person had already seen me in such a terrible moment, it didn't matter. "I'm okay," I said. And I *did* feel okay. Doomed, broken, but I didn't want to die.

The guy's hand was firm on my biceps. With the streetlamp glowing against his forehead, he looked like an angel.

"What's your name?" I asked him.

"Griffin," he said. "Griffin McCabe."

"I'm Laura," I said, feeling stupid.

He nodded. "How about I give you a ride home?"

"No, no, you've already done enough. Thank you. Really. *Thank* you."

The kid protested. He seemed uncertain and regretful as he walked back to his own car, like he was sure he was going to turn on the news tomorrow and see the story of a woman's suicide on the screen. I kept waving. All the way home, I repeated his name out loud. Griffin McCabe. Griffin McCabe. When all of this was over, when the dust had settled and my life was whatever it turned out to be, if I ever gained some semblance of peace again, I'd track the kid down at the university and send him a gift card or a case of beer as thanks. Griffin's been on my mind a lot, actually. When I spoke to Reardon, I offered up his name, saying Reardon should contact him to corroborate my alibi. But Reardon said that wasn't necessary. He believed me.

I come back downstairs, where Ollie is waiting. "I drove by Greg's house after the benefit, but I didn't go in. I would have never done something like that. I swear. Instead, I . . ." I shut my eyes, feeling a fresh onslaught of tears. Then I thrust the letter at him. "Read this. It explains everything. I should have told you a long time ago, but . . ."

I trail off, waving the letter in the air. Ollie doesn't reach for it. Slowly, his eyes rise to meet mine, and I get a jolt. All traces of confusion and concern are gone. Something sharp and inscrutable has taken their place, and it stops me cold.

"This is about the baby being Greg's, isn't it?" Ollie says in a low, defeated voice, glancing at the folded piece of paper in my hand.

My mouth drops open. My soul feels sucked away. "H-How did you . . . ?"

"You really think I had no idea?" Ollie lets out a laugh. "You really think I'm *that stupid*?"

"Ollie!" His name bursts out of me, a sharp, bright plea. "I-It was a mistake. The letter explains everything. And Greg was *threatening* me, after the fact!"

"So that makes you innocent in all this?" His voice cracks.

"Of course not! I'm not innocent, I know. But Freddie's *not* Greg's. I mean, he might be—but you're his father, where it counts."

"Is that what you tell yourself to make yourself feel better?" He edges closer. I can smell his minty breath. "I knew the truth from the moment he was born. And all this time, I've been trying to hold it together, just focusing on not splintering our family apart, not ruining Freddie's life, trying to pretend it isn't real, but it *is real,* Laura. This is really fucking real, and I can't *believe* you."

Tears stream down my face. This can't be happening. He can't have known. "I'm so, *so* sorry."

Ollie takes a breath. "And now our car's on camera in Strasser's circle the night he was killed. Right now, the cops on the case are running the plate report and talking about you. *Us.* Did you tell Reardon *why* you almost jumped from that bridge? Does *he* know you fucked Strasser?"

"No!" The words Ollie has chosen feel like knives against my skin. "I just said I was overwhelmed! I didn't tell him anything! I wouldn't do that to you!"

Ollie stares at me with heartbreak. In his arms, Freddie's brow furrows like he senses trouble. I stretch my arms out for him, so desperately needing him close. All at once, I'm acutely aware that Ollie's sadness could tip to rage. There's a gathering storm inside him. Unbidden, I think of him in the ring at his boxing gym, breaking people's arms. *But that's different,* I tell myself. *He'd never do that to me.*

"Put Freddie down," I say slowly. "Please."

Ollie thinks this over, then sets Freddie down on his play mat just out of my reach. Then he takes two thundering steps toward me, letting out a bullish snort. I hear the slap on my cheek before I feel the sting. The force of it knocks me to my knees, hard. I press my palms against my throbbing skin.

"Ollie!" I cry, my mouth instantly swelling. Hot tears spring to my eyes. Even though I deserve his anger, this is not the man I married—my heart drains.

Ollie stands over me. His fists are still clenched. He could hit me again, I realize. The way Ollie is quivering, so tightly wound with dangerous power, I'm certain that things might quickly twist and go even darker.

But then he takes a step back. Turns his back, hunches his

shoulders. "I have a right to be angry. Hell, I have a right to never see you again." He draws in a shaky breath. "You know, I wish you'd gone and done it that day on the bridge. I wish you were dead now, like that asshole Strasser. You would've both gotten what you deserved. And I'd have the kid all to myself."

And then, just like that, he strides forward and walks out of the house.

21

LYNN

MONDAY, MAY 1, 2017

*T*he mussels for monsieur." A waiter in a tuxedo places a steaming plate of slick black shells in front of Patrick. "And the oysters for madame. *Bon appétit*."

I shoot the man a tight, anemic smile, and then inspect my plate. Eight oysters sit on a bed of crushed ice. Little silver bowls of dipping sauce, smelling pungently of garlic and chilis and oil, are nestled on the side. The oysters look perfect, and they smell fresh. I shoot my husband a saucy look. "Want one? You know what they say about oysters . . ."

Patrick cracks a mussel. Steam rises into his face, bringing with it the scent of garlic and white wine. "Thanks, babe, but I'm good."

"More for me, then," I say playfully, and then, because I can't help it, add, "though I doubt they'll be as good as the ones at Lou's."

Patrick lowers his head guiltily, and I feel a stab of satisfaction. I'd been the one who'd had to make the reservation at Pistore's, a lush, excessive restaurant that's a favorite of the town's sports stars, politicians, and actors who come through during on-location shoots. I figured Patrick would have handled arrangements for Lou's, our usual anniversary spot, but when I asked him about it yesterday, he said it totally slipped his mind. When I called Lou's and begged for a table, the bitch on the phone told me they were all booked.

After we chat for a while about the kids—Connor has taken to video games, and I'm concerned that could be a slippery slope, and a girl in Amelia's class just got her period, which is terrifying—we fall into silence. Patrick uses a slice of bread to sop up some of the sauce. I try an oyster—not bad. Actually, better than Lou's, not that I'd admit it.

"So." I place the empty shell on the plate. "Did I tell you that two of the donors I met at the benefit transferred their endowments to-day? George is thrilled."

He chews his bread, not looking at me. "That's great."

"I know." I smile smugly. "I'm the only one in the office who seems to be making any headway. This hack is holding so many people hostage." I reach for my wine and take a long sip. Patrick's jaw is chewing furiously, steadily, like he's trying to murder the bread with his teeth. "We got numbers back from the benefit—they were dismal. The only donors we hung on to were the ones I dealt with."

"Is that so?" Patrick eats another mussel.

"You weren't there. You didn't see how disastrous it was."

Finally, he looks up at me. "What do you mean, disastrous?"

To our left, a maître d' seats an older, silver-haired couple. The woman wears a gray column of a dress and simple makeup, and her pearl necklace looks expensive. The man gazes at her adoringly, the corners of his eyes wrinkled with a smile. Hopefully, that will be Patrick and me, thirty years from now. Except I'll have better skin.

The discovery of Patrick's gift in the trunk the other day was a wake-up call. Now that I'm confident Patrick's love for me hasn't wavered, I feel I should get something off my chest. I could probably go for the rest of my life keeping what I've done a secret, but some-how, seeing that extravagant bracelet in that velvet box, I feel that I need to give Patrick something more than just an object. I need to give him a gift of vulnerability. I need to show him that I'm not always as perfect as I seem. It's got to be hard living with someone who handles everything with such ease, as I do. I read a few articles on the situation yesterday: how men with perfect, beautiful wives begin to question their place within the marriage—if they'll ever measure up, if they're even needed.

I want to make sure Patrick knows he's needed. I want to assure him that I'm human and make mistakes. And I also want to clear my conscience. I have to tell *someone.*

I clear my throat. "So many people were drunk that night. It was because of everything that was exposed in that hack. And my team had to scramble around to make sure the donors were shielded from most of it. Except there was this one person on our team . . . well, she was supposed to be pulling her weight, too, but instead . . . well, instead, she was a mess."

When I peek at Patrick, I see he's listening intently, his head tilted to one side.

"I could see it in her eyes the moment she stepped into the room," I go on. "She was hysterical. I eavesdropped on some of her first conversations with donors—it was all over the place, and certainly not good for Aldrich." I shake my head in dismay. "She shouldn't have come."

Patrick frowns. "Who was this?"

"Oh, no one you'd know." I slide another oyster into my mouth. "Just a colleague."

I can't give him any specifics. I've never vented about working with Kit, but he'll recognize her name because of Greg's murder. And I'm certainly not going to get into the reason the story about Greg broke wide open. When the hack started, I looked up Kit. Problem was, there was nothing *interesting* about Kit, so I got the bright idea to look up her husband. And there—well. Obviously, there was a treasure trove. I might have forwarded some of the e-mails to a few very gossipy people I know. And they might have forwarded them on. And on and on, until they got to Kit.

"Anyway, it's probably better you left," I go on, dabbing my mouth with my napkin. "How's your stomach been, by the way?"

"Fine," Patrick says cautiously. "So what happened with this woman?"

"Oh. Well, she was causing such a spectacle, but George was tied up with his other clients, so I felt that I needed to babysit her. And so . . . well, I'm not proud of this, but I made a decision. I did it for the good of the department. It was the right choice. I'm sure of it."

Patrick sits upright. "What did you do?"

I wave my hand. "I put Ambien in her drink. I had one in my purse, and I thought she needed to chill, and so . . ." I shrug. My heart thumps. Is this coming out okay? Do I sound blameless?

Patrick gapes at me. "Did she *know* you put a sleeping pill in her drink?"

"Of course." I can feel my lips twitching, a tell Patrick recognizes. "I mean, I *think* I told her it was in her drink. There was a lot going on." I push my lips out in a pout. "What would *you* do if you had a colleague that was being completely inappropriate at a public function?"

"Not give her drugs." Patrick crosses his arms. "You shouldn't mix sleeping pills with alcohol. The woman could have died."

The scent of seared steak wafts into my nostrils. The word *died* slices through me like a blade. "She's fine," I say quietly. "And it's not like I'm going to make a regular habit of it."

Patrick scoffs. "I hope not."

We fall into silence—but not the good, comfortable kind. I open my mouth, wanting to protest the way everything has just played out. *I'm* the good guy here. *I* saved the department. I want Patrick to tell me that Ambiening someone isn't a crime—and that there's no *possible way* that someone under the influence of Ambien and alcohol would go home and murder their spouse. I want Patrick on my side, but instead he seems . . . unnerved. Like he's sitting at the table with a monster.

"I thought you of all people would understand," I say. "I made a few mistakes."

Patrick looks at me carefully, and then something in his face softens. "I guess you're right. There are moments when your decision seems like the right one, even if it isn't totally ethical." He says this in a small voice, almost to himself.

"Exactly," I say. And here's the rush of gratitude I've been waiting for. The true, clean whoosh of absolution. "Nothing would get accomplished if people didn't take risks now and then."

There's a faraway look in Patrick's eyes. "I guess that's true."

"I bet I'm going to get a promotion. I mean, Patrick, I brought in *millions* last week."

Patrick's eyes crinkle, just like the old husband a few tables away. "I'm really happy for you, babe. You're so good at your job. You're so good at *everything*."

Thank you, I think, and once again, I'm on top of the world. "Anyway," I say, reaching into my bag and pulling out a small leather box. "Happy anniversary, baby."

Patrick eyes the box with surprise. When he opens it and sees the gold, antique Patek Philippe watch I've chosen for him, he sits back. "Lynn," he says sternly. "This is too much."

"Oh, stop." I wave my hand. "You deserve it."

Patrick bites his lip, looking like he wants to say something but then changing his mind. "Well, thank you." He slides the watch onto his wrist, then turns it this way and that.

Throat bobbing, he reaches into his jacket pocket. "Here. Happy twelve years."

The box glints in the light, the logo of the jewelry store winking at me. I smile at him innocently, pretending I have no idea what's inside. I wait in case Patrick wants to say something else—usually, when he gives me such a grand gift, he has a whole spiel about the process he went through to choose it. But he's just looking at me with a bland, faraway smile on his face.

I open the lid and let out a preemptive gasp I've been holding in since the soccer game. Yet when I look down, I see a thin gold pendant against the velvet backdrop. I blink hard. Where are the diamonds? Where is the platinum? My joy is quickly replaced with confusion.

"Do you like it?" Patrick asks. "It's three loops for you and the kids."

I touch the delicate gold loops hanging from the chain. Does Patrick not remember that he got me an almost identical necklace for Mother's Day? I picture that beautiful tennis bracelet I came upon in his trunk. I hadn't hallucinated it, had I? Did Patrick return it because he thought it was too expensive? Did he think I'd find it too ostentatious?

But that's ridiculous. I *love* ostentatious. I would have worn the shit out of that bracelet—to dinners, to galas, to school pickups, to fucking spin class.

"It's beautiful," I say. Because I'm too stunned to scream.

But a hot flame wells in my stomach as I remove the chain from the box and place it around my neck. I'm going to call the jewelry store tomorrow to check if Patrick returned the diamond bracelet, but I think I already know the answer. That bracelet didn't go back.

He just didn't buy it for me.

22

WILLA

TUESDAY, MAY 2, 2017

After a seven-mile run on the noisy Marriott treadmill, I drive to the house and set up shop at the kitchen table with my phone and laptop. My phone beeps with a few updates from work about the university hacks—a colleague from "The Source" has run with the story, and she seems compelled to keep me informed about some off-the-record stuff, perhaps because of my connections to one of the schools that was targeted. I read her report about how the hack has revealed that the Brown admissions staff inflated the SAT scores of its student body. I read something about how Princeton parents are pulling their kids out for the rest of the year. I almost, *almost* ping her and ask if she's dug up anything about Chi Omega at Aldrich—or any of the schools. I think of the rumors my boss intimated the other day. But I decide against it.

A *New York Times* story has also come out that the socialist group that authorities *thought* might have hacked the universities was a false lead. Apparently, hackers commonly used proxy machines and fake IP addresses and planted false clues in their malware to throw investigators off their trail. "The truth is, we might not be able to attribute this hack to anyone," an FBI agent named William Cornish told *Meet the Press.* "Hackers are clever. They know how to hide. What we need to do now is damage control and make sure this never happens again."

Heels *clack* on the wood floor. Kit has on a pencil skirt and blouse, about to go off to work. She looks toward the ceiling, then at me. "Can you check on the girls in a bit?" she asks, thumbing toward the ceiling. "With*out* grilling them?"

"I didn't grill them," I protest.

Kit rolls her eyes. "Of course you did. I shouldn't even be speaking to you."

"Kit, I'm *sorry*," I say, feeling frustrated. I thought we'd gotten past this. Kit and I had talked late into the evening last night, strategizing about how we wouldn't go to the police with this new information until absolutely necessary. We both felt conflicted—it didn't seem right to hide evidence—but I wanted to do some more digging before we pulled the trigger. "But look at it this way: Now we know. It was obviously tormenting Sienna to keep that secret to herself. And Aurora, too."

Kit shrugs. "I guess we know what they were arguing about the day of the funeral, anyway. And why they've been acting so weird."

"True."

Kit squeezes her eyes shut. "I don't know what to do now."

"What about Raina?" I ask quietly.

Kit grabs her handbag from the chair, her expression clouding. "She says she was at a party with Sienna when it happened."

"Are we sure? Was she there the *whole night?*"

Kit looks conflicted, like she's about to say something. Then she shakes her head. "If Raina stabbed him, I'm not sure I want to know."

I cross my arms. "So you'd rather everyone think *you* did it?"

Kit peers out the window, touching the stained-glass ornaments our mother hung there years ago. I wonder, briefly, if her fingerprints are still on them. Or has too much time passed? "Look, if you want to investigate, I can't stop you. But I also can't help. I can't handle something like this."

There is a cacophony of barks out the window, the kind of ruckus kicked up when a new dog comes onto common territory and interrupts the balance. I wonder if that's what Kit thinks I'm doing—interrupting the balance. Checking in the closet for ghosts. "Just be careful," she says finally.

"You, too," I tell her. After all, there's still a killer on the loose.

The easiest thing to do would be to interrogate Sienna more about Raina's relationship with Greg, but every time I knock on her door, she doesn't answer. Maybe in a day or two she'll settle down and forgive me for exposing her.

Instead, I spend the afternoon reading through Raina's e-mails on the Aldrich hack server. She has a tidy inbox with only about fifty messages, no specialized folders, and very few e-mails in the trash. She must be diligent about cleaning out her files, whereas I have tens of thousands of unread messages I'm never going to get around to reading. I parse through essays she's written for school, rants to friends, and a few messages from people asking for access to my father. In each of those, Raina politely replies that she no longer works for him, and she refers them to his new assistant, a girl named Angie.

Is it strange that Raina worked for my father for such a brief time? Back in the day, my dad kept his assistants on for a whole year, if not more—especially if they were pretty. So why was Raina cut loose so soon? Was it her doing, or my father's?

I pick up my phone to call Dad, but when I'm taken off hold, Marilyn O'Leary, his second-in-command, comes on instead. "Oh, hi," I say, caught off guard. I don't know Marilyn well—she's one of those polished, hyper, always-on cheerleader women who overuse catchphrases like "circling the wagons" and "think outside the box."

Today she seems a little guarded, too, but that's probably because of all the hack bullshit. "Alfred's in an important meeting," Marilyn chirps. "Can I help you with anything?"

"Do you remember Raina Hammond, Alfred's old assistant?" I ask her.

Marilyn pauses for what seems like a beat too long. "Of course," she says crisply. "Why?"

"Do you know why she stopped working for him?"

"You'll have to take that up with your father. But my understanding is that she wanted to focus on her academics. Can you hang on for a sec, Willa?" Before I can answer, she places me on hold again.

I can tell she's overwhelmed, so I hang up. *Focus on her academics?* Huh.

Still, there's nothing incriminating about Raina in her e-mails. She doesn't even seem to have a boyfriend, which puzzles me—she's too hot to be single.

Fifteen minutes later, and I still can't find anything. Whom can I turn to for answers? I comb through her e-mails for messages to her parents or siblings, even a cousin, but I don't find a single Hammond in her contacts list.

The bursar's files have been hacked, too, so I click on their files next, hoping this will give me some personal information. Raina's information pops up, and after parsing through her files, I discover a few disconcerting details: First off, she started at Aldrich only this semester, not last year. That's a red flag. As a rule, my father only hires students as his assistants, and I can't imagine him changing his policy even for Raina. And wait—how could she leave to focus on her academics if she wasn't even a student yet? Maybe *that's* why my dad let her go—he found out she'd tricked him? Only, *why* did Raina trick him in the first place? I don't understand why anyone would want to work for my father so badly as to lie.

Starting in January, Raina became a student for real. In her enrollment paperwork, she didn't list contact information for either of her parents. However, she did provide the necessary birth certificate and immunization records, and they say she was born in Cobalt, Pennsylvania, a coal town about an hour and a half from Pittsburgh. I squint at the words until they blur. From what I remember, Cobalt is quite poor. Is Raina on scholarship, then? I click through her records but see no awards. I do see, though, that she's paid her tuition on time. The last record the bursar has of her is from the beginning of the semester, in January. She paid $9,500.

I dig into Cobalt next. There are only three Hammonds in the Cobalt online directory. Only one couple about the age of people who have a nineteen-year-old daughter. Bingo.

I find the old Volkswagen Jetta, which Kit and I used to drive in high school, under a tarp in the garage. There is still a Jetta key on a pineapple-shaped ring by the back door, and I grab it, praying the car's battery isn't dead. It isn't, but a mile out of my neighborhood, I notice the gas light blinking. I pull into a station and hunch by the gas pump. Rain is blowing sideways, and fog is so thick that the minimart, only a few yards from where I'm standing, is eerily invisible.

"Hopefully, you're going somewhere worth it in this weather."

I jump and turn. A shadow of a man stands on the other side of the gas pump, hat pulled low and the top of his coat resting just below his nose. All I see are his dark eyes. I glance over my shoulder at the spookily empty parking lot. There's barely a car on the highway.

I grab the gas pump and wrench it from my tank, figuring I'm full enough to at least speed away. But then the figure steps closer. "Willa. It's Paul."

He takes off the hat, and I see the mop of brown hair, those haunting eyes. I breathe out shakily. "Oh. S-Sorry." My heart is still pounding.

"Where are you driving in this?" He gestures to the fog. "It's not exactly LA weather."

"I'll be fine." My fingers shake as I screw on the gas cap.

"Going anywhere good?"

An eighteen-wheeler barrels past, sending a splash of water dangerously close to our bodies. With his hat off, Paul looks vulnerable and almost small, but I'm still uneasy. Did he just randomly find me here, or has he been following me?

But that's crazy. Paul's an old acquaintance. Years ago, I would have died for a chance to hang out with him. I clear my throat. "I've decided to stay on for a while until Kit gets back on her feet. But to keep myself from going stir-crazy, I'm doing some sleuthing."

He grins. "So you're taking my advice, then."

"I guess so."

Paul glances at the highway again. "I don't know where you're off to, but you really should have someone driving who knows how to drive in this kind of rain."

I place my hands on my hips. "Dude, I grew up here. I've probably hydroplaned more times than you have."

"Okay, and there's also the fact that there's a killer on the loose, and no one should be alone."

"I can handle myself," I tell him.

Paul sticks out his lip in a pout. "I'm trying to come up with excuses for you to invite me along, but it's not going so well."

The wind shifts, and all I smell is gasoline, a scent I've never liked. Why is Paul so eager to hang out with me? "Do you want to protect me . . . or do you want to help poke around my sister's husband's murder case?"

"All of the above." Paul shrugs. "Look, I just got a big check for some freelance work, so I have a few days off. And I've always wanted to investigate a murder. And, well, I'd love for you and me to catch up."

His eyes meet mine, and I feel a flutter. But then I look away. It takes me a while to answer. I kind of want to make him sweat. "Fine," I say, "as long as you know it might not be very interesting."

"I know."

"And the cops might actually be really pissed at me, if they find out."

"I'm fully prepared for angry cops."

"Okay . . ." I glance at what I presume is his car, a blue Chevy, at one of the other pumps. "You want to ride with me, or do you want to follow?"

No surprise: Paul says he'll ride with me. He moves his car into a regular parking space, then climbs into my passenger seat—there's no way I'm playing damsel in distress and letting him drive. We pull out of the lot, the windshield wipers groaning to deflect the driving rain, the fog so thick we can only see the taillights of cars once we've almost crashed into them. Still, I white-knuckle it through the tunnel, and once we're in the city, the fog isn't quite as bad.

"So where are we off to?" Paul asks.

"Cobalt—up north. I think the woman Greg was sleeping with has family there, and I want to ask them some questions."

His eyebrows shoot up. "You mean e-mail girl? Lolita?"

"Sort of." I'm not sure I trust him enough to go into Sienna's role in the e-mails, so I say, "Kit's daughter is certain he was having an affair, and I have a strange feeling it might be one of her friends. Her name's Raina Hammond." I search his face, seeing if Raina's name rings a bell. He's Greg's ghostwriter, after all. But Paul just blinks. "Thanks to the hack, I was able to look into her. There are a lot of things about her that don't add up. So that's why I'm going to check out her family."

As we cross another bridge and get on the highway that runs parallel to the city and leads us to the northbound roads toward Cobalt, we discuss Raina: her good looks, her lies about being a student at Aldrich, and her strange behavior, including the naked, unapologetic grief when she came over the morning after Greg was found murdered. "It just seemed *odd*," I murmur. "She's his step-daughter's friend. It wasn't appropriate emotion."

"Yeah, but if she killed him, would she have carried on like that?" Paul asks.

The heat is blowing into my face, so I lower it a bit. "Unless she thought acting distraught was a good cover."

"Yeah, but you really think a nineteen-year-old girl is capable of murder?"

A fresh bout of rain pounds us, and I hit the stalk for the windshield wipers. "I don't know. But I feel like she's involved somehow. Sienna was so adamant to keep her out of the conversation. Maybe she was protecting her."

"Have you looked up Sienna's e-mails in the hack? Maybe she and Raina talk about it there."

I nod, careful not to say anything about how Sienna was Lolita. "There's nothing about Raina. No secrets whatsoever, actually."

Paul runs his hand over his hair. "I'm glad *I* wasn't hacked. I'm beyond careless with my e-mail. It really puts things in perspective."

"You?" I glance at him. "Got anything juicy about local rock bands you cover?"

"Nah." Paul shrugs noncommittally. "Just angry divorce stuff, mostly."

His face clouds over. I want to ask him about his divorce, but it's a level of intimacy I'm not ready for. In fact, even *this*—letting a near stranger into my car for a long drive up north—is usually too intimate for me. LA Willa would never have done such a thing. The past shapes much of why that is, but it's also that I've been such a loner for so long, I'm more comfortable doing things by myself. When I'm alone, I don't need to be anyone I'm not. I don't need to search for things to say. I don't need to have to anticipate reactions—or, in the worst-case scenario, be caught off guard by total changes in character.

"I can't believe you remember that dinner at the Indian place," Paul suddenly says.

I turn to him. "You can't believe *I* remember it?"

He smiles. "It was so long ago. And I never heard from you afterward, so I figured it didn't mean much to you."

I'm so surprised that I burst out laughing. "I think you have some of the details wrong."

He cocks his head. "How so?"

I let my gaze rest on a Massachusetts license plate ahead of us. The dinner Paul is talking about was an end-of-the-year lit mag celebration at Tandoori, an Indian restaurant in Blue Hill. Paul and I happened to get there at the same time, and we walked in together. As though sensing my greatest longings, he chose a seat next to me at the table, and we spent the evening talking. It was a funny, dazzling, seventy-two minutes of bullshitting about music and writing and his upcoming sojourn to Princeton, and how uncool most people were, and how there really weren't very many people worth talking to. It was one of those times when I was completely aware of the magic I was experiencing as I was experiencing it; I descended further and further into nostalgia as each course arrived, knowing that once everything was eaten, we would be one step closer to the meal's end. When our advisor, Mr. Hand, finally paid the check, I prayed that Paul would ask me to take a walk so we could continue talking. But then his mom showed up, and he ducked into the car with a crinkly smile, saying he'd see me around this summer.

I daydreamed about that dinner afterward. I picked apart everything Paul said to me. I tried to figure out everything I could about him—where he lived, what he was up to that summer—but because the Internet didn't exist yet, it wasn't easy. I prayed Paul would get my phone number from someone and call me, but it didn't happen. At the end of that summer, he went to Princeton. That fall, a drunk driver killed my mom. I started going to the punk clubs Paul used to frequent—basically, I *became* the cool, spidery girls he used to date. Not that he was there to see it. Though by then I stopped caring what he thought. What *anyone* thought.

Not long after that, the thing happened that ruined me for good.

In some ways, if I look back on it, that dinner with Paul was the last good day I had in this town. The last ray of sunshine.

"You didn't call *me*," I say now. I try to temper my emotions, keeping my gaze steady on the road. "Not the other way around." *And I waited,* I wanted to add. *God, how I waited.*

Paul frowns. "Why was I supposed to call you? You could have picked up the phone, too."

"But you were . . ."—I scramble for a word that doesn't sound too adolescent—"you were the head of the magazine. You were older. You were going to Princeton. I figured you were busy."

He crosses his arms over his chest. "I thought you were a feminist, Willa Manning." And then he looks at me with hesitation, almost like he wants to say something more but he's not sure. Whatever it is, he decides against it, shrugging and shutting his mouth and turning back toward the window again.

I study the way his hair curls over his left ear. Why *hadn't* I just called him? My mind reels for bigger reasons, too. I think about what Paul just said. *I thought you were a feminist.* Which means he thought of me, *period.* I feel a bittersweet smile creep across my lips. I wish I'd known back then how I could have just called him. I wish I'd known he would have answered.

———

Cobalt hunches like a feral animal alongside the Allegheny River. The town's main attraction seems to be a Dollar General, which stands next to a bunch of scrubby trees leading down to the river. Across the street is a hardware store that looks like it's been open for a hundred years in a building that seems on the verge of collapse. The rest of the buildings in the row seem like set pieces on a studio back lot—their facades are convincing from afar, but up close they're way too flimsy to be structurally sound. A very old sign marking boat rentals sags in the grass; a piece of paper pointing to a beer distributor is affixed to a stop sign with duct tape.

I pull onto a residential street. The houses are worn but occupied; a pink one a few doors down has cheerful Easter decorations peppered through the yard. "I wouldn't have thought Raina would have come from here," I murmur.

Paul nods, glancing at Raina's Instagram page, which he managed to find after some digging. The page is private, so he can see only a tiny thumbnail of her profile picture, a close-up of Raina's pretty face, red hair, and red lips. There's something glam about the profile picture, something expensive. This is the kind of girl who's told no one at snobby, class-obsessed Aldrich about her roots.

We step toward the house that's listed in the name of Judy and Bill Hammond. When I ring the bell, a dog inside barks. I shift from foot to foot, shaking out my hands. I'm always nervous before doing an interview. I'm always afraid someone's going to slam a door in my face.

The wooden door hefts open with a squeak. A redheaded woman with perky breasts and a thin gray T-shirt peers at us from behind a ripped screen. She has Raina's oval face and bright eyes, though her skin is traversed with fine lines. With a little pampering, though, she'd probably be mistaken for Raina's sister. "Help you?" She has the raspy voice of a smoker.

"Hi." I step forward. "I apologize for bothering you, but you're Mrs. Hammond, right? And you have a daughter, Raina?" The woman nods, looking nervous at the sound of Raina's name. "We're your daughter's advisors at Aldrich University. We have some concerns about her, and we thought we'd come to see you in person to talk them over."

"Wait." Mrs. Hammond looks startled. "My daughter's *where*?"

"Aldrich University." Paul smiles. "In the city."

Mrs. Hammond's eyes wander between the two of us. She lets out a bark of a laugh. "Raina's not at a university! That's bullshit!"

I glance at Paul. "Yes, actually, she is," Paul says.

"Do you mind if we come in?" I ask.

Mrs. Hammond stares at us hard but finally opens the door. Inside, the house smells like something meaty has just been microwaved. A small, fluffy dog barks from behind a baby gate in the kitchen. A man with thinning brown bedhead, wearing a shrunken Steelers jersey, ambles forward to scoop the animal up. His eyes narrow when he notices us standing on the patchy carpet. "Who're you?" he growls.

"Guess where Raina is, Bill?" Judy puts her hands on her broad hips. "A *university*!" She says it like a punch line.

Mr. Hammond's face sours. He gives a dismissive I-don't-give-a-fuck gesture and stomps down the hall.

Judy Hammond turns back to us and shrugs. "He's still sensitive about what happened."

I feel a prickle of excitement. "What do you mean, *what happened*?"

"You want to sit down?" Judy walks over to a small, upholstered couch and clears off some magazines and laundry to make room. "Can I get you anything to drink? We got pop. And water. Coffee?"

"I'm fine, thanks." I settle onto the couch. Paul sits next to me, declining a beverage, too. "So wait, you didn't even know your daughter was in college?" I ask carefully.

"Nope." Mrs. Hammond plops on a vinyl-upholstered recliner by the window. There's something fragile about her, like she's been broken and glued back together too many times. "She ran away in September. Just up and took off. We were worried sick. Bill, too, though he doesn't like to admit it." She clucks her tongue. "But *college*? Well, it's much better than sticking around this place. Though how's she paying for it?" Mrs. Hammond sweeps her arm around the shabby room. "*We* don't got the money."

Bingo. I glance at Paul, trying not to get too excited. I had a hunch Raina's parents weren't paying for college. "Maybe you could tell me a little more about the person she was when she lived here? And why she would have run away?"

Mrs. Hammond's gaze lands on me, suddenly distrustful. "Who did you say you were again?"

"We help out with students who are adjusting to Aldrich life. Sort of like therapists."

Mrs. Hammond turtles her chin. "*Therapists*," she repeats disdainfully.

"Listen, if you have anything to tell us about her, we'd be grateful," Paul urges. "Raina's doing great in school. Really on track. You want her to do well, right? Come home an Aldrich grad?"

Mrs. Hammond stares at her fingernails. Her hands are chapped and raw, her nails nibbled to the quick. "Raina was always smart. Way too smart to stay in this place. All the industry left this town decades ago. Now all you can get here are dead-end jobs. A lot end up hooked on opiates, meth. Get caught doing random shit. Hauled into jail for DUIs. That's who Raina was drawn to, but I could always tell she was smarter. She loved to read. And *write*. She was always writing stories." She sighed wistfully, but then her expression turned bitter. "Good at telling stories, too. That's what got her in trouble."

"What do you mean?" I venture.

"I guess she wouldn't have told you." Mrs. Hammond won't meet my gaze. "I doubt big-city smart people would find what she did particularly admirable."

Paul rolls his ankle, and a joint cracks. "Is there something we should know about? We want to set her up for success at Aldrich. She has a lot of promise."

A smile forms on Mrs. Hammond's lips. "She does have promise, doesn't she? But . . ."—she takes a breath—"her last few years of high school, Raina got into some . . . trouble. With this doctor fella. He's one of the only prominent people in these parts, not that he's from here—he just practices medicine at the hospital out here because *someone* has to do it." She sweeps her arm to the left. "He owned a huge lodge a few miles away. It sits on about six hundred acres of hunting land."

"And?" I ask.

"All of a sudden, Raina was coming home with a pretty new handbag, a new leather coat. I asked her where she got the money. She said she had some new job a few towns away, but I could tell she was lying."

I'm trying hard not to look at Paul. It's not hard to put the pieces together. "You think this man was giving her the money? This . . . doctor? Was Raina his . . ." I trail off, not knowing the appropriate word. Girlfriend? Sugar baby?

Judy Hammond sighs. "They were only together once. But as you probably already know, a grown man caught with a girl of sixteen is a criminal offense."

"Raina was sixteen when this happened?" Paul bleats.

Mrs. Hammond nods soberly. "She knew that law like the back of her hand. Made that doctor pay her in exchange for her not going to the police. And he did."

I run my fingernails against the rough threads on the couch. That's pretty slick for a high schooler.

"The only way we found out is because one day Bill caught him paying her in this little playground behind the grocery store. Bill was furious. He shook it out of Raina. Wanted to arrest that doctor, too, but that would mean getting Raina in trouble. In the end, we let both things go. But people found out all the same. Word gets around. The doctor switched hospitals. Sold that big property. And Raina?" She stares up at the ceiling, as though apologizing to God. "Well, she was the talk of the town. She had the grades to be valedictorian, but the principal revoked the honor because of the scandal." She clucked her tongue.

"She was dead to her father after that." Mrs. Hammond juts a thumb down the hall, where her husband disappeared. "He screamed at her for days. Screamed at me, too, because I insisted we pay back that doctor every cent Raina took from him."

"You didn't have to," Paul says. "He committed a crime, too."

Mrs. Hammond tilts her head skeptically. "This is terrible of me to say as her mother, but I think Raina was the instigator. She lied about her age all the time. Always said she was older, and from somewhere else. We went on a vacation to Niagara Falls once and found out that she was going around the hotel pool, talking to men, calling herself Madison." A sad smirk appears across her lips. "We sold her bags and fancy clothes, but it still wasn't enough to pay the doctor back."

"And how did Raina deal, after all of it was over?" I ask.

Mrs. Hammond shrugs. "You mean did she seem to understand that what she'd done was wrong? I don't know. She seemed angry, mostly. Probably that she got found out. I'm not sure she really learned her lesson, though."

Paul leans forward. "What makes you say that?"

Mrs. Hammond twists the hem of her T-shirt. "This January, not long after Christmas, we got some gifts from her. No return address, but fancy things. *Too* fancy, actually." She glances plaintively at us. "That's why you're here, isn't it? Because you know something? Because she's doing it again?"

I look at Paul, feeling uneasy. "We don't know. Not for sure."

"Do you know her address? Where we can find her?"

I lick my lips. Do we have the right to tell? But then I realize that I could give a hint without actually spelling it out: "The school's e-mail system has been hacked. Have you heard?" Mrs. Hammond shakes her head. "I can give you the website where all the e-mails were dumped. You can search Raina's name on there. Some of her e-mails list her new address."

Paul stands. "You've been really helpful. We appreciate your candor."

Judy Hammond gets to her feet, too. Her eyes are red-rimmed, and she touches my hand before I leave. The skin on her palms is cold, papery. "When I found out she'd run away, I thought she'd go somewhere far, like Florida. But only forty miles into the city? That almost makes it worse."

"People don't have to run away far to escape their problems," I say, a lump in my throat. "It's more about changing who you are. More about inventing a new life."

When we step outside, the air smells like exhaust fumes. Back in the car, we stare at each other for a long beat before exhaling. My mind is whipping fast. "Could she have been doing this with Greg?" Paul asks. "Doing things with him sexually, then flipping the script? Saying she'd tell on him, ruin his reputation? Making him *pay* her?"

I drum on the steering wheel. "And what if, the night of the benefit, he decided he didn't want to pay her anymore? He already knew his marriage to my sister was over because of the Lolita e-mails. Raina had nothing to hold over his head anymore. So he tells her the game is over, and Raina gets mad. That cash is affording her a brand-new life at Aldrich. It's not like she wants to go home to *this*." I point to the tired street.

"It could make sense," Paul says.

"Except it's all speculation right now. It's not like we have anything concrete to prove she was running a scam."

I get a thought and pull out my phone. I tap the app for the hack database, recalling that I've seen a few bank notifications in Greg's inbox. I click on the first few. His bank alerted him whenever he'd made purchases of five hundred dollars or more—there are receipts for fancy dinners, a Nordstrom shopping trip, car maintenance. I don't see anything suspicious. Certainly nothing to Raina.

Paul leans over to look, too. He's so close, his chin is almost touching my shoulder. I can feel his minty breath on my skin. It makes me go a little still. "These bank alerts don't say if Greg wrote any big checks. Or if he took out withdrawals in cash."

"There'd be no way for us to trace that unless we subpoenaed Greg's bank accounts." I chew on my lip. "Except . . . would he write her a big check? Kit told me that she and Greg share a bank account. She would notice something like that. She'd see a big chunk of cash missing, too."

"Did Greg have a secret account?"

"Not that the cops have found." I shift my weight. "Is there another way to siphon off nine grand—or more—in such a way that Kit didn't detect it?"

"Could Raina have set up a shell company?" Paul's tone is joking. "Maybe she's posing as Nordstrom-dot-com?"

"Or maybe he just gave her a few twenties or hundreds at a time?" I speculate. "Except I doubt they'd want to be seen together too often . . ."

Paul wrinkles his nose and stares out the windshield for a while. Then he turns back to me. "Did I mention that my ex-wife was thirteen years younger than we are?"

I stare at him, shocked. "She was twenty-four?" I can't hide my revulsion. "That's a *child*!"

"*Anyway*." Paul tugs on his collar. "One of the reasons we broke up was because we seemed on two different planets when it came to a lot of things. She didn't even have a checking account. Barely knew what to do if someone wrote her a check. She was always saying that no one her age had a checkbook—they all paid their bills online. She never carried cash. Never even had a credit card, half the time."

"Isn't that sweet," I say acidly. The last thing I want right now is to hear about Paul's prepubescent wife. "And that has to do with this . . . why?"

"Well, one of the financial things my wife *did* know about—which I didn't—was paying people through an app."

I frown. "What, like Paypal?"

"Yes. One of those."

I click back to Greg's e-mail in the hack. "I've heard of the apps, but I've never used them. I'm super old-fashioned when it comes to money—I still enter charges in a check register."

"Me, too!" Paul says, sounding almost overjoyed. Which makes me a little less angry about him being a cradle robber.

"So there's, what? Paypal? Venmo?" I start scrolling through Greg's e-mails, but I don't see anything. Nothing in his deleted messages, either. Then again, if Greg *was* paying Raina, he wouldn't have kept those messages around. They'd probably been doubly deleted ages ago.

I log into my own Venmo account, which I'd set up but never used. But it's not like I'm going to find a public note proclaiming that Greg Strasser paid Raina Hammond for *sex acts* or *hush money*. What would those emojis even be? But then, halfway down the screen, I notice a familiar photo of a man standing on a beach in Barbados. It's the very same picture shown at Greg's funeral a few days ago. He looks tanned, handsome, almost young. It's strange that the digital version of Greg has outlasted the man.

His screen name is *GStrass92*; Venmo has announced that Greg Strasser paid Kit Manning an undisclosed amount on April 25. That's the day before the benefit. So he does use his account, then.

But if I want to see more—and dollar amounts—I need more access. "Maybe I can sign into his account," I murmur.

Paul nods, watching me carefully. But before I do, I send a quick text to Sienna. *What was Greg's e-mail password?* I ask, remembering that she'd said she'd hacked into his e-mails to see if he was cheating. About half a minute later, Sienna responds: *StBarts081215*. The place and date of Kit and Greg's wedding.

"Let's hope he's the type who uses the same password for everything," I murmur, going to the login screen. Luck is on my side, because after a few variations of the password, I'm in.

"Whoa," Paul says, sounding dazzled.

I don't know my way around Venmo, but I decide to click on "Friends." I scroll through a list of people, my heart thudding hard. "There!" Paul cries, pointing at a name toward the bottom of the list. *RayRay09,* reads the screen name, and there's a tiny image of the same pretty, red-lipped girl that's on Raina's Instagram page.

I let out a whoop. "Holy *shit*." And then I click on her name. A list of payments appears. No explanations, no emojis, but still.

"This is it," I tell Paul, grabbing his hand before I realize that, well, we're holding hands. But I'm so excited, I don't care. "Paul, this is freaking *it*."

"What?" Paul cries, his eyes dancing.

"Greg was paying Raina through this app. In total, we have him on the books for giving her almost fifteen thousand dollars."

23

RAINA

TUESDAY, MAY 2, 2017

*T*his city is a strange place. One minute, you're driving through a neighborhood full of small, crooked houses smashed together like teeth in a mouth. But then, suddenly, you turn a corner, and *bam*. The houses look like castles, set on large, rambling lawns. Some of them go on forever, windows upon windows, garage doors for miles, circular driveways fit for a five-star hotel. That's how I feel when we get to Alexis's parents' place. Like I've landed on a very fancy planet. Like my ship has come in.

"This is nice," I say breezily, as if I'm surrounded by this sort of opulence all the time.

The Uber stops, and Alexis climbs out. I follow, gazing up at the towering brick-and-stone building. What must it have been like to grow up in such splendor? I want to hate Alexis for having such a plush life, but I don't. Maybe because she's looking at me like she really wants me to have a good time. Or maybe because, soon enough, I'll be profiting from all of this.

I gaze around the property. No lights are on, and there are no cars in the driveway. "Seems kinda empty," I say.

"Oh, my grandma's party isn't here." Alexis walks up the front lawn. "It's at a restaurant nearby." But then she frowns. "I'm surprised my parents aren't home, though." She pulls out her phone and studies the screen. "Shit. I missed a text from them. Their flight from France was delayed—they won't be here for another hour." She glances at me, her expression contrite. "Are you okay waiting outside until they're back? They're always changing their locks—they're security freaks—and I don't have the updated house key."

I shift in my high heels. They're already beginning to pinch my feet. "Couldn't we just go to the party without them?"

"Uch, no." Alexis makes a face. "I don't want to see Trip yet. Besides, it doesn't start until eight. Let's just party here."

In my world, being locked out of one's house would mean sitting on a cold porch, suffering stares and possible harassing remarks from the neighbors, and possibly inhaling meth fumes from the basement lab next door. In Alexis's world, it means sitting on a sprawling stone patio under a heat lamp, enjoying a good bottle of wine procured from a beverage fridge nestled into a rock in the outdoor kitchen. I sink into a canvas couch and gaze at the forest in the distance. Next to us is a burbling hot tub that Alexis says we can go in later if we want. Alexis starts a crackling, spitting fire in the pit in the center of the patio. She even turns on sexy music on her phone, which links to invisible speakers built into the walls. A soft blanket of sound surrounds us.

"Cheers." Alexis holds up her glass. "Thanks for coming. For *saving* me."

I sip. The wine is smooth, decadent, and surely expensive. It goes down easy, but I have to pace myself. I can't get drunk tonight. I need to stay on point.

The fire snaps and pops. I can feel Alexis staring at me. "So," she says.

"So," I say back, grinning.

Our eyes meet, and Alexis giggles. I do, too. The tension is gooey, thick, luxurious. We've talked a lot since the party. Things between us have started to shift from mere flirtation to something deeper and more confessional. Alexis has confessed about her eating disorder in high school. How she feels subpar next to her high-achieving older siblings. She's said how, most days, she hates her artwork, and she wonders if people take her seriously.

We also texted about Aldrich stuff—hack gossip but also our upcoming schedules for winter semester. *Let's rush a sorority next semester. Let's do it together.* Hell, I'd have the money to afford the dues soon. It's funny, earlier this year, when I was working for Manning, Sienna and I had considered rushing . . . but it wasn't something I was keen on doing with her, even if I had been able to afford it. Maybe it's because rushing requires a certain amount of vulnerability, and that was a part of myself I didn't want to share with her. Of course, that could be tangled up in the fact that I was scamming her family. With Alexis, things feel less complicated.

I've never actually had a friend like this. Sure, there were kids I hung out with in high school, though usually I used them because of what they had to offer: a sumptuous liquor cabinet, a forest full of four-wheelers, a Toyota Corolla that I could borrow. But I was never a girl who lay on the carpet of someone's bedroom and swapped secrets. I was always . . . well, scheming. So it feels kind of nice sending off a text and getting one back so immediately. It feels nice to have inside jokes with someone, upcoming plans. I feel rooted to Alexis in a way I've never been before. It makes me feel bad for everything I'm keeping from her. *Sort of* bad . . . but not completely.

We bob our heads to the music. With the wine and the setting sun and the roaring fire, it's hard for this setting not to feel romantic.

"Come a little closer," I murmur, patting the cushion. Alexis smiles and moves over, the warmth of her body dripping into mine. My other hand curls around my phone. *Go time.* I need to turn on the video recording function soon, so that it captures what's bound to happen. But I also have to be aware if her parents suddenly pull up. I can't have them catching us and ruining everything.

But before I can touch my phone, Alexis says, "Tell me a secret, Raina."

"A secret?" I draw both hands into my lap, intrigued. "What, like truth or dare?"

Alexis nods, her eyes gleaming. She's got her hair swept off her face, which accentuates her sharp cheekbones and the slope of her jaw. Her skin is milky, edible-looking. The wine has left a reddish stain on her lips.

"I'm not telling you a secret unless you do, too," I say, deciding on the spot.

Alexis shifts so close that our thighs are touching. She finishes off her wine, then looks at me, her mouth twitching. "Okay. Don't be mad, but my grandma's party isn't tonight."

I frown. "Wait, what?"

"And my parents aren't due back in the country for another week." Alexis ducks her head. "I just wanted an excuse to get away from campus. With you. So no one would see us. Do you hate me?"

I sit back and cross my arms. At least now I don't have to worry about her parents interrupting us. "You didn't have to make up an elaborate birthday party to get me alone." I wave my arms around. "This is gorgeous. I'm thrilled to be here."

She breathes in as though she wants to say something, then stops herself. Finally, she blurts, "You're beautiful, Raina. Like, I can hardly stand it."

I fumble with my wineglass. People have told me this my whole life, but somehow, her bluntness about it catches me off guard. "You're beautiful, too," I stammer.

Alexis's face seems to flower. She hinges a little closer to me, and I can smell the wine on her breath. My heart is humming. Is it going to happen *now*? Our faces are mere inches from one another. I can see the hope in her eyes. My fingers feel for my phone, but it's just out of my reach. As I'm fumbling, suddenly Alexis's lips touch mine. What comes next is soft, and warm, and delicate. It sends unexpected tingles through me, and then it's over. Alexis pulls back, her eyes wide, her lips parted.

"Sorry," she says in a breathless voice. "I just . . . really wanted to do that."

"It's okay." My voice is laced with wonderment. My mouth feels stung. I want to do it again, I realize. Again and again and *again.*

"Your turn," Alexis says softly, holding my hands. "Now you have to tell me a secret. Something you've never told anyone."

My mouth opens, then shuts again. My brain feels like it's moving through sludge. I need to think of a good secret, something that will intrigue her but not show my seedier side. All I can think about is the kiss. I want to touch her again. I want to explore those tingles. *Stop it,* my brain wills. I can't get caught up in Alexis. I can't start *feeling* something for her. I need to kiss her one more time so I can record it. I need to dangle that carrot a little longer.

"I know." Alexis's finger traces a flower pattern on the inside of my wrist. "Tell me why you were crying the day I met you in the coffee shop."

My mind freezes. I hadn't expected her to ask *this.*

There's no way I can tell Alexis the truth. Except she's looking at me so eagerly, so excitedly, her eyes gleaming, her posture straight and expectant. She knows I'm hiding something. Maybe she's worried about me. Maybe she just wants to know. The secret feels like currency—if I tell her, then she'll feel even closer to me. Then she'll kiss me again. Then I'll record it.

It's not like I have to tell her everything. I just have to tell her enough.

My fingers grapple for my phone, which I finally locate between two cushions. I will say this, and then I will press RECORD.

"You're right," I admit softly. "I was upset about that doctor. Greg. He and I were . . . close."

Alexis's whole body seems to thrum. "Were you *Lolita*?"

I arch my neck, staring at the constellations, and then I'm

transported back to the Mannings' kitchen. Greg was watching me, considering me. Our bodies were just inches from one another. I thought what I saw in his eyes was desire. I thought we were going to crash together, all lips and arms and torsos, and that I'd have him where I wanted him.

But then he crossed his arms over his chest. "You're better than this, Raina."

It felt like he'd dumped a bucket of water over my head. I stepped back. "*What?*" I spluttered.

"I wasn't Lolita," I tell Alexis now. "Greg and I weren't even together. But . . . well, he was giving me money. He was paying my Aldrich tuition."

Alexis blinks. "He *was*? How'd *that* happen?"

Greg guessed about me that night. He somehow knew I'd tried to seduce Alfred and was planning to try the trick on him next. When Greg questioned my motives, I spilled it all so quickly, almost like I'd been waiting for the chance. To this day, I don't know why. Maybe because of the caring in his voice. Maybe because I needed someone to listen.

I told Greg I'd come to Aldrich only to milk Manning; I'd done my research, reading up on a bunch of high-powered men in high-powered places, and I thought a university president would be the perfect, trusting mark, the sort of man who didn't have much experience with women or blackmail or anything treacherous and seedy. It also helped that Aldrich was only a simple drive away, *and* I could rent a hideout cheaply while I played out the con—something I couldn't do in a more expensive city, like Philadelphia or New York. And most of all, I knew I was smart. I knew I could blend in at a college better than at my high school. I wanted a better life for myself, and this felt like a stepping-stone. Okay, a somewhat questionable stepping-stone, but I had to make do with what I had.

To infiltrate Manning's life, though, I had to pose as a student. It wasn't much of a stretch. I'd applied to Aldrich the prior year—and

I'd even gotten in. But I'd torn up the admission letter. Aldrich was a place full of rich kids, entitled kids—I wouldn't belong.

But as it turns out, I liked pretending to be a student. A *lot*. I wished I didn't just audit the Aldrich classes—I wished I could go for real. Greg had looked at me with sympathy. "You're smart," he'd said. "You should." And then a light had come on in his eyes. Resoluteness. "*I'll* fund you," he said. "I'll send you to Aldrich. But you have to promise me two things: One, you can't tell anyone. And two, you have to use it for school—nothing else."

But I can't say this to Alexis—I can't show my hand. Instead, I describe my poor upbringing instead. How my parents didn't care about saving for my education. How I wanted a better life for myself, but they just rolled their eyes. Then I paint a picture of Greg and me hanging out in the kitchen alone and all of this pouring out of me. It isn't far from the truth.

"I told Greg the only thing I wanted was to stay at Aldrich—I'd fallen in love with it by then. But I couldn't afford the tuition," I explain. "And Greg said he was trying to make some positive, charitable changes in his life, and that funding me to stay at Aldrich would be one of them." A wistful feeling swoops through me, remembering how joyful I'd felt that night. It was like I'd been given a reprieve from the gallows. "He made good on his promise. We met every month. He wanted to see how I was progressing in my classes. He was like my advisor, in a way. And he always gave me the money. Sometimes through an app, but sometimes cash.

"But then . . . he was killed." A lump grows in my throat. "I couldn't believe it. He was such a good guy. That Lolita bullshit people found out about him—I don't know what that was all about, but I never saw that side of him. And now I'm stuck. I don't know how I'm going to stay in school after this semester. I'm so . . . *lost*."

The patio is silent, save for the chirping crickets. I glance at Alexis, figuring she'll move in for a hug. Or maybe, just maybe, she'll tell me that *she'll* pay my tuition. How wonderful would that be? I wouldn't have to scam her. I could just . . . *be* with her, and she'd pay my way through school, and we'd be so happy.

"So wait," Alexis says slowly. "You have no more money coming in?"

I shake my head. "Greg gave me just enough to pay for tuition, room, and board for the next two semesters—so summer and next fall. After that, I'll have to figure something out. I can try for financial aid, but . . ." I'll have to face my parents again if I want aid, and that isn't something I like thinking about.

Then I look at Alexis again. She's frowning. Actually, she looks pissed. "Why does this matter?" I ask tentatively.

Alexis's arms drop to her lap. She breathes out a plume of air, sending her bangs fluttering. "You were supposed to be loaded. I can't fucking believe this."

I frown, certain I've heard her wrong. But she still looks so furious. And not, I sense, at the situation—at *me*. "I'm sorry?" I squeak.

Alexis holds up her phone. The video app is on the screen—the very same video app I use. It reflects my image back to me. I see the time ticker in the corner, still running. "I just recorded you confessing your deal with Strasser," Alexis says in a low voice. "I was *going* to use it to blackmail you into giving me his money. And now I find out you have *none*?"

The heat from the lamp bores into the top of my head. I feel like I'm trapped in a dream, all of the puzzle pieces shifting. I scuttle away from her. "Y-You wanted money from me?" I look around at the house, the fire pit, the sparkling pool. "But *why*?"

Alexis's teeth gleam orange. The flames lick against her face, making her look ghoulish. "This isn't my house," she spits. "I house-sit for these people. I grew up in the city. In a shitty house probably not that different from yours."

I blink hard. "You don't live here? There's no birthday party? No . . . Trip?" I'm not making sense, even to myself.

She snorts. "Of course there's no Trip." She turns, stiff-shouldered, her hands balled into fists. "I made up a boyfriend because you seem like someone who likes a challenge—like I'd only be interesting if you could steal me away."

My eyes dart back and forth. Alexis's mouth is moving, but she's making no sense.

She goes on. "I've been tailing you for weeks. I saw you paying your tuition in cash a few days ago. I've seen you and Sienna Manning together. I knew there was something up with you that wasn't totally kosher. I knew you were getting the money illegally, I just didn't know how. But I thought he gave you *tons*."

I'm standing by now, backed up so far from the couch that my spine is pressing up against the stone wall in the outdoor kitchen. My brain scrambles. Alexis can't be using *my* methods. Recording someone's confession—that's *my* role, not hers. I run my hands up and down my arms, trying to feel if I'm still awake, still *real*.

Alexis is . . . *me*? I've been duped by another version of myself?

My hip bumps into the brickwork around the gas grill. "I have to go."

"No, you don't." Alexis holds up her phone; the video recording is still running, the time ticking away at the top of the screen. "Did you forget I have this on you? What will people think if they hear you got the murdered guy to pay your tuition? Did you tell the police any of this?"

My breath catches in my throat. Of course I didn't tell the police, but it's not like I did anything. It's not like I *killed* him. "I'll tell them," I insist. "I'm not afraid of you."

"You should be." She crosses her arms. "You really think they'll accept you at Aldrich if they find out you're the skanky scammer from the wrong side of the tracks?" She throws back her head to laugh. "It's pretty clear you want to be *part* of Aldrich, Raina, but if people know who you really are, they'll never let you into the inner circle. It's happened before. Check the hack—admissions rejected people with better records than you. After I release this video, they'll look at your file and stamp it with a big red *No*."

My jaw drops. It chills me how good she is at this—better than I am, even.

"What do you want from me?" I repeat, my knees shaking.

Alexis waves her phone. She's stopped the video. On the screen is a freeze-frame of my profile; I look scared and drawn, almost skeletal. All at once, I notice that the fire has died out. The cool, close, fragrant air billows around us. I want to run. I want to scream. These were the same words I used with Dr. Rosen, the same bargaining chips. Do I deserve this? Is this karma? My penance?

Alexis tilts her chin, slips her phone back in her pocket. When she takes my hand, it's almost kind and loving . . . but I know better. "You and I are going to team up," she says smoothly. "We're going to scam someone else as a team. And this time, it's going to work."

24

KIT

WEDNESDAY, MAY 3, 2017

I squint in the dim, dingy light of the Saloon. It's a bar right next to the giving department's building; I can see the parking lot from my office window. But I've never actually been here until now. The high-top tables are chipped and worn, the leather banquettes have what looks like a layer of grease to their upholstery, and signs for local beers hang on the walls. People, mostly men, have gathered around the TVs over the bar.

I choose a booth at the back near the bathrooms. One of the twenty TVs isn't playing sports, and I notice the closed-captioning on the news: *Authorities may have tracked the Ivy Hacker to socialist "hack-tivists" in New York who want free higher education for all.*

My father pops onto the screen. *Aldrich University President Alfred Manning Not Connected to Any Hack Scandals Thus Far, but Noted for Erratic Behavior.* What does *that* mean? I've barely gotten to speak to my father about all the stress he's under aside from the trading of e-mails on certain press releases I need to communicate to the donors. Most evenings, he's at meetings, or dealing with detectives, or addressing the board, trying to put out fires. Normally, *I'd* be in on some of these meetings, as so much of Aldrich's activities are things the donors want to know about, but it seems George is doing the bulk of the work.

I lean forward, trying to hear what Marilyn O'Leary is saying to the reporter. "Alfred Manning is fine," she insists. Her lipstick is a weird shade of orange. "He's understandably stressed by the situation, personally and professionally."

And then, inevitably, the reporter reminds the viewers of Dad's ties to me: "President Manning is also dealing with the death of his daughter's husband, Greg Strasser." The picture of Greg and me in Barbados pops on the screen. I slide down in my chair, covering my face with my hair.

"What's the matter?" Willa slides into the bench across from me.

I glance toward the TV. "Oh, you know. I'm just on the news again."

Willa wrinkles her nose. "They're saying Dad seems exhausted," she says. "Do you think we should be worried?"

"Marilyn says he's fine."

Willa snorts. "Marilyn's probably the one who planted the story in the first place. Something about her rubs me wrong. I think she's after Dad's job."

I ponder this for a moment, trying to imagine Marilyn O'Leary, a blond, slightly haggard, with a take-no-shit, Kellyanne Conway–thing going, taking over as Aldrich president. It makes me a little ill. Marilyn tried to date my father about ten years ago, when the stuff with my mom was still fresh. She threw herself at him. Acted completely ridiculous. I was surprised when, after he rejected her, she gracefully backed down. She's always struck me as one of those rat-sniffing terriers, stopping at nothing to dig for what it wants.

Willa looks disdainfully at the plate of fries I've ordered. I figure I'm going to get a lecture about trans fats, but then she sighs, plucks one from my plate, and stuffs it into her mouth. "Thanks for meeting me on your lunch break."

"It's not like I was busy," I mutter. "What's going on?"

Willa's throat bobs as she swallows another fry. "I thought you might want to know about some of the questions I asked Raina Hammond."

I stare at her. I just can't believe Willa cornered the feisty, slippery girl and got answers out of her. "Did she *admit* to something?"

Willa pokes a stirrer through the ice cubes in her water glass. "Greg was giving her money." She looks at me uneasily, maybe thinking I'm going to have some kind of ballistic reaction. I just gape. "All in all, he gradually transferred about fifteen grand into a Venmo account in her name."

"Fifteen thousand . . . are you *kidding*?" I splutter. A few guys at the bar look over. I hunch down in the booth, my head whirling. I feel hot, then cold, then dizzy. "Are you sure?"

Willa nods. "Positive. Raina scammed a guy in her hometown—some doctor. They had sex, she admitted to him she was underage, and got him to pay her. I have a feeling she tried to seduce Dad in a similar way, though she swore to me that it backfired. She turned to Greg next." She crunches another fry. "Except he didn't bite, either."

"So why did he still give her money, then?"

Willa picks at her nails. "She said he took pity on her. He wanted to offer her a way out of a life as a scam artist. She said her true dream was to be a real student at Aldrich. She wasn't even a matriculated student when she was Dad's assistant, if you can believe it. She lied her way into that job so she could get close to him to milk him out of some cash."

I stare up at the dusty, faux-Tiffany pendant lamp above us. How could my husband feel so much sympathy for someone he barely knew? He wasn't a bleeding heart. Maybe I'm biased because of those sickening e-mails, but I feel there's more to the story.

"I don't buy he was doing it just to be nice," I say.

"Yeah, I didn't at first, either," Willa says, shrugging. "No offense. But she seemed genuine—and believe me, I've interviewed enough liars. She even let me look at her bank accounts—the girl has about twenty bucks to her name right now. Apparently, she paid the bursar right before Greg died. I called the bursar, too—Raina's last payment, which isn't registered on the hack, actually took place the day all the systems were down. She paid cash."

"Do you think Greg paid her in cash, or she just withdrew cash from her bank account?"

"I don't know, though I'm not sure it really matters. But if she's telling the truth—and I think she is—if Greg was helping her pay for college, Raina has no reason to kill him. It explains why she was so upset about his death, too. You wouldn't have wanted to see the town this girl was from, so I get why she'd do anything not to go back there. Aldrich is a ticket to something better." Willa bites into another fry, then gives me another sheepish glance. "She also showed me empirical evidence that Sienna wasn't anywhere near your house all night, too."

I hitch forward in my chair. "Really?"

"The girls follow each other on Find My Friend. It's a pretty common app—"

"I've heard of it," I interrupt. "In fact, I've *used* it, with the girls. But I've become lax with it, lately. They're good kids . . ."

Willa drums her fingers on the table. "Raina's app has a history of where Sienna was that whole night—it's a little square around campus, and that's it. Though she did say that if I made public what I'd figured out about her, she'll delete the evidence. I tried to bluff, saying Sienna's alibi doesn't matter, but Raina must know Sienna isn't innocent in all this. Maybe Sienna slipped that she wrote the Lolita e-mails. Raina knew it was a good bargaining chip."

"Shit," I whisper. Then again, proof that Sienna wasn't anywhere near the murder was good. Just in case the cops ever figure out she's Lolita. Then I lean forward. "Did she say anything about why she lied to me about when she found out about Greg's death?"

Willa frowns, confused, and I explain to her how Raina said she was right next to Sienna when she actually wasn't. "That's why I was suspicious of her in the first place. I thought she was trying to cover up for having snuck to my house and killed him."

Willa shrugs. "She showed me her own data for Find My Friend. She really was at that party. Same as Sienna. I guess they just were in different rooms or something."

"Is there a way to *fake* Find My Friend?" I ask.

"I mean, I *guess*." Willa takes another fry. "One of them could have planted their phone at the party, I suppose. But that requires quite a bit of forethought. Also, Raina's data shows the phone moving around, like someone naturally would at a party."

I settle back, trying to think this through. Maybe Raina was just confused, then. Or maybe she said she'd found out with Sienna because that's how she wanted it to go down, even though it hadn't. It was hard to know.

Willa twists her mouth. "How do you feel about all of this?"

"I don't know," I say, and it's the truth. Getting the news about Sienna being Lolita was brutal enough. I still can't wrap my mind around it, and I still don't know if not saying anything to the police is the right move. A few times, I've peered at the card Ollie Apatrea gave me at the funeral, wondering if I should call him. Maybe he'd be a good sounding board. Maybe we could talk off the record. But then, he's still a cop. It's probably still too dangerous.

But now finding out Greg was paying a random girl to go to Aldrich? Couldn't he have used that money for charity? For *us*?

I shut my eyes, grief pounding down on me again. I can't ask Greg why he did this. I'll never really know. His absence is surprisingly staggering. It also makes me want to smash things, because this is a person I was supposed to know well, but maybe I didn't know him at all.

I take a breath. "So now what?"

Willa stands and slings her purse over her shoulder. "I'll let you know soon, but I have to go. I'm late for something."

"You're leaving? *Why?*"

"Just . . . a meeting." Two red blotches form on Willa's cheeks, almost like she's embarrassed. "I'll see you later, okay?"

She's about to get up when her gaze lingers on something else on the TV screen. *Aldrich Students Hint at Assault Allegations Post-Hack.* The closed-captioning reads that a few e-mails have surfaced on the hack about things happening to girls at fraternity parties on Aldrich campus. Two girls have shared their stories on closed groups on Facebook, and the posts have quickly circulated.

"Oh dear," I say.

But my sister doesn't answer. She shakes her head with disdain. After a final glance in my direction, she zips up her jacket, and ducks her head. "I'll see you later," she says, and hurries out to the street.

I watch her rush across the avenue, my head propped in my hand, my feelings all over the map. In the past week, I've basically found out everyone in my world is a stranger. I love Willa for doing this for me.

But I hate what she's figuring out.

After I pay my bill, I walk around campus. The sky is a cloudless blue, but the temperature hovers somewhere around the fifties, which, after the beautiful weekend, has thrown everyone into an impatient funk. Students hunch around in big coats with frowns on their faces. Two girls in running shorts shiver outside Starbucks. Everyone seems to have taut, tense expressions. Are they *all* affected by the hack?

A stream of kids emerges from the science building, and I assess the faces, bracing myself for a run-in with Raina. But she isn't there.

I try to imagine Greg systematically Venmoing Raina cash for college tuition. If she's telling the truth, it's certainly a noble gesture on my husband's part, and we had enough money that I didn't even notice thousands of dollars going missing. But why hadn't Greg just *told* me about it? Was he that afraid that I'd jump to conclusions and get the wrong idea? But if he really *wasn't* having an affair with Raina, why would he hide it?

Unless, of course, he *was* having an affair with someone else. Maybe he didn't want to arouse my suspicions in any sort of way, and he figured it was better not to say anything about Raina, even if the whole transaction was innocent.

I feel a hand on my shoulder and tense. Someone pulls me into an alleyway between the buildings. I let out a muffled cry, preparing to fight.

But when the person spins me around, it's Patrick Godfrey holding my forearms.

"What the hell?" I wrench away from him. Light shines in from the street, but no one has seen him pull me into the alley. "W-Were you following me?"

"I need to talk to you," Patrick pleads. He's wearing a dark gray suit and shiny loafers but no coat. "It's important."

I step toward the sunlit sidewalk, stabbing a finger toward the building across from the bar. "Have you forgotten your wife works right up there?"

"Come for a drive around the block with me, okay? It'll take five minutes."

There's something in his posture that tells me he isn't going to take no for an answer. Unbidden, my thoughts flip back to our hot, hurried kisses in that elevator. I whisk the image away.

"Fine," I decide, hating myself a little for giving in. "Five minutes."

Patrick's car, a white Acura crossover, smells like basil and fresh leather. I climb in tentatively and buckle my seat belt. Patrick's hands tightly grip the wheel. He's wearing a wedding ring today. The sight of it sickens me, even though I know it shouldn't. At a stoplight, I consider jumping out. This is a bad idea. I need to keep out of trouble.

Patrick grabs my arm as if he senses my hesitation. His eyes are pleading. "There's this thing that I found out that's been weighing on my mind. I feel like you should know."

I cast my mind about for answers: He's going to say something about *us*. Maybe he's leaving his wife. Maybe he's never felt a connection like the one he felt with me.

The light changes, and he hits the gas hard, shooting us back in our seats. "You know that benefit last week?" he asks.

I almost laugh. "You mean the one I got home from and found my husband dead in my kitchen?"

He tugs awkwardly at his collar. "Yeah."

I study the print shop whizzing by, then a sandwich place.

"I was watching you," Patrick goes on. "You seemed . . . well, you seemed drunk." He holds up his hands in quick apology. "Not that I blame you. That night was a shitshow, and I'm sure my showing up there didn't help any. So I left, figuring my absence might help. But now I'm just wondering . . . how much did you drink that night?"

At first, I'm annoyed—what business is this of his? He doesn't have any right to judge my life. But the question makes me uneasy, because I realize how specific it is. I stare at the blinking LED lights on the dashboard. "I only had one martini that night—well, that I can remember. I guess it hit me strangely."

"Does that often happen?" Where is he going with this?

"No." I peek at him. Is he trying to gauge if I'd been drunk when we kissed in Philly?

"And did you get the drink yourself, or did someone get it for you?"

A muscle in his jaw twitches. His eyes are on the road, but I can tell he's steeling himself for my answer. "Your wife did, actually."

And then it's like a light goes on—for me, and for him, too. Patrick looks crushed. When he turns to me, I think I know what he's going to say before he says it.

"Lynn put an Ambien in that drink," Patrick says quietly. "I'm almost positive that's why you got so drunk."

For a few moments, the only sounds are the rumble of the engine and the swish of the road. I don't know what to say. I don't know what to feel, either—betrayal, obviously. Embarrassment. Finally, vindication. I knew Lynn was a bitch.

"Did Lynn *tell* you, or did you figure it out?" I finally ask.

"She told me she gave someone Ambien, but she wouldn't say who. I put two and two together." The car halts again at a light, and he turns to me with a look so sincere I feel a flip in my chest. "She's crazy, Kit. There's always been something about her that's off." His throat judders as he swallows. "She could have *killed* you."

"Wait a minute." My heart stops. "Do you think Lynn knows about . . . *us*?"

Patrick shakes his head. "I doubt it."

"But you're not sure. She *could* know. She could have known at the benefit, even. She could have been out to hurt more than just me that night."

His eyes widen at what I've just suggested. "Are you thinking maybe *she* stabbed your husband in revenge?" He runs his hands through his hair. "Jesus. I never thought of that."

We whizz through three green lights in a row. I almost *want* Lynn to be the murderer—then she would go to jail. Justice would be done. It would free up Patrick, too, though I feel dirty recognizing this silver lining.

Finally, Patrick stops in a parking lot and shifts into park. About five minutes have passed since we got into the car—he is making good on his promise of not keeping me long. I feel disappointed. Maybe I've misinterpreted his intentions. Maybe he really is just trying to warn me.

He reaches into the side pocket on the door of the car and pulls out a small, gray, handled bag from a jewelry shop whose name I recognize but have never visited. "This is for you. I saw it, and I realized you had to have it."

I back away as though it's made of poison. "What are you doing? Don't give me things."

He drops it in my lap. "Open it. Seriously. I'm not taking it back."

"You should be with your wife. Your family." As much as I hate Lynn right now, I can't take her husband away from her.

"You're going through a lot," Patrick says. "And I feel guilty about what Lynn did. And . . . well, I'm unhappy, Kit. Miserable, in fact. I can't stop thinking about you. *Us*."

"Patrick . . ."

He leans toward me just as he did that day at the bar—with interest, with need. Maybe I'm too exhausted not to pull away, but if I am honest, he entrances me—his sadness, his wanting, the way he seems so bedazzled by me. So I lean in, too. Our lips crash into one another, and it is everything I've yearned for. I push harder into him, moaning, spinning, my heart thundering. When Patrick pulls away, I can feel tears on my face that I can't explain. He looks at them worriedly, but I just wipe them away and laugh. I'm upset. I'm joyful. I'm ambiguous.

When our phones start pinging, we look at one another mournfully. "Back to work," I say quietly. I already feel the ache of his absence. By his expression, I can tell Patrick feels the same.

He nudges his chin toward the jewelry box still on my lap. "Go on. See what I got for you."

I let out one more note of protest, but it seems clear that Patrick isn't taking no for an answer. Slowly, I open the box. I gasp at all the diamonds twinkling at me and shut it tight, glaring at him. "Jesus," I whisper. "*Why?*"

He grins boyishly, grabbing the box from me and lifting the bracelet off the velvet. The chain is delicate, and the diamonds are plentiful and flawless. "It's a bracelet fit for a queen. Didn't you say you were part royalty?"

I try to speak, but I have no words. Is it possible our coming together *is* fate? Can I allow my brain to go there?

I reach for him, then pull away. Maybe I've been too burned.

Maybe I need to sort out my feelings about Greg, which are still largely unexplored.

Or maybe I should just take the leap. Maybe the third time is the charm.

And so I stretch out my hand once more, and Patrick takes it. And then I lean toward him, living out the fantasy I haven't been able to get out of my brain since the day we met.

25

RAINA

WEDNESDAY, MAY 3, 2017

That evening, I walk down a hallway of an old brick apartment building. The air smells like garbage. A light above me flickers, threatening to go out. A couple screams behind one of the doors; from another, I hear death metal.

I find apartment 22 and knock. On the other side, I hear the metallic clink of a latch being undone. The door opens, and here is Alexis. Not a resident of Hudson dorm, as she first told me. Not even a student at Aldrich University, period. The Facebook page she created, the one I fell for hook, line, and sinker? It's all a lie. Even her style has changed—today, instead of crisp Tory Burch and Burberry everything, she wears a ripped cotton T-shirt and threadbare skinny jeans. Her eyeliner is thicker, messier; her hair falls across her face. And yet I still find her hot. Even though she could ruin me.

Alexis steps aside for me to enter. The apartment is dim and sparsely furnished. Dishes are piled in the sink, and there's a rancid smell in the air. The blue couch is stained, the coffee table looks like it's on the verge of collapse, and my eye goes to a framed picture of Alexis and some dude on the mantel. I almost want to point out that this dude isn't Trip, until I catch myself.

"Drink?" Alexis asks from the kitchen, a dingy little galley that looks infested with bugs. She unscrews the cap of a large jug of vodka and glugs some into two glasses. As she passes me one, she rolls her eyes. "Don't look so miserable. So I caught you." She flops down in the chair opposite me. "*I* should be the miserable one. You were supposed to be my meal ticket."

"Sorry to disappoint," I say bitterly, knocking back the vodka. It tastes like rubbing alcohol.

I want to leave. Alexis is no longer the only person who knows what I did. I recall the fresh fear that went through me when Willa Manning cornered me on the street yesterday. Willa knew *everything* about me, down to the amount Greg had given me, down to where Dr. Rosen used to live. She'd even spoken to my mother. The fear shot straight to my bones. Everything I worked so hard for, everything I thought I could still achieve—was it about to be taken away? Willa held all the cards. It would be so easy for her to ruin me.

But Willa was questioning me because she thought I killed Greg. The thought astounded me, but seeing it from her perspective, it isn't so crazy. There was nothing I could do but tell her the arrangement Greg and I had. I didn't want to be on her suspect list—having the police question me would blow my secrets wide open. And I came up with a good bargain to ensure Willa would keep quiet, too—I hated using Sienna's whereabouts as bait, but after seeing my friend the day after Greg's death and at that party where she was guzzling wine into oblivion, I had a feeling she was keeping secrets. By the way Willa snapped to attention, I assume she thought so, too. But the idea of Willa telling Sienna the truth hurts. I value Sienna's friendship more than I realized.

But I have no advantage with Alexis. Nothing to ensure she keeps *her* mouth shut. I've racked my brain all morning, but besides the wine we stole from that mansion on Tuesday, I don't know anything about her.

Alexis places her hands on her knees. "We'll find a guy with money. We'll seduce him. He'll pay us off, and we'll both get what we want—you'll get to go to Aldrich, don't worry." She assesses me over her tumbler. "You're good at this. You got Strasser to pay your tuition. I found out about your little deal with that doctor up north, too."

I bite my lip. "I'm guessing this isn't your first rodeo, either?"

Alexis shrugs noncommittally, her gaze returning to the laptop.

"Are you going to tell me *anything* true about yourself?" I ask. "It's only fair."

"Fair how?" She watches me, her long, slender fingers hovering over her keys. And then she laughs. "What, you're trying to tell me you were your real self with me? Come on. You're full of shit, too."

I pretend to study an ugly landscape painting hanging on the far wall. The thing is, I *was* honest with Alexis—about some things, anyway. Like what I told her about Aldrich. What I told her about how she and I should do everything together. And that kiss was sure as hell honest, unfortunately.

The screen on Alexis's laptop lights up, and she types something into Google. After a moment, a website appears. I figure it's going to be the hack site—we could probably easily find out someone's net worth and sexual proclivities through their e-mails—but instead, it's a meet-up page. *Naughty Pittsburgh* reads a red, sexy font at the top. There's an image of three women shot from the neck down in bondage gear, and a description talks about how the page is for people interested in BDSM and other naughty behavior to connect.

"Okay . . ." I say, wrinkling my nose.

"Oh, don't be a prude." Alexis clicks through to a login site. After keying in her user name and password, she's into the group, and the page directs to a message board with post titles like *Dom looking for a Sub* and *Pet looking for a Master.* "This place is a gold mine to find people who are up to no good but don't want anyone to know about it—they all use stupid code names. And I think I've found the perfect mark." She clicks a message thread and scrolls down to a screen name: BigDaddy23. Some guy has written a post asking if there's anyone near Aldrich College looking for "unusual role-play."

"There's no way we can tell this guy has money just based on his post," I point out. "For all we know, he lives in this building."

Alexis doesn't seem amused. Then she looks back to the screen. "Lucky for you, I've already done some research. Last weekend, I went to a munch."

I inch away from her on the couch. "What is that, a disease?"

She rolls her eyes. "It's a casual get-together for people into this stuff. The organizer of the meet-up reserved a back room at Ali Baba's, and people dropped in to hang. It's for people who are curious. To make the whole thing less scary. I didn't talk to anyone, but I did a lot of watching. And I found someone. I looked him up, and he has a lot to lose—his reputation at his job, his wife, family . . ."

"Do you have a picture?"

She scoffs. "Uh, no, he wasn't really up for a photo at a secret sex role-play get-together. You'll just have to trust me on this one. He's the real deal. Plus, he's cute."

"So what are we going to do?" I ask warily.

She clicks back to the meet-up page. "I've already put a post saying that there are two hot girls up for anything, ready to meet. A lot of people have replied, but I'm waiting for *him* to bite. It's just a matter of when."

"So you and I are going to have to do something . . . together?" I say slowly.

Alexis gives me a sly look. Slowly, her hand encircles my wrist. "That kiss we shared the other day? I know you want to do it again."

Heat rushes through me. I want to push her away. But she's right. I push a lock of hair over my shoulder. "And you're sure he'll pay up?"

"Positive." Alexis leans back, but she's still watching me. "You can't chicken out."

I think of the papers I still need to write, the commitments I still have, even the intimidating questioning from Willa Manning this morning. I shouldn't be getting into more trouble. Yet at the same time, how else will I get to stay at Aldrich? Without Greg, there's no money coming in. My bank account is almost at zero.

And if I can't stay at Aldrich, that means . . . what? The answer is clear: If I don't do this, how else can I work toward what I promised Greg I'd become—a different person?

"Fine," I say, standing up, ready to go. "Just tell me when."

26

WILLA

THURSDAY, MAY 4, 2017

I squint in the early afternoon sunlight, shading my eyes to get a better view of the apple trees. A tractor pulling an empty trailer filled with hay rumbles over the pitted ground. It stops close to where Paul and I are standing. A man in muddy jeans, a plaid shirt, and a Pirates ball cap jumps out of the cab and undoes the back latch so we can climb aboard.

I turn back to Sienna and Aurora, who are poking around the huge bin of leafy broccoli at the farm stand. "Are you sure you don't want to come on the ride?" I ask them for the third time. I'd invited Paul to come along to discuss some things I'd found out about the case, but at the last minute, I'd invited Sienna and Aurora, too, figuring a trip to Round Acres Farm would at least get them out of the house.

"At least go into the butterfly tent." I gesture to a little structure behind the bin of pumpkins. Years ago, when my mother used to bring Kit and me here, we would spend hours in that little tent, letting all sorts of butterfly species land on our arms. It's why I wanted to come to the farm today: It's a good connection I have to my mother's memory, and thankfully, very little about the place has changed aside from the fact that they finally take credit cards and they now have a donkey in the petting zoo.

With that, Paul and I climb onto the trailer behind the tractor and sit on spiky hay bales. I wish Kit could be here, too, but she seemed determined to go to work. That's ballsy of her, considering that she found out a colleague, Lynn, slipped her a pill at the benefit. How Kit found this out, I'm not sure—but when Kit told me that news, it took me a long time to respond, so long that Kit asked if there was something wrong. "People are shitheads," I finally croaked out. My voice sounded strange. My hands, I realized, were curled into fists.

And yet it made sense. It never quite added up how drunk Kit had become that night on only one cocktail. Now at least we know why.

I'd asked Kit if we should report Lynn to the cops. Kit thought it over and said she wasn't sure—which surprised me. I would go after a person who spiked my drink for their own professional gain—it violates all sorts of workplace bullying regulations. But Kit seemed distracted, almost like it was an annoying side problem.

Then I looked up Lynn on Facebook. I found tons of photos of her—she's one of those people who posts about *everything*. It took me mere seconds to know why she looked familiar: She's the wife of the man Kit was talking to outside the funeral. His name, Facebook tells me, is Patrick.

"Are you *sure* we shouldn't put Lynn on our suspect list?" I asked Kit pointedly, later that day. Was there more to this Lynn-Kit-Patrick triangle than met the eye? I flash again on the charged way Kit and Patrick were staring at each other in the parking lot after the funeral. Was there something else for Lynn to be jealous of?

"I made an inquiry about Lynn with Detective Reardon, and her alibi is clear," Kit explained. "Dozens of people saw her at the benefit long after the coroner determined Greg had been stabbed. There's no way she could have been in two places at once." She shrugged. "It sucks that she poisoned me, and she's crazy, but she didn't kill Greg."

After that, the conversation ended. My sister didn't offer anything more about Patrick. I don't know why, but I couldn't bring myself to ask point-blank. For as much as we'd come together in this past week, it still felt like there was a barrier between us. Perhaps there are too many years to make up for.

Paul seems nervous as the tractor jerks forward, gripping my arm to catch his balance. It gives me a pleasant tingle. Once he lets go, I smirk at him. "Never been on a tractor ride before?"

"I already told you no." Paul rights himself and brushes hay off his jeans.

"You never came here as a kid?" When he shrugs, I add, "Actually, of course you didn't. You were too cool for hayrides."

Paul raises an eyebrow. "Are you trying to say I was cool when I was younger?"

I turn away, feeling my heart flutter. "You're kidding, right? You were *Mister* Cool."

"Mister Cool? *Me?*"

I feel my eyelashes batting at him, but then feel a little silly. This is *not me*. I'm not flirtatious. I don't put myself out there. I can't believe I even invited Paul today—though, in other ways, it's necessary. We're here to brainstorm about Greg's death. This is business.

The tractor begins to ascend a bumpy slope toward the apple orchards. "So," I say, my tone suddenly professional again. "Any luck with that data on snowstorms from last winter?" We're trying to track down the exact date Greg came home drunk and stinking of perfume. Sienna said there had been a big snowstorm that day, so I asked Paul to look into last year's weather history.

Paul nods. "We had only three really big storms last year. One was the first week of January, one was the third week in February, and one was late March." He nods thoughtfully. "I remember that late March one, actually—because of Greg. I was supposed to meet him to work on a piece I was ghostwriting for him, but then some of the roads were shut because of downed power lines, and we had to do a Skype session instead."

"And he never talked to you about anything personal?" We're passing a huge patch of wildflowers now. I dwell on them, my gaze resting on the tangle of pinks and yellows.

Paul shakes his head. "We didn't have that kind of relationship. I told him more about myself, actually—I was in the thick of the divorce at the time, and I remember my lawyer kept calling with updates from her lawyer."

"Your wife thought to get a lawyer?" I ask.

Paul's face clouds. "Just because she was young doesn't mean she was stupid."

His tone is harsh, defiant. I turn away, digging my fingers into the straw. "Sorry."

"It's fine," Paul says after a beat, so quietly I almost can't hear him over the roar of the tractor's engine. "I should be used to people's opinions about it by now. And I know it seems kind of . . . stereotypical—older guy, super-young woman. But I really *did* love her. And sometimes it doesn't make much sense who you fall in love with. That's happened to you, right?"

I concentrate for a moment on the patches of sunburned skin on the back of the tractor driver's neck and arms, suddenly feeling sad. There's a lot Paul and I really don't know about one another. "Not really," I admit.

"Oh." Paul seems surprised, then awkward. He folds his hands in his lap.

"It's been . . . hard," I hear myself saying. "Something happened to me when I was younger. Something that made me not trust people."

I can feel him watching me. Why have I just opened this door? It's something I've told no one—and I've liked it that way. And now Paul is waiting for me to say more.

The tractor chugs to a stop in the fields where, in the fall, there is a corn maze, a pumpkin patch, and a bunch of bounce houses. Today there are only a few plots of crops and a pick-your-own-flowers pavilion, which I intend to check out. I stand quickly, making my way toward the back to climb off. Paul follows me, and I can tell his mind is churning, formulating ideas about me. I paste a smile on my face and head for the flowers. "I love wildflowers," I call to Paul over my shoulder. "You're not too cool to pick some, right?"

We buy bottles of water and pick some wildflowers until we have a big bunch. I'm pleased to see that Paul has gotten into it, arranging his bouquet by color and adding a few random weeds and sprigs of hay to "dress the whole thing up." Afterward, he presents the sloppy bouquet to me, and I blush. "It's really something," I mock gush. "You've really outdone yourself."

"You think?" He grins. "Do I have a future as a florist?"

"Oh, definitely."

We sit down on the logs that, in colder weather, would be in front of a roaring fire. I put Paul's bouquet to my face, inhaling the sweet, springy scents. I can feel Paul looking at me with concern. *Please don't ask me any questions,* I silently will. *Please just pretend I never said anything.*

"Anyway," he says, his gaze falling to the dewy grass. "If we could talk to Sienna again, see if we can pinpoint the month when she remembers Greg coming home drunk, then we could cross-reference that with Greg's calendar. Maybe he put who he was out with on there. It's not as if he thought the thing was ever going to be public."

"Sounds great." I want to hug him for moving on so seamlessly. I pull out my phone, getting an idea. "Actually, we might be able to look through all those dates and see if there's anything suspicious on his calendar right now."

But when I try to access the hack site, the little wheel in the corner of my phone screen just spins and spins. We're too far out in the country to get service. I slip the phone back in my pocket. It will have to wait until later, then.

The air smells like dirt and manure, and I'm transported to the last time I was here. I was twelve, maybe thirteen; we'd picked apples. I have glimpses of my mom in my memory, but I can't remember a thing she said to me. We must have talked about *something*. I hate how cruel memory can be, hanging on to the things you'd rather forget, dropping those you're desperate to hold on to.

"I didn't mean to get all intense with you before," Paul says suddenly. "About my ex, I mean. I get too sensitive about it, I guess."

"It's okay." I hug my knees, feeling my body tense. "We all have our things."

"Yeah, but I have too many things, probably." Paul stretches his arms over his head. His T-shirt rises up just a little, and I get a peek at his taut, smooth belly. I glance away before he notices. "I take myself too seriously. Just like I did in high school. I should have been doing more bullshit like this, but you're right—I *was* too cool."

"We all took ourselves too seriously," I tell him.

"You didn't."

I stare at him. Who *was* I, to him? "Of course I did. I mean, maybe I didn't scowl as much as you did, but I was still . . . *me*. I was a personality. I fit into a box. There wasn't much leeway for that back then, being too many things, especially when they were contradictory. It was weird for me to be in lit mag, actually, and also do sports." Paul nods, thinking about this. "I remember agonizing about the first meeting before going. Thinking, *Shit, they're going to see me as this jock; I'm not going to be welcome.*"

"We wouldn't have done that," Paul says emptily. I'm not sure he believes his words, though. He looks unsettled by the conversation.

"It's why most people stay in their little box and don't venture out. And by the way, it follows you into adulthood, if you let it. Especially around here."

"Especially anywhere," Paul says.

I think about the women at the country club, with their set personalities and little boxes. But maybe Paul is right that everyone falls prey to getting stuck in a rut. After what happened to me happened, I didn't change. I remained fixed, stunted, unable to move on.

"But I believe people can change, too," Paul adds. "People can grow. They can become better versions of themselves. You just have to be bold sometimes; you just have to get up and shake yourself off and be like, *Okay, I'm going to do this even though it goes against every ounce of who I think I am. Because I want to try. Or because I think it's right.*" His eyes lower. "That's the pep talk I gave myself before talking to you at the funeral reception."

I burst out laughing. "You had to give yourself a pep talk to speak to me?"

He shrugs. "My marriage burned me. And honestly, I didn't think you liked me much. But I'd always wanted to get to know you. For the record, when you came into that first meeting a zillion years ago, I noticed you right away. I didn't think you were a jock who didn't belong. I found you interesting. Thoughtful." He looks sheepish. "And beautiful. You're still beautiful."

The wind shifts, blowing my hair into my face. It's been a long time since someone's called me beautiful—or maybe, since I've wanted to accept the compliment. When I look up, Paul is staring at me adoringly. My breath catches. I glance to the right and left, but we're pleasantly alone, the tractor having disappeared down the hill. I meet Paul's gaze again, my heart suddenly pounding. He cups my chin and brings his face closer to mine. The touch of his lips on mine feels surreal, like something out of a dream. I probably *have* dreamed something close to this. He shifts his whole body closer and places his hand on my arm. His other hand wraps around the back of my neck. And that's where something snaps. My brain doesn't reject the touch, but something in my body does.

But then I jolt away. Paul is breathless and looks confused. "What?" he asks, searching my face. "Are you okay?"

My face is hot—with embarrassment? Passion? Shame? I try to push the spiky feelings and memories away, but they're flooding in

SARA SHEPARD

anyway. This angers me. Paul didn't do anything wrong. And I *want* this. I gave permission.

But still, I just . . . can't. "I'm sorry," I say in a small voice, standing up. "I should go."

He blinks, blindsided. "W-Why?"

"I . . ." What can I say? What can I do? "I don't live here, Paul," I blurt out, grasping for something, even if it's bullshit. "I shouldn't string you along."

Paul looks confused. "What does living here have to do with anything?"

But there's nothing more I can say. I wave my hand and turn for the rutted path that leads back to the farm. Paul stands, too, but I turn away, indicating as best I can that I need space—lots of it. My boots squish in the soft earth as I walk away from him. I can feel his eyes on my back, and it's then I realize, too—I've forgotten the bouquet he made for me.

But I don't turn to retrieve it. Really, he should give it to someone else.

27

LAURA

THURSDAY, MAY 4, 2017

After just an hour of my shift at the hospital, I step into the bathroom and look at myself in the mirror. I've put on a lot of makeup to cover Ollie's slap marks from three days ago, but I can still see the imprint of each red, angry finger. No one has asked me about it, though. I guess they all have their own problems.

Suddenly, dread comes over me. *Freddie,* my intuition pings. *Something's wrong with Freddie.* Maybe Ollie has done something terrible. I've been *waiting* for something to happen, for his stony, punishing silence to spill over into the anger he hinted at a few days before. And he knows Freddie's my weakness. What if he decides to take out my betrayal on the baby? Would Ollie *do* such a thing? Days ago, I wouldn't have dreamed of it. But now, I'm not sure. My husband is now both utterly himself—big, strong, relentless, emotional—and utterly a stranger.

I need to get home.

I tell my supervisor I don't feel well and drive home so quickly I nearly rear-end someone on the parkway. As I open my front door, horrific possibilities of what I'm about to behold flood my mind.

But then I see Freddie in his Pack 'n Play in the living room.

His babysitter, Lucy, kneels next to it, waving a plush spider in his smiling face. Both of them glance up at me as I walk in; Lucy seems startled by the frantic look on my face.

"Oh," I cry, rushing toward Freddie and scooping him up. I'm swarmed with desperate, aching joy.

"Is everything okay?" Lucy stands and brushes off her jeans. "I thought you were going to be back at five."

"I, um, I've come down with something," I lie. "So I figured I'd come home. Sorry to drag you over here. I'll pay you for the whole day."

I press Freddie to my cheek, inhaling his sweet baby scent.

I write Lucy a check. She scoops up her things and heads for the door. "You need me here tomorrow, or do you think you'll be staying home?" she asks as she steps onto the porch. "I don't have class until five."

I hesitate. "You should come, just in case." It's probably safer if I don't tell the truth yet. I'll call her tomorrow, early, and cancel.

After Lucy leaves, I catch sight of myself in the round mirror in the foyer. On the surface, I look fine. My hair is clean. My makeup isn't smudged. The thick foundation over the slap is doing its job. I bring my hand up to touch it, wincing at the tender ache.

Time has stood still since everything went down. Ollie has barely spoken to me since he found out. For three nights, he has slept in our bedroom, while I've retreated to the pull-out couch in the office. This morning, he dressed quietly, babbled to Freddie, and then left without saying a word to me. The other shoe is going to drop— but *when*?

And I have questions. *Ollie knew.* He knew about Greg and me this whole time, but he said nothing. *Why?* Is it really because he didn't want to believe it was true? *You really think I'm that stupid?* he'd said. And then, later: *I'm glad that guy is dead.*

He'd known when Greg's Lolita e-mails broke wide. Hell, he might have thought *I* was Lolita. And he'd known the night he sent me to the benefit alone. What *else* did he know that night? And where was *Ollie* the night of the gala?

I'd come home from my near suicide attempt at 2:00 A.M. Ollie hadn't been here—I'd had to wake Lucy from the couch. I figured, of course, that he was still at the police station, working on the hack . . . but now I'm not so sure. If I'd idled my car for a little longer in Greg's circle that night, might I have seen Ollie come along next?

I imagine the rage roiling through him after finding out about Lolita. Reading those e-mails, presuming I wrote them, imagining Greg and me doing those disgusting things. I picture Ollie pacing the floor, breathing through his nose, groaning. Did he worry about being made a laughingstock, a cuckold?

Am I living in a house with a murderer?

Fear shudders over me. Ollie's motive is perfect. And he has the strength to overpower someone like Greg. It's the perfect crime, too, because after all those e-mails breaking in the hack, Kit looks like the obvious suspect. How deeply are the police searching for other people's motives? Is there any way they could find out about what Greg and I did? I remember, too, how cavalierly Ollie had said, "Oh, they'll find the murder weapon."

One thing's for certain: I can't stay here any longer.

I snap off the bathroom light and scurry into the living room again. As Freddie pokes at a small, plastic lion toy with noisy buttons, I locate my phone in my bag. My mother's number is at the top of my contacts list, but my finger hesitates over the screen. What do I tell her? That we're simply going to take a drive up north for a visit? Or maybe I shouldn't call at all. Maybe I should just grab Freddie, pack a few things, and call her while I'm on the road.

I hurry upstairs to the baby's room and start throwing things into a bag. Next, I scuttle into my bedroom. I open my closet and toss the first things I see into a duffel. It doesn't matter what I bring, really. I can buy new things later.

And then I hear a cough.

I shoot up, the bag's handles slipping from my fingers. I can just make out Ollie's silhouette in the dim light of the hall. Fear shoots through me like fire.

"Oh," I say, my voice too loud in the silence. "W-What are you doing?"

"What are *you* doing?" It's not a question. Then I feel his gaze drift to the suitcase. My heart sinks. Once again, I feel foolish for thinking I could trick him.

In a blink, he's across the room, right next to me. I shrink against the wall as Ollie—well, he doesn't touch me, exactly. He just stands there . . . *threatening* to touch me. The energy crackles off him like lightning. There's an eerie smirk on his face that turns my blood to ice. He's pressed so close to me that our torsos are mere millimeters apart. For the hundredth time, I don't recognize the man I married.

"Don't do it," he whispers.

"Please," I eke out. "Please."

Downstairs, Freddie lets out a squawk. Ollie glances toward the sound and then, mercifully, steps away. I collapse to the ground as though he's just tried to strangle me. He bends over me, jutting up my chin to force eye contact. "Don't do it," he growls, hate in his eyes. "Or you'll regret it."

28

LYNN

FRIDAY, MAY 5, 2017

*M*orning, Lynn!" Amanda chirps as I walk into the office on Friday. "Ready for the weekend?"

I stare at her as though she's just spoken in Dutch. I want to rip off her perky barrette. I want to pull out her fake nails. But instead, I smirk and say nothing.

"George wants you, Kit, and some of the others in his office in fifteen," Amanda adds. "That okay?"

I murmur a note of consent, then close myself inside my office. I sink into my couch; my eyeballs feel freeze-dried from lack of sleep. My nerves are jumping from . . . well, from nothing *specifically,* except the fact that my husband is cheating on me and it's been four whole days and I still haven't figured out who the bitch is.

I've combed through Patrick's things. Every pocket of every blazer. Every receipt in his wallet. Every text on his phone. I tried to re-create his schedule, figuring out exactly when he might have seen whoever she is—and when he could have given her that bracelet. Or perhaps he hasn't yet? Perhaps it's still hidden somewhere and he's going to give it to her on an upcoming business trip?

Yesterday, early evening, while I'd been tidying the house and getting the kids ready for soccer practice, I noticed Patrick in the foyer, putting on his coat. "Where are you going?" I knew there was a paranoid wobble to my voice, but I was already teetering over the edge, trying desperately not to explode.

Patrick worked the buttons of his coat, his head down. "I need to do a few things in the office before I head to Detroit next Wednesday. That okay? I figured you didn't need me for soccer."

Call a private detective, my brain blared. What if he was meeting *her?* I rose to full height. "Maybe I'll come to Detroit with you."

He looked up at me in surprise. "You want to come to *Michigan?*"

"I've never been." I tried to sound flip and airy. "It sounds fun."

"But what about the kids?"

"You know my parents would love to have them."

I watched his face. His straight mouth, his darting eyes. But then he shrugged and said, "Sure, if you really want to. I could probably get you on my flight, though I'm not sure about first class."

That was the final nail in the coffin. The Patrick I know would be like, *Lynn, don't be ridiculous, Detroit is a cesspool and you'll be horrified at its idea of a five-star hotel.* He'd reiterate that there was absolutely no good shopping and the weather was shit and all the people there were ugly. He'd say that we should go somewhere swanky and lovely the following weekend instead; he'd make reservations on the spot.

It was a guilty Patrick who'd given in. He caved because, perhaps deep down, he knew I was suspicious, and he wanted to lead me off the scent. Maybe I should have pushed the issue and asked for something even more extravagant—a new Chanel purse, hell, maybe even a whole new house. If Patrick felt so guilty, he'd probably cave to anything.

But all I want is for him to get rid of *her.* And that, unfortunately, has no price tag.

I can't just sit back and let this happen. I'm not going to be a wife who just smiles and pretends. Do I explain that I've found the bracelet? Is it possible that I'm misinterpreting this and that the bracelet *is* for me . . . just for another occasion? Christmas, maybe. My birth-day, in four months.

There's a knock on my door. I shoot up, my head feeling cottony. "Lynn?" Amanda's voice is muffled. "You ready?"

I heave a sigh. The meeting. I stand and smooth my skirt. Amanda smiles at me as I open the door, and she leads me down the hall into my boss's office, which is huge and bright and faces a scruffy bar at street level that seems to cater to drunks and people who like to dress in head-to-toe Steelers gear. I sit down on the couch, noticing that a few of the other people on the donations committee are here as well. There's a knock on the door, and Kit Manning-Strasser hurries in, too.

"Sorry I'm late," she says, falling into the last available chair.

"It's fine," George beams at her, the favorite child. I want to vomit.

There's something different about Kit today. Her hair is oddly shiny and there are two bright pink spots on her cheeks. Her whole face seems lighter, like someone has tied a string to her forehead and sharply yanked upward. She looks . . . *pleased,* I realize. What kind of woman is pleased after her husband is found dead? Distaste roils in my gut.

I turn to her, mustering a smile. "How are you doing?" I simper.

"Oh." Kit's eyes are cold. "You know. Tough time."

"The police figure out any leads yet?"

Kit shrugs. "Not really."

Then she angles her body toward Rory. Her rudeness shocks me. Kit's never been icy before.

"Okay, let's start." George peers at a legal pad, then turns to Roz Pepperdine, who works with the art museum that's linked to the college. "I hear we've made some headway getting the Bonners to donate a few of their works into the permanent collection?"

Roz launches into a talk about oil paintings and sculptures and transport costs, but my gaze is still on Kit. Her whole body is angled away from me. It feels purposeful. She couldn't know I gave her that Ambien, could she? Maybe I shouldn't have told Patrick about that in a public place. Maybe someone overheard.

"And what's the status with the alumni?" George now looks at Ivan, a slight, young guy in the corner.

Ivan moves his head from side to side. "Well, with some of the hack news, a lot of the alumni are a little less than impressed. Especially the stories that span when they were students here. Like the stuff about admissions fraud. Or the, um, rapes."

George frowns. "We aren't sure the rapes happened."

Kit looks at him sharply. "Did you really just say that?"

George raises his hands in surrender. "They're only hinted at in the e-mails. Nothing's concrete."

"Yes, but a few girls came forward with stories of things happening to them at frats," Kit blurts incredulously.

"Those posts don't give specifics," George says weakly, but then backs off as if he realizes what he's just said. "Not to minimize things if they *did* happen . . ."

"Absolutely," I jump in.

I haven't completely paid attention to what's been said—I only agree with Kit to gauge her reaction. But Kit stares stonily ahead as if she hasn't heard me. Maybe she *does* know, then. I curl my toes inside my shoes. *Shit.* Is she going to call me out on it? I can't get in trouble for this, can I? I mean, so I slipped her an Ambien. I thought it would just loosen her up. I was trying to help.

And then I see it.

It's Kit's turn to give an update. As she's talking, the sleeve of her blazer rides up, revealing a bare wrist and a glitter of diamonds. My heart stops in my chest. That bracelet is the same delicate chain I'd laid eyes on last week. The very same piece of jewelry, I'm almost positive, that lay in that little velvet box tucked in the back of my husband's trunk.

It can't be. But then I look again. The glinting diamonds. The delicate chain. It's *identical.* My stomach lurches.

I must make a sound, because suddenly, everyone is looking at me. I clutch my stomach as though suddenly ill. "Excuse me," I say, leaping to my feet.

I run into the bathroom and shut myself in a stall, my breaths coming erratic and fast. It's *the* bracelet. The same unique color of gold. The same small, glittering diamonds. Is this her way of saying she's in charge? But . . . *Patrick?* Why would he be into Kit? And when did this start? As I once saw in a text window on my daughter's cell phone: IDEK. *I don't even know.*

My scalp feels greasy with sweat. My whole body is throbbing. I suddenly realize, it must have been *Patrick* who told her about the Ambien. No doubt he'd been watching Kit the night of the benefit, noting how drunk she became, maybe even worrying about her. Maybe they'd even talked about it afterward. Maybe she'd been like, *Geez, I feel like someone drugged me.* And there I sat at the restaurant, playing into their hands. I feel like a fool.

But wait. Patrick barely saw drunk Kit at the benefit. Oh, maybe he saw her staggering a little, but the really good stuff only happened after he left. All at once, I feel uneasy. I never bought that he had a stomachache. He'd sprinted out of that gala like an Olympian. I'd thought he was running away from me, but maybe he was running *to* something. Or to *do* something.

I think of his missing car in the driveway when I got home later that night. I think, too, of someone sneaking in and murdering Kit's husband during those very same hours. But no. No *way.* I can't go down that road.

Because married to a murderer? That's *not* who I want to be.

29

WILLA

FRIDAY, MAY 5, 2017

I pick up takeout and drop by my dad's house, which brings on a barrage of memories in itself, because after my mother passed away, takeout was pretty much our mainstay. It's hard to remember how we got through those years. Our father must have scheduled Kit and me for regular doctors' appointments and made sure we had all the paperwork to apply to college, but I find it hard to believe *how*, exactly, because we were all so frozen with grief. And obviously things fell through the cracks with us. Especially with me.

I'm ready to dig into who Greg might have been having an affair with. For once, my father is home. When I ask if he'd like some pad thai, he smiles wanly and says he isn't hungry.

I frown. "Are you eating enough, Dad? You look really pale."

He nods vaguely. "I had a big lunch. Really."

He pads off to his office. I exchange a look with Kit, who's unloading plates from the cupboard. The stress is really getting to him. He's had to fire so many people. Give so many press conferences. And he's not getting any younger. But my father's always been stubborn—he works through the flu, through snowstorms, even right after my mother's accident. It's like he thinks the school's future rests solely on his shoulders.

We open the cartons of food and call for the girls to come down. Just as Kit's spooning some rice onto her plate, her phone pings. She glances at the screen, and something in her expression brightens. "I have to go," she murmurs.

"Go where?" I ask, suddenly on alert. Kit has barely left the house except to go to work. The news crews are still prowling the circle, and I can tell they make her uneasy.

"Work thing." Kit hurries out of the room, her feet clonking heavily on the stairs. "I'll be back."

"*What* work thing?" I yell after her. But she doesn't answer.

Sienna and Aurora wisp into the room like ghosts, glancing at me uneasily. They silently fill their plates with food and are about to retreat back upstairs—I guess they don't have any weekend plans—but then I clear my throat. "Hang on. I have a couple of questions for you girls."

Their faces fall. They're so sick of my questions.

"I'm sorry, I'm sorry, and it won't be about anything crazy," I assure them. "I'm not trying to cause trouble. You know that, right?"

Neither answers that question, probably because all I've *done* is cause trouble. But they dutifully sit, which is a relief. As I'm pouring the girls sparkling water—they asked for diet soda, but I said no freaking way, refraining from a lecture on what soda chemicals do to one's insides—Kit returns from upstairs. She's now wearing a soft, fitted linen dress and smells like freshly spritzed perfume. I watch as she studies her phone again and slips on a pair of high-heeled shoes. As she's heading for the mudroom toward the garage, I scurry after her.

"Kit," I say in a low voice so the girls can't hear. "This has nothing to do with that woman at work, does it?"

Kit frowns. "Of course not."

But she won't look at me. Is she lying? *Does it have anything to do with that woman's husband?* Kit leans in and pecks me on the cheek, something we never do. "I'll be back soon."

After the door slams, I trudge back to the kitchen, scoop some takeout onto my plate, and take a few bites. Normally, I'm not a fan of hole-in-the-wall takeout, as everyone knows the food is filled with MSG and other chemicals, and I'd planned to make myself a salad tonight, but after the stunt Kit just pulled, I feel undone and in need of comfort. Should I follow her?

"Aunt Willa?" Sienna gives me a pained look. "I really want to go back upstairs. What did you want to ask us?"

"Oh." I swallow a mouthful of oily, delicious noodles, trying to bring myself back to the task at hand. Kit will be okay. I have to believe that. "So, um, you mentioned hearing Greg stumbling around that one night, and you also mentioned it was around the time of a snowstorm. I was able to pull up storms from last year—if we look at Greg's calendar, maybe we can figure out who he was with that night. Can you remember if the storm was in January, February, or March?"

Sienna pops a chicken satay in her mouth and chews thoughtfully. "I want to say January. I don't think Valentine's happened yet."

I glance at the notes Paul gave me today at the farm, feeling a stab of regret when I see Paul's small, neat, rounded handwriting. I wonder how confused he feels at the way I rejected him. Hell, *I'm* still confused at myself . . . and, at the same time, totally unsurprised.

"January tenth," I read off the list. "Eight inches of snow. Sound right?"

"I don't know. I guess."

I click to the chunk of data I've exported to my laptop from the hack database. It's Greg's data—I wanted to have it accessible at all times in case I'm ever in a spot without a cell signal again. Greg's calendar is in a subfolder, and I open it and scroll back to last January.

According to his calendar, which is jammed with surgeries,

meetings, and business events, he didn't have anything scheduled for the evening, but there was a quadruple bypass slated for 11:00 A.M. for someone named P. Vitrillo. I sometimes forget that Greg used to pry open people's chests and work on their hearts. Kind of an ironic line of work for such an unfeeling person.

I look at the girls. "Did Greg often go out after tough surgeries to blow off steam?"

They exchange a glance. "I don't really know," Aurora says. "Maybe?"

I stretch out my legs under the table. "If he did, who might he go with?"

"Other doctors?" Sienna suggests. "Friends?" It's clear she has no idea.

Aurora makes a face. "Greg always whined about the other doctors, though. Said he'd be happy if he were the only doctor on call." She picks at her nails.

"Someone else from the hospital, then? An administrator? A nurse?"

The girls look at one another and shrug. "We didn't know much about his life at work."

I only recall Kit telling me about one nurse on Greg's staff: that woman who came to the funeral with her baby. Laura . . . something. A thought pings in my mind. *Laura Apatrea.* Perhaps she knew Greg well?

I hold a finger up for the girls to tell them to bear with me for a moment, then pick up my phone. The first thing I see on the screen is a news alert for a few more posts from some girls who have made references to assaults at Aldrich frat parties. I feel a knot in my stomach, guilty that I'm swiping past these testimonies. Reluctantly, I navigate to the hack site and dig up Laura's folder.

Turns out I was right: Greg and Laura e-mailed quite a bit, though it was mostly scheduling stuff, or sometimes a funny GIF. There certainly aren't Lolita-esque missives between them. But I do notice something strange: Laura wrote something cryptic to Greg just days before he died. *I've received your research. Definitely taking into consideration. But I have all I need for now—thanks.*

Curious, I flip all the way back to a year and a few months before, around the time of the January snowstorm. Laura had written Greg a non-work-related note that day, too: *Thanks for being there for me.*

Three minutes later, Greg shot back, *Always.*

A frisson goes through me.

I stare at Laura's message again. *Thanks for being there for me.* Was this a response to a friendly conversation they'd had in the break room . . . or was Greg with Laura that night of the snowstorm? Were they just friendly colleagues . . . or something more?

It would be too easy if Laura had just written in her calendar, *January 10: Drinks with Greg.* And when I flip through Laura's e-mails from February and then March, I can't find another e-mail to him besides bland administrative stuff. In fact, the only other e-mails Laura has saved from that time are a few notes from her mom, a few messages from her husband, Ollie—who mentions the police station, so this *is* the same person from the funeral—and a whole bunch from a site called BabyCenter. *Congratulations, you're pregnant!* says the first one.

I click on it to find a lot of *What to Expect When You're Expecting* nonsense. After that, BabyCenter sent her an e-mail once a week, updating her on her developing fetus's progress. Each week, the fetus graduates to the size of a new fruit: *Today, your baby is a blueberry! This week, your baby is a cantaloupe!* I scroll all the way forward to late September, when the baby is the size of a watermelon. *Happy due date!* bleats an e-mail on October 3. *According to your calculations, you are forty weeks pregnant today!*

I frown. Calculations? Do most women know the exact day they conceived? I don't recall Kit knowing, but then, I didn't pay much attention.

I open a window in the Internet browser and type *due date*

calculator into Google. A site appears that predicts when a woman will give birth. It seems you can calculate your due date from your last menstrual period, an IVF transfer, or an exact date of conception. On a hunch, I type *January 10* into the search field. The night of the snowstorm.

The little wheel spins, and the results come up. I can't even say I'm surprised when I see that Laura's projected due date is October 3. But what does this *mean*? Laura's married. It's very possible Laura didn't go out with Greg the night of the snowstorm but instead went home to her husband, lit some candles, and did whatever else people do to get in the baby-making mood. It's possible I've got this all wrong.

But it doesn't *feel* wrong. I can't say why, exactly. Something nudges me at the edge of my consciousness.

I click to Laura's sent messages, searching around October of last year. Bingo: Laura, sent out an e-mail to her friends shortly after her baby was born. *Frederick Thomas Apatrea, eight pounds, six ounces, twenty inches long,* it reads. A picture is attached. When the wrinkly, squinty-eyed newborn appears on my screen, I study him hard, suddenly understanding what has been nudging me. The baby has Greg's same sloped nose and cleft chin.

But how to get more information? Should I call Laura? I'm a reporter, after all. I can lie about my motives. I can figure out what to ask her without giving too much away.

I click back to her received e-mails. Some Amazon purchases show that she lives on Armandale Street, which isn't that far from here. From there, it isn't difficult to find her phone number. I stab in the digits, then press the phone to my ear.

"Hello?" says a gruff, impatient voice on the other end. It must be her husband.

I straighten up. "May I speak to Laura, please?"

There's a long, crackling pause. "She's not here."

"Any idea when she'll be back?" I ask, my voice pleasant enough.

"Who is this?"

I frown, startled by his rancorous tone. "It's Willa Manning. I'm—"

"I know who you are." And then, almost imperceptibly, I hear him mutter under his breath.

Next thing I know, the line is dead.

I call back, hoping it's a mistake. There's the same gruff, annoyed *hello*—I say, "Sir, is there another number I can reach your wife at?"

"*No*," he growls. In the background, I hear the faint sounds of running water, maybe a TV, and then a baby's cry. "I don't want you calling here, *ever*. Got it?"

He disconnects us once more. I stare at my phone as though it's just given me an electric shock. I can understand Laura being unwilling to talk to me, but her husband? What stake does he have in this? Unless he's covering up for Laura. And then a cold rush cascades down my back. No, that's not it. Maybe he's covering up something about *himself*.

I think of Laura's husband's towering height. His thick arms, his catcher's-mitt hands. This kind of über-masculine man brings up old wounds for me. He's the kind of guy who might not be able to handle the news of another man fathering his wife's baby.

I rake my hands through my hair. I don't want to make assumptions. And yet the lead feels more credible than anything else I've considered. There's just one problem. I have no idea how to prove it.

30

RAINA

FRIDAY, MAY 5, 2017

*A*lexis calls me between classes. Well, between *my* classes, since I now know she's not an Aldrich student. "It's happening. There was another munch today, and I sidled up to our guy and asked if I could have his number. Then I AirDropped him some kinky photos of you and me, and he was into it. He wants to meet us tonight."

I stop in the middle of the sidewalk so abruptly that a group walking behind me almost bumps into my back. "Where did you get a sexy picture of *me*?"

"I had one of your face, and then I did some Photoshop work. But it's basically your same proportions, don't worry."

I start walking again, feeling shaky. "So what's going to happen, exactly?"

"He and I got to talking about porn. Well, not *talking*—texting. You know. And anyway, our dude said his favorite plot in porn movies is when the woman's in the house alone, kind of scared, and the burglar breaks in. But then it turns sexy, and the burglar's totally turned on because she's afraid, and she gets off, too, because almost being killed is sexy. In a man's mind, anyway."

"He's going to pretend to *rob* us?"

"Not *really*. It's all an act, though we'll have to act afraid. But, I mean, we got off easy. He could have asked to do bondage stuff . . ."

I shudder. "Still. It seems . . . *demeaning*."

"Most porn is demeaning to the woman, Raina. Don't be naïve."

"But don't you think this hits a little too close to home? Someone broke into Greg Strasser's house . . . and *killed* him. Unless he lives under a rock, this guy has to know that. It's not kinky—it's sort of sick." And then another thought strikes me. "Are you sure this isn't a trick? Like maybe he's setting *us* up?"

"For what?" Alexis sniffs. "What we're doing isn't illegal. We're all consensual adults."

"I know, but . . ." So much dirty laundry has been aired recently that I'm paranoid all of our actions are being watched, even those that are off-line.

"So listen, he wants to meet us in this house near Aldrich at eleven P.M. He said he's going to leave the door unlocked. I'll go early and set up the camera." I can hear the excitement in her voice.

I turn the corner to the Aldrich University green. In the daytime, this long, sprawling patch of grass is a buoyant hotbed of activity, but at night—and especially on Friday nights, when this part of campus clears out—it's creepy. The streetlamps don't adequately illuminate the walking paths. The middle of the green is a vast thicket of darkness. Someone could be standing ten feet away from me and I wouldn't know. I think about Greg's murderer, still roaming the streets, and shiver.

"I don't know," I say. "This gives me the creeps. Maybe we find someone else."

"Are you fucking kidding me?" Alexis sounds livid. "I already did all the legwork!"

"Well, then, maybe *you* find someone else. I'll help out with the next guy. Surely you have some kind of underground network of skanky girls who'd be into this."

"But we had a deal!" Her voice is shrill, and I hold the phone away from my ear. "Look. He really wants *you*. He made that clear—he has a thing for redheads. I'm not sure he'd be up for it if it was me and somebody else."

I listen to the static on the phone, saying nothing.

"Do this for me, and we're even," Alexis says begrudgingly. "You're off the hook. I won't expose you, and I won't make you do anything else."

I lean against the cool brick of the science building, getting an idea. But I must take this very, very slow. "Okay, then I get a slightly bigger percentage. Sixty-forty."

"What the fuck?" Alexis spits. "No!"

"*And* you tell me your real name."

She snorts. I hear her breathing in like she's about to speak, but then she changes her mind. Finally: "Why does it matter?"

"Because I want to know."

Across the campus, the bells in the clock tower strike the half hour. The wind lifts the leaves from the brick-lined streets, blowing them in a circular pattern. There's a discarded protest sign lying facedown next to some trash cans across the street: NO MORE SILENCE FOR RAPE VICTIMS.

Alexis breathes out. "Fine. Sixty-forty. And it's Jane."

"Thank you, *Jane*. See you soon."

And then I hang up. A smile stretches on my face. I can still manipulate with the best of them.

31

KIT

FRIDAY, MAY 5, 2017

*W*hen Patrick and I finish making love, I roll over and listen to the Aldrich clock tower chime. We are lying in a king-size bed in the Kingsland Arms, an understated, modest hotel near campus. It isn't the Duquesne Club or the Omni William Penn, which are the hotels a woman of my status would expect—or, rather, where a man like Greg might have taken me, but I'm beginning to feel a little turned off by status symbols. Where did they get me, after all? Wealth certainly didn't make me much happier.

The blinds are thrown open, exposing a view of the river and the Pittsburgh Point. The sun is beginning to set, turning the room a dusty pink. Patrick leans toward me, and I feel the warmth of his body against mine. "You know that box you carry around containing the meaning of life?" he murmurs.

It takes me a moment before I get the reference—it was a detail from my Philly persona. "Mm-hmm . . ."

"I think whatever's in there can't be better than this."

Just his touch makes me dissolve. I reach for him again. I want to never leave this bed.

Patrick's phone buzzes. We're still kissing, but I can feel him pull back. He rolls over, sits up, and reaches for the device. A tired expression comes over his face. It's Lynn, then. She probably wants to know where he is. I lick my lips. I have every right to hate Lynn Godfrey for drugging me. I have every right to feel justified about doing this with Patrick—though that's not why I'm doing it.

Patrick drops the phone back on the desk. "I have to go."

I nod. "I understand."

"I certainly don't *want* to." He touches my cheek. "I'd rather be flying into hurricanes with you."

"Hurricanes," I murmur. Right, right, he was the hurricane pilot. "Or even just lying here. For the rest of our lives."

"Mmmm." He leans over, his lips brushing my shoulder. His eyes are pleading and hopeful. "If I left her . . . would that be something you'd want?"

I blink. *Do* I want that? I barely know Patrick. But isn't it also true that when you know, you just *know*? It's an instinct I had with both Greg and Martin. Or at least I *thought* I did.

"I don't know," I say quietly. "I'd have to think about it."

"But you wouldn't rule it out."

I lick my lips. "No. I wouldn't rule it out."

He takes my shoulders in his hands, lightly massaging my muscles. When we kiss, I close my eyes, letting him fill me.

A few minutes later, after he's disposed of the condom we've used and we've taken a quick shower and dressed, we're kissing again at the door. But as I move to walk with him to the elevator, Patrick touches my arm awkwardly. "Actually, I should probably go downstairs first. You wait here, if that's okay."

It gives me an oily feeling, but it's not like I can argue. After enough time, I slip into the hall and shut the door behind me. The corridor is eerily empty. Even the lobby is deserted, the lone attendant at the front desk busy with something on her computer, though as my heels tap across the marble floor, she looks up and gives me a warm smile. After a moment, something in her eyes sharpens. I keep my head down. Can she sense what I've done? Or maybe she recognizes me from the news? I think of the lie I told Willa before I left: I'm at a work meeting. I picture what my daughters would think if they found out what I'm really up to.

The double doors open, and I emerge into the night. The sky is the color of a bruise. Lights twinkle atop buildings. The downtown street is as vacant as the hotel's lobby, and I feel a chill. I wish Patrick were walking me to my car.

I turn left, then right, momentarily disoriented as to where I'd parked. I'm ultra-aware of my lone shadow gliding along the sidewalk. Is this a safe neighborhood at night? I'd thought so, but it isn't like I come here very often.

I find the parking lot, a flat square of pay spaces usually guarded by an attendant, though it seems he's left for the day. I rustle in my bag for my keys, then hear a click to my left. I raise my head, turn. Someone's there.

A streetlight makes a lone gold circle at the edge of the lot. Far in the distance, a car alarm blares. I squint past the rows of cars, watching shadows and movement that may or may not be real. My fingers curl around my keys. Shakily, I hit the unlock button, and my taillights illuminate. I hurry to the driver's door, but there it is again. A rustle. A footstep. I glance over my shoulder once more. Maybe Willa was right to warn me to be careful. My fingers clamp around my phone. Maybe I should call 911. Maybe I should call Ollie Apatrea, considering his open-ended offer that I could reach him at any time.

I wrench the door open, fall into the seat, and lock the car fast. My breathing is quick, and I can feel my pulse heavy in my throat. I glance in the back seat, remembering those horrible campfire tales of killers lurking there, ready to pounce on lone women. Nothing. I run my fingers through my sweaty hair. Maybe I'm losing my mind.

Buzz.

My phone buzzes in my palm. An unlisted number flashes on the screen. "Hello?" I answer, praying it isn't a reporter.

All I hear is breathing. "Hello?" I say again. "Who's there?"

"I know you did it," says a voice. A gravelly voice, asexual and slinky like a snake.

"Did . . . *what?*" I ask. The hotel room strobes in my mind. My limbs entangled with Patrick's. I think of the desk clerk's eyes on mine, seeing me, knowing me.

"You killed him," says the voice.

My heart drops. "*What?*"

"You know you did it," it repeats. "And I know, too."

There's a click, and the line is disconnected. I let the phone fall from its cradle between my shoulder and ear. My fingers curl tightly around the steering wheel. *You know you did it.*

I glance out the window to the dark square of asphalt. Those clicks, those footsteps—is that who called me? *Is* someone watching me?

I hit the start button, and the engine roars to life. The headlights illuminate the chain-link fence, the building next door, a line of dumpsters. As I back out, the headlights bounce off the cars, the attendant's little kiosk, the pay machine. No one is there. No one is hiding, at least no one I can see.

32

LYNN

FRIDAY, MAY 5, 2017

It's past nine by the time Patrick gets home. I arrange myself in a casual pose, but I feel anything but casual right now. My brain is a swarm of bees. My heart is like a hamster running frantically on a wheel. It's Friday night. There's no way Patrick can use working late as an excuse. He was with her. I can tell.

Patrick walks through the hall but stops when he spies me in the living room. "Hey?" He sounds uneasy. I'm sitting in the dark. Unmoving. Just staring.

"W-Where are the kids?" Patrick asks.

"Sleeping."

"*Already?*"

I sip from my glass of wine. "I drugged them."

"You *what?*"

I set the glass down on the table with a sharp clink. "With melatonin. It's perfectly safe. I figured they wouldn't want to hear this. And don't look at me like that. You've done far worse."

The grandfather clock, a gift from my parents for our first anniversary, ticks in the hallway. Next door, I hear our neighbor's weed whacker—that psycho tends his lawn at the weirdest hours. I don't like how caught Patrick looks. I want to say my heart is breaking, but I've become so convinced that Patrick is a shithead that I'm almost desensitized to all feeling.

"I know what you did to Greg Strasser." My hand curls around the pocketknife I found in the drawer. I have it with me just in case. "You disgust me."

Patrick's mouth drops open. A choked laugh escapes from his throat. "Lynn . . ."

"You were with his wife tonight, too. Don't try and deny it. And you weren't home when I got back from the benefit. Where did you go?"

"I-I told you." His eyes search my face. He looks trapped. "I was getting Pepto. For my stomach."

I cross my arms. He's not a good liar. "I could tell them you have motive. I could tell them you were missing when I got back. I could put you away for life."

"What the fuck, Lynn?" Patrick's voice is a string held taut. "Why are you doing this?"

"Or I could keep this all to myself. But only if you stop seeing her. She's not a good person, Patrick. She arranged with Greg to kill her first husband on the operating table. Did you know that?"

Patrick's eyes roll back in his head, revealing slick, white membrane. In a blink, he's advancing toward me, his steps long, his nostrils flaring. I reel back, surprised by his sudden movements, my fingers grappling around the knife's shaft. "Don't you say that about her," he growls. His breath smells like wine. "Don't *ever*."

Rage floods me. So that's how I get a rise out of him, then, by insulting Kit.

"You gave Kit a diamond bracelet," I hiss in his face. "I found it in your car—I thought it was for me. But she showed up to work with it on today, plain as day, the moron." He steps back. The blood has drained from his face. "I can track down the receipt from the jewelers to prove it. I've heard the police like proof."

"Stop talking about the police!" Patrick cries. His jaw is twitching.

"Did you kill Greg to get him out of the way? Or did Kit *tell* you to do it?"

"For all I know, *you* killed Greg!" Patrick stabs a finger at me. "You're crazy enough to! You fucking drugged her at that event—I could tell the police that! Who's to say you didn't rush back to her house and stab him to frame her? Maybe *you* wanted *her* out of the way!"

I scoff. "*What?*" I'm astonished Patrick has come to such a crazy conclusion. Has he been mulling this over since I told him about drugging Kit? "Good try, but I have witnesses putting me at the benefit the whole night. Don't try and pass this onto me."

"But I didn't do it, either." His eyes are pleading, suddenly. "I swear, Lynn. I *swear*. Please don't talk to the cops."

"Stop seeing her, and I won't."

I give him a level gaze. I hate that, so far, he hasn't denied that he's seeing Kit. Maybe he doesn't see the point. And maybe I don't even really care. I just want the upper hand. I want Patrick under my spell again. Like things used to be. He thrives under my spell. He *soars*.

It gives me a perverse rush just thinking about it. Before I know what I'm doing, I drop the knife, lurch toward him, grab the sides of his face, and kiss him hard. I feel his body resist at first, but then he lets me in, cupping the back of my head, pushing his groin into mine. I dig my fingers into his upper arms. I'm kissing him with the passion of someone who has the control but also as a relieved wife. He's mine.

I'm the first to push away. Patrick pants lightly, his eyes searching mine. But where he is flustered, overwrought, our kiss has steadied me. Sex has always done that.

"I'm your wife," I say evenly. "I'll keep it a secret. But I need you to stop seeing her. Otherwise, I'll ruin you—in ways you don't even know."

Patrick nods weakly. His posture has even changed from a few minutes before—his face is more open, and he stands erect, like an eager dog waiting for his next command. *Here* he is, I think. The man I married. The man I know.

"Do you understand what I'm telling you?" I ask, my voice a coo. Sadness flickers across Patrick's features. "I-I don't want to break up our family. I don't want to lose our kids."

"You don't have to, darling. As long as we have a deal."

He gives a head bob and falls into me. I wrap him in my arms. "It's okay," I coo, stroking his hair. "I know you didn't mean to do it. You're just confused. You've just lost your way."

"I did." Patrick has his head in his hands. "I guess I did."

There's a confession in there for sure. I catch sight of myself in the mirror across the room and give my reflection a victorious smile. Actually, take away a few faint wrinkles around my eyes, and I look young, badass, and in charge. Some things never change.

A creak startles me awake. I look around the bedroom and wait for my eyes to adjust. The fan whirs in the corner. There's a rustling sound off to the left. "Patrick?" I call out.

I hear swishes of fabrics, cracks of joints. Then I see Patrick's shape looming on the other side of the room, watching me. Startled, I sit up in bed. "What are you doing?" I ask groggily, pushing aside our mountain of pillows.

His dark form twists away. "I can't sleep. I'm going for a run."

His voice is cold, empty. I check the clock on the nightstand. "It's almost eleven at night."

"I got water," Patrick says. "You want some?"

He thrusts a glass under my nose. There's not much I can do but take it and drink. The water is cold and refreshing for my cottony mouth. I swallow three gulps, four. I offer it back to him, but he waves his hand, already heading for the door.

"Patrick." I leap up to follow him. "Don't go." Intuition tugs at me. The killer might be out there. Ready to jump someone else. "Stay here. Run on the treadmill. We have a whole home gym down-stairs."

"I need fresh air. I'll be fine. See you in a bit."

And then he's gone. I stand in the dim hallway light, rubbing my eyes. Out the window, I catch sight of Patrick cutting across the lawn, hands on his hips, the reflectors on his sneakers glowing. But he doesn't head toward the pavement. Instead, he circles around to the side yard, like he's going around back. That certainly isn't his normal running route.

For a long minute, nothing happens. But then, what seems like a year later, the lights of his car flash on. I watch as his SUV backs out of our driveway and rolls quietly around our circle.

My skin prickles. Of course he isn't going for a run.

"God*damn* it," I mutter. He has no intention of stopping things with Kit. He's going to do something rash tonight. Steal Kit out of town. *My wife is onto me. We have to go, now.*

Or maybe he's snuck out to do something worse.

All at once, my throat feels like I've swallowed knives. I reach for the doorknob to the side yard—do I risk following him? Will my kids be okay alone for a few minutes? But there's something wrong with my depth perception, and I swipe only air. I try again, this time turning the knob, but as I walk over the threshold, my legs feel like they're filled with sand. It feels like I've stood up too fast, too, so I lean against the wall and wait for the feeling to pass.

Except it *doesn't* pass. Stars whirl. The dizziness is nause-ating. *Deep breaths,* I tell myself. Is this a panic attack? But that's ri-diculous. I'm not the panic attack *type.* My kids' faces pass through my mind. Am I dying? Is this a stroke?

But then I think of the water I've just drunk. My mind halts at even *thinking* such a thing, but then I cross the bridge anyway, letting the idea in. Of course he did. It was his only way to escape. *An eye for an eye.* Patrick dissolved an Ambien in a glass of water just like I'd plopped one into Kit's martini.

I feel my eyelids drooping, but I fight against it as hard as I can. I'm so angry I want to wail, except I'm also so exhausted I can barely manage a whimper. But if Patrick thinks I'm going to give up without a fight, he clearly doesn't know me very well. I'm not going to descend into oblivion. I run to the powder room, shove my fingers down my throat, and watch as bile and liquid come back up. It will erase some of the medicine from my bloodstream. I need to be the smarter one here.

I need to stop the murderer from getting away.

33

LAURA

FRIDAY, MAY 5, 2017

I've drifted off just as my alarm buzzes. I shoot up, silencing it quickly, not wanting to alert Ollie. My eyes adjust to the darkness. I'm lying in our king-size bed. Ollie let me back into the bedroom, I suspect, because it's easier to keep track of me if we're sharing a room.

But as I turn, I realize that Ollie's side is cold. My heart jolts. I spring out of bed and run to the baby's room, my heart in my throat. Freddie is snoozing away, his lips parted, his eyelids fluttering. I place my hand over my heart as if to slow it down.

I creep downstairs, knowing that at any moment, Ollie could step out of the shadows. He could ambush me in the living room and strangle me to death. I pad through the foyer, past the couch, into the kitchen, my body on high alert. No lights are on. Outside, nothing stirs.

And then I see it: Ollie's car isn't in the driveway. I blink, dumbfounded. He's . . . gone?

I stand stock-still in the middle of the kitchen, opening and closing my fists. What does this mean? Has Ollie *left*? Hope fills me. Maybe he took off for good. But in the next breath, I doubt this is true—after all of Ollie's threats to keep me here, it makes no sense that he'd randomly give up.

But still, he's given me a window. This is my chance. I need to get out of here before he comes back.

Stealthily—I still don't trust what's happening—I tiptoe back into Freddie's room. His crib mobile spins gently, emitting soft, tinkling bedtime music. My heart pounds as I carefully lift him from his crib. "Shh, *shhh*," I whisper as he stirs and grumbles.

Freddie is a heavy lump against my chest, but he remains asleep. Trembling, I creep out of his room and maneuver down the stairs. Before I went to bed, I left my purse and keys by the door, where I could easily find them—and miraculously, they are still here. I peek out the front window again. Ollie's side of the driveway is still empty. Is this truly happening? Am I going to get to slip out of here?

The baby snores as I loop the purse and baby bag over my wrist and silently undo the front bolt. The door opens soundlessly, as though greased. Cold air assaults my face and I wince, pressing Freddie tighter to me, willing him not to react to the change in temperature. His eyes remain closed. His breathing is steady.

Only a few more steps. First down the front porch, and then across the walk, and then unlocking the Subaru. The sky above me is the color of ink, and all the stars are out. A streetlamp casts my long shadow across the grass. I glance down the street, but Ollie's SUV doesn't appear through the darkness, ready to catch me out. Hurriedly, I place the baby in his car seat and strap him in. Freddie smacks his lips and stirs for a moment, but then drifts back to sleep. I slide into the driver's seat and jam the key into the ignition.

I pull away from the house. Pause at the stop sign at the end of the street and look both ways, though it's asinine to think anyone would be out at this time of night. I turn two more times, and then I'm on the highway going north. At this rate, we'll get to my parents' house at about 1:00 A.M.

I breathe out, feeling the tears drip down my cheeks. The tension I've been holding in for days explodes from me, and I let out a few wrenched, wretched sobs. But I'm happy, too. Relieved. Because I've done it. I've escaped.

And maybe, just maybe, I'm safe.

34

RAINA

FRIDAY, MAY 5, 2017

A driver drops me at a house in Blue Hill with a long, sloped, unkempt front yard littered with wildflowers, weeds, and political candidate signs of races long past. The driveway has dandelions growing through the asphalt cracks. A dim light glows from the porch, but otherwise, the house looks shut and dark.

I knock tentatively on the door, my skin crawling. Alexis—and I've decided to call her that in my mind, despite the fact that it isn't her real name—opens it right away, her long blond hair cascading over her shoulder. "Does *he* live here?" I splutter. "Or is this place abandoned?" The last thing I want is to get arrested for trespassing.

Alexis shrugs. "He said it belongs to a bunch of the people in the kinky community. You pay a fee to play here. Think of it as a co-op."

"More like a *gross*-op," I murmur as she opens the door.

The hallway is empty and smells like feet. The living room is also empty save a ratty couch in the middle of the room. The kitchen faucet drips noisily. I walk to the back of the house and look out the window to the overgrown yard. We are only one street away from the Strasser-Manning house . . . where the murder went down. I think of Sienna. I can't recall the last time I heard from her. Is that on purpose, or is she just busy? All at once, my friendship with Sienna seems so uncomplicated and safe. I regret not putting more effort into it. Maybe we'll be able to start over, once I collect this money and repair my life.

"I might be having second thoughts, *Alexis*," I murmur, my throat tight.

Alexis's mouth pinches. "Don't call me that."

"I should call you Jane, then?"

"Don't call me anything."

She turns and struts up the stairs. I try not to stare at her butt, but it's difficult. She's wearing a skirt so short that I keep seeing snatches of her ass. Her shoulders are bare, too; I can see the delicate knobs of her spine. Her skin glows. I want to bite into it.

The bedroom she leads me to is generic and stripped down. In it is a bed with a mattress, sheets, and a comforter, though I wonder when they were last washed. Alexis flops down and glances at her watch. "He'll be here soon. I've got everything set up."

I look around. "Where are the cameras?"

"Hidden." Alexis crosses her arms. Her eyeliner is thick today, and her lips are extra pink. "I'm not going to tell you where they are. You'll stare at them and give everything away."

I scoff. "I'm just as good at this as you are."

"Says the girl who tried and failed *twice* in the past six months."

Her eyes are gleaming. Is she flirting with me? But when I look again, she seems impassive, even annoyed. Like this is just a job to her, nothing more.

I smooth my hands on the comforter, then realize how dirty it probably is and pull away. "So what's the plan?"

"We're supposed to act like we're at a sleepover. And then, I guess, he breaks in"—she makes quote marks with her fingers—"and pretends he's robbing us. We need to act scared. He has to believe that we're into this, too."

I bite my lip. This is *so* weird. "What next?" I want to know when we reveal we're blackmailing him.

"And then wait for my signal." Alexis's voice is businesslike. "Leave everything to me."

I nod, though I don't like putting my trust in someone else's hands—I've always worked alone.

We kick off our shoes. I want to suggest that we watch something on my phone, but I don't know if that's allowed. I pick at my nails. Alexis rolls on more lipstick and presses her lips together with a smack. She gets up and paces around. She seems nervous, too. I wonder if she's thinking about our proximity to the Strasser house, like I am.

"You really are acting like this is your first time," I remark.

She shoots me daggers. "It's not, don't worry."

"So what was your first time?" I lower my lashes. "Your first con . . . *or* your first time having sex. I'll accept either answer."

Alexis stops with her back to me, facing the window. "We're not here to have a little chat. We're not friends."

"Okay, okay. Jesus." I grit my teeth. "I'm just trying to act like we're friends at a sleepover. I'm trying to get into character."

But Alexis doesn't buy it for a second. "Don't you know the best way to succeed at this is to not actually become attached to people? That's when mistakes get made. That's when people get hurt."

"I guess that's the difference between us." I turn away, not wanting her to see the emotion on my face. "I'm not really cut out for this world. I *want* to make attachments."

Alexis snorts.

But I don't believe her. I *can't*. So I position myself so we're looking at each other again. "You mean to tell me you and I had absolutely *no* connection? When we were hanging out—when you thought I was different, and when I thought *you* were different—you felt absolutely nothing for me?"

The gooseneck lamp on the side table illuminates her sharp

jawline. A muscle in her cheek twitches. She seems to be gnashing her teeth.

"What happened to you to make you like this?" I ask. "I mean, for me, it's because I always went without. It's not really my parents' fault—they only did what they knew. They weren't smart enough to climb out of their situation. But I wanted to change things. I wanted a better life. Is that what happened to you, too?"

Alexis's mouth is pinched. "You really want to know?" she challenges.

"Yes. I really do."

"Okay. Fine." She turns to me, and her eyes shine in warning. "I didn't *have* parents, Raina. I never had a father. I found my mom's dead body when I was fourteen. Suicide. Pills. She was always a mess. After that, I was in foster care—which means I was abused, picked on, and sexually assaulted. I did whatever I could to survive. I cheated. I stole. I fucked people over. And I learned that you should never trust anybody. The worst thing you can do is make friends, because no one has your best interests in mind."

Her tone is taunting as she tells me this, like she knows just how uncomfortable it will make me, though when she raises her head, her eyes are shiny, maybe with stress, maybe with tears. "You happy now?" she spits, her teeth clamped together. "Is this *bonding* enough for you?"

My jaw trembles. "I . . . I'm sorry," I whisper. "I didn't know."

Boom.

The door to the bedroom flies open. I'm so surprised I back up against the headboard, the blood rushing to my ears. Alexis lets out a scream. A man with a ski mask over his face rushes toward us. "Don't move," he growls. All I can see are his wild, narrowed eyes.

"Don't hurt us!" I whimper. I'm only half acting. Real fear shoots to my gut.

The man aims something black and blocky at us. A gun? I try to breathe. This is just part of the role-play, right? It can't be real.

The man grabs Alexis's purse, then mine, and dumps their contents on the bed. Lipsticks fly everywhere. Alexis's phone hits the ground with a thud. We both beg for mercy, pleading for him not to hurt us. But as the man shifts, it's clear he's turned on. When he grabs me hard, it's not to hurt me, but to ravage me. His hands travel up and down my body. His mouth, surrounded by the woolly mask, travels over my neck, the base of my throat. I don't like it, but I try to get through it. It will all be worth it, I tell myself. Only a few more minutes.

The man turns to Alexis and kisses her, too, but he moves back to me within minutes. His kisses are unwelcome and pushy, all teeth and lips. Aggressively, he takes off my top and slides down my underwear. Out of the corner of my eye, I see the shiny wrapper of a condom. All at once, I'm naked in this dingy, empty room, facing a man in a ski mask. I glance at Alexis, hating that she's witnessing this. I feel small. Undignified.

The man's pants fall to a twisted heap on the floor. He grabs my hips, spins me around, and pushes our bodies together. I shut my eyes, trying to think of something pleasant and innocent. His thrusts are so forceful and rough that the crown of my head slams against the headboard. I accidentally bite down on my tongue and taste blood. I open my eyes for a moment and see my palms flat on the mattress, my boobs flopping, a big stain on the sheets. Revulsion ripples through me.

"Stop," Alexis says suddenly.

He doesn't listen. My head knocks into the headboard again. The lone picture hanging on the wall falls off its nail, clomping to the floor. It doesn't even have glass over the image anymore, and the frame is plastic. I wonder how many other times it's fallen because of this very reason.

"*Stop!*" Alexis growls. "Goddamn it, *stop!*"

The man turns sharply to her. I can smell sweat seeping from his skin.

"We're done," Alexis says.

"Huh?" he grunts. I look at her quizzically, too. He hasn't taken off his mask. It would be better if the camera recorded his face.

But Alexis doesn't seem to care. She crosses her arms over her chest. "This is weird. And it's not worth it."

"Alexis," I murmur impatiently. And then, impulsively, I twist around, sit up, reach forward, and pull off his balaclava. The man flails, trying to grab it, but I whip it across the room. "There," I say to Alexis. "*Now* tell him."

The man frowns. He's much better-looking than I would have expected. I feel like I've seen him before, too—though I don't know where. "Tell me what?" he demands, making an ugly, surly, coitus interruptus face. His penis has gone limp. His chest heaves from exertion and excitement. "Tell me *what?*"

Alexis looks nervous, so I clear my throat. "We're filming you. Everything's on camera. And if you don't want your wife to see—or anyone you work with—we're going to have to negotiate."

The man blinks hard like we've punched him. He wheels backward, covering his penis with his hands. "What the fuck?" he splutters, scrambling to pull on his underwear. Then he looks around the room. "Like hell you're getting a video of me. Where are the cameras?"

I swallow hard. Alexis lowers her eyes. The man leaps off the bed and storms for her, flattening her against the wall. "Where are they? Where the fuck did you hide them?"

Why he's taking this out on Alexis, I'm not sure, but in an instant, she's flat on her back, and this *stranger* is over her, trapping her. His hands aren't on her, but they could be on her in moments. His eyes are wide. His mouth is a straight, angry line.

"*Tell* me!" he pleads.

Terror spikes through me. I leap onto his back, pawing at his T-shirt. He whips around and he shoves me away—not that hard, but the effort surprises me. I tumble to the carpet.

He turns back to Alexis. "*Tell* me," he says again. Alexis shakes her head stubbornly.

"Just tell him," I urge. I'm afraid things are going to escalate. Maybe I should make a run for it.

But then I think of Greg Strasser. How he'd stepped back from me that night in his house, that beatific, pitying smile on his face. How he'd said softly, "You're better than this." It pisses me off that I'm thinking of him right now—it's because of him that I'm in this mess in the first place. But I remember how inspired I'd felt. Someone finally believed in me. Someone had thought I transcended where I came from, how I acted, what I was.

You're better than this.

I launch myself onto the man's back once more, wrapping my arms around his neck and digging my fingers into his eye sockets. He lets out a squeal and rolls onto his side, and Alexis springs up. A sharp elbow to my ribs jolts me away, and when I open my eyes again, the man is coming for me.

His shoulders hunch. His face is flushed with blood. I back up into the corner—with nowhere to run. He advances toward me, hands on his hips. He's at the end of his rope. He's had enough.

35

LYNN

FRIDAY, MAY 5, 2017

It's been a bitch of a drive. Puking up whatever my husband spiked my drink with certainly took the edge off, but I still feel blurry, and twice now I've steered the car into the opposite lane— thank God there isn't any traffic. Part of me wonders if I've even followed the right vehicle, but then I see my husband pull up to a dark house only a few streets over from our own and get out. My vision wobbles. This must be Kit's place. I've never been. It's certainly grand enough, a typical Blue Hill craftsman made of old stone and slate and copper. The yard needs a cut, though. Then again, I'm sure landscaping isn't at the top of Kit's list.

I press my phone to my chest, grateful that I've remembered it in my languid stupor. I can't quite feel my feet on the pavement as I walk up the driveway. Something suddenly stabs at me: My children are at home, *alone*. Am I nuts? Something could happen to them.

But then, perhaps Greg's murderer is *here*.

I reach the front door and hesitate, not sure what to do. Ringing the doorbell seems ridiculous. I twist the knob, and, surprisingly, it opens easily. Idiots. Perhaps in the throes of passion, Kit forgot to lock it behind her.

Acid burns through my chest. I *hate* them.

The first floor of the house is so dark that I need the flashlight app on my phone to move forward. A thud rings out from somewhere above, and I freeze. But when I crane my neck upward, I'm so light-headed, I have to feel the wall for balance. A wave of nausea sweeps over me, and I stop and shut my eyes, gasping in breaths. *You can do this. You have to power through this.*

And then I hear the scream.

It's a yelp—quick, surprised, scared. But it's quickly subdued, almost like someone has clapped a hand over a mouth. The haziness shakes off me. It came from upstairs. Then I hear heavy thuds, the sounds of breath, and then a crash. Is it Patrick in there? Are he and Kit fighting?

Another thud sounds. A sharp crack, like bone hitting wood.

I start to shake.

To think I have any control over him. I'm such a *fool*.

My feet feel like blocks of cement as I haul myself up the stairs. I creak down the hallway, following the sounds. At the end of the hall is a closed door with a little strip of light peeking out from the bottom. My hands tremble as I tap my phone's camera function, getting everything ready. I need to record this—maybe for more reasons than one. But what am I walking in on? What if Patrick turns his attention on me next? I know the same things Kit does, after all.

Maybe it's the drugs in my system, maybe it's the adrenaline coursing through my veins, but when I reach the door, I rap on it hard. The crashes inside continue. They haven't heard me. So I jiggle the knob—it's an old-fashioned crystal knob, probably original to the house. Locked. But I need to get in there. I hear another yelp. Another growl. Someone whispers, "No."

I fumble for my wallet. I find an Amex in one of the front card slots and pull it out, the little hologram chip catching the orange overhead light. I push it into the door, wiggle it appropriately, and I

hear the lock give and feel the doorknob turn. My nerves are crackling. I'm in. I push against the door quietly, but as soon as it's open
even an inch, the sound rushes at me like fire. Growling. *Whimpering.*

Shakily, I press the record button on my phone. I take a tentative
step into the room, wrinkling my nose at a lacy red bra flung haphazardly against the baseboard. My foot kicks something else, too—
something that looks like a black wool hat. I frown at it, something
sparking in my memory. It's not a hat but one of those face masks
one uses in frigid winter weather so as not to get windburn. Patrick
uses it when we go on ski trips in Colorado.

Why has Patrick brought a ski mask?

In the room, a lamp has been knocked to the ground, and light
spills across the carpet. I see the mattress moving, but I don't yet see
bodies. I take another step but then realize my mistake—I've let the
heavy door to the room go instead of carefully shutting it. It bangs
shut noisily, the sound ricocheting off the thickly plastered walls.

The room goes silent. I take another step, my phone outstretched
in front of me.

Then I see a figure. *Two* figures, actually—women, one of them
in the bathroom, the other cowering against a wall. I blink hard,
wondering if this is the drugs at work. But I don't see Kit. I see a
slight, beautiful redhead and a tall, broad-shouldered blonde. They
see me, too. The shock rolls through all of us like wildfire.

Patrick leaps away from the corner, where he's standing with one
of the girls. "*Lynn?*" His pants are around his ankles, though he's
still got on his boxers. He blinks hard at me—not menacingly, exactly, but certainly shocked. "What the hell?"

"You *drugged* me," I whisper. "Who *are* these people? Where's
Kit?"

Patrick's eyes darken. He opens his mouth, but no sound
comes out.

"Put on your fucking clothes!" I gesture at his bare legs. "What
the hell are you doing? Who the hell are these girls? What's with that

mask?" I stab my finger at it. The empty eye and mouth holes look ghastly, ghoulish, on the floor. My skin is snapping. I've never been so disgusted and humiliated in my life. And still: *Where* is Kit?

Patrick yanks up his pants. Behind him, the girls are scrambling to get dressed, too. As they lean over, I see they're both wearing thongs. I also notice that one of them is putting on an Aldrich University T-shirt. It's then that I realize that I know who she is. She sat in the front pew at Greg Strasser's funeral—with Kit's *daughter*.

I glower at Patrick again. "Are these girls even legal?"

Patrick stands in front of them to block my view. "We can talk about this later."

I roar with laughter. "I'm not going anywhere!" I notice that the girls have moved far away from Patrick, all the way to the opposite corner of the room. "Are you two all right?"

The girls have baby skin. Long baby eyelashes. They lower their eyes and nod mutely. Both of them look shaken but not beaten up. The blonde looks more pissed than anything else.

Patrick grunts. "They were trying to get money out of me," Patrick snarls. "These bitches were trying to play me—*us*."

The girls exchange guilty glances. The blonde breathes in. "We made a video. But I'm going to destroy it. I-I promise."

A *video*? But before I can ask, the blonde scuttles over to the television. She reaches on top of the screen and pulls off a little device no bigger than a button. I can see that she's about to drop it into her purse, so I clear my throat.

"Give it here," I say, extending my palm. "If there's anyone who's going to screw Patrick over, it's his wife."

36

LAURA

FRIDAY, MAY 5, 2017

A sign above me flashes that a turnpike interchange is coming up and that I need to get my E-ZPass ready. I fumble for it in the glove compartment before closing my fingers around the hard plastic square. I place it on the dashboard and feel relief as the green light flashes, saying that it still works. The last thing I wanted was to have to slow down and fumble for change. I just want to keep moving.

My plans have changed. On the road, I suddenly had a change of heart: There's no way I can go to my mother's. Ollie would look there first, and then I run the risk of him hurting not just me but my parents as well. So I'm going to drive all the way to New Jersey. I have enough gas for that. From there, I'll buy a plane ticket out of here. Ollie will see the charge on my credit card, but by that time, we'll be long gone.

When I arrive, I'll change my name. Freddie's name. We'll disappear. We *need* to disappear. I hate that I'm leaving behind my family, my job . . . but it's the only way. The only thing that matters to me is Freddie. I glance at him in the rearview mirror, and my heart breaks. *This is the right thing,* I tell myself. Freddie will grow up without a father, but it's better than being around someone who's violent.

I'm sure Ollie killed Greg. I would have never believed it a few weeks ago . . . but then, there's a *lot* I would have never believed a few weeks ago. Like the slap marks on my cheek. And those sharp, acidic words whispered in my ear. This isn't the behavior of a rational man. It isn't even the behavior of someone whose heart is broken. Ollie snapped. Maybe he's always been this way and just hidden it well, I'm not sure—that's something I'll have to work through later. And while I wish I could tell the police what he did, it also doesn't help that Ollie is revered at the station. No one will believe my story—or, at the very least, they'll have to jump through all of the hoops in order to make a conviction stick. And in the time it takes them to do that, Ollie will have his way with me. I probably won't live to see the end of it.

Rain spatters the windshield.

I don't even notice the flashing blue and red lights behind me until they're almost on my tail. At first, I move toward the shoulder, figuring the police car wants to pass me, but he keeps pace, the sirens still whirring. I stare at the gauges on the dashboard. Have I been speeding? Is a taillight out? This is *not* what I need right now.

Nervously, I pull over to the side of the road and stop the car. Freddie's eyes pop open in the back seat, and he starts to whimper. "It's okay, bubba," I coo, rummaging in his diaper bag for a bottle, one of the few things I actually brought with me. I pop it into his mouth and hold it there—he's not old enough to hold it on his own. I remain this way, cramped and twisted, as the police car doors open and two officers step out. *Two?* Is that some sort of new policy? Usually, when people are issued a ticket, they only send one guy . . .

A flashlight beam shines in my face. I roll down the window and offer a polite smile. "Hi, and I'm sorry," I say preemptively. "I had no idea I was speeding, I guess because there's no other traffic out here and I wasn't paying attention—"

"Ma'am," the officer in front interrupts. The glare from the flashlight obscures his face, but I know that he's tall and broad, maybe even broader than my husband. "Can you step out of the car?"

I gesture toward the baby in the back seat. "B-But I'm giving him his bottle. He'll start crying."

The officer's light moves toward the back window. When it shines on Freddie, I feel a surge of protectiveness. "We need you to step out of the car," he repeats.

"Here's my license and registration . . ."

"Ma'am," the second officer orders. "Get out of the vehicle. *Now.*"

I release the bottle from Freddie's lips. No surprise, he starts to wail. "It's okay," I tell him, a hard, solid ball suddenly clogging my throat. Then I unlock the door and step out. The night is cold, and the rain bites at my skin. The officers shine their lights up and down my body, taking in my pajama pants, my untied shoes, my tangled hair. I don't like how long they're looking at me. I don't like how vulnerable I feel, standing on the shoulder.

"What's this all about?" I ask shakily. "Can I get back to my baby now? He needs me."

"Where are you headed just now, Mrs. Apatrea?" the second officer pipes up. Bossily. Angrily, almost. "The middle of the night, with your baby?"

"I . . ." I search their dark, shadowed faces. *How do they know my name?* I haven't given them my information yet. "Why are you asking this? What did I do wrong?"

"We have a report of child endangerment, Mrs. Apatrea. Your husband has a report from a psychiatrist that you're suffering some pretty serious postpartum depression and that you're at risk to harm your child."

"*What?*" I blurt.

"We need to get the baby back home," the first officer says. He takes my wrist, and his big, broad body forms a shield around me, preventing me from running. "And you, too. You need help, Mrs. Apatrea. Your husband is very worried."

My heart bangs in my chest. *Your husband.*

My head starts to spin. I'm afraid I might be sick. And Freddie, in the back seat, has reached a fever pitch. "Y-You can't take me back there," I whimper, the tears streaming down my face. "My husband hurt me! He's dangerous!"

"Ma'am." My eyes have adjusted now, and I can see their faces more clearly. They're craggy, bland, generic, uncaring men, and as they look at me, I can tell they see only what they want to see—what Ollie has told them. The first guy puts his other hand on my shoulder, guiding me toward the waiting vehicle. "The only dangerous person here is you."

37

KIT

SATURDAY, MAY 6, 2017

I sit on the side of my old bed from childhood, staring at the braided rug. There's no way I can sleep. I watch as the clock ticks from 1:20 to 1:21. Then 1:59 to 2:00. Then 2:12 to 2:13.

I haven't heard from the anonymous caller again, but those few words, that bald threat—*I know you did it*—is enough to send my mind spinning. Who was on the other end? Why would they say *I* murdered Greg? I try to reconstruct the night of the benefit as best I can, but it's pointless. The whole night is a jumble of sounds and images I'll never get back, a dark, formless room with a door shut tight.

But if I could open that door a crack, what would be in there?

I was certainly angry enough. Humiliated that Greg had ruined our family. Rejected, too, because I'd expressed again and again that I wanted to save the marriage. And then I'd seen Patrick at the benefit, the fresh lust making things hurt even worse. What might have happened in my yearning, needy, hopeless, irrational brain? Did betrayal plus wanting plus rage plus embarrassment plus extreme intoxication equal murder?

Stop it, I tell myself, punching my pillow. *You didn't do anything.* But

I don't know for sure. I don't have certainty, and it's that tiny shred of doubt that makes me uneasy.

I rise from the bed, pull on a cardigan, and push my feet into a pair of slippers. I can't be in this house right now. I'll take a flashlight, I'll take some pepper spray, but I at least need to stand on my father's front porch and look at the stars.

I creak down the stairs, not wanting to wake the girls. I disarm the alarm system and push open the front door. The air feels good on my skin, and I tilt my face toward the sky. The moon shimmers above me. The only sounds are faint gusts of wind and far-off traffic.

I wonder if the neighborhood was this still the night Greg was killed. I shut my eyes, trying to recall padding across this lawn, poisoned out of my mind. Staggering into the house. Not heading straight into the bathroom but instead into the kitchen and finding Greg at the fridge, casually reaching for a beer. Could we have fought? Maybe everything burst to the surface, and I just . . . snapped? I don't remember, though. There isn't even a glimmer.

I turn and look at my parents' house, the stonework towering toward the sky, the aged copper roof tiles intricately shadowed in the moonlight. I'm sorry, I want to tell my sleeping father. The last thing he needs is a shock to his system. I want to tell my daughters I'm sorry, too. I'm sorry because I don't remember, and I don't have a good excuse, and I can't know for sure if I'm not a killer. And I'm sorry to Willa as well. I dragged her out here. Put her through this. And it turns out it was me all along.

I swallow hard. Plunge my hands into my cardigan pockets and locate my phone. I need to run this by someone. I scroll through my calls and find the number. It rings a few times, and when he picks up, he sounds disoriented. Which—obviously. He was sleeping. It's the dead of night.

"Please come," I tell him, my voice cracked and dry. "There's something we need to talk about."

38

WILLA

SATURDAY, MAY 6, 2017

I snap awake and look around confusedly. It takes me a moment to realize I dozed off on my parents' couch in the back room—I'd wanted to wait up for Kit when she came home to ask where she really was tonight, but I guess my sleepless nights got the best of me. I sit up and rub my eyes. My heart is still banging in my chest. Something woke me. A sound? Kit?

A car engine growls outside. Frowning, I hurry to the front window. Headlights glow on the circle. Kit drifts, sylphlike in a white cardigan, toward an open door of a white SUV. There's a nervous, conflicted look on her face, almost like she isn't sure she wants to get in. The car chugs. It's too dark to see the driver. After a beat, Kit seems to gather her courage and climbs into the seat. The car door slams, and the car peels away noisily, tires screeching.

"Kit!" I cry out uselessly. But there was something so unsettling about the way the car just left the house. It was almost like a . . . *getaway*. Worry spirals through my gut. I know someone with a white SUV: I saw him, his wife, and her baby climb from it the day of

Greg's funeral. Ollie Apatrea. The cop. The *murderer*? Is that *his* car she just climbed inside?

"Oh my God," I whisper, my hand flying to my mouth. Is this because of the call I made to their house earlier? Does Ollie know we know? What on earth did he say to Kit to tell her to get into the car *willingly*? I curse my choice not to text Kit with my hunch about Ollie. News that your dead husband had a child with another woman seemed like a callous thing to find out through text, but maybe I shouldn't have waited. Clearly, Kit trusts Ollie enough to get in the car with him. But she's dead wrong.

I rush down the path, but there's no way I'll catch the car; even before I reach the curb, it's already turned off the street. I scramble back into the house, snapping on lights in the kitchen, wondering what to do. I can't let them get far. I grab the VW keys from the table and hurry to the garage. The engine springs to life, and I'm backing out of the driveway and turning in the same direction the vehicle went—toward the college. If I drive quickly, I can hopefully catch the SUV. Where could it be going?

With one hand, I stab at the green phone button on my screen and dial Kit's number, putting the call on speaker. But it rings and rings, then goes to voice mail. I press END, then do it again. Voice mail. My stomach swoops with worry and dread. Do I call a third time, or is this making the matter worse? If Ollie is the driver—and if Ollie is the murderer—he might hurt Kit faster if he's aware someone knows she's missing.

Far ahead, two taillights blaze at a stop sign. It's *them*. I ease up on the gas now that I've got them in my sights—and then it hits me. What am I *doing*? Am I really going to do whatever this is, alone? As much as I want to handle this all on my own, maybe I'm being foolish.

My eyes are still on the car—and my sister's shadowy figure in the passenger seat. I feel around for my phone in my cardigan pocket. Glancing from screen to road and then back to screen again, I click on the window I need, and then the phone number. The time between rings feels like an eternity. I hold in a breath, praying that he answers.

"Hello? Willa?" And here's Paul's groggy voice, full of concern and confusion. "I-Is everything okay?"

I swallow hard. "No. I need your help."

39

KIT

SATURDAY, MAY 6, 2017

For a few minutes of the drive, I don't speak. My heart is thumping with doubt. It's like there's a Ping-Pong match going on inside my head: One minute, I worry I killed my husband. The next, I'm certain I never could have done such a thing. Does even suggesting my guilt open doors I should keep shut? Maybe I should keep quiet?

Except that phone call. Someone's trying to get to me. I need someone on my side.

So I look to my left to the man I've dragged out of bed at this time of night. Patrick. "Thanks for coming," I say shakily.

He gives me a sidelong look but says nothing. It makes me uneasy. I climbed into Patrick's waiting SUV because I thought he'd be full of concern and sympathy and comforting words with what I'm going through, but the vibe in the car is the opposite of that. Also strange: He hasn't asked me yet what I want to talk *about*. Is it possible he knows already? Is it possible the person on the other end of the line called him, too?

I eye Patrick cautiously. His eyes are vibrating. His hair is mussed.

He looks like he's been electrocuted. I clear my throat. "So, um, were you awake anyway, when I called?"

Patrick speeds through a traffic light without answering. Blue Hill is eerie this time of night, and Patrick's white SUV, when reflected in the shop windows, looks like a drifting ghost. At the main intersection before the college, he reaches over and gives me a small nod of recognition. "Actually, yes," he finally says. "It's been a weird night."

"Me too," I say, the unsettled feeling in my gut sharpening. The caller *did* reach him, then. That has to be what this is about.

And yet he still doesn't ask me what's wrong.

We take a sharp turn on a yellow light and head up a road I haven't been on in years. It leads to a back neighborhood of newer homes, but we pass though the main entrance and head toward a sign that points to a wooded park with a running trail, an outdoor ice rink, and a dog run. I know this park. Years ago, my mother, Willa, and I used to skate at the rink. We were all terrible skaters, holding on to one another for balance, relishing the moment when we'd completed a few laps and could dive back to the benches and drink hot chocolate.

Patrick pulls into the lot and chooses a space by the entrance to the trail. After he hits the button to cut the engine, he climbs out of the vehicle swiftly and with purpose, as though he's keeping to some agenda. He walks to the front of the car, hands on his hips, and stares at the towering trees.

I follow him, my sneakers crunching in the rough gravel. Wind snaps around us. The woods are as dark as death. "This sure is private enough," I say, laughing nervously.

All I can see of Patrick is the edge of his profile, backlit by the moon. "I just figured we both needed somewhere quiet to think." His voice is empty. Hollow. I think of those old horror movies where a patient's brain has been removed and yet he can still talk, respond, react. But his whole essence has been removed.

It hurts to swallow. I walk around to face him, forcing him to meet my gaze. "Is everything all right? You're kind of acting—"

But I'm interrupted as my phone lets out a beep. I glance at it, terrified it might be something from the strange caller, but, to my surprise, Lynn Godfrey's name pops up on the screen.

Patrick notices before I can tuck the phone back into my pocket. His features darken, and he looks at me with disdain. "Why is *she* calling you?"

"I-I have no idea," I stammer.

"Are you guys *friends* now?"

"No!" I stare at him like he's gone crazy. "Of course not!"

"So she hasn't spoken to you tonight?" His eyes are wild. "She hasn't *told* you anything?"

His face is so close that I feel the need to back up a few inches. What is he *talking* about? "No," I say. "Told me what? Did you and Lynn have a fight?"

Patrick turns away. His jaw is twitching, and he's drumming his fingers on his thighs. "Lynn's insane. Don't believe a word she says."

My stomach sours. I don't like the way Patrick said *insane*. "Okay . . ."

"And she's onto us. She knows." His mouth twists into a smirk.

I bite down hard on my lip. "H-How?"

He rounds on me, admonishingly. "What possessed you to wear that bracelet to fucking *work*, right in front of her?"

I struggle to think. "The . . . bracelet? That's how she figured it out?"

"Did you just want to rub it in her face a little? Need to mark your territory?"

"Patrick, what the hell?" I screech. This all feels wrong: standing in this dark, deserted park, Patrick's jitteriness, that walking-on-eggshells feeling in my gut, the fact that I haven't even talked about *my* thing, which is why we're supposed to be out here in the first place. "I haven't talked to Lynn. I'm sorry she found out. I'm sorry I wore the bracelet. But why would she recognize it?"

Patrick breathes out. He looks like he might shatter into pieces, but then he turns away and puts his head in his hands. I stare at him for a few beats, trying to figure out what the hell is going on. My thoughts zoom back to Lynn. God, she must have lost it when she put the pieces together. I can't imagine the rage that whipped through her—or the revenge she has planned. I mean, if I got a sleeping pill in my cocktail just for stealing her clients, what does she have in store now that I've stolen her man?

But suddenly, I realize: I *know* what Lynn has in store. She's already done it. *She* was the voice on the other end of that phone, insinuating I killed Greg. It's brilliant, actually—she knows I have no memory because she's the one who drugged me. She also knows that if I begin to believe what I've done, I'll either lose my mind or confess. I'll go either to a mental hospital or to prison. And then, Lynn will have Patrick back to herself.

It's elegant, actually. Diabolical. The relief floods over me, too, because as soon as I let in this little crack, I realize how crazy the notion ever was. Of course I didn't. Even in my wildest dreams, even in my drunkest state, I wouldn't snap like that.

Except why is Patrick acting so strangely, then? Just because I accidentally wore the bracelet and Lynn figured it out? I guess that *is* kind of a big deal. His marriage is crumbling. He probably didn't expect it to happen. And he definitely didn't expect us to get caught—especially by his scheming, conniving wife.

My phone buzzes once more. I wince when I see Lynn's name once again on the screen. Instead of calling, this time she's written a text. I don't intend to read it, but my settings are such that the message appears on my locked screen, like it or not:

I know you're with him right now. Get out of there. He has no alibi
for the night your husband was killed. He isn't safe.

Shivers zing through me. I press the phone to my chest to hide it. My heart is thudding. This is another one of Lynn's tricks—it has to be. She's just trying to drive Patrick and me apart, that's all.

But then something strange occurs to me. After the funeral, Patrick found me and said, *I know* you *didn't kill Greg*. He'd seemed so certain. So resolute. At the time, I'd thought he was being chivalrous, even romantic . . . but how did he know for sure?

Don't think that way. But all at once, I can't help it. I consider what happened at the benefit, too. Patrick had been so shocked when he saw me, but later, he told me that he'd felt something change in him that night—and that he had to have me, no matter what. Patrick left the benefit so early that night. Ditched Lynn, actually. Where had he gone?

My heart goes still.

Patrick lifts his head. I don't know what he sees in my expression, but whatever it is, it must give me away. He knows what I suspect. He knows I might *believe* it. Hell, maybe he thought I knew this before I even got in the car—maybe he thought *this* was what I wanted to talk to him about.

Panic overtakes his features. He grabs the phone from my hands and tosses it into the woods. I see the glow of the screen disappear into darkness. "What the hell?" I shriek.

"She did get to you," Patrick cries. "And you . . . believe her."

"Patrick." I have my hands clutched against my chest like armor. "I-I . . . I won't say anything. I won't tell anyone. I'm sure it was a mistake."

He steps closer. He seems so tall, so imposing, and all of a sudden, I can't breathe. "You really think I did it? You really think I'm that kind of person." He looks so astonished. Then he points at me. "I was hoping you called me to talk about it and say you *didn't* believe. And I came to get you so we could run away. Be together. Escape all this . . . *bullshit*." He shakes his head, his expression sharpening. "Forget that now. You're just as judgmental and quick to accuse as the rest of them."

Hot tears stream down my face. I don't know what to think. But I don't like being out here, all alone. I don't like the fraught feeling between us. And also—I don't like the doubt that's now in my mind. I need to get out of here. I feel the need to *run*.

"Freeze!"

At first I think I've imagined the voices, but as I look across the parking lot, I see two dark shapes. The shadows scuttle out from the bushes, and as they come closer, I recognize a familiar woman's shape. The man she's with points a gun at Patrick.

I blink hard. *"Willa?"*

Willa shoots me a grateful look, but then steps forward. "Freeze," she barks at Patrick, who's backed away from me. "Don't fucking move, asshole." But then she stops. "Wait a minute. Who are *you?*"

40

WILLA

SATURDAY, MAY 6, 2017

I stare at the man next to Kit. He's got a full head of hair, narrow shoulders, and a square jaw—in other words, nothing like bald, hulking Ollie Apatrea. As he lifts his head, it all crystallizes. It's *him*. The husband. Patrick Godfrey.

Kit runs to me, and I wrap my arms around her protectively. "What the hell is going on?" I ask.

"Don't let him leave." Kit points shakily to the shadows. "Call the police. He's the killer!"

Patrick lowers his hands for a millisecond, but Paul straightens the gun, and he stiffens once more. I balked at Paul bringing a rifle tonight—his dad used to use it to hunt, he said, and though he never used it, he still knows how to fire it.

Patrick glares at all of us. "Look, will you put that thing down? I didn't kill anyone!"

Kit is shaking her head. "Lynn just texted me. Patrick has no alibi for the night Greg was stabbed. He has motive."

"Of *course* she's going to text you that!" Patrick roars. "That's what I was just trying to explain! She hates me! She wants to break us up!"

I frown. So Kit *is* with him, then. I don't know where to direct my whirling thoughts, what to concentrate on first. Then Patrick adds, "And I do have an alibi for that night, okay?"

"Oh yeah?" Paul calls, the gun still raised. "And what would that be?"

Patrick shakes his head as if to say *I can't believe I've gotten myself into this.* A long few seconds elapse. There's no sound out tonight, not even any bugs.

"I was at this after-hours club," Patrick finally mutters. "I stopped at home first, and then I went there."

"What kind of after-hours club?" I demand.

His shoulders heave. "It's just this . . . place. I'm part of this online community that gets together every once in a while. I knew they were getting together that night, and I made an excuse to my wife, and . . ."

He lowers his head. A sour feeling rushes through me. I once did an investigative report on certain after-hours clubs; a woman who frequented one was murdered. By the shame on Patrick's face, I'm pretty sure he wasn't going to one to play poker and drink. He was going to have orgies, maybe some sex play. Bondage, extreme violence, rape fantasies, and worse. The interviews nauseated me, plunging me back into memories I didn't want to consider. I'd almost had to give up the story.

But this is someone Kit was *sleeping with*? I glance at her, registering the shock on her face. It's clear she didn't know, either. She takes a small step back, and her lips pucker into disgust. I can see it all over her face: *Who* are *you?* But she doesn't say it out loud.

"I didn't touch Strasser," Patrick goes on. "If you need a witness to corroborate that, I have someone you can call."

His eyes lower. I exchange a glance with Paul. I presume he means the woman he was with that night. I check Kit's expression about all of this once more. She looks shattered.

"I just didn't want to admit where I really was," Patrick grumbles.

"I have a wife. Kids. A business reputation." He glances uneasily at Paul. "Can you stop pointing that gun at me?"

Paul goes to lower the rifle, but I catch his arm, telling him to wait. "You were still hurting my sister," I growl. "Care to explain *why*?"

I watch as Patrick's eyes widen and he holds his arms in front of his chest like a shield. But then Kit sighs. "Forget it, Willa," Kit mumbles. "Let's just get out of here."

Patrick makes a small, beleaguered noise, but Kit doesn't look at him. I nod for Paul to stand down. Patrick hurries into the SUV I'd mistaken for Ollie's; within seconds, he's out of the lot. Darkness swarms over us. Paul and I had parked our vehicles down the road, and without any lights, I can barely see a few inches in front of my face.

But I can still sense Kit's presence beside me. She's oddly still, like she's thinking—or trying not to cry. I try to process what I've just witnessed—and how Kit must be taking it. I have so many questions. How long has Patrick meant something to her? A while? Before Greg? And who steals into the woods at two in the morning?

But I can't ask any of that, because Kit's shaking so badly. I touch her shoulder. "Are you okay?"

"No," Kit says. Her voice is thick, maybe on the verge of collapse. Had she *loved* this guy? I feel hurt that she felt she couldn't tell me about him. I feel heartbroken, too, that he's turned out to be such a dick.

I reach over and hug her hard. Kit's body is stiff, but I can feel her heart beating quickly through her thin chest. "Thank you for coming," she whispers. "I don't know how you figured it out, but . . . thank you. That guy . . . he was a big mistake, I guess." She starts to walk into the woods. "He threw my phone in here. Can you help me look for it?"

I hesitate a moment—does her phone *really* matter right now? But it also seems easier just to look for it, so I switch on my phone's flashlight and shine it over the forest floor. "You know, we followed you because we thought you'd gotten into someone else's car. The man I'm pretty sure *did* kill Greg," I say softly.

Kit's eyes widen. "W-Who?"

Somewhere in the distance, a large truck rumbles down the road; because of the stillness, it seems so much louder than usual. "Ollie Apatrea."

Kit is bent over, peering into the fallen leaves, but when I say this, she rises and stands very still. It takes Kit a minute to wrap her head around it. "The cop?"

I nod. My heart is beating fast. There's so much that I haven't told her yet. So much I wasn't even *sure* of, though when I floated my theory to Paul just now—going through the dates of Laura's tryst with Greg, outlining the exact conception date of her baby, telling him about Ollie's hostility on the phone when I tried to call his wife—he said my hunch seemed right. But once again, this will be another blow for Kit. Maybe the *worst* blow. It means her husband has a child out there. It means another secret she has to absorb.

But I take a breath, and I tell her anyway. After I'm finished, Kit slumps to the cold ground and is hugging her knees. "Jesus. Are you sure?"

"We aren't, unfortunately." I glance at Paul, who has followed us into the woods. "And it's sticky because Ollie's a respected officer—if we go to the detectives, they might be less likely to look into him, I'm not sure. So we'll need some kind of proof."

"What kind of proof?" Kit asks.

"I don't know," I say. "But I'll figure it out."

Kit nods, but then adds, "Just make sure it doesn't impact the baby." She makes a strange noise at the back of her throat. "I've *met* that baby. Those blue eyes. I mean, I never *thought* . . . but it was right in front of me. All along."

We nod quietly. Then, Paul breathes in. "There." He shines his phone's flashlight on something wedged in the leaves. It's the edge of Kit's glittery iPhone case. She pounces on it and presses it to her chest. I feel grateful we were able to solve *something*.

After that, we slowly walk Kit back to the VW. Paul heads back to his own car, but before he can get there, I grab his sleeve. "Hey. Thanks."

He turns and looks at me. "Of course," he says.

There's a lump in my throat the size of a baseball. There's so much more that I want to say, but I don't know how to say it. I realize the preciousness of finding a man who will wake up from a dead sleep in the middle of the night to drive to an abandoned park with you to save your sister—and that's *after* you've rejected him. I realize how good a person he could be for me—for so many reasons, including helping me through the things I'm keeping from him. But that's just the thing—I've never considered *anyone* helping me.

I reach out and give his hand a squeeze. It's all I can do right now. Tomorrow I'll call him, and we'll talk more, but now I have to get my sister home. Paul seems to understand this, and he waves at both of us and disappears into his car. I don't really remember the drive home except that it was very quiet. Kit sat slumped in the passenger seat, arms clenched tightly across her breasts. I keep picturing the strange, angry man in the woods, trying to configure him with someone Kit could love. It just goes to show there are so many sides to a person. It's always so hard to know whom to trust.

We pull alongside the curb and Kit leans into me one more time, letting out a whimper that seems to be her way of saying thanks. "Come on," I say, climbing out of the car. "Let's get to bed." We walk across the lawn arm in arm, shivering in the middle-of-the-night chill. The police car sitting at the back of the driveway has its lights off, which is why I don't notice it at first. That's what I'll tell myself later, anyway. It's only when I hear a slam and footsteps ringing out that I whirl around.

"Freeze!" voices bark. "Hands up!"

Kit and I stop in our tracks. They're right next to us now,

grabbing my arm, twisting Kit around, and—inexplicably—snapping handcuffs on her wrists. "What's going on?" Kit bleats, trying to wrench away. "I'm Kit Manning! I *live* here!"

"We know you're Kit Manning," one of the officers says, pinning Kit's arms behind her back. "We've been looking for you."

Kit's eyes bounce all over the place. "Why?"

"Ms. Manning, you're under arrest for the murder of Greg Strasser. We found the murder weapon in your garage."

41

WILLA

SATURDAY, MAY 6, 2017

"This is impossible," I repeat again and again as I pace around the police station waiting area the following morning. "Freaking impossible."

Then I look helplessly at a man named Colton Browne. He's Kit's lawyer, a fact I only vaguely recall my father sharing with me when I first came into town. It's my first time meeting the guy. He's dressed in a suit and bow tie as though this is his normal attire for a Saturday. He also looks a little bewildered, like he isn't ready to defend someone who's on trial for murder. It doesn't give me much confidence.

"Can't you see what's taking them so long?" I hiss at him. The guy's sitting comfortably in a chair in the waiting area like he's hoping to take a little nap.

Browne glances toward the closed door that leads to the booking area, a bunch of interrogation rooms, and the jail. My poor sister spent the night in a *jail*. And that was after they took her mug shots, fingerprinted her, and filed her into the system. Now we're just waiting around until the magistrate gets off his lazy ass this morning and decides to hear her case.

But there *is* no case. It's such bullshit. Clearly, *clearly* the kitchen knife, with the dried blood on its blade and with Kit's fingerprints on the handle—because of *course* Kit's fingerprints are on the handle, *she used it to cook with*—had been planted. Obviously, Ollie took the knife with him the night he'd murdered Greg. Maybe he held on to it for a while because he felt conflicted—he wanted Greg dead, but perhaps he didn't necessarily want an innocent person charged. But I have a weird feeling my phone call changed his mind. How he figured out I was onto him, I'm not sure. But once he knew I'd put two and two together, he dropped the knife into the garage, called in an anonymous tip, and we were off and running.

The lawyer's phone beeps, and he studies the screen. "That's your dad. He's on his way. He'll attend the bail hearing, and then we'll get her out. It'll all be over soon."

But not soon enough. I shift closer to the lawyer. "Look, someone else killed Greg. I might have proof."

His eyes widen. "*Who?*"

I give a sidelong glance to the young cop at the front desk *clacking* on his computer keyboard. I'm not so idiotic that I'm going to accuse a fellow officer in a police station. "Greg impregnated another man's wife," I whisper. "And I think the husband found out about it . . . and snapped. We could run a paternity test to make sure."

Colton looks skeptical. "Are you *sure*?"

Of course I'm not sure—if I was, I wouldn't be sitting on my ass, helpless. But I've done enough reporting on murders and jealous spouses and terrible crimes that these sorts of things begin to take on a pattern. If we had proof the baby was Greg's, it would be a great start. But why would Laura offer her baby up as a piece of evidence? I don't know if *she* knows Ollie knows. Nor do I have any idea how she would take the news that her husband killed a man. For all I know, she will want to protect him. Even warn him that I'm onto him.

Browne eyes me with pity. "I hate to say this; you might need to start really considering the fact that Kit might have done it."

Bile rises in my throat. "Are you kidding me?" I rise and slam out of the building. *Note to self. Find Kit a new fucking lawyer.*

I walk across the parking lot, unlock the car, and climb in. Kit's handbag, an expensive leather bucket that gapes open at the top, is still in here from last night. Inside it, I see her leather wallet, a pouch full of makeup, a pack of Trident gum. Her phone's tucked into a little pocket in the side; the screen keeps lighting up with texts. I haven't checked the news this morning, but I bet there are reports that she's been taken into custody. Are these texts from nosy people seeing if it's true?

I glance at the phone, feeling curious . . . about more than just the texts. What if there's a message buried in there that indicates culpability? Maybe I have it all wrong—and she and Patrick planned something together? But no. I don't trust that Patrick guy, but I do trust Kit. I really do. Yes, she was hiding the Patrick thing from me . . . which is disappointing. But she doesn't have it in her to kill. And she'd certainly never devise a scheme to run away, leave her daughters.

Tires crunch. In the rearview, I notice my dad's BMW pulling into the lot. My father's, Sienna's, and Aurora's faces flash behind the windows, their expressions grave. My heart aches for all of them. I know I should wait with them for Kit's hearing, except it feels so inactive. I want to do something beyond sit on a bench and wait for a judge to decide Kit's fate. I need to *prove* something.

I scan the parking lot. Lines of police cars flank the perimeter, but what I figure are the officers' civilian vehicles sit farther to the back near a small grassy island and a picnic table. In a sea of vehicles, I instantly locate the white Subaru that Ollie and Laura Apatrea climbed out of the morning of the funeral. He's here, then. In this very building. Working on the weekend. A shiver runs from my neck all the way to my tailbone.

I get out of the car, but instead of heading toward the main entrance with my family, I walk to the Subaru and peer inside. The inside has been freshly vacuumed; not a single receipt or gum wrapper remains in the cupholders. The baby seat in the back looks like it's just come out of the box. If Ollie tracked evidence into his vehicle the night he killed Greg, he cleaned it up. Luminol spray would show stray droplets of blood, but it wasn't like I had access to that right now. Maybe I could *get* access, somehow? Maybe Colton Browne would have an idea?

I stride back to the station. When my phone rings, I pick it up without checking the caller ID. "Willa." It's Paul. "I just heard about Kit. Where are you?"

Guilt stabs through me. So Kit *is* news, then. I feel bad that I haven't told Paul myself. "At the station," I admit.

"Do you want company?"

"Wait, no," I say. My mind scrambles. It's better if I work alone with this one. Paul was helpful with tailing Kit last night, but this Ollie stuff . . . I don't want to drag him into something dangerous. "I'm about to go into a magistrate meeting. Can I call you later?"

"Oh." Paul sounds a little disappointed. "Yeah. Sure."

I squeeze my eyes shut, feeling awkward and shitty, because all Paul has done for the past week is help me, and I don't want him to think I'm pushing him away. "I *do* want you here," I add. "There are too many people here as it is. I'll just call you and let you know how it goes, and then we'll think about next steps." I'm careful to use *we*—to let him know that he's still included.

But I've lied. I didn't want him to stay away because of the crowd. I didn't want his company because I have no intention of going into the magistrate's office. And, as luck would have it, when I push into the lobby, it's empty. I guess the magistrate was ready for my family early. This rules out asking Browne about luminol, but maybe I can explore another avenue now that I'm free to investigate without my family asking questions.

I approach the front desk and clear my throat. The officer working there has the face of a high school kid playing dress-up in a cop uniform. "Is there a larger restroom than the public one in the lobby?" I ask, trying to sound sheepish. "Maybe something with a room that gives someone a little privacy?" I mean, there's no way I can just ask to see Officer Apatrea. He'd see that coming from a mile away.

The kid looks at me quizzically, and so I add, sotto voce, "I'm waiting to hear the results of my sister's bail hearing, but I'm a nursing mother, and I really need to pump." I don't know what made me think of leaky boobs being the very thing that would embarrass a kid this age the most, but by the mortified look on his face, I think I've hit the jackpot.

He tugs uncomfortably at his collar. "Well, it's against station policy to let civilians behind the gated door without special permission."

"Please?" And then, yes, I touch my breasts. I'm fully against this sort of manipulation, normally, but I figure it's an emergency.

The kid is turning red. He thumbs the door. "There's a handicapped stall in the women's room for the staff. We'll have to check on you every ten minutes or so, but is that good enough?"

"Perfect," I shoot him a grateful look. Something else buoys my spirits, too: Behind him, on a printed chart, are the cube and office numbers for everyone who works in the building. Oliver Apatrea is there in plain, bold ink. *Office 205*.

Now I know where to go.

42

WILLA

SATURDAY, MAY 6, 2017

I climb to the second floor. No one else in this precinct works on Saturdays, it seems, as every door I pass is tightly locked. Some of the hallway lights aren't even on. But the door to room 205 stands open. I inch against the wall outside it, trying not to breathe. Is Ollie in there? Is this crazy?

After a few seconds, I muster the courage to peek into the room. Ollie's chair is empty. Light from a single banker's lamp shines on his desk. My pulse rocks even in my eyeballs.

Slowly, I tiptoe inside. Pictures of Ollie's son fill the bookshelves. One newborn shot, wrinkled and baby bird–mouthed on a pale blue blanket. Another shows Ollie proudly holding the baby against his chest, his big hand splayed along the baby's tiny back. A more recent one on his desk shows the baby sitting up, giving the camera a gummy smile and popping his big, brilliant, blue eyes wide.

I mean—those *eyes*. Of course Ollie knows it.

A click sounds, and I freeze, my fingers spread wide at my sides. Nothing. *You're okay,* I tell myself. *Nothing's going to hurt you.*

Drawing deep, even breaths, I head for Ollie's desk. File folders lie in disarrayed stacks, some of them open, some of them fastened closed. Ollie has two computer monitors, though they both show Excel spreadsheets that mean nothing to me. If only I could click over to his e-mail.

A clock ticks on the wall. When will the young cop at the front desk come looking for me? When will they send out an APB that the woman who'd received special permission to use a breast pump in privacy has gone missing?

I scan the room. Ollie's police cap sits atop a small filing tray. There's an assortment of pens splayed near the keyboard. Three mostly empty coffee cups perch near the window. I lunge for a red ceramic mug with the Starbucks logo emblazoned on the side and drop it into my tote. It has DNA on it for sure. I could find a lab to analyze it, and then get my hands on the forensics report of the crime scene. Ollie couldn't have cleaned up *everything* as well as he cleaned the murder weapon. Something has to turn up.

I back up, itching to leave, when a gaping file folder near Ollie's second monitor catches my eye. There's a name written on the top tab. *My* name. *Willa Manning.*

I do a double take. What is *this*? I move toward it. With one trembling pointer finger, I open it up. And . . .

"Excuse me?"

Ollie's bulky shape fills the doorway. I jerk away from his desk, hiding my hands behind my back. A strange, high-pitched, borderline hysterical laugh comes from somewhere deep inside me. "Um, hi. I . . . I was just leaving."

"Willa Manning." Ollie looks surprised. "*This* is interesting."

His tone stops my heart. He knows why I'm here, obviously. And suddenly, this floor seems dangerously desolate. I strain to hear sound elsewhere in the station, but the air is airlessly, porously still.

I try to push around Ollie, but he shoots out his elbows, blocking the door. "How'd you get up here?"

He's at least a head taller than I am—so tall, in fact, I can see up his nostrils. His chest is solid and leaden, and brute strength seems to crackle from within. But I can't be afraid of him. Not now.

I meet his gaze. "I was looking for something."

He nods. "And did you find it?"

"Maybe." *As soon as I test that DNA on the coffee cup, you're dead.*

"So how much did you read? Is my research correct?"

I frown. *Research?* What does he mean? I notice Ollie's gaze drifting over to the pile of folders on his desk. On the very top, probably now marred with my fingerprints, is the file with my name on it.

I blink, trying to understand. *Research.* Research . . . about *me?* And then it hits me. Oh my God. Oh my *God.*

I'm so stunned, I can't quite believe it at first. I step backward. My vision tunnels. There's absolutely no way Ollie could have a file on me about *that.*

Ollie's knuckles make a loud crack on the doorjamb. He knows, and he knows that *I* know. And then he says, "Did you know I grew up here, Willa? Well, not in Blue Hill proper—I'm not from that side of the tracks—but on the outskirts. But I hung out with Blue Hill kids my whole life, partied with guys at Aldrich. I went to a lot of frat parties, in fact."

It feels as though the blood has drained from my body. I wheel around, needing to escape from what I'm afraid he's going to say next. I look for a window.

"Now hold on a second," he says, lightly touching my wrist. "Let me finish. First off, if you think I'm *that* guy, you're wrong. I wouldn't do that to a woman. But I was at that same party. I only found out about what they did afterward—it's not like they did it to the girls out in the open."

It feels like I've swallowed razor blades. This can't be happening. *Please tell me this isn't happening.* "I don't know what you're talking about," I try to say, though the words sound garbled, nonsensical.

Ollie ignores me. "But the morning after, I saw this guy smooth-talking a couple of skittish girls as they left. Him being like, *It's all good, nothing bad happened.* One of them was you."

I quiver. My mouth opens and closes soundlessly, like a fish.

"And then I asked the dude what it was all about. He laughed, told me everything, though he couched it as 'they were asking for it, they loved it, it was a good time.'" He shakes his head, disgusted. "I guess he wasn't afraid *I'd* say anything—his dad was, like, the CEO of some billion-dollar company, and my dad was working part-time security."

The humiliation rakes through me like a trail of slime. "I don't know what you're talking about," I insist again. "You have me confused with someone else."

But Ollie snorts like I've told a joke. "Nah, I remember you from that party. Those dudes were such idiots—didn't even realize you were the new president's daughter. But I did."

"I don't . . ." I whisper, closing my eyes. But I can't deny it anymore. Not when it's so clear he knows. It is horrifying, but he knows. The memories pound me, wet and hot, not just flickers anymore but with true, hard edges.

God, it was long ago. I certainly wasn't the type of girl who went to frat parties—because, Jesus, frat parties were for idiots. But this girl I knew from the punk club, Andrea, said it might be "ironically fun." And so I'd thought, *What the hell?*

Ironically fun. I dressed up like a girl going to a frat party, buying a tight red dress from Goodwill, applying sparkly eye shadow goopily all over my lids, sliding on platform heels, and practicing my dumb-girl laugh. This would be a performance piece, I figured. I'd be an undercover reporter. When I crossed the threshold into the house, I must have passed the skank test, because the frat guys— brothers? I didn't fucking know—looked at me approvingly. Someone handed me a beer, and I chugged it.

For a while, it *was* fun. I drank beers. Guys came up to me and said they liked my dress, my shoes, my tits, my ass—totally unapologetically, like they thought they were being chivalrous and loving. It was all so despicable, but strangely intriguing—I felt like I'd gone undercover into a strange new land.

But then the room tilted. I was drunk so suddenly, in a sickening whoosh. I laughed loudly, found myself taking part in one conversation and then abruptly I was elsewhere, talking to someone else. Eventually I found myself with someone cute. He was tall with a face like a heartthrob on a reality dating show. Not my kind of guy, but then, I wasn't really in my right mind.

I rose to my tiptoes, scanning the crowd for Andrea, but I couldn't find her. I should have left then, but the guy I was talking to placed a hand on my arm like he owned me. *No. You can't leave yet.* I almost slapped him—I certainly wanted to. But my limbs felt unsteady, and my aim was off. I felt weak. Scared, even. I'd never been scared of anything in my life.

What happened next was a toxic, confused blur: that same guy taking me by the hand, kissing me. I kissed him back at first, but then I had enough. Except the guy didn't take no for an answer. We were in a dark hallway. The music was far away, a distant bass line. He backed me into a dark room even though I kept slurring that I wanted to go home.

My butt on the mattress. My shoes falling off with a *thunk*. I tried to fight because I'm a fucking fighter and this did *not* happen to people like me—liberated women, strong women, women who didn't take any shit.

And then. The feeling of being split open. Wanting to scream, maybe actually screaming, but the sound being swallowed up by laughter and music and indifference.

Later, I woke up in a twin bed with dark sheets in a room I'd never seen before. I was wearing the short, trampy red dress from the thrift store, though the skirt had been hiked over my naked butt. It was like someone had used me up and then tossed me away.

As soon as I sat up, pain rippled through my body. A half memory rushed back, and I gasped. I heard snippets of loud music from the night before. I tasted the beer on the roof of my mouth. And then pain rocketed through me. I clutched my throat, remembering someone pressing his weight on me. Remembering screaming, fighting. The rest of the evening rolled back in vomitus, disjointed pieces. Except it couldn't have happened to me. There was no way.

The hallway of the frat house was eerily silent. The living room was trashed with empty cups and bottles, cigarette butts, and an inflatable dildo sticking out of a lampshade. People were snoring on couches and chairs and even the sticky, grimy floor—was Ollie one of them? He must have been.

I wanted to throw up again at the sight of them. Had they all known what had happened to me? Did they just not give a shit?

A kid on the couch opened one eye. "Hey." Then he sat up straighter. "*Oh*. Hey."

He had broad shoulders and squinty eyes. The day before, I might have found him somewhat hot . . . but now, he repulsed me. I didn't think this was the guy who had hurt me the night before, but what if he'd watched? Because suddenly, I had the distinct feeling that other people were in the room as witnesses. Cheering. Laughing.

"Sleep okay?" The guy walked around the couch toward me. He was at least six three. His biceps were gigantic. There was something predatory about his smile. "Want some coffee? Hair of the dog?"

Get away from me, I wanted to scream. But I felt dizzy, like I might pass out. Fight or flight—I'd learned about it in health class. *Please don't faint,* I willed.

The guy must have sensed my fear because he stopped. "Hey now. You're okay, aren't you?" When I didn't answer, he frowned. "There's cool-girl code about what goes on here, you know." His smile morphed. "You're a cool girl, right? You certainly *seem* cool."

"Y-Yes." By this time, I'd backed up to the door. There was a menacing smirk on the guy's face, like he found all of this entertaining.

Stop thinking about it, I scream at my brain now, but it's like Ollie hit a switch. Here are all the thoughts that have been crowding my mind for years, suddenly running free.

"I didn't think much about you until recently, though," Ollie tells me, dragging me back to the present. "After the hack broke, when President Manning gave all those speeches. I remembered what those guys did to President Manning's daughter. And then I realized nothing had ever come of that. It seemed even more poignant after those rape stories surfaced."

I shut my eyes.

"And *then* I saw you at Manning's funeral—and I was like, *Holy shit. I remember her.* You've barely aged—good for you. And you seemed uncomfortable being back here, almost like you were so afraid it was going to happen to you again. Am I right?"

My lips part, but it's like my voice box has been slashed. I need out of here.

"Why didn't you go to your father about it? Bigwig at the school, you'd think he would have been able to help."

Rage fills me. "Why didn't *you* say anything? You were there, too. If you thought it was so disgusting, you should have turned them in."

"I wish I could have, but I didn't see it happen. Besides, those guys would have lawyered up and made me look like a fool. I wouldn't have had a leg to stand on." He leans in. "Is that what your father said to you, too? That the frat has a lot of political pull within the school, and you shouldn't cross them? Lotta big donors within those ranks. Lotta old-boy money."

"No." I wrench my head away. "It wasn't like that."

I'd thought about saying something to my father, afterward. I *wanted* to. In an ideal world, my mother would still be alive, and I could have gone to her first . . . but unfortunately, I didn't have that luxury. It wasn't that I was afraid of confronting my father . . . but no matter how eloquent my monologue, I couldn't blurt it out. It gave my dad such pride when I brought home stellar grades, high SAT scores—and despite my cynicism about a lot of things, that still mattered to me. I didn't want to cause him complications or strife; I dreaded to think how this might affect his brand-new position if we prosecuted. For all I knew, the guy who raped me had parents whose donations to the school had built the new science building last year. I wasn't stupid. I knew political connections were everything at Aldrich. I also knew how much my father relished his job, how hard he'd fought to become president. It was his saving grace now that my mother was gone. To threaten his position seemed cruel.

But even more than that, I didn't want to be the girl in the news. I'd read enough about girls who cry rape—the shame people put on them, how people seem to circle the wagons around the guys, saving them. My face and body, every choice I made, every guy I'd hooked up with in the past, every beer I'd drunk and dumb thing I'd done— people would dig up all of it. I'd be under a microscope, each damning fact compounding toward a verdict that this was my fault, not the guy's. I'd led him on, I'd wanted it, I shouldn't have gone to the party in the first place. I didn't want to go to trial. I didn't want this bullshit to follow me around. I didn't want to be marked as the girl who was stupid enough to be raped in the first place.

And so I said nothing. I didn't tell anyone. I drew further and further into myself, blaming myself, even hating myself. It was only last year, when I was reporting on a story of a young woman who'd been raped at another prestigious university, that I got involved in the online forum. I'd been astonished when women also having attended Aldrich parties came forward, too. Some of them were closer to my age, and some of them were younger, but it was always the same frat—Chi Omega. Some of them had tried to complain, but it had gone nowhere. That was what scared me the most. That even if I'd tried, I would have been silenced.

"I don't blame you for wanting vengeance," Ollie says, and he sounds almost empathetic, like he's on my side. "You snapped, didn't you? That's why you did what you did."

I wrench away and make a break for the door, but Ollie quickly runs for it, once again blocking the exit. His body is rank with Axe spray. "You're not just back in town to fight for your sister's innocence, are you? You want to witness the downfall of Aldrich firsthand. The school that ruined you—you want it to go down."

I stare at him, not sure what he's talking about. Ollie smiles. "Please. You initiated the hack, and you know it. Your boy? Blue Parker? We traced it to him. The whole shebang."

I blink hard. The words don't even make sense at first. "Wait. *Wait.*" My thoughts are whirling. *Blue? My Blue?* But that makes no sense. Except then it hits me. There's a file about me on the desk. There's evidence in those pages. A trail I didn't even realize I'd created.

"He said someone encouraged him to look into Aldrich," Ollie went on. "It'll lessen his sentence if he tells us who kicked this all off. I did some digging about what the guy was all about, where he's from. And guess what I found. California. Not far from you, as a matter of fact. Even more interesting? Your number is in his cell phone."

"I-I don't know anyone named Blue," I stammer.

"Sure you do! I got records from your editor. Richard, is it? You wrote a piece on hacks last year, but he killed the article before it published. That's the saying, isn't it?"

My jaw falls open. Ollie spoke to *Richard*?

"You got to know some hackers. Got to know how evasive they could be, how they could infiltrate a system without a footprint. And you still had this old wound, an old crime gone unsolved—hell, you wanted to punish people, right? *I* would." He crosses his arms over his chest. "Well, you certainly punished a *lot* of people. Four whole universities' worth! Guess you figured you might as well expose everyone's sins, huh?"

"No." My heart beats so fast, I'm afraid it's going to explode. "I didn't . . ."

I don't know how much to say. I do know Blue. We met for coffee a few times in LA. And, during those meetings, I'd idly mentioned the corruption within the frats at Aldrich, how I was afraid it was some sort of Chi Omega tradition.

And then Blue had leaned back in the booth, a supercilious smile on his face. He told me he could find out if that was really true, if I wanted. No strings attached. He had the skills. "Those Ivies and their hoity-toity frats, they deserve what's coming to them," he said, bemused.

Jesus.

Except that's where it ends with me. I wanted the e-mails for myself, not for the world. I just wanted to know what I was dealing with. I thought I could go to my father on my own, try to handle matters from within. And I certainly, *certainly* didn't have issues with other universities. That's just . . . *insane.*

But maybe Blue did. And Blue had taken matters into his own hands.

"Do you realize what you're responsible for?" Ollie says in an eerily calm voice. "How many failed marriages? How many lost jobs? How many kids who'll never get a college education now because of one stupid mistake in their e-mail that now *everybody* knows?"

"No," I stammer. "I didn't . . . you don't . . ."

Ollie looks at me pityingly. "It's not like I don't understand what you must have gone through. When someone you love betrays you . . . it's crushing. Your bottom drops out."

My throat catches. Is he comparing my situation to his with Laura?

"And so you acted on it," Ollie adds.

There's disgust in his voice. But guilt, too? I imagine Ollie bursting into Greg's kitchen and slashing him through the kidney. It's simple, maniacal, coldhearted killing. Who's to say he won't do something like that again? Do it *right now*?

My body quakes. But slowly, I plunge my hand into my purse. My fingers curl around a cold, ceramic handle. I pull the coffee cup from my bag, whack Ollie across the face with a solid, ringing *thud,* and run.

43

WILLA

SATURDAY, MAY 6, 2017

I skid down the hall. Glimmers of dull, fading light from a window spill across the floor. The stairwell is ahead, and I pick up my pace. If I can just get to the first floor, I'll be safe. Safe from Ollie, at least.

I hear footsteps and Ollie's heavy breathing. All at once, he's on top of me, tackling me to the floor. My cheek slams against cold linoleum. I'm able to get out a muffled scream before Ollie claps his hand over my mouth. "You can't resist arrest. I'm going to read you your rights."

I wrench away from his grasp. "On what grounds?" Ollie's body on mine sets off all kinds of triggers—I feel as powerless and as trapped as I did all those years ago in that dark, dingy room. The horror of it undulates inside me, bringing fresh sobs to my throat.

My muscles contract. Even though I'm exhausted and terrified, I manage to get an arm out from under Ollie's body. I use it to sock him in the balls. He leaps back in a yowl of pain. I roll out from under him, jump to my feet, kick him in the stomach. Ollie wails, then lunges at me murderously. I feel white-hot pain as he connects with my shoulder blade. I'm on my back in seconds, my lungs screaming for air.

Through blurred vision, I catch sight of Ollie towering over me.

"Are you trying to shut me up?" I croak. "Because I know what I know about you?"

He rolls his eyes. "What do you know?"

"I know that baby isn't yours. I know about your wife and Greg Strasser. I know *everything*. And now you want to silence me so no one else finds out."

The color drains from Ollie's face, and his mouth forms an O. Is it possible he had no idea I knew this? Did he truly think I was only pawing through his office to save myself?

He crouches down until he's next to me, and then, quick as a wink, he smacks me across the face. Stars flash before my eyes. I taste blood in my mouth. I clutch my vibrating cheek, then feel the tears dripping down my face.

"Don't you ever, *ever* say that again," he growls, his eyes wild.

I wipe away my tears. "I'm not afraid of you. And you can't keep me quiet. No one is going to keep me quiet again."

"Shut *up*," Ollie roars.

A door bursts open. "What the hell?" a deep voice growls. And suddenly, the hallway is filled with officers—and *all* of them have their guns drawn.

Ollie turns to them. "She's our hacker! She was rifling through my office, trying to get rid of the evidence I had on her! And she gave me a full confession, and then she attacked me!"

Boots squeak as the officers approach me, and someone yanks me to stand. "Please," I beg. "*He* killed Greg Strasser! *That's* why I was in his office! I was looking for proof!"

Ollie glares. A muscle in his jaw twitches.

"Ask him about his motive!" I plead, staring at the line of cops in their starched uniforms. "Does he have an alibi for the night Strasser was killed?" I lift the coffee mug from my bag. "Test this for his DNA!"

Ollie faces the officers, drawing to his full height. "I have no idea what she's talking about. But I have all the data that she initiated the hack. And she's got motive, too—a rape at an Aldrich frat, years ago. She never reported it, but clearly never got over it, either. We've got her."

"It's not what it looks like," I plead. "I didn't do what you're accusing me of. But *he* has motive to kill Greg Strasser. His wife had an affair with another man! His baby isn't—"

Two officers hurriedly surround me and snap cuffs on my wrists. I struggle at first, but then I realize that resisting only causes the cuffs to dig in further. My shoulder blades ache. This is all wrong.

The crowd parts, and Reardon, the lead investigator in Greg's murder, presses through the mob of cops. Unlike the others in their crisp blue uniforms, he looks almost rumpled, his button-down wrinkled, his cuffs sloppily rolled to his elbows. I expect him to head for me—maybe he also was part of the hack committee—but instead, he turns to Ollie. "My office. Now."

Ollie's shoulders stiffen. "Why?"

"Downstairs," he says.

The detective's back is to me, so I can't see his face, but Ollie lets out an incredulous snort. "You *believe* her?" He points at me. "Are you fucking kidding me?"

Reardon almost looks like he wants to roll his eyes. "We *heard* you, Mr. Apatrea. We heard everything you said just now. And . . ." He glances at my face, which I'm guessing has already reddened with a bruise. "Not exactly protocol, Sergeant. So downstairs. *Now.*"

The blood drains from Ollie's face. "I can't fucking believe this."

For a moment, Ollie seems paralyzed, but an officer behind him nudges his back, and he staggers forward. The rest of the department doesn't move a muscle until the two disappear, but then everyone disperses at once. That's when I realize—it isn't just the police witnessing what happened. A few more figures besides the cops who were restraining me remain. The first is my father, his mouth a slack O. The second two are Kit's daughters, the blood drained from their faces. Finally, I see Kit, her hand pressed over her mouth.

But that doesn't make sense. Shouldn't Kit still be in the holding pen? Still in court with the magistrate? She isn't even handcuffed.

"Kit?" My voice is hoarse. "You're . . . okay?"

"I was set free," Kit admits. She looks intensely distressed.

"B-Because of Ollie?"

She doesn't answer. She seems uninterested in that, actually. But she's staring at me with intensity, the amazement and disbelief evident. And then it hits me: Kit witnessed Ollie's claims—that I hacked the school. That I had motive. They heard why, too.

I turn to our father, and Aurora and Sienna, who lurk behind him. By the shock on their faces, obviously they heard, too. They watch me as if I'm an animal they no longer trust.

"Willa," my father croaks sadly. "Did you . . . the hack . . . ?"

I shake my head, hating how this is being misconstrued. "*No*," I blurt. "Or, not exactly, anyway."

The two officers grip me tightly. "Okay, Ms. Manning. You need to come downstairs, too."

But then a strange gurgling noise echoes through the hall, and when I turn, I see my father's knees buckling. "I . . . I have to . . ." he ekes out.

"Dad?" Kit turns to him in panic. "Dad, what is it?"

"Grandpa?" Aurora looks terrified.

"I have to . . ." Alfred Manning points at his chest. His skin has rapidly turned an alarming shade of gray. "I'm . . ." he tries again, but then his neck snaps back, and he crumples to the floor.

44

KIT

SATURDAY, MAY 6, 2017

*J*ust past 8:00 P.M., an ER nurse bangs into the tray by the bed, and I jolt awake.

I blink, disoriented. I'm curled in a chair, bone-cold under a thin, hospital-issued blanket. My body aches, and my head throbs. My wrists still hurt from where I'd been handcuffed hours before.

"Oops!" the nurse cries as she scuttles about. It's a woman I recognize—Wendy somebody. I think she used to be in the cardiology department, assisting on Greg's surgeries. I may have even seen her at Greg's funeral. I wonder if she was one of the women whispering about me.

I stretch, wishing I could have stolen a few more moments of sleep, then immediately feel guilty for that wish. I glance at the immobile shape at the head of the bed. "How is he?" A single, dim light shines on my father's cheek. I can't tell if he's breathing.

Wendy checks his monitor. "I just came on shift, but he seems stable."

"When is someone going to tell us what's going on?"

She smiles tightly. "I'll check." She clicks something on the computer monitor that stands near the door and is gone.

I turn to my daughters. Sienna looks awake, though perhaps it's from all the coffee she's drunk. She's tapping on her phone. "Who are you talking to?" I ask.

Sienna looks guilty. "Raina. She was worried about Grandpa . . . and you."

I feel a pinch of irritation, now knowing all of Raina's secrets. But maybe, in the grand scheme of things, Raina is the least of my worries. Then again, what's the *most* of my worries? Dad? Willa? Patrick? I suck in my stomach, thinking of Patrick's surprising wrath. My heart feels flattened. How could I have been so stupid *again*?

"I'm going to go down to the cafeteria for more coffee," Sienna adds. "Want some?"

I'm about to say no, but then I shrug. I might as well stay awake in case a doctor comes in to explain what the hell is happening with my father. As Sienna leaves, I call out, "Honey, wait."

Sienna turns. I want to say something to her about the e-mail scheme she concocted—I haven't forgotten, and we haven't had a proper talk about it. Yet Sienna looks so guilty right now, almost like she's readying herself for a blow. Maybe now isn't the time.

I sigh. "Grab me two stevia packets, okay?"

She nods and disappears. Then I turn to Aurora in the corner. I expect her to be asleep, but her eyes are open and haunted, unblinking. I shift closer to her. "Hey. It'll be okay."

Aurora nods like she's trying to convince herself. But she's chewing hard on her lip. Her knee is jiggling crazily. Her gaze shifts to her grandfather, then back to her lap again. "I just . . . there's no chance of you going back to jail, right?"

I shake my head. "No. I don't think so."

"Are you *sure*?"

When I heard about the murder weapon being found in our garage, hidden behind some drop cloths, I thought, *Well, maybe I did do it. Maybe it wasn't Patrick . . . or Ollie . . . or anyone else.*

I sat in the filthy holding cell, awaiting my time in front of the magistrate, and decided to come to terms with what I'd done. Crazier things had happened than a woman stabbing her unfaithful husband in the kitchen, right? Maybe Greg had gotten violent with me, or maybe he'd snapped in the same way Patrick did in the woods. I'd felt such revulsion for Patrick, and shame in myself for trusting him implicitly. Coupled with disappointment because I was supposed to be a smart, careful, protective person, and there I was, believing in the wrong person once more. Those feelings were startlingly similar to how I'd felt about Greg when I'd been made aware of those e-mails. Maybe violence isn't so difficult to imagine.

But then, just as I was beginning to take ownership over my rage, a female officer rapped on the bars. "Your bail hearing has been canceled."

The officer unlocked the cell door and gestured for me to walk toward her. "Turn of events." Her expression gave nothing away. "Forensics found a print on the murder weapon—but it's not yours."

Ollie's, I'd presumed—especially after Willa told me what she'd figured out. I should probably be more emotional about the fact that my husband fathered a child with another woman . . . but, well, it's all too much on top of everything else. I feel like nothing in my world, *nothing,* is in the place where I left it. I wouldn't be surprised if I opened up my wallet and found another name on my driver's license. If I opened my eyes and saw a different man than my father lying in the bed.

An hour ago, another strange turn of events: Detective Reardon called to say that, yes, there was a print on the knife, and yes, it wasn't mine. But it wasn't Ollie's, either. It was a print that *isn't in the system at all.* I had them check on Patrick, who'd been fingerprinted for his job—nope. So *whose,* then?

There's a murmuring sound from the bed. My dad shifts on the mattress, his eyelids fluttering, his lips making small, fleshy, popping sounds.

"Dad?" I rush over to him. "Dad?"

He squinches up his eyes, smacks his lips, but then drops back into sleep.

I glance at Aurora, who flew to his bedside, too. She looks so shattered. "It'll be okay," I say softly, patting her arm. I need to be the strong one for once, even though I'm reeling.

I study my father's eerily gray skin, the white stubble on his chin, and the tubes running into his veins and nostrils. I've barely seen him sick, but hours ago, he'd collapsed to the floor as though made of glass. The paramedics worried he was having a heart incident. They gave him a sedative to bring his heart rate to normal levels. His body gave out because of what Willa did, I'm guessing. Because she'd ruined his school. Or maybe it broke because of what happened to her.

"Kit?"

I whirl around, and my heart flip-flops. And lo and behold, here is Willa in the flesh. She's wearing the blue sweatshirt and joggers she had on from when she rescued me from Patrick. Her eyes are bloodshot. That ugly mark from where Ollie hit her looks like a lightning bolt across her cheek. But she's here, unhandcuffed, staring at the group with deep, tortured remorse.

"Hey," Willa says tentatively. "Can I come in?"

45

WILLA

SATURDAY, MAY 6, 2017

My father's machines and monitors hiss like snakes, and the mattress seems to swallow him. His eyelids are blue and paper-thin. As I look at him, nausea rises in my gut. Hospitals have always sickened me. The last time I'd been in one was after my mother's accident, and she'd already been pronounced dead.

I look at Kit. "How is he?"

Kit's gaze is glued on our father's monitors, which blink a bunch of unintelligible numbers. "Well, it's not a problem with his heart. That's about all I know. But no real doctor has come in with an update yet."

I nod, uneasy at the distance in her voice. She's mad. Maybe I deserve it. No matter how you slice it, I'm culpable for the hack. I got the wheels turning. I should have never arranged for Blue to dig into a private university. I wanted information. Maybe even revenge. But I didn't want to ruin anyone's life.

Greg's. Kit's. Maybe even my father's.

I sit down in an orange plastic chair two seats away from Kit. The fake fluorescent light buzzes above us. "Look," I say, my voice cracking.

"Willa," Kit says at the same time. I gesture for Kit to speak first. Kit glances at me, then heaves a sigh. "So. You're out of jail."

I nod. "I was released without being charged. It doesn't mean I *won't* be charged—I've already called a lawyer—but not now." I turn my hands over, staring into the lines of my palms as though hoping they might give me a prophecy. They don't. "I did something, Kit. But not what Ollie was accusing me of."

An expression of disappointment flashes across Kit's face, and I feel yet another zing of shame. "Greg's dead because of me. The hack affected your job, affected students, teachers—it's awful. It's been weighing on me since this all happened. I understand if you don't want to speak to me ever again."

Kit stares at the brown squares on the linoleum floor, looking disgusted. Defensiveness rises in me. *Yeah, but I'm damaged, too,* I want to snap at her.

As though sensing this, Kit clears her throat. "I wish you would have said something. About . . . you know. What happened to you. I think that's what hurts the most." Her eyes quickly flick to Aurora and Sienna, who's standing in the doorway, cups of coffee in her hands. I wonder how much she's told them. "Why did you think you couldn't come to me about this?" she asks, her voice breaking.

"I didn't come to anyone about it."

"*Why?*"

I scoff. "Because it's not exactly *flattering.*"

She looks stunned. "Who cares? It's not *your* fault! You could have prosecuted! You could have taken those kids down!"

"But I didn't see their faces. I couldn't have accused the whole fraternity."

Kit mutters something I can't hear under her breath. Next to her, Aurora and Sienna shift uneasily. I can't even look at them. All my life, I've wanted them to admire me, but I'm a failure. Certainly no role model. I hate that they're growing up in this world.

Out the window, the early evening sky is a soft navy blue. I linger on it a moment, trying to put myself in another place, another time. On the other hand, maybe it's important that I'm here, finally explaining all of this. And maybe it's good that Kit's daughters are here to listen. Maybe they won't make the same mistakes I did.

I take a breath. "I didn't tell anyone because for a long time, I blamed myself. I felt so stupid. Like, *How did I get myself into this mess? And, Is this my fault?*"

"Jesus," Kit spits. "*No.*"

"I've come around since then, though. I know I did nothing to deserve what happened. I've gotten in touch with other women who went through the same thing. I heard all kinds of stories. Most of the women were at other schools. But I met a few who were at Aldrich. The very same frat house where it happened to me."

Kit stares at me, her eyes wide. "You're kidding."

"I wish I was." My head drops. I can smell my unwashed skin and oily hair. I can feel the makeup caked under my eyes and the swollen bruise on my cheek. Almost as palpably, I can feel that guy's hands on me, pressing me down, making me his. It's incredible how that sensation has stayed with me all these years, no matter how much I've tried to suppress it.

"When that sort of thing happens to you, it's like they steal your identity," I murmur into my chest. "You don't know who you are anymore. You don't react the same way to things. It just . . . *lives* with you. So for a long time, I buried it. It was my only way to get through. I moved away from here, I came back as little as I could, and I just . . . changed my whole life. I know it's not healthy, but it's what I did." I take a breath. "But then, after enough time, I got angry. Especially when I found out that this happened to other women at Aldrich. And some of them actually *reported* it."

Kit looks stunned. "To whom?"

"To Marilyn, actually."

Kit's eyes boggle. "Dad's *assistant?*"

"Yep. And she *said* she'd pass it up the ladder—to Dad. But then things got muddled. The story shifted. Instead, she reached out to the victims again. Had private meetings. Cut deals. I don't know why she was trying to handle it herself—maybe she thought Dad was too busy? Maybe she thought he'd make the wrong choice, make too much out of it?"

"But she's a *woman!*" Kit cries. "How could she do this?"

"I don't know. I guess not everyone sees it like we do. And all the victims I talked to said she could be pretty scary in person. Anyway . . ."—I glance at my father in the bed—"I had to know for *sure* that he wasn't involved. That this was *her* secret, not his."

Kit puts her hands on her hips, ready to defend him. I cut her off. "I don't think he was. Not anymore. There's nothing about it in his e-mails. Then again, there isn't much from Marilyn in the e-mails, either—whatever she said, she said it face-to-face, and it wasn't logged anywhere. I only know from personal accounts. Every woman told me Dad wasn't involved. But I just—I needed to know for sure." I clear my throat. "I didn't tell Dad what happened to me, so I didn't know how he'd handle it."

"Why didn't you tell him?" Kit demands.

"I just . . . it's complicated," I fumble. "I would have told Mom. I just . . . you know. She wasn't there."

The clock ticks loudly in the corner. In another room, someone's monitor keeps dinging, a tone that's impossible to tune out.

Kit shifts. "So you decided to hack the entire school because of that?" Kit's voice is shaking. "Four whole universities?"

"Don't be ridiculous." I shake my head. "It was never my intention to expose anyone except Marilyn, if I could. But a few months ago, I was working on this story for 'The Source' about hackers, and this guy, Blue, was one of the people I interviewed. I still had his number, so I asked him to meet me."

I remember the chrome sheen of the diner where we met. Blue, a short, thin man in a bomber jacket, who was no older than twenty, slid into the booth across from me with such an arrogant smile that I'd almost felt uneasy—it reminded me, I realized, of my attacker.

"I told him in vague terms that something happened to me at a frat house when I was younger—and that I was afraid it had happened to other girls, too, and that there was a cover-up. Blue said he could look into it for me. He said he hated colleges like Aldrich—he was thrilled to sniff out a scandal. He seemed so self-assured about how easy the Aldrich system would be to hack—which I guess it was."

"So you asked him to hack . . . who?" Kit asks.

"Just some of the higher-ups' e-mails. I told him that if he found anything, I'd pay him for his time."

Kit looks crestfallen. "Oh, *Willa*."

"I know. But worse, I heard nothing from him after that. I figured that's the last I'd hear of it—so imagine my surprise when, a few months later, *all* of Aldrich is hacked. And it's all out there on that server for everyone to see." I feel the same stomach clench I did the day the hack broke. I'd been standing in my hallway, still wet from the shower; after reading the news on the TV screen, I'd vomited on the carpet. I prayed for it to not be too bad—for Dad, for Kit, for Sienna, for anyone.

Kit runs her hands down the length of her sweater. "How do you know it was even Blue who did it, then?"

"When I confronted Ollie in his office—crazy move, I know—he said the investigation led back to him. I don't know how he'd have come up with that name otherwise." I run my hands through my oily hair. "No money changed hands, but I still asked him to do it. There was still a verbal contract."

Meaning I still could be held accountable. What would my punishment be for this? Would I be fired from "The Source"? Would I ever get another job again? These questions have swirled in my mind ever since the hack broke—though, hideously, it had felt good to push them to the back burner while we were figuring out what had happened to Greg. But now, Ollie had exposed everything. There was nowhere for me to hide.

Kit presses the heels of her hands into her eyes. "I can't believe that Ollie was a link to your past."

"I can't either. But he was there. And he thinks it happened to other girls that same night. And he might know the guy's name who . . . you know. Did it."

Kit watches me, resisting asking the obvious question. I don't want to know the guy's name. It's not because doing so will make it seem more real—I *know* it's real. It's more that I don't want to give what happened any more importance. Knowing a name means I'll inevitably look the guy up—see where he works, if he has a family, what he looks like. I'll cling to what happened. I won't be able to let it go. I'd rather he just be anonymous. That way, he matters less.

The bed creaks. I whip around to see my father's eyes now open. He stares into the middle distance as though possessed.

"Dad?" Kit rises and scurries to his side. "Dad, it's Kit. Willa's here, too. You're in the hospital. Do you remember?"

My father's eyes land first on Kit, then Aurora and Sienna, and then me. His eyes narrow when he sees me, and my stomach clenches. He remembers what I've said. He's furious.

"Dad?" I step a little closer, feeling tears well in my eyes. "I—"

He shakes his head to cut me off. "I didn't, Willa."

"What's that?"

His voice is sandpaper-rough, the voice of a one-hundred-year-old. "I had no idea about the rapes. You have to believe me."

Kit's eyes widen. Sienna's mouth falls open.

"No one ever told me. Not that that's an excuse. It's never an excuse. I should have been aware of everything that happened, bad and good. But I didn't. You have to know that. I would have never let that happen."

Shame rocks through my body. I bend my head so that it's almost on the mattress beside his leg. "Okay." There's a lump in my throat. I shouldn't have doubted him. *Why* had I doubted him? All at once, hot tears are on my face. "I'm sorry, Dad," I blurt. "I'm so sorry."

His machine beeps. "It's all right," he says quietly. "Maybe it's good that the hack happened. There was so much going on. So much we needed to get rid of."

"Don't say that," I insist. He can't let me off the hook that fast. It feels too easy.

Feet shuffle behind me, and a tall, bearded, exhausted-looking doctor peeks into the room. He carries a clipboard, and his expression is guarded. "Miss Strasser?" he asks, glancing at my sister.

"Yes." Kit straightens her spine.

"Dr. Stein." He shakes Kit's hand. Kit introduces him to the girls and me. Then he shifts awkwardly. "So. Your father." He glances down at our dad, too, and his expression turns sober. "Something came up in the MRI we just ran. There's a large mass in your pancreas, Mr. Manning."

For a moment, I can only concentrate on details of the man's face: the large pores on his nose, the gold accents on his glasses. Kit bursts out laughing. "Wait, what?"

"*Cancer?*" I ask quietly.

"Actually, yes. Not that we've had a chance to run any tests—but we did call around to other hospitals. Apparently, your father has been receiving pancreatic cancer treatment since January at Allegheny General? His oncologist team treated him with an on-site injector a few days ago—it helps increase white blood cells after strong chemotherapy, cuts down the risk of infection so a patient can go home instead of have to stay in the hospital?"

He says this like we're supposed to know, but we all just stare at one another.

Kit smiles as if it's a joke. "No. My father had a *panic attack*. He's had a very difficult few weeks. It's not cancer."

"We think it's likely that his incident in the police station was a side effect of the injector medication," Dr. Stein explains. "It can cause lung issues, trouble breathing, and combined with stress . . ."

"Wait, wait." I realize something. "Are you saying that our father received a strong dose of chemotherapy only a few *days* ago? When the hell would he have done that?"

"Right," Kit says. "He was at Aldrich University. Dealing with the hack." Then she looks at me. "*Wasn't* he?"

But how would I know?

Dr. Stein lowers his clipboard and regards us with sympathy. "Sometimes, patients conceal their diagnosis and treatment as long as they can. They don't want to be pitied, or to be taken less seriously at their job. Many feel their reputation would be affected if people found out they were going through something so debilitating." He glances at our father in the bed. "Mr. Manning didn't lose his hair. He looks thin, but not *that* thin. He probably thought he was hiding it well. Has he suffered any memory lapses lately? Mood swings?"

I just stare.

"I can understand that this is a shock," Dr. Stein says. "But we're in touch with his medical team from Allegheny, so at least we know what we're dealing with. We'll be back in the morning with our goal for what's next—I was told that this round of treatment was to be your father's last. I'm not sure the therapies have been very effective."

And then, after giving us a long, heartfelt look, he's gone, the door swishing closed.

The light in the room seems to have dimmed. All of us stare at one another. There are tears in Kit's eyes, but I'm too numb to feel much of anything.

Kit looks at our father. "Cancer, Dad? And Allegheny? That isn't even a good hospital!"

"It's fine," our father croaks. "They're very nice to me there."

It feels like he's just shot a bullet though the room—all of us recoil. "So it's true, then?" Kit says. "You were having treatments? *And not telling us?*"

"It seemed easier that way."

"Are you *serious*?"

"I didn't want you to worry. I didn't want to be trouble."

"What the *hell*, Dad?"

I place my hand on Kit's arm to stop her. I understand why my father did what he did in not telling us about his illness. It's the same reason I had to not tell my story, years ago. It's easier not to be a burden. It's easier for everyone not to know. Then, everyone would know.

Kit places her hands on the sides of her head. "I don't believe this." Then she looks rabidly at the group. "Does anyone *else* have a secret they've been keeping from me? Anyone? You'd better say it now. I can't take much more than this."

The room is silent. Even the A/C has clicked off. Suddenly, there's a small, weak cry in the corner. Everyone whirls around to look at Aurora. She's in her seat again, her knees pulled up to her chest. Her face has drained of color.

"What's the matter?" Kit's eyebrows shoot up.

Aurora glances desperately at Sienna. There's that strange exchange between the two of them, and my skin starts to prickle. "Tell her," Aurora pleads.

Alarm registers on Sienna's face. She gives a slight shake of her head.

"Tell me what?" Kit asks, straightening, her tone verging on panic.

The girls watch one another. For a while, no one speaks—maybe no one even *breathes*. Finally, Aurora looks down and breathes in raggedly. "It was me," she says softly, into her shirt.

"What?" Kit asks.

"It was me," Aurora repeats. "I did it."

"Aurora, stop it," Sienna snaps. "Stop talking."

Kit turns slowly so that she's facing her daughters. "What are you talking about?" She whips back to Aurora. "What did you do?" She grabs the girl by the shoulders. "*What did you do?*"

Aurora shields herself with her hands. She's bawling now. "It just happened! I read the e-mails, and they disgusted me, and I was just trying to protect her!"

Kit's jaw goes slack. I'm so stunned I have to sit down. *What is Aurora saying?*

"Protect who?" Kit asks. She looks at Sienna, then back at Aurora again. "Aurora knew you wrote the Lolita e-mails, is that it?" Neither girl reacts. Kit keeps trying. "But why did you feel like you needed to *protect* Sienna? You didn't want anyone to find out? You thought Greg was going to hurt her?"

All I can see of Aurora's lowered head is her crown. She shakes miserably. "No. *No.*"

"No *what?*" Kit's voice has risen to a shriek. She looks desperately at Sienna. "What is she talking about?" But Sienna is stricken, motionless in her chair.

"Sienna didn't plant those e-mails," Aurora mumbles into her chest. She sounds both angry and devastated.

We look back and forth between the girls. Sienna is hiding her face in her hands, her long, elegant legs crossed prettily at her ankles. Even though I can't see her face, I can practically feel her shame. It oozes out of her the same way it oozed out of me. And then I think of what Sienna told me after Greg's funeral, about why the two sisters were fighting: *We had a fight about this guy . . . it's dumb.*

My skin goes cold.

I turn to Aurora slowly. "You thought the e-mails between Greg and Sienna were real."

Aurora shrinks in the chair, but after a pained few moments, she nods. "I . . . I saw him, once. He touched her . . . inappropriately. And she didn't pull away." She glances up at her sister, and there is fear in her eyes.

"Is this *true?*" Kit gasps.

Sienna lowers her hands just a little. Her face is a mask of pain. "I couldn't," she whispers. "I couldn't pull away."

Kit's body is rigid. "Those e-mails really *were* from him? You didn't write both sides? The e-mails . . . *were* real?"

Sienna's eyes flit to her mother's for only a second, then lower again. "I can't do this," she blubbers, and then gets up and runs out of the room.

46

KIT

SATURDAY, MAY 6, 2017

For a moment, everyone is too stunned to move. Then I wrench away from the bed after my daughter. Willa catches my arm. "Wait. Just let her . . . decompress."

"Decompress?" I run my hands down the length of my face. My heart is racing so fast I can hardly see straight. "What did she just tell us? Did she just *confess* something?"

Willa blinks. There are tears in her eyes. "I-I don't know."

I walk to the door, touch the knob, and then pull back. Pace around. Yank the door open and peer into the hall. It's empty.

Is it really possible that Greg was involved with my *daughter*? But then I think of Lolita's e-mails—in the beginning, they were fun and flirtatious, like she was enjoying herself. So Sienna played along, then. Sienna fell for him. *Fell for my husband.* Just like I did.

But then I think of how the e-mails shifted, Greg's words becoming more aggressive and suggestive. All those dirty scenarios he presented. All that sex talk. I can feel the bile rising in my stomach. I stagger to the bathroom and throw up in the sink.

When I'm finished, I wipe my mouth and eyes. My father's room is quiet. Willa is sitting on a chair staring, dumbfounded, at the blank whiteboard. Aurora is sobbing in a corner. I turn to her, realizing what she's admitted to. It was nearly buried under Sienna's horrible truth.

"Honey," I squeak out. But I can't go closer. It's almost like I'm afraid to touch her. "Aurora. What happened that night?"

She shakes her head. "I . . . can't."

"You have to tell me. You have to tell me before things get worse."

She glances up at me, terrified. "Worse *how*?"

How can she not know what might happen? The police will circle back to us. They'll question everyone whose prints aren't on record. They might even focus on Aurora first, being that she was at a neighbor's house the night it happened. Hell, I'd thought she was *home* that night.

And she was, I guess. For a little while, anyway. And I guess she hid the knife in the garage, hoping—praying—it would never be found.

My thoughts, unbidden, turn to how it might have gone down. Aurora must have let herself into the house with her key, which explains the lack of a forced entry. And then . . . what? She found Greg in the kitchen? Stabbed him in a blind rage, furious for what he'd done to Sienna? But I can't quite buy that. Aurora is moody, but she's not stupid.

I turn to her. "What happened that night?"

Aurora wipes her eyes. It seems to pain her to speak. "We . . . argued."

"About what?"

"The e-mails." She sighs. "I knew they were to Sienna. I felt . . ." Fresh tears spill onto her cheeks. "It's *gross,* Mom."

I'm nodding. There is a boulder on my throat, making it almost impossible to swallow.

"And then what?" I ask gently.

Her face breaks, and something inside me does, too. I guess it isn't so hard to figure out what happened next, now that we have all the pieces. "I told him I thought he was disgusting," she whispers. "I said I would make him pay. I never wanted him to touch her again. And then . . ." She takes a breath. "He *lost* it. He came at me. Started denying stuff, started calling me all these names . . . I didn't know what to do."

"You were afraid. You had to defend yourself."

Aurora looks pleadingly at me, her eyes wide, her mouth small, her body curled so tightly in the chair. She's so *young,* I realize. Younger than I was when I met Martin. Younger than Willa was when she was raped. Still so innocent.

"I don't want to go to jail," Aurora whispers between sobs. "Please, Mom. I can't."

I feel my life disassembling, piece by piece, until there is nothing left. Where can we go from here? What can I even *tell* her? This is the worst possible outcome. No lessons are learned here. No justice is done. It was a hideous thing that we don't even entirely understand yet—and a child's impulsive decision. My baby is going to be gone forever. It's one thing if it's me in jail, but it's another thing entirely if it's one of my daughters. There's no way I can let that happen.

"I'll go for you," I say in a near whisper. "I'll say I did it. The police already think so, anyway. It's what everyone wants to believe."

Willa frowns. "It's not your prints on the knife. There must be another way."

Irritation rises inside me. Who cares about holes in the story? I just need to save my daughter. "No. This is the only way."

"*I'll* take the blame."

My father is propped up a little in his bed and staring straight at us. A jolt goes through me—he's been so out of it the last few hours that I keep assuming he hasn't heard much of what we've said. But now, he stares at us with resigned intelligence. Even a little color has returned to his face.

"I'll take the blame," he says again. "I'll say I did it."

I blink hard. "*You?*"

"You heard the doctor. I don't have much time to live."

"But . . ." Willa sounds dumbfounded. "No, Dad. *No.*"

"You don't have to," I interrupt. "This is ridiculous to even think about."

"They won't put me in prison." He breathes in raggedly. "I'm dying, girls. Where am I going to go?"

He almost looks mischievous as he says this. I'm dumbstruck.

"Dad." I shake my head. "I'm not letting you confess to a murder you didn't commit. It's . . . preposterous."

"It'll ruin your legacy," Willa pipes up.

He waves his hand, but his voice is suddenly full of remorse. "What kind of father doesn't know that something terrible has happened to his daughter? That something has happened to his grandchildren? You *are* my legacy."

"Dad." Willa shuts her eyes. "Stop."

"It's true. I put Aldrich on the front burner for years, and that made me lose sight of keeping my children safe." He shifts so he's sitting a little higher. "Let me do this. Let me keep you safe. It's the least I can do."

Aurora lets out a squeak. Willa stares at me with a look that seems to say, *How can we stop him?* Tears drip down my cheeks. My father looks so at peace with his decision. It's all happening too quickly—realizing we're going to have to say goodbye, and now hearing of the sacrifice he's going to make for us.

I walk over to Aurora and put my hand over hers. My heart is beating quickly, and I don't want to get my hopes up that this could work, and I feel conflicted even considering letting him go through with it. I feel her press against me, her body shuddering with pain. Even if she isn't going to jail for this, she's going to have to live with it for the rest of her life, just like Willa has lived with her rape.

And maybe that's prison enough.

EPILOGUE

47

LAURA

FRIDAY, MAY 12, 2017

Mother's Day dawns warm, sunny, and fragrant, which is a delight. Last Mother's Day, almost halfway through my pregnancy, I woke up to six inches of snow. Ollie and I went through with our picnic plans anyway, shoveling off a patch on the lawn of Phipps Conservatory, our fingers frozen as we sipped sparkling cider, the snowflakes landing on my slightly swollen belly. We were both so happy, though, the weather barely mattered.

Well. Actually, I guess neither of us was. I was afraid. And Ollie was quietly, secretly furious.

But this is my first official Mother's Day as a mom. And as I swing into the car, I hear Freddie kicking at his dangling car seat toy in the back, and my world is filled with light and life. I understand the gift I've been given. That if things had gone differently, I might not have my son at all. I might not be alive.

The day the police stopped me on the turnpike still comes back to me in horrific flashes. The cops took me into their cruiser, arranging for a separate vehicle to follow behind us with Freddie. I'd begged them to let us ride together, but they refused. The whole drive, I rocked with psychic pain, sensing Freddie's lonely screams as though they were needles drilling into my skin. I was furious, too. What doctor had signed a bogus note that I was a danger to my child? How long in advance had Ollie planned this? What if Ollie got sole custody of my child? That's what frightened me the most, I think—that my baby would be with a man who had it in him to kill.

The drive back to Pittsburgh was excruciating. We finally pulled up to the station in Blue Hill, and the police escorted me to a small, isolated interrogation room and told me to wait. I strained to hear Freddie's cries, but the office was as silent as a tomb. I pleaded with an officer who came to check if I needed something to drink. The baby still nurses, I urged. He's going to need a diaper change. He's got to be scared.

But they didn't listen to me. My paranoia spiraled. I went from thinking they'd sort out the mistake to being certain that I was never going to see my baby again. This was how far Ollie was going to go to ruin my life. I cried loudly, hideously, but no one opened my door.

After what seemed like hours, a door swung open. I cringed, expecting more officers barging in with handcuffs, ready to haul me off to jail or court or the hospital. When I saw a female officer and a plainclothes woman, I lifted my head a little. Then I realized the woman was holding my child in her arms. I let out a relieved, broken little bleat, jumping to my feet and stretching my arms out for my child. "We're sorry," the officer said, her voice full of genuine regret. She handed the baby over. "Mrs. Apatrea, we are so, so sorry we put you through this."

I didn't ask how they'd figured out what had happened. I didn't care. I nuzzled Freddie, sobbing, grateful. After a moment, the officer said that they had Ollie in custody for assault. But I wouldn't really grasp what had happened until much later.

Now my phone dings. I muffle it, not wanting to wake the baby, and glance at the screen. It's a reminder of an upcoming appointment tomorrow: *Ollie, lawyer's office.* We're meeting on neutral territory to sign the divorce papers. It certainly wasn't difficult to schedule: Ollie was fired from his police position almost immediately after that showdown with Willa Manning. There are also charges against him that I filed—one for domestic assault, and another for lying to Child Protective Services and the state troopers. I don't think he's going to get that promotion anytime soon. I won't let him back in the house; rumor has it he's living with his mother on the other side of the city. He calls me regularly, begging me to take him back. Says he screwed up, says he forgives me for what happened with Greg. Says he misses Freddie. Still considers him his child.

What's crazy is that these phone messages tug at my heartstrings. But then I think about those last few days we were together. The fear I felt. And the betrayal, too—I had been so, so certain that Ollie, as impulsive and hotheaded as he could be at work, would never, *ever* be that way around me. For him to flip, for him to change—albeit provoked by my betrayal—it made me lose faith in almost everything. So I can't take Ollie back.

I've explained all of this to detectives and a new therapist. They said that I can file a restraining order that will legally forbid Ollie from coming within a certain distance of me—and Freddie. But I know how flimsy those things can be. I know that if you want to violate an order, not much is stopping you.

It's why, then, I have a plan.

I flip on the radio, wanting to catch the news before I switch over to the nursery rhyme songs I've downloaded for Freddie. I find a local station, and someone is just finishing the weather report. Then, another anchor announces a new story: *"Aldrich University president and self-confessed murderer is dead at sixty-nine."*

A ball clogs my throat. I turn up the volume.

"Alfred Manning, the president of Aldrich University and *the murderer of Greg Strasser, is dead from complications with pancreatic cancer,"* the voice goes on. *"Manning was undergoing hushed treatments for the disease at an Allegheny Hospital branch thirty miles outside of town. He fell gravely ill shortly*

after the murder weapon was found on the premises of his daughter's home. He regained consciousness after his medical episode and offered a full confession. Mr. Manning leaves behind a tarnished legacy not only with the murder of his son-in-law but also of his beloved school, which was rife with scandals that came out in the famous Aldrich hack."

I feel a wave of sadness. I've never met Alfred Manning, despite his being Greg's father-in-law. In news clips, though, he always seemed like such a nice man. So gentle. I remember reading how he'd lost his wife suddenly, how hard that must have been. But I guess appearances can be deceiving.

I glance at Freddie in the back seat. "Okay, enough of that." And in seconds, we're listening to "Baa, Baa, Black Sheep," his favorite. The sun streams in through the windows. We wind through the old brick streets toward the park. I'm going to miss this neighborhood, I think, glancing around at the handsome brownstones. I'm going to miss Pittsburgh in general.

But it's almost time, and I am ready. A U-Haul will be here tomorrow night to pack up the simple furniture like Freddie's crib, my bed, a table. The U-Haul I've arranged is the kind that will hitch to my SUV; I'll be like a turtle, carrying my whole house around wherever I go. I'm not sure where we *will* go yet. Somewhere I won't easily be found. I've made a few contacts that will get me the right paperwork to change my name, make my details untraceable, even online. Once your life is threatened, the world seems to change shape. You do what you have to do. Certain choices suddenly become easy. And this is one of them.

"Ba!" Freddie exclaims from the back seat, and a smile spreads across my face.

"Ba!" I say back, turning the wheel. "We have such a fun day planned, boo! The park . . . the aviary . . . but just a quick stop first, okay?"

I have to rely on GPS in Blue Hill; despite having worked there, I never had much chance to drive through its back streets. I pass the hospital first, though I barely glance at it before driving by. It doesn't bother me that I'll be giving notice over the phone; there's no one I really want to say goodbye to in person. Next, I drive by the museum where the benefit took place. It seems like a million years ago that I was there. I try to remember the fears that had gripped me that night. All the things I was trying to hold on to. All the things that had now changed.

I drive on, coming to a street whose name I recognize. *Hazel Lane.* A red light stops me before I can turn, so I gaze down the long drive, spying Greg and Kit's house a few lots down. There's no more police tape around the front door. Rumor has it Kit moved back in, though someone else said she probably wouldn't stay. Her porch light is on, though, meaning she's home. My fingers twitch on the steering wheel. Do I dare?

I feel like I owe Kit something. An explanation, an apology. Or maybe I just present Freddie to her, saying, *here.* Some kind of acknowledgment. And yet I'm not sure if this is what Kit wants. I know she knows about Greg and me—Detective Reardon explained that her sister, Willa, accused Ollie of Greg's murder, having figured out about the baby herself. But it's not like she's reached out to me. I probably wouldn't either, in her shoes.

Maybe it would be better just to leave this be. Maybe, years from now, I can track her down, for Freddie's sake.

The light turns green, and I drive on.

The GPS tells me to take another right, and then a left, and then I drive down a hill to a series of weathered apartment buildings in the shadow of the Aldrich University science lab. It doesn't take me long to find a parking space, and I turn off the car and heft Freddie out of the seat. "This'll just take a moment," I murmur, adjusting him in my arms.

The address I've been given is a building without an elevator. The corridors are dark, and loud music escapes from underneath quite a few of the doors. The third floor, his floor, has a beery stench to it, like someone held a party here the night before. I check my watch before ringing the bell. Is it too early?

But I'm here, so I do it anyway. The bell has one clear note and one sour one. It takes a while for footsteps, but then I hear the click of latches and bolts, and the door swings open. When Griffin Mc-Cabe sees me, his forehead creases. "Hello?" he says tentatively.

"It's . . . me." I realize I haven't planned what to say. "Laura. The woman you . . ."

His eyes widen. He looks from me to the baby, to me again. "Of course," Griffin says. And there is that earnest smile, that helpful, hopeful light in his eyes. He looks both younger in this light and much older and wiser. He glances behind him, then at me again. "What are you doing here?"

"I don't want to come in or anything," I say quickly. "I just . . . I was in the neighborhood. And I wanted to thank you. I never got to."

He waves his hand dismissively, like it doesn't matter, but I shake my head because it does. My mouth opens, and I consider telling him everything—why I stood on that ledge that night, the despair I felt, the shame and entrapment. But then I shut my mouth again. My story of suffering is just another story in a sea of many. And anyway, maybe it's not worth dwelling on.

"Well, you're welcome," Griffin says after an awkward pause. And then: "How is everything?"

I'll ask myself that question a lot in the years to come. Sometimes, I'll be far from okay. Sometimes, I'll feel the same despair I felt that night on the bridge when I wanted to end it all. Those feelings will chase me, never quite evaporating completely, a faint film always on my skin. But I'll fight through them. I have to. I press Freddie closer to me, hugging him as tightly as I can.

"I'm getting there," I tell him.

48

RAINA

AUGUST 14, 2017

Since I've moved off campus into a dumpy, suburban apartment shared by four people that I struggle to pay for on my brand-new salary as a coffee barista, it takes longer to get anywhere. I finally make it through the tunnel, off the bridge, and down the long boulevard, passing the history museum, the art center, and the huge Aldrich University library, where I still owe fines for overdue books. Near my stop, I press the button to get off. The bus huffs to the curb, and I hurry down the stairs. I'm late. Part of me worries if this is even for real. Maybe I've schlepped over here for nothing.

The bursar's office hasn't changed since I was here last. Same red-and-gold Aldrich flags, same sticky door, same cranky women behind the desks. I feel a pull in my chest as I look around. She isn't here yet. It's a joke, then. I mean, of *course* it's a joke—I should have known it the moment her e-mail came in last week. I should be arranging for scholarships, or maybe applying to other, cheaper schools, or speaking to my parents one more time to see if they have any more money stashed away under a mattress. We've been back in touch, a little. I got a good dose of perspective after that incident with that Patrick guy. I realized that my parents were just Podunk and uninformed, not bad people. Not like Alexis's family. Not like Alexis's life.

But anyway, I should be planning and preparing for next semester, when my Greg Strasser funds run out—not following a wild-goose chase that's only going to end in humiliation. Shouldering my bag, I pivot and head for the door just as it swings open and someone comes inside. She and I collide, and I step back, my breath catching in my throat.

Lynn Godfrey appraises me, hands on hips. "Going somewhere, Raina?"

My hand flies to my throat. "No. I was just afraid I was late, and . . ."

". . . and that I wasn't going to show up?"

Well, yeah, I want to say as Lynn walks to the first unoccupied partition window. I mean, yes, Lynn first reached out to me after that whole bullshit debacle went down; I guess she found the secret e-mail account her husband used to set up his sex-play trysts, and then got my contact information through Alexis. And yes, she spoke to me at length about what happened that night with Patrick, and if anyone had seen, and if I thought he'd done it with lots of others, and what I was after that night, anyway.

I'd been honest with her back then. I'd even told her about my arrangement with Greg Strasser, which seemed, interestingly, to break the ice. I told her the only thing I wanted was to continue going to school. But I didn't think anything would come of it. After that, Lynn gruffly ended the call, and I figured I'd never hear from her again. But months later, she called me. Said she'd done some thinking and wanted to pay my tuition herself. I almost fell off my couch when I heard those words.

"Help you?" the bored woman behind the window asks, eyeing Lynn and me.

Lynn sits down in the chair facing the window and explains to the woman that she wants to set up an account to withdraw funds to pay for the rest of my schooling here. The woman slips her the appropriate form, and Lynn picks up a pen. Then she looks at me. "What's your last name again?"

"H-Hammond," I stammer.

"Date of birth?" Then she rolls her eyes. "Actually, here. You fill this in."

Lynn's posture is straight. She stares rigidly ahead. I write in my important details—my student ID and social security numbers, the address where I'm now living, how many credits I have left, et cetera. At the bottom, Lynn provides a bank routing and account number for the bursar to use to make automatic withdrawals.

She slides the completed paperwork back through the slot in the window, and the woman on the other side of the glass begins to type it into the system. Lynn places her sunglasses back over her eyes, preparing to go back outdoors.

"Lynn," I cry, my voice squeaking unpleasantly.

Lynn eyes me coldly. Almost like she doesn't like me—which, I mean, why *would* she? I swallow hard. "I don't understand why you're doing this. You know I'm not going to say anything." Exposing Patrick Godfrey would mean exposing myself. I thought Lynn understood that. After everything I've gone through, I still put myself first. I have to.

Lynn snaps her handbag shut, a prim, no-nonsense expression on her face. "I'm doing it because my husband will hate it."

I blink.

"He doesn't want to be reminded of that night. This is my way of sticking it to him."

I stick my tongue in the gap where I had the tooth pulled, long ago. I'm not sure I like the idea of being a pawn in someone's marriage. It makes my position precarious, like Lynn could take away the gift she's given me when she gets tired of torturing Patrick.

Her face softens. "And you remind me of me when I was your age. I did strange things for money when I was young, too. And my mother also wasn't particularly supportive. But I don't want you to do that stuff anymore. Because, I mean, my God. You could have been killed."

I lower my head. That bedroom in that house haunts me. The situation could have become so ugly. It's something I could never do again. I wish I could say that things have worked out with Alexis, but we haven't spoken since that night. I still think about her, though. I wonder if she thinks of me, too. I wonder if we'll ever see each other again. Sometimes, I still think I see her on campus . . . until I remember. She was never a student here.

But Sienna is. I've tried my hardest to be a shoulder to cry on. That's not to say I'm taking the news about Alfred in stride. I never, *ever* thought that dude had it in him. In fact, something about it seems kind of fishy—could a man battling cancer really overpower someone as virile as Greg Manning? But that isn't a question for me to ask. The old Raina might have tried to dig it up—and scam Sienna for it, maybe—but that's not me anymore. I guess Greg was right: I really *am* trying to be a better person.

"We're all done," the bursar officer says, passing Lynn a receipt. "Have a nice day."

Lynn folds the receipt and places it in the front pocket of her purse. "Just be careful, all right?" she says as we move away from the window. "You're smart. I can tell. You're going to be something someday. So I guess it's about that, too. I'm making an investment in a future. Maybe someday you'll cut me in on a business deal. Stock options before you go public. How about that?"

"S-Sure." And it's not out of pity, either. She thinks I have a future. She thinks I *belong* here, at Aldrich. Maybe even more than Greg did.

"Anyway." Lynn checks her watch, then raises her chin. "I need to be somewhere." She places a hand lightly on my arm, but then seems to think better of doing anything affectionate and pulls away. "Be good to yourself, Raina. And remember, I'm always watching."

And with that, she pushes through the door to the outside. I trail behind her. Lynn's high heels *clack* down the sidewalk.

The August sunshine beats down on my head. Has this actually just happened? I can feel the smile widening on my face. And then I revisit what she's just said: *I'm always watching.*

I bet she is. I bet she's going to make sure I make good on my promise not to get into trouble. But you know what? I don't mind someone watching out for me. I don't mind that at all.

49

LYNN

AUGUST 15, 2017

*A*nd the oysters for monsieur and madame." A waiter sets a beautiful plate of bluepoint oysters on the table. *"Bon appétit,"* he adds, and then discreetly backs away.

I admire the shells for a moment, and then glance around the room to see if anyone is ogling our meals, too. It's something *I* always do at restaurants—I always love to see what other people eat. Then I push the plate toward Patrick. "Here, darling. Have the first one." I wink, adding saucily: "You know what they say about oysters."

Patrick eyes the plate, then picks up an oyster shell and knocks it back. I watch him chew and swallow. He pushes the plate to me. His movements are a little forced and wooden—if it gets any worse, I'll talk to him about it later. I slide my foot up his leg under the table. I feel him flinch, but then he goes still, letting it happen.

We're at Lou's, our old favorite. We try to do this once a month. It's a date night of sorts, though we call it that only because that's what husbands and wives do. It's a nice shorthand; when I drop into conversation with colleagues or friends that Patrick and I have a date night coming up, they look at me appreciatively, acknowledging that I have an ideal marriage, something to aspire to.

It feels good to be out and about. I recognize a few people, like Dahlia Root, from the Duquesne Club, which I've pushed Patrick to join. She sits at the bar across the room, and I give her a finger trill, mouthing that I'll come talk to her in a bit. And there's Frannie Waites, who's on the board at Aldrich University—since my promotion after Kit left, I've been much more involved in such meetings. She's sitting with a girl who looks like her daughter, by the window— I make a mental note that Amelia's probably old enough to dine here now; perhaps we'll do a mother-daughter date soon. And there's Annette Darling, who lives down the street from us and has a girl in my daughter's grade—not long ago, Annette drove past Patrick and me just as we were having a small argument on the street. Did she draw conclusions?

I shift closer to Patrick and try to look loving and content. When I notice Annette turn my way and watch us for a beat, I fake a laugh at an imaginary thing Patrick has said. *See? We're all good.*

Patrick places his oyster shell on the plate and folds his hands in his lap. "Was it tasty?" I prod, my smile effervescent.

"Excellent."

He doesn't quite look me in the eye, and his smile is a touch soulless, but I don't think anyone notices. As long as he's sitting here with me, looking fantastic, as long as we give this public performance, I don't care what sort of emotional maelstrom is happening inside his head. It's just like old times, actually: I'm back to controlling his every move, making him do exactly what I want. And he's keeping his life. We're both getting what we need.

What I have on Patrick is ruinous, after all. It's one thing if I leaked his disgusting habits online, like I did with Greg Strasser's affair. That would lose Patrick most of his clients. His respect. His life. But Patrick is far more indebted to me than that.

The night I caught Patrick in that house with those girls, I'd made him tell me exactly what he was up to—every last disgusting detail, including the other times he'd done such things, which, unfortunately, horrifyingly, were numerous. Hearing that he wanted to playact a robbery, I was sure he was the murderer, but Patrick revealed his hideous alibi, saying he had many ways to corroborate it.

"You have an illness," I told him. "You need to see a doctor."

"I've tried therapists," Patrick said miserably. "They've explained to me, again and again, that I just like the fantasy of becoming someone else. Even if that person is a bad person—like a burglar—I can't get enough of playing a role." He lowered his eyes. "It's why I moved us to Pittsburgh last year. Not just the business opportunities—I thought that if I started over somewhere else, maybe I'd change." He took a deep breath. "I mean, even with Kit Manning—that wasn't real. We had fake identities. And I got off on it. I didn't think of her as a real person. A wife, a mother. That stuff's boring to me."

I stared at him, arms crossed. Was he seriously trying to rationalize Kit Manning? I wonder what *she* would think if she heard this theory.

"And look—with those girls, in that house . . . I just need to control something, Lynn. To *dominate*. To feel like a man."

I'd laughed out loud. His words combined with his hangdog, pitiful expression—he really expected me to feel bad for him!

I could have kicked him out that night. I could have deposited Patrick in some shitty motel where he would muddle through the rest of his days, sans wife, sans girlfriend, sans ever being able to see his children. But instead, I responded with kindness. "Look, I can't let you ruin your life," I said. "I've invested in you. I have a responsibility to get you back on track."

He'd looked at me confusedly. His eyes were bloodshot. His jowls hung down like a hound dog's. "Okay," he blurted, sounding suspicious. "But what if I don't *want* to get back on track? What if I want something different?"

I crossed my arms over my chest. "Like you'd ever leave your children."

A pained look flashes over his face, and I know in an instant I'm right. "There are . . . ways," he said quietly. "I have rights."

"Well, for your information, I'm not talking about our marriage, Patrick—though I have no intention of granting you a divorce. No children of mine are splitting their time between two homes. I'm talking about your career. Or are you okay with walking away from that, too?"

His eyes narrowed. "What are you talking about?"

At this point, I was enjoying myself. "You know, Patrick, it strikes me as funny that you've never wondered who your angel investor was, all those years ago."

Patrick blinked. "Angel investor?" he parroted.

"You know. The anonymous person who invested millions in your company before we married. It's so interesting you never cared about the person's identity."

Patrick's face was clouded in confusion, but all of a sudden— maybe because of my smug smile, maybe because I was literally vibrating with glee—the clouds began to lift. The blood drained from his cheeks.

"*You* know?" he said slowly, trembling a little.

"I do know." My smile was catlike, satisfied. "Because it was me. That little marketing management business I ran? My friend who got famous got *really* famous? A big talent agency bought out my client list back in the day. I made quite a killing."

Patrick let out an incredulous laugh. "And you never thought to tell me?"

I shrugged. "It was money I earned before the marriage. My lawyers insisted I get a prenup, but I didn't want to emasculate you. And anyway, I poured quite a bit of that money into your company. Though I made sure to own a fifty-one percent stake in your business. Which means, actually, I already *control* your business. I can do with it whatever I want. Meaning I could fire you. But I'd rather keep you around."

Patrick's mouth hung open. It wasn't a very attractive look for him.

"I'd rather give you another chance, allow you to shape up a little," I went on. "I really think that if you listen to me, you'll make all kinds of improvements."

Patrick fell heavily into a chair and stared blankly at the opposite wall. I'm not surprised he felt so blindsided—he doesn't take the time to really look at people, really figure out what they're hiding. I watched him look around our big, beautiful house, understanding that everything he thought he'd built was all actually mine. He was nothing without me. I could make him nothing again. Easy as that.

I wouldn't make things too hard for him, I said. All I needed were some public appearances. Some regular social media content. Family time. Sex, sometimes—I'd even indulge in his stupid robbery fantasy. I wanted a man on my arm. A dutiful father mowing the lawn on Sundays. You know, the works. The dream.

It's not like the status quo is even *bad*. Because look at us. Look at the stealthy glances people are sending our way. We are perfection, Patrick and I. We are going to rule this town, be the envy of everyone who lives here. No one will see our cracks. No one would ever imagine what we're hiding beneath. I'm keeping Patrick in line, making sure he's being a good actor.

Because respect, envy, a good reputation? It takes a little work—but it's so, so worth it.

50

WILLA
OCTOBER 17, 2017

Our homes are within walking distance of the surf break at Venice Beach, but because of all the equipment we're hauling, it's easier to drive. At this time of day—the sun just rising, the sky an ombré of pinks and oranges—the public parking lot is nearly empty. The only other vehicles here are banged-up Jeeps or Subarus of fellow surfers, also hoping to catch a few waves before the day properly starts.

I drag our boards off the top of the car and drop them to the concrete with a thump. Sienna and Aurora pounce on theirs and slather them with wax so naturally, you'd think they'd been doing this all their lives. Their full-body wet suits are unzipped to their waists, and their long hair has become sun-streaked. They already look the part of California girls. It didn't take long.

"How about you, Kit?" I point to my sister. "Swim today?" But she shakes her head. She's wearing shorts and a sweatshirt, as always. "Come on," I goad. "The water is great. I promise."

"It just looks so *cold*," Kit murmurs, shivering. "And what about sharks?"

"Thanks for the mental image, Mom." Aurora hefts her board and tucks it under her arm.

"Oh, go easy on her," I scold Aurora. It doesn't really matter to me if Kit surfs of not—what's more important is that she's *here,* in California, with me.

I still can't believe Kit and the girls made the move, that they're now living a few blocks away in a cool, small house along one of Venice's canals. We're so close in proximity that we can meet for coffee every day and have brunch on the weekends if we wanted, which we sometimes do. I can attend the open-mic nights Sienna started doing at a space in West Hollywood. I take Aurora to tae kwon do and therapist appointments. I take Kit to therapist appointments, too, and try to calm her down as she drives through the crazy city traffic.

Basically, we're a family again. And to think that it rose from the ashes of such tragedy and lies.

Sienna hands Kit her phone. "Hey, can you take a picture of me? I want to send it to Raina."

"Raina, huh?" I say, surprised. Kit raises the camera and gets Sienna in the frame. "You guys are still texting?"

"Here and there." Sienna glances at me guiltily. "Is that weird?"

Kit snickers. "A little weird, but probably not the weirdest."

I zip up my wet suit to my chin and slide on booties, humming to myself. I feel good. Better than I've felt in a long time. It's hard to believe there were a few days back in April when I wasn't sure if I'd be arrested. Finally, several days into our dad's stay at the hospital— the cancer had indeed spread to other organs, including his brain, and because he'd confessed, there was now an armed guard sitting outside his room—the NSA agent who had taken over the hack case, a stout man with a perpetual five-o'clock shadow, named Carruthers, met with me, Kit, and my new lawyer.

Carruthers said that the charges against me had been dropped. It wasn't right that I'd had a discussion with Blue, and it wasn't right that I'd put the idea to hack Aldrich into the hacker's mind, but because no money had officially exchanged hands, I couldn't be held accountable for everything Blue did. Blue had hacked the Ivies and Aldrich because *he'd* wanted to; he'd exposed the universities due to a vendetta he had against institutional learning as a whole.

The news of Blue's arrest would hit airwaves and the Internet the next day, Carruthers went on, but Blue and only Blue would be to blame. My involvement, including what prompted me to want to look into Aldrich's files, wouldn't be part of the story. I was free.

And my story was still a secret.

I paddle over the shallow breakers. Farther out, a few of the younger guys twist around and break into broad grins at Sienna and Aurora, who are only a few steps behind me. Nothing sexier than surfer girls.

Cold, salty water splashes my face. We reach the break, push up onto our boards, and bob. A wave crests toward me, and I start to paddle for it, but the current's too weak, so I stop midway through.

Both girls wait back at the sandbar. Sienna meets my eye as I sidle up next to her. "So have you seen what's been going on online?" she hesitantly asks.

I spit out a column of water. "Another hack?" In the months that have passed, dozens of other businesses, institutions, political campaigns, and celebrities' private photo albums have been hacked and released to the world. More reputations have crumbled. More people have been shamed. Practically every week, I cover another one at "The Source." You could say I'm sort of the hack expert these days.

Sienna shakes her head. "No. All those posts on Facebook. The MeToo stuff."

Out at sea, a pelican dives for a fish, coming up with the thing flopping around in its jaws. "Oh. Yeah." The posts began popping up on my Facebook feed a few days ago. They've even been one of the meeting topics at work.

"Have you thought about writing something?" Aurora asks quietly.

The girls' shoulders have broadened since they've moved to

California. In the evenings, when I come home from work, I often find them hanging out in my apartment, wanting to show me a new poem they wrote, or a funny Instagram post, or to tell me about a new cold-pressed juice place they tried. It is hard to imagine I was afraid that after finding out I'd initiated the hack—and ruined so many lives—they'd never speak to me again.

I stare into the sky, thinking about Sienna's question. Water streams through my fingers.

"I mean, it's okay if you don't." Sienna's response is quick, apologetic, like she's spoken out of turn. "It's your experience to post or not post."

Another wave breaks over us. A couple of guys to our right catch it and ride it all the way to shore, but I hug the board with my inner thighs to stay put. Aurora and Sienna know everything about what happened to me the night at the frat—I've even told them more details than I disclosed that day in the hospital. I haven't quite known how much weight to give it. It's certainly not something I want to glamorize or exploit. I want to be an empowering figure for the girls, not a tragic one. Too many women have been cast in that role already. At the same time, what's the difference between what happened to me and what happened to Sienna? Not much. My situation was perhaps more violent, but we were both forced into corners—and into silence.

Since coming back to California, I've tried to make strides to heal—*really* heal. I found a new therapist. New medication. A support group. I took up surfing again. I've opened up to my family— slowly, because old habits take time. I've opened up to Paul, too, who is an excellent listener—patient, kind, intuitive. I guess it's turning into something, considering that Paul is moving out this way in two weeks' time. He's been hinting at it for months, but I staved him off, saying I felt more comfortable with the long-distance thing—we'd meet at a central point in Chicago or Minnesota and spend long weekends together. But he applied for a job at a music website out here and got it . . . so here he comes. I'm nervous about it, though Kit, Aurora, and Sienna are all cheering me on.

I guess the worst that can happen is that it doesn't work out. But maybe I should think positively for once.

There are other new things, too. After the news of the frat broke, Marilyn O'Leary was under formal criminal investigation, and the Feds came up with a number of just how many rape accusations she'd buried and deflected: *sixteen.* That's more than I even knew of in my Facebook group. It probably isn't *everyone,* either—considering *I* didn't come forward, I'm guessing others didn't as well. But still: *sixteen.* It's shocking. Their names weren't released, but I felt like I knew them all the same.

They whispered to me, those girls. They felt like sisters. I couldn't help but imagine where it might have happened for them: in that same dingy upstairs bedroom.

I wanted to find these victims, though I had no idea how. They weren't on the hack database. They aren't nestled in my father's files—and for that, I'm eternally grateful. Even the ones I spoke to on Facebook did so anonymously, through shell profiles.

But then, #MeToo started. I've torn through the stories that have come out so far, even though many are triggering. The stories range dramatically from rapes to hideous comments to a grown man's hand on a girl-child's thigh on what was supposed to be a happy airplane trip to a tropical vacation. But the message to everyone is the very same thing that was ingrained in me: *Do nothing. Say nothing. It doesn't matter.*

It was affirming in the most terrible of ways. I don't want to be part of this club, but here we all are. I admire the bravery of the women who've tweeted and Facebook-posted and personal-essayed the truth. And the outpouring of support and unity is staggering.

"Actually, I already did write something," I admit now, during a spell of flat water.

Sienna blinks big, fat water droplets off her lashes. "Really? On Facebook?"

"No, an essay. I'm going to send it to an editor friend. She's going to publish it on their site. But the thing is . . ." I take a breath. "It tells everything. Including stuff about the actual frat and the school. I even talk about how I had a hand in hacking the school. I thought about doing it more anonymously, giving shaky details, but, well . . ." I shrug. "Go big or go home."

"Wow," Aurora says softly. "Good for you." Sienna nods, too. There's pride in her expression. This will be a good thing. This is what I'm supposed to do.

A wave rises up, and I'm grateful to hold up a finger, indicating *Hang on, I'm taking this one.*

I paddle hard, feeling the board catch, and then I'm skidding quickly down the wave. I stand up, gain my balance, and shift my weight onto my back foot. *Yes.* This is always such a life-affirming rush. Here I am, balancing on a flimsy fiberglass board propelled by the full-throated power of the ocean. If I can do that, I can do anything.

The wave peters out quickly, and I plop into the water. On the shore, Kit's sitting up straighter, applauding. I wave back, and head out again.

The world shimmers at its edges. The ocean swirls beneath me, dark and unknowable, but that's okay, too. I dive in, my board trailing behind me—not heavily, but oddly light and free. And when I surface, cold water dripping from my face, the beautiful horizon rounds above me, promising and powerful, truthful and terrible, wide open for whatever comes next.

51

KIT

OCTOBER 17, 2017

I sit on the sand, watching the three people I love most in the world battle a force of nature that seems way too overpowering and impossible to vanquish. My toes curl every time a wave pulls them under, but they pop up each and every time, like answers to my prayers. After one particular ride, Aurora turns around and grins at me. I smile back and give her a thumbs-up. And it hits me for the millionth time: I still can't fathom that my daughter did what she did. It's also hard to believe she *recovered* from the trauma of it.

When my father slipped away a week after taking the blame for Greg's murder, I was bombarded with conflicting emotions. Grief. Guilt. Shock. Sadness. Even anger—I hated that the gossipy public, who'd glommed on to the story of his confession and wouldn't shut up about it, would never know how selfless he really was. In the future, there would never be any statues of Alfred Manning on the Aldrich campus. He'd be excised from the Aldrich history books, known as *that* president, the scandalous one. I wished I could tell everyone the truth of the sacrifice he made for Aurora. I wish I could describe the peaceful look that came over his face after he'd said he'd take the blame for Greg's murder. It had filled him with grace, almost like a renewed reason for living—or, rather, for dying. But I couldn't do any of that. I had to just sit by and let the barrage of negative press roll in.

The only consolation was that Marilyn O'Leary could no longer swoop in and take his place—after a few carefully placed anonymous tips to the press that Marilyn was perhaps trying to make behind-the-scenes deals with rape victims without the president of the university knowing, reporters dug into her hacked e-mails and started asking questions. It didn't take her long to crack; she resigned shortly thereafter.

After Dad took his last breath, Willa and I sat with his body in the hospital room in silence. I still felt so distanced from her. So much had been cleared up about why Willa was the way she was— why she abruptly left Pittsburgh, why she'd stayed away for years, even why she held us at arm's length. But I also felt cheated. If Willa had told me about the rape, we might have been able to solve it together. We might have been close instead of the kind of sisters who occasionally traded texts. It was because of that history I turned to her in the hospital, saying, "We're coming to California with you."

Willa waved her hand. "You don't have to take care of me."

"No, we need to take care of each other. And, well, I think we need the escape."

My house didn't sell for what it should have—but then, I wouldn't want to live in a place where a man had been stabbed, either. When I packed up to go, I tossed everything into a rented dumpster, easily parting with my past. I did the same with my father's house, too. To my surprise, Dad had saved boxes and boxes of our mother's things in the attic—old pictures, marked-up calendars, sketchbooks, even moldering art supplies. Every card she made for him, every little drawing—it was all there, squirreled away, tucked into desk drawers or bureaus and sometimes even the pockets of his jackets. I had no idea how close he kept her at all times.

Fat tears fell on the drawings. I missed my family. I even missed

Greg—though I let that emotion pass quickly. I still couldn't reconcile what had happened between him and Sienna. Whenever I tried to fully confront what Greg had done—the fury and frustration, the disappointment and betrayal, the shame in myself for choosing a man who'd do such a thing—it felt like I could only go so far until a wall came up, and I had to turn away. My chest physically clenched at how badly he'd hurt me. It ached, too, with how happy we'd once been . . . and how strange it was that it was both a sham and the absolute truth, all at once.

But I'd been about to do it all over *again* . . . with Patrick. I had absolutely no idea who he was—and yet I would have tumbled wholeheartedly into a new relationship. I should have realized Patrick's MO the *very first moment we met,* when we had that long conversation about our alter egos. But I guess I'm a romantic at heart. I thought that even in our lies, we were admitting important things about ourselves. Now I know that only *I* was doing that. For Patrick, it was all just a game to pass the time—a new identity to try on for the evening. Just like all those other women he saw. Just like all those other role-plays he was part of. Just a void to fill.

I grieve the *idea* of Patrick, but not the actual man—because that guy? I never met him.

I want California to feel like a new start . . . but to be honest, I still feel adrift. I could apply to another giving department—there are certainly enough universities around here—but my heart isn't in it. I don't care about snaring wealthy people and squeezing money out of them. All I can think of is the secrets that new university might have. Lies, betrayals, bad behavior, cover-ups. It was human nature to conceal.

So mostly, I just go to yoga. I cook elaborate meals for my kids on weekends—Sienna has transferred to UCLA, but she lives at home. I try to talk with her about what went on between her and Greg, but it's more useful in front of a therapist. From what I've gotten out of her, Greg's flirtation started out innocently enough not long after we married. She didn't really see him as her *family member*—more like my boyfriend, and often not even that. They started e-mailing, but Sienna felt weird about using her regular account, so she opened another one, using two characters from books she'd recently read as her handle. She hadn't meant it as anything, she said, though in the words of Freud, there are no accidents.

Greg's flirtation was flattering, but then, as it began to get more sexual, Sienna started to feel trapped. She didn't want to do the things Greg was asking her to do—the MRI machine and all that—but at the same time who could she talk to about it? Greg's e-mails implied that if Sienna *did* tell, he'd twist things around and make her out to be the instigator. Why he thought I'd choose to believe him over my daughter, I don't know. Then again, I was in the throes of love—of Greg, and of my new life. What *would* I have done?

But then, about a month and a half before Greg died, Sienna had enough. She was interested in Anton; she wanted to go into the relationship with a clean conscience. I remember her talking about him—and Greg asking her a lot of questions about Anton. At the time, I'd appreciated his interest. Now I see it another way.

She'd told Greg her decision to stop what they were doing, in person, in the kitchen one night when I was at a dinner. Greg replied by telling her how special she was, how beautiful. He'd come toward her, touching her leg—that was what Aurora had seen. But what Aurora didn't see: Moments later, Sienna pulled away. Said Greg couldn't touch her like that anymore.

Greg retaliated by icing her out—especially on that Barbados vacation. So *that* explained his mood, anyway. How annoyed he'd been at Sienna's peppy attitude. It also could explain why he'd rebuffed me when I'd suggested—once again—that we try therapy. Greg was rejecting me because Sienna rejected him. Maybe he was done with all of us.

But it got worse. After that trip, Greg threatened to take away Sienna's college tuition, to take away her car, her nice clothes, to drive a wedge between her and me. He said once again that he'd spin things so that she was the one who looked guilty—after all, he had lots of e-mails to prove it. Sienna's last e-mails to Greg pleaded with him to put things back the way they used to be, not because she wanted the relationship to continue, but because she needed to be back in his good graces.

This had occurred only a few weeks before the hack. Right around that time, Aurora had noticed how on edge Sienna seemed, and she brought up how she caught Greg touching her, expressing that she was pissed that Sienna had just stood there, unresponsive. "Are you *into* him?" she'd asked, disgusted. Something in Sienna's behavior must have given her away, and Aurora drew some damning conclusions. When the e-mails were leaked in the hack and Aurora read them, she was horrified—but she had an inside track to exactly what was going on. This man, her stepfather, was a predator. She needed to stop him from doing this to her older sister.

And that was that.

How do I feel about this, now that I know? Like I've failed as a mother for not giving my daughter better guidance about flirtation, appropriate touch, crossed boundaries—even with a family member you're supposed to trust. I hate that Sienna was afraid of what Greg might take away, even for a moment—because I understand wanting things. But would it have been that big a deal? She always would have gone to college—my father would have made sure of it. But kids learn from their parents, don't they? Maybe Sienna coveted those things because *I* did. And maybe, if I hadn't been so caught up in what I had or how I looked to others, perhaps Sienna would have been brave enough to come to me about what Greg was doing, no matter the consequences.

And there's a part of me that deeply admires Aurora. I want to think I would have sought vengeance for Willa, back in the day, had I known of what happened at that frat house. This alone restores my faith that maybe I have done something right as a parent. The thing that matters most is standing up for the people we love. And for that, I'm glad Aurora was there when my father volunteered to take the blame for her. Alfred Manning's public reputation was tarnished for the ages, but in my family's heart, he's golden. A martyr. A hero.

Far out at sea, my sister and daughters bob like sleek, black seals. The sun hides behind the cloud, giving the air a welcome bite. I get a burst of optimism so pure and unexpected that I almost laugh. Not long ago, I used to be consumed with how people saw me . . . and I did everything possible to remain that person. But these days, after the hack, the murder, the rumors, my arrest, my father's choice—I have no idea what people think of me anymore. Terrible things, probably. I imagine the country club all atwitter—and the people at my job, and all my old clients. And Lynn Godfrey? She's probably pleased as punch. All those people who gossiped when Greg and I got together. All those people who criticized my father's reign over Aldrich. People who didn't like me, and people who did—I'm forever changed in their minds.

But you know what? I don't care.

Maybe the best reputation is no reputation. Maybe it's best not to care whatsoever how people see you. Maybe the only thing that really matters is how you see yourself.

ACKNOWLEDGMENTS

Like all books I write, this one took a while and had a lot of moving parts. It actually began as development for a TV series, though figuring out what the story should—or shouldn't—be helped tremendously in mapping out how to make things as dramatic and juicy and satisfying as possible in book form. So for that, I'd like to thank Sara Shandler, Josh Bank, Gina Girolamo, Les Morgenstein, and Melissa Carter for working with me to crack these characters, their secrets, how the hack worked, and the world the hack shattered. It took a while, but we finally got there!

Thanks, next, to Andy McNicol for believing in the project. And to Maya Ziv—my favorite editor ever—for loving *Reputation* in its raw form and working to make it even better. It is truly a delight to be partnered with you again. Thanks also to Laura Barbiea at Alloy, Hanna Feeney at Dutton, and Althea Schenck at WME for your keen eyes and tireless efforts. Thanks also to Christine Ball at Dutton for being an early fan—I'm so excited you saw the potential.

I also owe a great deal of gratitude to Rick White, for donating to the Childhood Leukemia Foundation—and for Rick's partner, Lynn Nordstrom, for allowing me to use her name in this novel.

Thanks also to Amanda and Jeff Manning for being okay with me using their last name. Many thanks to Michael for being his Michael self. And much love to Kristian and Henry. Stay good, my boys! And please, if you learn one thing from this book: Never e-mail what you're actually thinking! *People will always find out.*

ABOUT THE AUTHOR

SARA SHEPARD is the #1 *New York Times* bestselling author of the Pretty Little Liars series. She has also written other series and novels, including The Lying Game series, *The Heiresses*, and The Perfectionists series.